More praise for
A FLUSH OF SHADOWS

By Kate Wilhelm:

A FLUSH
OF
SHADOWS

**Five Short Novels Featuring
Constance Leidl and
Charlie Meiklejohn**

Kate Wilhelm

FAWCETT CREST • NEW YORK

A Fawcett Crest Book
Published by Ballantine Books
Copyright © 1995 by Kate Wilhelm
Introduction by Robin Wilson copyright © 1995 by Robin Wilson

"With Thimbles, with Forks, and Hope" copyright © 1981. First pubished in *Isaac Asimov's Science Fiction Magazine*, November 1981.
"Sister Angel" copyright © 1983 by Omni Publications International. First published in *Omni*, November 1983.
"All for One" copyright © 1995.
"The Gorgon Field" copyright © 1985. First published in *Isaac Asimov's Science Fiction Magazine*, August 1985.
"Torch Song" copyright © 1995.

http://www.randomhouse.com

Library of Congress Catalog Card Number: 95-96156

ISBN 0-449-22434-1

This edition published by arrangement with St. Martin's Press, Inc.

Manufactured in the United States of America

First Ballantine Books Edition: June 1996

10 9 8 7 6 5 4 3 2 1

To Jon, Kitte, Roxy, and Mo,
with love

CONTENTS

INTRODUCTION

HERE'S SOME HISTORICAL comment about novels, some personal history about novelist Kate Wilhelm, and a little pedantry to link the two; I'm a professor and this is allowed. You need not take notes; you will not be tested, but I think when you open a new book by an artist as accomplished and versatile as Kate, ready to savor (with some deliberation, please!) five of her best, you might want to ponder briefly the literary tradition in which she has practiced her remarkable skills and the pedagogic triumph she has realized along the way.

First, start with the fact that all of us—readers, writers, and pedants—are ardent coworkers in humanity's age-old attempt to limn our condition with language. Relatively late in this process, the printing press and spreading literacy freed us from dependency on bards and the boards they trod, the theater ceded primacy to the novel, and millions of paperbacks in thousands of newsstands testify that television and the Infobahn have yet to win it back.

As literary forms go, however, the novel is a newcomer. In the English-language tradition, it has been around only about as long, say, as national debts, some three hundred years. Earlier, narrative fiction—other than chapbooks, didactic tales, and such rogue romances as *The Triumph of*

God's Revenge against the Crying and Execrable Sin of Murther in Thirty-Severall Tragicall Histories—consisted of continental imports, particularly French. These were mostly great, gassy escapist "romances," averaging eight to ten volumes in length, full of supernatural heroics, courtly love, and aristocratic artificiality. Made-for-TV stuff.

But the new form of fiction was aborning. In 1666 Mrs. Aphra Behn, a mysterious woman of amorous reputation, retired from a stint as an English spy in Antwerp (where she bore the code name "Astrea"), returned to the London of Samuel Pepys, and wrote nineteen plays and perhaps a dozen novels, emulating the shorter fictional form current in Spain. She was the first Englishwoman to earn her living with her pen and ought—I think—be considered our first novelist. She was not long alone; the sixty years after her death in 1689 brought us Defoe, Richardson, Fielding, Sterne, and Smollett, and the medium for our contemporary discourse with ourselves was firmly established.

Now the more personal history. My association with Kate began nearly thirty years ago (a tenth of the English novel's life span!) when she was codirector (with spouse Damon Knight) of the Milford Science Fiction Writers Conference. I was a new professor, a new writer with a few sales under my belt, and like Mrs. Behn newly retired from the espionage business. I was flattered to be invited to Milford, awed by the experienced professionals I met there, and dazzled by the workshop process, and by Kate and Damon. There was this heady mix of psychological insight and precise expression, of passion and cool analysis, of scientific rationality and the outré, of fascination with folly and the heart to chronicle it with compassion. Boy, was I dazzled!

And so I did my best to hijack as much as I could—

process and persons, the workshop method and Kate and four others. I was bent on establishing a creative writing program at my institution, Clarion State College, and—with a little fiddling here and there to better suit the process to students and to make it look good to academic bureaucrats—there it was. The Milford Conference, of course, survived my depredations and continued until Knight and Wilhelm moved to warmer climes.

This was in 1967, and Kate and Damon have been the major factors in the success of the Clarion Writers Workshop (at Michigan State University since 1972) every year since then. They have been directly responsible for polishing up hundreds of neophytes into professional writers, each of whom can remember some moment of calm, penetrating wisdom that is Kate Wilhelm's hallmark as teacher *and* writer.

Back to Aphra Behn's era. When young playwright William Congreve made a stab at the new fiction in 1692, he prefaced his novel with this interesting insight: "Novels are of a more familiar nature; Come near us and represent to us Intrigues in practice, delight us with Accidents and odd Events, but not such as are wholly unusual or unprecedented, such which not being so distant from our Belief bring also the pleasure nearer us. Romances give us more of Wonder, Novels more Delight."

Look back over Kate's work: there is wonder enough and delight in all of it, but lately—over the past fourteen years, through Constance Leidl and Charlie Meiklejohn—Kate has made a quiet shift away from "odd Events . . . unusual or unprecedented" toward matters "not . . . so distant from our Belief." In genre terms, this is a tilt from the fantasies of the science fiction in which Kate early distinguished herself toward the verisimilitude and immediacy of the best contemporary novels of crime and detection, of which she is now an acknowledged master.

A last academic point and a caution: The novella is a challenging form. Some writers stretch a narrative like a Rodeo Drive limo in order to convey dark didactic or propagandistic themes, or to dwell endlessly on parochial manners and morals, or to meet the space needs of an editor. Others compress a novel's worth of events, racing from incident to incident, not pausing to explore character and cause, the meticulous representation of life that Henry James claimed as "the only reason for the existence of a novel."

Cutting the cloth of human experience to novella size is an exacting art. By employing two continuing principal characters whose loving but complex relationship is a stable focus of her narrative (and more is revealed about it in each story), Kate is able to use the novella's limited space to portray a parade of malefactors and their victims, the incidents that illuminate their humanity, and the settings within which good and evil contest. This is not escape fiction, not "romance." It is important stuff. Take your time with it.

You may be tested after all.

—Robin Wilson
January 1995

WITH THIMBLES, WITH FORKS, AND HOPE

THE FARMHOUSE GLOWED in the late-afternoon dusk, like an old-fashioned Christmas card scene. Low evergreens crowded the front porch; the sidewalk from the drive curved gracefully. It was all scrubbed-looking, the white clapboard freshened by rain that had started to fall. Charlie felt a twinge of guilt at the cleanliness and the comfort of it after spending most of the day in New York. He parked in the garage and entered a small side porch that led into the back of the house. The porch was a catchall for the bottles to be returned to the store, newspapers destined for a recycle center, some wooden seed flats that had gotten only that far on their way to the barn, an overflowing woodbox. When the clutter got so bad that he could no longer make his way through it, he cleaned it up, but not until then, and he never had finished cleaning everything—the seed flats had been there since June.

Inside the house, the fragrance of soup was tantalizing; there were the odors of wood fires, of onions, of cats—three of them—cedar paneling, and other things he had not been able to identify, leftover things from when the house was built, or from the first seventy years of its occupancy.

"Hello," he called out, but he knew Constance was out. The house felt empty when she was outside. Two of the three cats stalked over to sniff his shoes and legs, checking credentials before they accepted him. The third one, Brutus, glared at him from on top of the upright freezer. It was Charlie's fault, obviously, that the rain had started again. Brutus turned his back and faced the wall.

Charlie went through a narrow hallway, through the utility room, all the time dancing to avoid squashing a cat. He heard the soft plop Brutus made when he left the freezer, and he knew the evil old tiger cat was following along, his tail rigid, daring either of the other two to get in his way. They would keep an eye on him and scamper if he got near. Brutus was a New York cat; he had not, would never approve of country life. In the kitchen, there was a copper-colored electric range with a stove-top grill, a dishwasher, a disposal that had never been used since they had moved in—meat scraps went to cats, and everything else went on the compost; there were rows of hanging pots and pans, all gleaming copper-bottomed, seldom used. What was used every day for nine or even ten months of the year was a forty-year-old wood cookstove. On it now, there was the iron kettle with soup simmering so low that a bubble broke the surface once every five minutes or so.

The orange cat rubbed against him and complained about things generally. He rubbed its ears for a moment, then said softly, "She's going to be mad as hell, Candy." Brutus swiped at the gray cat, Ashcan, in passing and settled himself on the rocking chair nearest the stove. His eyes gleamed yellow as he narrowed them in the way that made him look Mephistophelian. Candy went on detailing her awful day, Ashcan licked the place Brutus had nabbed him, and Charlie tried to think of a way to break the news to his wife that he had practically taken on a job for them both. "She will be mad as hell," he said again under his breath, and he put down the briefcase filled with reports that he planned to read that night and have her read.

On the slope overlooking the house and yard, Constance was on her knees planting daffodils under the half dozen apple trees that made their orchard. Next year, they should start bearing. "Goddamned rain," she muttered, "had to do it now, couldn't wait another fifteen minutes, had to be right now." Rain trickled down her neck, icy fingers that made her skin flinch, trying to turn itself inside out. She plunged the bulb planter into the yielding earth, twisted it viciously, lifted out the plug, and laid it down. With one hand, she scooped up wood ashes and bonemeal and sand and tossed the mixture into the hole; with the other, she groped in her pail for another bulb and dropped it in, no longer taking the trouble to put it right side up. She returned the column of dirt topped with newly cut grass and jabbed at the ground a scant six inches away to repeat the process. It was impossible now for her to summon the vision of apple trees in bloom on a golden carpet.

She had heard the car and knew that Charlie was home. She had known when Charlie left that morning that when he got home he would hem and haw around for a while and finally blurt out that he had taken the job, that it would be a milk run, nothing to do, nothing dangerous, et cetera, et cetera. Her stomach would churn and her blood would chill, making her fingers cold, and she would nod silently and try to find words that would tell him she hated it but that she was willing for him to do it because she knew he couldn't just quit the business cold turkey. She knew that now and then he would go see Phil Stearns and come home to tell her that he had agreed to do just this one job, this one last time. "But it isn't fair," she muttered. For twenty-five years, Charlie had worked on the New York City police force, and he had come out scarred but intact, and it wasn't fair to risk everything again.

The worst scars were the ones that could not be seen. Invisible scar tissue had formed, protecting him where he had been hurt too often. In the beginning, he had been possessed by zeal, a sense of mission, holy justice; over the years, that had become cynicism and simple dedication to sharpening his skills of detection. Then he had become different again, had developed a cold fury because nothing changed, or if there were changes, they were for the worse. His rage at the criminal began to extend to the victim. Constance had known then it was time for him to get out. Surprisingly, he had agreed, and three years ago, at forty-seven, he had retired.

She looked with dismay at the pail, at least twenty more bulbs. The rain was coming down harder; there was a touch of ice in it. Her fingers were red and swollen-looking and her nose had started to run and she couldn't wipe it without smearing mud across her face. "It isn't fair!" she cried, looking at the house.

By the time she finished the job and put away her equipment, the rain was a downpour and the day was finished, with the gray sky lowering toward the ground. Charlie met her at the back door and drew her inside, pushed her gently into a chair, and brushed a kiss across her nose as he leaned over and pulled off her muddy boots. He helped her out of the sodden jacket and then took both her hands and pulled her across the kitchen, through the hallway, to the bathroom, which was steamy and sweet-smelling from bubble bath.

She sighed and did not tell him she would have preferred a shower in order to wash her hair also. Since her fingers were stiff with cold, he ended up undressing her and then held her elbow firmly until she was in the tub, only her flushed face and wet hair above water.

Charlie was perplexed about the hair; she was not the image he had anticipated, with mud on her cheek and her hair dripping and clinging to her cheeks and her forehead.

"Be right back," he said, and left, taking her wet clothes with him.

As soon as he had vanished, she stood up and pulled a towel from the rack and tied up her hair. It was silly for Charlie to baby her; she was taller than he was, and almost as broad. Her face was wide, Slavic, her eyes pale blue, her hair almost white, it was so blond. The gray that was already showing here and there blended in, and no one but Charlie knew she was turning. She knew she neither looked nor acted like the kind of woman a man would baby. She sank back into the suds and thought again it was silly for him to go through this to ease his conscience, but she was glad he did. Sometimes he babied her and sometimes she babied him; it worked out.

He came back carrying a tray with two frosted martini glasses, the shaker, a plate of garlic salami, the kind you could get only in a good New York deli, and strips of cheese. He sat down cross-legged on the floor so that his eyes and hers were level, poured the drinks, handed her a towel and then her drink, and began to tell her about the job. While he talked, he ate the salami and held out pieces for her to bite.

Constance watched him and listened and she thought: He was night to her day, all dark and brooding and secret. His hair was a mop of tight black curls, his eyebrows so heavy, they made his face look out of proportion. There was a gleam of gold in his mouth when he laughed, one gold cap.

His teeth were crooked, an orthodontist's nightmare, but they were the whitest teeth Constance had ever seen.

"Lou Bramley," Charlie said, eating cheese, "will be fifty-one November first. That's Saturday. He's got a wife that he cares for, two good kids, treasurer of Tyler and Sacks, Incorporated, no debts, everything going for him. And Phil's sure as sin that he's going to suicide before the end of the day Saturday. And leave him, Phil, holding a five-hundred-thousand-dollar insurance policy."

"So why doesn't he just not issue the policy?"

"Because it's too big to piss away without more than an itch to go by. And nothing's come up. He's had his best working on it for the last three weeks and they haven't come up with anything—no motive, no problem, no woman, nothing."

"Why does Bramley say he wants that kind of insurance?"

"His story was that at a party a screwball astrologer told him the next six months are the most dangerous of his life, that unless he takes extreme care, the odds are good that he will be killed in an accident." Charlie poured the last of the martinis and laughed. "Phil even hired an astrologer to do a horoscope for Bramley. Nothing to it. He's riding a high wave, nothing but good things ahead. Can you imagine Phil going to an astrologer?"

Constance laughed. They had known Phil Stearns since Charlie's college days. Phil believed in nothing but actuarial tables. "Charlie," she said then, "it's an impasse. In time, a good psychologist or psychiatrist could give Phil his answers, but if his people couldn't find anything in three weeks, what does he think you can do in three days? He has to gamble or cut loose."

Charlie nodded. "I more or less told him the same thing.

Midnight Friday, the policy goes through automatically if he doesn't reject it. By midnight Saturday, we both think Mr. Lou Bramley will no longer be with us, and Mrs. Bramley will come into a sizable fortune. Phil is ready to cut him loose, but he wants a backup opinion from a good psychologist. From you."

She shook her head. "I'm retired. And you are, too, if you'd just remember it from time to time."

"Bramley's gone down to a flossy resort in Florida, in the Fort Myers area. That raises the possibility of a vanishing act instead of suicide. In either case, it has to go down on the books as accidental death for the big payoff. All Phil wants you to do is go down there and observe him, talk to him, and on Friday give Phil a call. He needs something more than an itch to refuse a policy like that."

Constance glared at him. "You can't take jobs for me. I'm not an indentured servant or something."

"I didn't tell him anything definite," Charlie said reproachfully. "I did say that if we agreed, we'd want a week's vacation at the flossy resort after we finished this little job. On Phil, of course."

She shook her head. "Go stir the soup or something."

As soon as he was gone, she opened the drain, pulled the towel from her hair, and turned on the shower. She hated bubble bath; this was a gift from their daughter. Of course, Charlie would be hooked on Lou Bramley—they were the same age. He would never admit it, but the idea of stopping everything now when there was so much to do, time enough finally to do it, that would frighten him. He was not a coward—he had survived too many encounters with near death and had gone back too many times—but he was cautious. He was not ready. His own unreadiness would make it impossible for him to sidestep Lou Bramley, who evidently was ready. Charlie would have to know why. He would have to stop him if he was stoppable.

Constance had called Charlie late in the afternoon of her first day at the luxurious hotel. She had managed to talk briefly with Lou Bramley, she reported. "He's withdrawing, Charlie," she had said soberly. "Anyone with half an eye could spot it. He's not eating, not sleeping, doesn't finish sentences. He stares and stares without moving, then jumps up and walks furiously on the beach. Nervous energy. He's so obsessed, he doesn't even realize he's got two women pursuing him."

"Two? What do you mean?"

And she had told him about the woman who was openly stalking Lou Bramley. The bellboys and waiters were betting on when she would land him, it was so obvious.

Charlie did not like having a woman appear. It was possible they planned to skip out together.

He was going to like it even less, she thought. She had learned that the woman was June Oliveira, from Brazil, and Lou Bramley was the first man she had paid any attention to in the week she had been in the hotel. Wherever Lou Bramley went, she was so close that she might as well have been attached to him. Constance had watched her sit at a table next to his and start edging her chair toward him. When she got within whispering distance, he apparently had become aware of her for the first time, and he had moved out to a beach chair in the sun. His action had been almost absentminded. The woman had continued to watch him intently, and moments later when he jumped up and started to walk, she had followed.

It would have been easy to miss, Constance knew. The terrace was usually a busy place, especially during the late-afternoon happy hour. Waiters were rushing back and forth, groups forming, breaking up, re-forming. If she had not been watching closely, she might not have noticed, partly because the woman was so brazen about it; somehow that screened her intentions even more than secrecy would have done. When she first mentioned the woman to Charlie, Constance had realized she could not describe her beyond the most obvious features—long black hair and slender figure. Her face was smooth and unreadable, expressionless; she wore no jewelry, no makeup, no nail polish. Probably she was in her thirties; she was too self-assured to be younger, but there were no visible signs that she was older.

Up to this point Charlie would be willing to accept her assurance that Lou Bramley and the woman were strangers. And then she would tell him that last evening the woman had moved to a room next to Bramley's.

The bellboy who was willing to sell information had rolled his eyes when he told her that. Later last night, Constance had gone for a walk, and in the shadows of a sea-grape bush, she had stopped and looked back at the hotel, studying it until she found her own room, counting up and over from it to Bramley's. On the balcony next to his, she had made out the dim figure of the woman as close to the joint rail as she could get.

Constance remembered the chill that had shaken her, and she felt it edging up her arms now. She looked at her watch; he should be home, she decided, and dialed the number.

Charlie sounded pleased; he was running down a good lead, he said, but the woman continued to worry him. She could be a complication, he admitted.

"I'll see if I can get anything from Bramley about her," Constance said. "I'm having a drink with him in a few minutes. I doubt that we'll be able to talk, though. That woman will be in his lap practically. Charlie, she . . . she really bothers me."

"Okay. Keep your distance from her. Don't get in her way. She's probably got her own little racket going. Just watch the gazebo from a distance. Right?"

She agreed, and in a few minutes they hung up. She had not thought of the gazebo for a long time, but this didn't feel at all like that. There was something strange and mysterious going on, but she felt no danger; this was not the way she had felt when she had made the workmen move the little structure—hardly bigger than a playhouse. Nine years ago when they were in the country on weekends and part of the summer only, she had looked out the kitchen window one Saturday morning and had felt her skin crawl. I have to move the gazebo, she had said to herself sharply, and without another thought she had gone to the phone and called Willard Orme and had told him to bring someone out to do it. He had protested and tried to arrange a date a week away, and she had said she would get someone else to do it and remodel the house and build the garage and all the rest of the work he was figuring on doing for them. Reluctantly, he had come out and moved the gazebo. That afternoon, their daughter Jessica and two friends had been sitting in it drinking Cokes and eating hot dogs when a storm had blown down the walnut tree near the barn, and it had fallen on the newly bared spot of earth.

This was nothing like that, she told herself sharply. It was time to go down and meet Lou Bramley, see if they could find a place where she could get him to talk a little, a place where there would be no room for June Oliveira to be at his elbow.

The terrace was very large, and even though there were

forty or more people on it, many tables were vacant. The hotel was between seasons now; after Thanksgiving, through spring, it would be jammed and then it would be impossible to wander out and find a table. She sat down and shook her head at the waiter. She would order when Lou Bramley joined her. She spotted him as soon as he walked from the lobby through the wide doors. He hesitated, looking around, then nodded and started for her table. He had taken perhaps ten steps when he paused, looked past her, and changed his direction to go through the terrace, out to the beach chairs in the sand, where he sat down next to June Oliveira.

"For heaven's sake," Constance muttered to herself. "He's falling for her line." Bramley was facing the Gulf, away from her. June Oliveira was at his left, talking to his profile. Constance watched them for several minutes and then decided not to let Oliveira get away with it so easily. She picked up her purse and put on her sunglasses; it was still very bright out on the sand. She hated going out in the sun because her nose was burned, her cheeks, her chin. She walked across the terrace and down the three steps, turned toward them, and then veered away and headed toward the beach instead. She began to feel the heat of the sun on her nose and cheeks, and abruptly she turned and went back, without glancing at Lou Bramley and June Oliveira.

In her room again, she began to shiver and started to adjust the air conditioner, but she had turned it off when she arrived and it had not been on since. She went to the balcony to let the late-afternoon sun warm her. She realized that she was cursing under her breath and suddenly she laughed. A tug of war over a man! She had not played games like that since her teens. Now she began to look over the people on the sand below. Finally, she found Lou

Bramley and June Oliveira, exactly as before. She stood thinking and then went back inside and dialed Charlie again.

"I just want you to call her and keep her on the line a few minutes."

He didn't like it, he said many times, until she said she would hire a bellboy to do it, and if she paid him ten, that woman would more than likely pay fifteen to learn the identity of the hoaxer.

"And if you get him out of her clutches, then what?"

"I'm going to try to get him drunk enough to sleep tonight. If he doesn't, he just might go through with it, no matter what you tell him. He's desperate for sleep."

Charlie grumbled some more, but he would make the call to Oliveira in five minutes. "Honey," he said before hanging up, "just be damned careful."

Lou Bramley sat in the afternoon sun with June Oliveira and on her balcony Constance shivered. It was crazy, she told herself sternly; there were fifty people down there, and that many more on the beach, dozens of people swimming or sunbathing. It was a mob scene down there.

Almost thirteen years ago, Charlie had given her a present of one year of self-defense classes. He had insisted over her protests, saying further that as soon as Jessica was ten, he was going to enroll her also. Months later, she had come home one afternoon upset and unwilling to continue. "Charlie, what Kim is teaching us now are lethal blows. I don't like it."

He had held her shoulders and regarded her soberly. "If anyone ever lays a hand on you, hurts you, you'd better kill him. Because if you don't, I will. You'll get off with self-defense, but it will be murder for me." They both knew he meant it.

What her classes had not prepared her to do, she thought decisively, was to stay in her den and shiver when she had agreed to do a job. She waited in the dark, cool bar for the bellboy to summon June Oliveira for her urgent long-distance call. The bar adjoined the terrace; it had ceiling-to-floor smoked-glass windows that let the patrons see out and kept those on the outside from seeing in.

The day the walnut tree fell was the day that Jessica had given up junk food, had, in fact, become a health-food fanatic. The girls had come running in, talking shrilly, caught up in a nervous reaction to the storm and the crash of the tree, and the realization that they could so easily have been under it. Jessica had stopped at the door and looked at her mother across the kitchen. There had been beads of sweat on her upper lip. Wordlessly, she had crossed the room and hugged Constance very hard, shaking, saying nothing. Strange, Constance thought as she watched, how memories like that one pop up, complete, every detail there, as if it were a little scene one could raise the curtain on at any time. She was glad she had been with her daughter on the day she learned how short the distance was between life and death.

Presently, June Oliveira appeared, walking fast toward the lobby. Constance left the bar through the terrace door and went straight to Lou Bramley. The woman had left her scarf on the chair; she did not intend to be delayed very long.

"Hi," Constance said. "Want to take a walk?"

Bramley jumped up and looked around swiftly. "I certainly do. Let's go."

They started for the beach, then he stopped. "It's no good. She'll just tag along."

"I've got a rental car in the lot," Constance said, taking his arm. "Let's go somewhere else to walk."

They went to a flagstone path that wound between the swimming pool area and the tennis courts, up past the terrace, to the street-front parking lot. Not until they were on the busy highway heading south did Lou Bramley relax.

"I really wanted to talk to you professionally, but I'm not quite sure of the etiquette of the situation. And I owe you an apology," he said. "I'm sorry."

Constance laughed. "I'm retired. Any advice I give these days is just that, advice, like you might get from sweet old Aunt Maud."

She glanced at him as she spoke; his mouth twisted in an attempt to smile, then settled back into a tight line. His sunglasses were mirrors that completely hid his eyes. She turned her attention once more to the road. Incredibly busy, she thought; probably many of them were on their way down to the Tamiami Trail, through the swamps over to the east coast.

A straggly line of pelicans flew across the road; she admired pelicans more than all the other birds. They were scruffy-looking on land, ungainly, comical, but in flight they were supreme. So little effort seemed to go into it. They just opened their wings and sailed.

"I came down here to think through a problem," Lou Bramley said after the silence had stretched out long enough to be almost unbreakable. "A business problem," he added quickly. He turned his head away, as if afraid that even with most of his face hidden behind the sunglasses, he might reveal too much. "Lucky, my wife, says that we constantly signal to each other, all people, and that we learn to read the signals as kids and get sharper at it as we grow up. She says that women don't make passes at me because I'm not signaling that I'd be receptive." He paused, waiting for her response.

"That's really very good," Constance said dutifully.

"Yes. And now especially, with this problem, I know I'm not hunting. So why is it that I can't turn around without having that woman at my side? Earlier, I wanted to have a talk with you and I went to her instead. I don't even like her. I actively dislike her, more than anyone I've met in a long time. And I can't stay away from her."

"I wonder what she wants," Constance said.

"That's the stumbling block for me, too. There must be some kind of con game that she's going to pull when the time's right."

"She isn't right for a con artist, too blatant, too uncaring about appearances." She spied a good place to leave the highway at a small restaurant with beach access. "Finally, we can take our walk."

They walked on the hard-packed wet sand at the edge of the water. Lime green waves rose knee-high before they lost themselves in the froth. Flocks of sandpipers probed the sand, scattered at their approach, settled again as soon as they passed. Now and then, a large white heron fluttered up out of their way, or a bunch of seagulls screeched at them. Constance did not push the conversation or try to direct it as he talked about the woman, June Oliveira. She got little from it; he was not a good observer, not an attentive listener, not at this time in his life, anyway.

They turned back as the sun was setting in a gaudy display of reds, golds, ivory, green. . . . Offshore, a large yacht was moving south. They watched it.

"I don't swim," Lou Bramley said suddenly.

"My husband doesn't swim very well," Constance said. "He paddles a little."

"I saw you heading straight out into the Gulf this morning; it gave me a sinking feeling in my stomach when I realized I couldn't see you any longer."

"I don't think June Oliveira swims, either," Constance said. "At least I haven't seen her doing it."

"She thinks it's dangerous. She doesn't do anything dangerous. She thinks people are crazy who do."

He did not break the silence again until they were drawing near the tiny restaurant. "Would you like to have dinner here? I understand almost all the seafood restaurants are pretty good."

They got a booth by a window and she ordered a martini; they watched the end of the gaudy sunset while they waited for it.

"What happened after you published your articles?" he asked. He had not ordered a drink, and he watched her sip her martini with poorly concealed desire for one just like it.

He was punishing himself, she thought, making himself live through every minute of this week without help of any sort. The hollows under his eyes were alarming.

"I had already quit the hospital when I began to write the articles," she said. "They brought a little pressure on the university. I had tenure and they couldn't have touched me, but it was uncomfortable. I finished the semester and dropped that, too. It wasn't as if I sacrificed anything," she said easily. "I was busier than ever doing consulting."

"They made it look like a continuation of the old battle between the psychologists who aren't doctors and the psychiatrists who are," he said thoughtfully.

She shrugged. "A plague on both their houses. I'm researching a book right now that will damn the psychologists just as much as those articles damned the holy psychiatrists."

"I'd like to see that," he said almost regretfully, and his eyes went distant as his fingers began to tap on the table-top. He was back in his own hell.

"It's heady stuff," she said, "taking an opponent that much bigger than you are." His gaze remained fixed. She pulled the menu close to the candle and tried to make out the faint print.

When the waiter came to take their orders she asked to see the wine list and was disappointed by the selection. She did the best she could with it and said firmly, "two glasses." Lou Bramley started to protest, then became silent again. For the first time, he seemed to be uncomfortable with the silence.

"I'm surprised that they're still treating so many people with electroshock," he said.

"Several hundred thousand a year. For a while, they thought they had a better solution with psychodrugs, but what happened was, they ended up with addicts. Mostly women."

"And the difference in the treatments for men and women. That was shocking, too."

"Shocking," she agreed. "That's the word."

Suddenly, he smiled, the first time. "I'm not very good company. I'm sorry. Thanks for rescuing me, though. I'm glad we got out, away from that woman."

He ate little, but he drank the wine, and she kept refilling his glass; when the bottle was low, she signaled the waiter, who immediately brought a new one. The food was delicious. She was sorry he had not eaten.

They both ordered key lime pie and while they waited for it, he said, "I really wanted to talk to you about a favor. You mentioned that your husband is joining you this week-end and you'll be around next week?"

She nodded.

He leaned back as the waiter came with their pie. For a minute, Constance was afraid he would reconsider and withdraw again, but as soon as the waiter left, he went on.

"I thought I might miss you tomorrow. I have an important call I have to wait for in my room, and I thought you might have plans to go out. Anyway, that woman has made me jumpy, and I don't want to leave anything in my room. For all I know she might find a key somewhere, let herself in." He tried to laugh to show that he did not really mean it, but the effort was wasted. "It's something I want kept safe for me. I'm going deep-sea fishing, but I mentioned that already, didn't I?"

He knew he had not. The lie evidently made his mouth dry; he had to drink some of the awful water before he could continue. Constance was missing nothing: his sudden thirst, the way his fingers tightened and relaxed, tightened again, the way he avoided her gaze. He was still too dry to go on and he reached for the wine this time.

Constance took a bite of the pie and drew in a deep breath. It was sinfully good, made with real whipped cream, real lime juice.

"I don't want to leave confidential papers in the hotel safe," Lou Bramley said finally. "I know they have to turn things over to the police in case of accident or anything," he said in a rush.

He stopped again and this time Constance thought he would not go on. "This has to do with your business problem?"

"Yes. That's it. I would like to know that someone responsible has the papers, just in case."

"I'll be glad to hold anything for you."

"Thanks. And if—I mean there's always a chance that

something could happen—and if it does, would you just drop the stuff in a mailbox for me? There will be two envelopes ready to mail. Inside a larger envelope."

She nodded.

"I can't tell you how that relieves my mind," he said. "I know it must sound crazy, but I've got a hunch that I should make sure that stuff is safe." He put his fork down and looked past her out the window and instantly his face was set in that distant look she had come to know.

"I believe very much in hunches," she said. "I used to wonder why everyone in my profession paid so little attention to intuitions, hunches, things that we all experience and no one wants to talk about. Some of those patients committed to years of institutional life, ordeals of drugs, shock treatments, hours of psychodrama, group therapies, the works, are there because they couldn't bring themselves to ignore their intuitions. They got out of control. Others, even sicker people on the outside, pretend there is no such thing. There has to be a middle ground; there has to be a handle to it, a way to look into it without being labeled crazy. I haven't found it yet," she admitted. "But I'm convinced that you can't treat neurotics, psychotics, psychopaths, any of them, unless you admit that part of the psyche is still uncharted, unknown, and powerful."

She had brought him back; he was regarding her with interest.

"They'll crucify you," he said softly.

"They might try. I'm hammering my nails as hard and fast as they are hammering theirs."

He smiled with her.

She made a waving motion. "Enough of that. Why is your wife nicknamed Lucky?"

It was a silly story—her father had won a daily double

the day she was born—but it started Lou Bramley talking. It was all about his wife and two children now, the trips they had taken, the strange and wonderful things the children had done. Nothing current, nothing about the future, nothing more recent than a couple of years ago. When he paused, she told a story about Jessica, or about Charlie.

They were the only customers still in the restaurant when it closed. He was yawning widely. At the car, he stopped and looked back at the small dining room, the beach beyond it pale under a new moon. He nodded, then got in.

It was shortly after twelve when they walked into the hotel lobby and saw June Oliveira studying travel folders near the desk. Lou Bramley groaned.

"Jesus Christ!" he muttered. "She's just waiting. She knows and she's waiting."

On Friday, Charlie arrived at the hotel at 6:30 and went straight up to their room, where Constance was waiting for him. He kissed her fervently.

"You had me worried," he said then, holding her at arm's length, studying her. "Have you looked at your nose?"

She had; it was shiny and red as a plum tomato. It was also hot.

"You know what he's running away from?" she asked.

"I think so. He needs to confirm it; I don't have a stitch of proof."

"If he doesn't, we have to kidnap him or something. We can't let him go through with it, Charlie. I like him; he doesn't deserve that."

"And I like his wife a bunch, too. We'll see. Now, what about that mystery woman?"

"I wish I knew. Look, Bramley hasn't left his room all day. He's waiting for that phone call. He was supposed to get a package to me for safekeeping, and he hasn't done that, either. It's that woman. She's got some kind of control over him. I know, I know . . ."

Charlie watched her pace to the window, back. He had seen her like this before, but not for a very long time. He tried to pull her to the sofa next to him; she was too restless to sit down.

"Charlie, you'll have to get him out of here to talk to him. Tell him he's insured. Tell him you have to have something to eat, say in the coffee shop, that he has to sign papers and can do it there. She'll follow. In the lobby, I'll distract her, and that's when you have to get him out. There's a place down the road, south, Jake's Fish House. I'll meet you there. You rented a car, didn't you?"

"Yes. You told me to, remember? Constance, what is all this? You're nearly hysterical, you know?"

"I'm not hysterical, but there isn't much time. There's an eleven o'clock flight out of Miami and I want him on it. Charlie, he won't talk here! That woman is hanging out on his elbow. Believe me."

He kissed her again and went to the door. "Okay. Jake's Fish House. It'd better be good, sweetie, real good."

He would have recognized Lou Bramley from the photographs, but they had not prepared him for the muddy color of his face. He had blanched when Charlie said he represented the insurance company.

"You have the policy, Mr. Bramley," Charlie said. "There are some formalities, of course, a few things to sign."

Bramley sank into a chair, staring at him blankly; very slowly, the mud color changed to a reddish suntan. He moistened his lips. "Something to sign?"

"Yeah. Would you mind going to the coffee shop? I got a lousy headache on that flight down here. Cup of coffee and a couple aspirins, that's what I need. We can get the paperwork done there."

Bramley nodded and stood up. He went to a chest, opened a drawer, and withdrew a manila envelope. "I have to drop this off at the desk," he said, looking at the envelope.

The woman was standing at the elevators when they arrived. The Dragon Lady, Charlie thought, and nodded to her. At his side, Lou Bramley had gone stiff. He looked straight ahead, as if he had not seen the woman at all. No one spoke.

She got off before them but was walking so slowly that they passed her within a few feet of the recessed elevator bank. They went to the desk, where Bramley handed over his envelope and watched until the clerk deposited it in Constance's box. He took a deep breath.

"The coffee shop's over there," he said dully, turning from the desk.

The woman was less than fifteen feet away. Constance appeared and walked between them, and when the woman stepped aside, Constance brushed against her.

"Hey, what are you doing?" Constance yelled. "She had her hand in my purse!"

June Oliveira started to move away faster; Constance caught her by the arm and turned her around. "I know you did! I saw you and I felt the tug on my purse. It's happened to me before, just like that."

"Let's get the hell out of here," Charlie said, taking Bramley's arm. There was no need to tug; Bramley was already nearly running for the wide entrance doors.

In Jake's Fish House, they took a booth and Charlie ordered.

"One scotch on the rocks," he said, pointing to Bramley. "One very dry martini for me."

"Your wife said that's your drink," Charlie said easily.

"You saw my wife? Why?"

"Routine."

"You told her about the policy?"

"Nope. Told her I was a headhunter scouting you out for a new job."

"She believed that?"

"She sure was trying hard to believe it. She showed me your computer. Neat, real neat."

Bramley ran his hand over his lips. "Who are you?"

"Actually, I really am doing a bit of headhunting for Jim Hammond."

Bramley looked as if he might faint. The waiter brought their drinks and Charlie said, "Drink up." He sipped his martini and knew he wanted another one very fast. Bramley drank most of his scotch without pausing. They regarded each other. Bramley looked haunted, or maybe treed. Charlie had seen that look on other faces. Sometimes if the person with that look had a gun, he began shooting. If he was on a ledge, he usually jumped.

"If you've done what we think you've done," he said softly, "Jim Hammond wants to hire you, starting now, tonight, or next week, next month, whenever you can arrange it."

"He doesn't even know. No one knows."

"Five hundred thousand dollars' worth for openers," Charlie said.

"For openers," Bramley said. He finished his scotch.

"Hammond wants you; you can work it out together. You found a glitch in his foolproof gadget. You could even say he needs you." He signaled the waiter to repeat the first round and then leaned back, watching Bramley. "Of course, it was the dumbest thing you could do, get a policy like that and take off, I mean. Like a neon announcement."

"I never claimed to be smart. I was desperate. It would have worked. Lucky would have paid the money back and would have collected fifty thousand from Hammond. His offer is still good, isn't it? The reward for anyone who cracked his system? I wrote out exactly what I did to prove . . . Oh my God!"

"Now what?"

"I've got to retrieve that envelope from the hotel desk!" He shook his head, then asked, "How did you find out?"

"The old Sherlock Holmes method. If it's all that's left, it's got to be it. Or something like that. We couldn't find anything on you, so I looked up your company. Two years ago, they got a new Hammond computer system. I read about the guarantee and the reward. As soon as I saw that computer setup at your house, I knew."

Their new drinks had arrived before Constance showed up. She came straight to their booth and sat down next to Charlie. Bramley looked completely bewildered by her arrival.

"It's okay," Charlie said to Constance, putting his arm about her shoulders and squeezing slightly. "You put on a good show. How did you get out of it?"

"I apologized and explained many times that I had been robbed in New York by someone who casually brushed against me. She was not happy."

"You two . . . ? You're with him?"

"This is my husband," Constance said. "I have your envelope. I suppose you want it back?" She took it from her purse and slid it across the table.

He looked from her to the envelope, back to her. "You've been working these past couple of days?"

She nodded. "I had planned to kidnap you and make you see how unfair you were being, if Charlie hadn't pulled it off."

"It's too easy to make judgments from the outside," Bramley said. "It would have ruined her life, too."

"And what about the load of guilt you were planning to dump on her? Wouldn't that have ruined her life? Ruin, despair, humiliation, those were your burdens, but you know she would have shared them. Who would have shared her guilt?"

"She would have grieved, but she would have gotten over it. It was going to be an accident. Everyone would have accepted that."

"She already knows," Charlie said. "I don't know how, but she does."

"Just as I'd know," Constance said.

"She would have tried to stop me if she suspected," Bramley whispered.

"Maybe she feels she can take the guilt trip better than you could stand the humiliation and ruin from whatever you did. Maybe she wanted to save you from suffering," Constance said coolly.

"Stop it!" His voice broke and he gulped his drink. "You've made the point," he said.

"Lou, there's an eleven o'clock flight out of Miami for New York. You can take my rental car and turn it in for me at Miami. You have a reservation for that flight."

"This feels like a bum's rush," he said, but his eyes gleamed, and there was a look on his face that she had not seen there: boyish, eager.

"The hotel knows you're going out fishing tonight; they

won't think anything of it when you don't come back. Call them from New York tomorrow."

He was nodding. "I really don't have to go back there. I could drive over in a couple, three hours. What time is it?"

"Seven-thirty."

"I'd better get started."

"I got some sandwiches, and a thermos of coffee. They're on the front seat. Here's the agreement for the car, and the key." Constance handed them to him.

He folded the paper and stuffed it in his pocket and brought out another slip of paper. He looked at it, then let it fall to the table. "My receipt for the fishing trip. Paid in full." Now he stood up. He looked down at Constance. "I don't know yet what I think about you. I owe you a lot. Thanks." Suddenly, he leaned down and kissed her forehead. He reached across her to shake Charlie's hand. "You don't really have anything for me to sign. That was all done a month ago. Right?"

"Right. Good luck, Lou. Hammond's waiting for your call." He hesitated, then asked, "Fill me in on one thing, before you go. What do you think the Oliveira woman was up to?"

"I think she knew I was going to die and she was hanging around to watch," he said without hesitation. "She'll be disappointed. Keep out of her way," he added, looking at Constance. "She's a ghoul, probably crazy, and I think she's very dangerous."

They watched him leave, then Charlie turned to Constance.

"Okay. What was that all about? He's right—it was the bum's rush. Why?"

"I don't think he would have been able to leave again if

he had gone back to the hotel. I don't know how or why, but that woman does have some kind of power over him. I think he's right, Charlie. She knew. That's what she was waiting for."

Charlie took a deep breath, blew it out again in exasperation. "Tell me," he said.

When she kept it all very objective, as she did now, Constance knew there was nothing frightening about the woman. She repelled and fascinated Lou Bramley, nothing too unusual there; except, she told herself, both she and Lou Bramley knew it was more than that, even if neither of them could ever demonstrate it.

"Now, you tell me. What did he do? He's not a crook."

"Not in the usual sense, anyway. His company got a big multimillion-dollar computer system two years ago, guaranteed safe against illicit access. And Bramley couldn't resist trying to break into it. It was a game, puzzle solving. And he did it. Eighteen months ago, he got his own computer at home, and it's been like having a mouse in the cheese cupboard ever since. God knows how much money he's diverted, where it is. Hammond, the computer company president, wants to hire him." He shrugged. "I think I got out of the crime business at a good time. I just don't understand things anymore. Hammond said half a dozen companies would hire him if he actually got access to that computer. And I guess he did."

Hours later when Charlie fished for his keys, he felt the receipt for the charter boat and brought it out also. "Let's do it," he said. "Let's go fishing."

"He's going to take off at high tide, at three or a little after," she said. She thought of the glassy water of the Gulf. "We have to sleep aboard if we're going." They began to hurry, like children rushing to a picnic.

For a moment or two, Constance was aware of another feeling, the same one she had felt years ago when she had looked out her kitchen window that Saturday morning. The same, but intensified, and also directionless.

"You know," Charlie said, driving, "this is something I've wanted to do all my life. Never thought the chance would drop into my lap like this. Freezing rain was falling when I left the city. . . ."

Beside him, Constance was caught up in his infectious gaiety; she pushed the intrusive feeling of dread and fear out of her mind.

At the docks, she and Charlie went into an all-night diner to ask directions, and they met Dino Skaggs there, one of the brothers who owned *Dinah's Way.* He was a wiry brown man with sun-bleached hair, his face so wrinkled, it was hard to guess his age, which Constance thought was about thirty-five, give or take a few years.

Dino scowled when Charlie showed him the receipt. "You sure he isn't coming?" he asked suspiciously, studying the receipt.

"I'm sure," Charlie said. "Look, if there's an additional charge because there're two of us, we'll pay it."

Dino bit his lip as he studied Charlie, then Constance. "Shit," he said finally. "Hundred per head, in advance. We shove off at three. No checks," he added as Charlie pulled out his checkbook.

"I have cash," Constance said. She counted out the hundred and handed it to Dino, who recounted it.

He stood with the money in his hand, still frowning glumly. "Shit, I guess you won't be eating all that much." He peeled off five tens and thrust the bills back to her. "Don't bother to come aboard until two-thirty, and keep it quiet when you do. We've got a sleeping passenger aboard already." He slouched away.

"Well," Constance said. "You're sure about this?"

"Shit yes," Charlie said, grinning. "Want some coffee?"

Dino met them on the dock where *Dinah's Way* was moored. It was too dark to tell much about the boat, except that it looked small, and very pretty, sparkling white, with blue letters, blue trim, gleaming copper rails. It looked less like a fishing boat than Charlie had anticipated.

"You'll want to watch the lights and all, I guess," Dino said morosely. "I'm going to settle you in the stern and you stay put. When you've had enough, you go on to your stateroom. And no talking in the galley. Inside your room with the door closed, it's okay, just keep it low. Right?"

Charlie said, "Aye, aye," and Dino groaned. Constance felt a stab of impatience with Charlie. He was too eager, too willing to let this pip-squeak boss him around.

"I'll take her out from up on the flybridge," Dino went on. He led them aboard and to the rear. The boat rocked gently. "Grandstand seats," Dino said, pointing to two fighting chairs. "Back through here," he said, motioning them to come to the cabin, "you go down the stairs, and turn right at the bottom. There's a yellow light over the door; that's your room. Light switch on the wall. Head at the far end. Bathroom," he added, glancing at Constance. "You'd better take your seats. I'll see you in the morning." He waved to a man who was leaning against a piling and vanished around the side of the boat.

Constance leaned toward Charlie. "What's a flybridge?"

"I don't know."

They sat back in their chairs and watched the gleaming black water laced with ladders and bridges and arcs of light. The engines started up and Charlie found

Constance's hand and held it; lights came on above and around them, running lights, Charlie thought with self-satisfaction, and then they were moving easily, backing away from the dock, out into the bay. Here and there, other boats were moving, small boats with lights hardly above the waterline, larger fishing boats, a yacht that made everything else look toylike. Charlie sighed with contentment.

When they finally went to bed, after all the lights had disappeared in the distance, they shared one of the bunks. Sometime during the night, Charlie moved to the other one and again fell asleep instantly.

He woke up first and was amazed to find that it was nearly eight. The motion of the boat was very gentle, nothing like what he had imagined. He had never been on a boat before, except for a rowboat when he was a kid. He thought of the seascapes he had admired, always stormy, threatening. Another time, he decided, and was glad that today the Gulf was like a pond, the boat's motion hardly noticeable. As soon as he got up and started toward the head, he realized the motion had been effectively concealed while he had been horizontal. He held to the bunk and groped for the door. He had just finished showering when he heard Constance scream.

He flung open the shower door and stopped. Standing in the open doorway to the galley stood June Oliveira, staring at Constance.

"Where is he?" she demanded.

"Why didn't you tell us she was aboard?" Charlie snapped.

They were in the galley, where Dino was making breakfast. June Oliveira had gone forward, he told them.

"I don't recall that you asked me," Dino said, breaking eggs, his back to them.

"We have to go back," Constance said.

Now, Dino turned. "Lady, get this one thing straight. This is my boat. I'm the skipper. I say when we come out and when we go in. I made a contract with Mr. Bramley, all signed, paid for, everything. You and your husband said you wanted to use that contract. That means we do it my way. And that means we fish until this afternoon. I pick up my brother Petie, and then we go back. That's in the contract, and I'm following it to the letter. You don't want to fish, fine. You can look at scenery. I'll fish."

"When did she come aboard?" Charlie asked, his voice easy now. His working voice, Constance thought.

"Last night. I was checking things out and there she came. What's this? What's that? I'm going, too, you know. I'm his guest, you know. He wants to pretend it isn't planned, so just don't say anything to him, so he won't have to lie about it. That's her story. How was I to know anything?"

Charlie nodded in sympathy. "I've seen her operate. But you could have mentioned it to us," he added reasonably.

"Yeah. I should have. I was afraid you wouldn't want to go, and I sure as hell didn't want to go out alone with her. She's . . . I don't know. Anyway, I had to go out to pick up Petie, and I'm sticking to the original schedule. Now let's eat." He motioned toward the table, where there was a coffeepot. "Help yourselves."

The galley was sparkling with copper fixtures, everything so compact and well planned that in an area hardly more than five feet square there were a two-burner stove, a refrigerator, sink, cabinets. The table and a right-angled bench could seat half a dozen people. Behind it, there was a wall separating off another stateroom, and beyond that the pilot's cabin. The boat was moving slowly, on automatic pilot while Dino did the galley chores.

Charlie began to wonder how much it all cost. Opposite the galley was what Dino called the saloon, with three chairs and a bench-sofa and coffee table. The walls were mellow, rich paneling. Teak? Mahogany? It looked expensive.

Dino served up ham and scrambled eggs and fluffy cinnamon rolls.

"Are you going to call her?" Charlie asked.

"She said she'd have coffee a little later. I think she's mad as hell." He looked at Constance, who was eating nothing, just drinking the coffee. "Look, I'm sorry. But the boat's big enough for four people not to get in each other's way. You and Charlie just stay in the stern, do a little fishing. I'll see that she stays forward, or up on the flybridge. I can run the boat from the pilot's bridge down here, or from up there, either way."

He showed them the pilot's bridge. "Dual controls," he said, "for the two diesels. This is clutch; this is throttle. Midway, that's idle, forward for going ahead, back like this to reverse, down all the way to stop. That's all there is to that. And the wheel here, just like a car, only you allow for more time and space for everything to happen. Okay?" He glanced around at the instrument panel. "You won't need more than that. In case Charlie gets a big one, I might have you run us while I help him. Oh, yeah, here's the starter, just in case you need it. Just flip it on."

Again, Charlie was struck by the simplicity and the beauty of the boat. He was very much afraid the Skaggs boys were running more than fish out of the Gulf waters. And he told himself to forget it. He wanted no part of the drug business; he was retired.

Dino got Charlie baited up, urged Constance again to give it a try, then went below. In a few minutes, he said, they'd start trolling. Constance looked at the water, almost too bright to stand; there were long, smooth swells, and now and then there was a soft plop as water broke against the side of the boat. She had grown used to the lesser slaps of water; the larger sounds broke the rhythm. Something splashed out of sight behind her and she wondered, prey or predator? The sea stretched out endlessly, formless, exactly the same everywhere, and yet different under the lazy swells. It would be terrifying to be out there alone, she thought; they were so small and the sea was so big. Another splash sounded and this time she swiveled to see what it was. She could not even see ripples. Prey or predator? She caught a movement from the corner of her eye and turned farther and looked into the eyes of June Oliveira up on the flybridge. She's frightening because her expression never changes, Constance thought, and abruptly swung back around. She felt cold in the hot sunlight. She should have known that woman would be aboard. It had been easy enough to figure out that Bramley had planned his accident to take place at sea.

"Why didn't you argue with Dino at least a little?" she asked bitterly.

"Wouldn't have done any good. I'm afraid we're on a drug run, honey. So let's just play it real cool. I'm in the insurance racket and you're a housewife. Period. We don't know from nothing. Right?"

"Oh for heaven's sake!" she muttered helplessly, and stared at the brilliant water until her eyes smarted.

Dino brought her a big floppy straw hat and a long-sleeved shirt. "You're going to cook," he said. "You're already burning. People as pale as you can get sun poisoning without ever getting warm."

"Thanks," she said, and he ducked away quickly, back to the pilot's bridge. Soon the boat began to move a little faster through the calm waters. "He's hard to hate," Constance said, tying the ribbon of the hat under her chin.

Charlie nodded, and thought, But he's a drug runner. Sometimes he tried to sort out the criminals he hated most on a scale from one to ten. Usually, he put arsonists first, but he knew that was prejudice. He had had to get transferred from the arson squad when he had started having nightmares, had smelled smoke where there wasn't any, and suspected smoldering rags behind all locked doors. Child molesters came next, then rapists, and drug pushers, murderers. . . . But he always changed the order even as he composed it, because some of them obviously had to be second, and they couldn't all be. He glanced at Constance; her eyes were closed.

He woke up with a start. Dino had touched his shoulder. "Sorry," Charlie muttered. Constance was coming awake also.

"Doesn't matter," Dino said. "If you'd gotten a strike that would have waked you up pretty fast. Just wanted to tell you, might as well reel in. I'm taking us to a place to try some reef fishing. Might get something there. Good place for scuba diving." He looked at Charlie hopefully, shrugged when Charlie shook his head.

Dino sent June Oliveira down from the flybridge, and then the boat stood up and raced through the water. Charlie nodded at Constance. He had suspected there was a lot more power in the engines than they had witnessed before.

June Oliveira braced herself in the doorway to the galley; she looked terrified. Constance remembered what Lou

Bramley had said about her: she did nothing dangerous. Obviously, she thought what they were doing was dangerous. Constance was glad to see that she did have at least one other expression.

When Dino cut the engines and came down, he looked happy, as if this was what he liked to do, open it up and roar, leaving a wide white wake behind them as straight as a highway through a desert.

"Lunchtime," he said cheerfully. "Then you'll get a snapper or two, Charlie. Bet you a ten spot on it."

He would have won. Charlie caught a red snapper within the first fifteen minutes of fishing over the reefs.

"It's a beauty," Dino said. "Catch its mate and that's our supper. Go ashore, build a little fire, roast them on a spit. That's good eating, Charlie. Just you wait and see." He was keeping an eye on the progress of the sun, evidently timing their day carefully. "You've got half an hour." He watched Charlie bait his hook, patted him on the back, and left with the first snapper, to put it on ice. The boat was again on automatic, moving slowly over the shadows of the reefs.

Charlie was excited and pleased with himself, Constance knew, standing close to him, watching the water. The live fish on his line went this way and that, then vanished. Charlie was muttering that it was pulling; maybe he had something—no, it was just the bait fish. Something splashed behind them. Charlie let out more line as his bait fish headed deeper. Constance was watching, looking down, when she caught a glimpse of a larger motion. She jerked her head around and saw Dino in the water behind them.

"Charlie! Look!"

He dropped his rod and grabbed at one of the life preservers clamped in place against the side of the cabin. "Get this thing back there!" he yelled to Constance as he moved.

She raced through the cabin, through the saloon, to the pilot's bridge. Put it on manual, she thought clearly, and flipped the automatic control off. Pull the control back to reverse. She pulled the lever back, heard a slight click as it passed neutral, and then the engines stopped. She groaned and hit the lever back up to the neutral position, aligned the clutch control. She pushed the starter. Nothing. She repeated it several times before she gave up and ran back to the stern, where Charlie was standing rigidly, staring at the water behind them. Their momentum was pushing them forward slower and slower.

"I killed the engines," Constance said, tearing off her hat, loosening her sneaker with her other hand.

"What are you doing?" Charlie asked. His voice sounded strange, forced.

"I'm going in after him."

Charlie's hand clamped painfully on her arm. He was still looking at the water. Now Constance looked. There was the life preserver, nearly two hundred feet away, bobbing easily. There was no sign of Dino.

"I almost hit him with it," Charlie said in that strained, thick voice. "He could have reached out and touched it, caught it. He never made a motion toward it. He wasn't even trying to swim."

"I can still get him up," Constance said, jerking her arm, trying to get loose.

"No! He went down like a stone. He's on the bottom, already dead. He wasn't even struggling."

Constance felt her knees threaten to buckle. She turned to look at the flybridge: June Oliveira was standing up there facing the life preserver. Her eyes were closed.

"She did it," Constance whispered. "She killed him."

"Take it easy, honey," Charlie said. "She was up there

the whole time." He turned away from the water now. "He must have had a stroke or something, couldn't move, couldn't swim. He didn't even yell. Maybe he was already dying before he fell in."

"You don't just fall overboard," Constance said, watching June Oliveira, who hugged herself, opening her eyes. She looked at Constance; her expression was as blank as ever. She moved to the ladder and descended from the flybridge.

"I think I'll lie down now," she said.

They watched her enter the cabin. "Let's go up there and see if we can get this boat going," Charlie said. He sounded tired. Wordlessly, Constance started up the ladder to the flybridge.

The flybridge was built over the main cabin; the front was enclosed, the rear open, with another fighting chair. There were wraparound windows and a control panel exactly like the one below, the same wheel, dual controls for the engines, automatic pilot. The same array of dials and indicators that neither of them understood. Charlie sat down behind the wheel and looked at the controls: The automatic was turned to off; it must have moved when Constance turned it below. The dual controls were both at midpoint, in neutral. He turned on the starter. Dead.

"I thought it might be like a car engine," Constance said. "Maybe I flooded it when I moved the throttle too fast." She knelt down and tried to see behind the control panel. It was all enclosed.

"What are you looking for?"

"A wire. She must have pulled a wire loose or something."

Charlie shook his head. "Knock it off, honey. I'm telling you, she was nowhere near him. Let's go find the engines.

Maybe we can tell if it's flooded, or if a battery connection is loose."

"See if the radio works," Constance said.

Charlie had no idea what most of the switches and knobs were for, but he did know how to operate a radio. It was dead.

At three, Charlie called June Oliveira to the galley. He had made coffee and was drinking a beer. Constance watched the other woman warily when she drew near to sit at the small table. She said she wanted nothing when Charlie offered her a drink.

"We're in a spot," Charlie said. "I don't think it's especially serious, but still, there it is. I can't make this boat go. I don't know how, and neither does my wife. Do you know how to run it?"

She shook her head. "It is the first time I am on a boat."

"I thought so. Okay. So we have to wait for help. We have no electricity, and that means no lights. Someone may spot us before dark; if not, we'll have to take shifts and keep a watch. I'm afraid we might be run down, or we might miss a passing ship or small boat. I found a flare gun to signal with if we see anything." He poured more coffee for Constance.

"His brother, he is expecting us," June Oliveira said. "When we do not arrive, he informs the authorities. Yes? They come for us then."

Charlie shrugged. He was trying to place her accent. Not Spanish, not anything he had heard before. Portuguese? He did not think so; there had been some São Paulo students at the crime lab, eight, nine years ago, and they had not sounded like her. He said, "Eventually, they'll come, but I doubt they'll hear from Petie right away." Little brother, he thought, would have to hide something first, bury it, sink it at sea, do something. Depending on where he was, little brother might have to be rescued also. "We'd better prepare for an all-night wait, and a daylight search tomorrow."

"If there is more beer ..." June Oliveira said then.

He took one from the refrigerator and handed it to her. Already the ice was melting. They would have to eat before dark, before the butter melted, the other food spoiled.

"If you two will start keeping a watch now," he said, "I'll gather up everything I can think of that we might need during the night. I found one flashlight only, so we'd better have things in one place." He handed a pair of binoculars to Constance. "You take the flybridge. Yell out if you see anything. Miss Oliveira, you go forward and keep an eye open for a ship. Later we'll switch around, choose lots or something. Okay?"

Constance watched her go around the cabin to the forward deck before she started up the ladder to the flybridge. Charlie handed up the coffee and the binoculars to her.

"Be careful," she said softly.

Charlie felt a twinge of impatience with her. He nodded and turned to his task. When Constance got a notion, he thought, she played it to the bitter end, no matter how ridiculous it was. He scanned the water briefly before going back inside. He could no longer see the life preserver and he was glad, even though he could not tell if the boat had drifted or if the wind had simply taken the doughnut away. He was glad it was not there, a constant reminder that he had done nothing at all, and had prevented Constance from trying to do anything. She swam like a fish; she might have saved him. He did not believe it, but the thought came back over and over. He remembered his own feeling of terror at the idea of letting Constance go over the side after Dino: What if she got out there and just stopped swimming, as he had done? He knew he could not have helped her; he would have watched her look of incomprehension, fear, disbelief. . . . Angrily he jerked up a life jacket and stood holding it. Where to put things? Not on the table, which they would be using off and on. Not in the saloon; probably they would take turns sleeping on the couch. Finally, he opened the door to the stateroom he and Constance had shared the night before. He put the life jacket on her bunk and went out to continue his search; a first-aid kit, what else? He was not certain what they might need; he could make no list and then go search. All he could do was collect things he saw that looked useful. He felt the same helplessness now that he had experienced when Constance had said they did not even know what switch to throw to put out an anchor to stop their drift. He did not know where they were, how fast they might be drifting, or in what direction, not necessarily pushed by the wind, although they might be; it was also possible that they were in a current from the Florida Straits. He simply did not know.

Constance made a hurried scan of the horizon in all directions, then a slower search. She saw birds, and she saw porpoises in the distance. A few hours ago, the sight would have thrilled her, seeing them leaping; now it was depressing that only the creatures of the sea were out there. Charlie clearly thought Dino's death was the result of a seizure of some sort; she knew she would not be able to convince him of anything else. Up here, examining the problem logically, she agreed that it had been an accident, but she rejected the logic. She knew June Oliveira had been responsible, even if she did not understand how she had done it. She knew, and accepted, that she would not have been able to save Dino. It would not have been allowed. She could not see the woman from on the flybridge, and she could not hear Charlie moving about. She bit her lip and strained to hear something, but there was only the slap, slap of water on the side of the boat, and a faraway birdcall. She went down the ladder and met Charlie coming up from the cabin.

"What's wrong? Did you see a ship?"

"No. I just came down for my hat." She had left it in the saloon. She retrieved it and started up again. "Charlie, say something to me now and then, or whistle, or something. Okay?" His nod was perfunctory and absentminded. He was tying a self-inflating rubber raft to the side rail, out of the way of traffic, but available if they needed it. A second raft was already tied in place. Constance returned to her post and did the entire search again.

The sun was getting lower. A couple more hours of daylight, she thought, and then the long night wondering what Oliveira would do next, if she could do anything as long as Constance was awake and watching her. She leaned over the side of the flybridge and called, "Charlie, is there plenty of water?"

"Yeah, I checked. And plenty of coffee," he added, as if reading her mind. She smiled slightly and looked at the sea.

They should eat something before it started to get dark, she decided a little later. Oliveira could come up here while she made something; she started down the ladder again. There was only the gentle sloshing sound of water. Charlie was still below, maybe swearing at the engines. . . . She took a step toward the cabin door, paused, and instead went to the side of the cabin and looked forward. June Oliveira was standing at the rail near the pilot's cabin windows, and beyond her, ten feet away, Charlie was swinging one leg over the rail.

Soundlessly, Constance dashed the fifteen feet to the

woman and hit her with her shoulder, knocking her flat. She kept going and grabbed Charlie, who was hanging on to the rail, dangling over the water. She hauled on Charlie's arms and he pulled himself up, got purchase with his foot, and heaved himself back aboard. He was the color of putty.

June Oliveira was starting to sit up.

"You move another muscle and I'm going to throw you overboard!" Charlie yelled at her. He unfastened the inflatable raft he had secured to the rail and tied the rope to one of the loops on it. Holding it over the side, he pulled the release and then dropped it, keeping the rope in his hand, letting it out as the raft fell and settled.

"Now get up!" he ordered. "Over the side, down the ladder. Move!"

She shook her head. "I am hurt! Your wife attacked me! I think my back is broken."

"You'd better be able to swim, lady. You go down under your own power or I'm going to throw you in and let you swim for the raft. Right now!"

"You are crazy," she said.

"Hold this," Charlie said, handing the end of the rope to Constance, taking a step toward the woman. She was on her knees, and now she scrambled up, clinging to the side of the boat, then to the rail. She looked terrified, the way she had looked when Dino had roared at full speed over the water. "There's the ladder," Charlie said, stopping within reach of her. She backed away, stepped up the two steps to the rail, then over it, down the ladder. Charlie maneuvered the raft closer and she stepped into it, clutching the sides. "Get down low," he said. "I'm towing you to the other side." He didn't wait for her to crouch down, but yanked on the rope and hauled the raft, bumping and rubbing against the boat hull, around to the other side, where he tied it securely.

"Let's go below," he said to Constance then. "I sure God want a drink."

Silently, he poured bourbon for them both, added some shrunken ice cubes, and took a long drink from his.

A long shudder passed over him and his knees felt weak. He sat down and pulled Constance to his side, put his arm around her shoulders, and held her tightly against him.

"Oh, Charlie," she said softly, "I'm afraid we've caught ourselves a boojum."

He held her tighter. He still saw himself going into the water, not struggling, not trying to swim, going under, down, down. . . .

"I think you're right," he said. His voice was so normal that few people would have detected the difference, the slight huskiness, the almost too-careful spacing of words.

"Do you know what happened to you?" Constance asked. She drank also and welcomed the warmth; she had become icy cold now that the woman was in the raft and she and Charlie were side by side.

"I was going to go over just as if I had decided to do it. I was doing it and I was watching myself do it. Watching her watching me, pushing me, not even trying not to go, not even trying to resist. I was just doing it."

She nodded. Neither of them said, Like Dino. "What are we going to do?"

"Remember when I read *The Hunting of the Snark* to Jessica? Remember what she said when I asked what she'd do if she caught a boojum?"

Constance nodded again. Jessica had said the only thing to do was cut it loose and run.

"It might come to that," Charlie said grimly. "It just

might." He took the last swallow of his bourbon, then pushed the glass away. He got up and put the coffeepot on the burner to heat it. "Start with the first time you saw her, the first thing Bramley said about her," he said. "You were right, honey. I should have paid attention. Let's try to make some sense out of it now."

He stopped her when she told again how Lou Bramley had bypassed her to sit at a table with June Oliveira. "Exactly what did he do?"

"You know the wide doors? He stood there looking around until he spotted me and then started toward my table." She closed her eyes, visualizing it. "Then he looked past me and he didn't look at me again. His face changed a little, became set, almost like a sleepwalker, or someone in a trance." She opened her eyes. "She did it then, too. I was blind not to realize."

"You couldn't have known," Charlie said. "Then what?"

"I waited a minute or two. Then I decided to spoil it for her, to join them. I got up and started toward their table. . . ." She stopped, remembering. "I thought it was my decision to take a walk instead. Oh my God, I wasn't even aware . . . I didn't even wonder about it!"

Charlie squeezed her shoulder. "Try to remember exactly how it was, honey, I think it may be important. What was he doing when you started to walk?"

"His back was to me. He was staring at the water. I got pretty close to them before I changed my . . . He hadn't moved, I'm sure. Then I turned right." She stopped, eyes closed. "I think he might have stood up; there was a motion. I just caught it from the corner of my eye, and I was thinking how hot it was on the sand. It was sunny, and I had been trying to avoid the hot sun. I went a little farther and decided I didn't want to walk after all."

"You were thinking it was hot, all that, close to their table?"

She nodded. "What is it, Charlie?"

"She couldn't hold both of you," he said. "She got you past the table and lost him, grabbed him back and lost you. What do you think?"

She considered it and nodded. "But we can't be certain. We can't count on it."

"No, but it's something." The other thing she had said, that the woman did nothing dangerous, alarmed him. No doubt she thought it was very dangerous out there on the raft with night coming on fast. She might even be right; it could be dangerous. He didn't know.

"I'd better start making sandwiches," Constance said. "We're all going to be hungry eventually."

"Okay, but keep talking. What else was there?"

She talked as she rummaged in the refrigerator and the cabinets. When she stopped again, Charlie was staring fixedly at the tabletop, deep in thought. She did not interrupt him, but continued to assemble the sandwiches.

It did not make any sense to him. If she had that kind of power, to control people like that, why use it in such a perverse way? Murder was so commonplace, never really dull, but not exciting, either; it was always sad, always futile, always the action of ultimate failure. It was the final admission that there was no solution to a problem, no human solution. But no one needed her kind of power to commit murder. A gun, a knife, poison, a brick, a fire . . . he had seen them all; death that looked accidental—a fall, car exhaust in a closed garage, a leaky gas stove, overdoses of everything that could be swallowed. All filthy, all irreversible, all committed by ordinary people for ordinary reasons: money, sex, revenge, greed. . . . All committed without her

kind of power. That was the puzzle. Why use such a gift
for something so mundane? And why out here in God
knew what part of the Gulf? She could be knocking people
off every day of the week—running them in front of trains,
making them jump from high places, forcing them to put
bullets through their brains. Who would suspect? Each and
every one would go down as accidental, or suicide.

He remembered what Lou Bramley had said, that she had
known he was going to die and wanted to watch. He nodded.

Constance, seeing the nod, stopped all movement, waiting, but Charlie continued to stare through the tabletop.

Bramley had been broadcasting death and she had picked
it up somehow. She had planned to watch for whatever insane pleasure that gave her, and she had been cheated.
Again, Charlie nodded. She had had her death through murder, not suicide. And she planned to kill the witnesses. Now
he shook his head. No one had witnessed anything. What
could he or Constance say that could damage her? She
could make a better case against them. Of course, if she
was a psychopath, none of the best reasoning in the world
would apply to her. He rejected that also. She was the boojum, an *it*, not like other people. He could not fathom her
motives in either event—a whacko, or something inhuman.
And, he thought, motives were not the issue. What she
might try next was the only issue now. She had tried to kill
him, damn near succeeded, and she no doubt would try
again.

But she had not come out here to kill, he said to himself,
and he held on to that one thought as the only clue he had
about her, the only thing he was reasonably certain about.
If the original plan had worked, Bramley would be dead
now, a legitimate suicide passing for accident, and she and

Dino would be back ashore. Their stories would have been accepted: Dino was well known; the insurance would have entered into it. Finis. Dino's death was a different matter. No one would believe he had fallen off his own boat in a dead calm, in the first place. And it was less plausible to suggest that he had not gotten back aboard, even if he had managed to fall. Although no one could prove anything else, no one would ever believe that story. What if there were others, like her, who would know the story he and Constance could tell was true? His skin prickled all over at the thought that his people would never believe his story, but that this woman's people, if she had people, would.

He was certain she planned to be the sole survivor of a ghastly tragedy. No one knew he and Constance were aboard. If they vanished, no one would know that. The contract would be found with Bramley's name, and he was in New York, out of it. She could say anything to account for Dino's disappearance, and he was the only one she would have to account for, actually.

Constance froze in the motion of cutting through a sandwich; Charlie lifted his head and listened. June Oliveira was calling them in a shrill, panic-stricken voice.

They went out together, staying close to each other. Constance still carried the butcher knife.

"There is a shark! I saw it! You cannot keep me out here! I will stay in the little room. You lock the door. Please, I did not do nothing. You know I did not!"

In the west, a spectacular sunset was blossoming; the light had turned deep pink, making June Oliveira look flushed, almost ruddy, very normal, ordinary, and very frightened.

"Who are you?" Constance demanded.

"I see him starting to climb over the rail, and I am petrified. I cannot move. I am terrified of water. I cannot to help him or call out or anything. I am coward. I am sorry."

"You don't just watch them die, do you?" Constance said. "You weren't watching Dino. Your eyes were closed. You feel it, experience it. Why? Why don't you feel your own people's deaths? Why ours?"

"She crazy," June Oliveira wailed to Charlie. "She crazy!"

"I saw you," Constance said. "You knew exactly when Dino died. We didn't; we couldn't know, but you did. You planned to experience Lou's death. You come here to feel death without dying yourselves, don't you? Do your people ever die? Just by accident, don't they? Isn't that why you're so terrified of water, of fire, of anything that might be dangerous?"

"Please give me jacket or sweater. I am cold. So afraid," June Oliveira moaned.

"For God's sake," Charlie said, and turned away. "I'll get her jacket."

"How many of you are there?" Constance asked furiously. "How many murders do you commit? How many accidents do you cause?"

The woman was huddled down, her arms wrapped about herself. Suddenly, Constance realized what she had done; she had separated them. She turned, to see Charlie in the narrow passage between the rail and the cabin, coming toward her, carrying the heavy gaff, the iron hook Dino had said they used on the big ones.

Constance put the knife to the rope tethering the raft. "Let him go or I'll cut you loose! You'll drift away. He can't bring you back; he doesn't know how." She began to cut.

She stopped the sawing motion and watched as if from

a great distance as the knife turned in her hand, began to move toward her midsection. In the stomach, she thought, so death wouldn't be too fast. There would be time to feel it all, to know it was happening. . . .

Charlie leapt at her, grabbed the knife, and threw it out into the water. His hand dripped blood.

Constance sagged, then straightened. "My God, oh my God! You're hurt! Let's go fix it." Neither of them looked at the woman in the raft as they hurried away, back inside the cabin.

"What are we going to do?" Constance whispered. "Charlie, what can we do? We can't even cut her loose!"

"Get the first-aid kit," Charlie said calmly. "You'll need the flashlight. The kit's on your bed. Bring a clean towel, too."

Constance snatched up the flashlight and ran to the stateroom for the kit and towel. When she returned, Charlie was washing the blood from his hand. She dried and bandaged it and neither spoke until she was done.

"I'm going to kill her," Charlie said. He reached out and gently touched the shirt Constance had on. There was a slash in it; she had not even noticed, had not realized how close it had been.

This was why some people murdered, Charlie thought, because there really was no solution, no human solution. How easy it was to step across that line. He felt as if he had always known that, had denied knowing it, had pretended it was not true when of course it had been true from the beginning. When he had transferred from the arson squad, it had been because he had dreamed too many times that he was the one arranging the materials, pouring the oil or the gasoline, setting the match. The thrill of the pursuer, the thrill of the pursued, who could tell how different they were? Now that he had crossed that imaginary line, that arbitrary line that each cop drew for himself, he knew the thrill was the same, the desperation the same, the fear, it was all the same.

"We can't cut her loose," he said in that deceptively calm voice, "so we cut ourselves loose. We have to go out in the other raft, get the hell away from her. She'll try again, maybe soon. Before it gets much darker." He glanced about the galley. "Start packing up everything you think we might need for tonight and tomorrow. We might not be picked up for hours, maybe a couple of days. Fill whatever you can find with water."

Thank God she didn't argue, he thought, going into the stateroom. She knew their chances of escaping as well as he did, knew their only chance was in getting distance between them and June Oliveira. He lifted the mattress of his bunk. Foam, he thought with disgust. There was a plywood board, and beneath it there were cabinets with linens. He nodded. It would do. He cut a circle out of the foam mattress with his pocketknife and tucked the extra piece under the pillow on the other bed. He had seen a can of charcoal starter in a cabinet in the galley; he went out to get it. He took the flashlight back with the can. He soaked the plywood board and let it air out before he replaced the mattress. In the hole, he now put a folded towel and then added a layer of crumpled toilet paper, then another towel, this one folded in such a way that the paper was exposed in the center of it. He studied it for a minute and sighed. The fumes were gone, the odor so faint that he might not have noticed it if he was not sniffing. He had seen cigarettes somewhere, in one of the cabinets in the saloon. Dino did not smoke, but maybe Petie did, or their guests. He went to the saloon and found the new package and opened it, lighted a cigarette with the flame from the stove. Constance was filling a plastic water bottle, a collapsible gallon jug. There were two at the bottom of the stairs, already filled. She looked startled at the cigarette, but she still asked no questions.

"About ready?" Charlie asked.

She nodded. "It's getting dark fast."

"Yes. Come on, let's tell her our plans."

"Charlie . . ." She stopped; there was not enough time to spell it out. She followed him to the door.

Charlie went to the corner of the cabin and yelled, "You, you can have the goddamn boat! We're taking off in the other raft. Before we go, I'm going to toss the portable ladder over your side so you can climb aboard. Just leave us alone and let us take off. Is it a deal?"

He puffed the cigarette hard. It was not yet dark, but within half an hour it would be. Already the water looked solid, impenetrable, and there were two stars in the deep violet sky. She must be calculating her chances of getting one of them before dark, making the other bring her aboard. He was not even sure she could make someone do anything as complicated as that; she was not a telepath. Her power was cruder, a total assault, a complete takeover. She cannot read our thoughts, he said to himself, praying it was true.

"If you leave the flashlight. Put it on the flybridge, turned on, so I can see it." She sounded calmer and was controlling her accent and syntax better, but her voice was still tremulous.

He let out his breath. "Okay. We're taking provisions with us, water and stuff. It'll take us a few minutes, ten maybe."

He nodded to Constance. "Let's get the life jackets and other stuff over by the ladder."

As Constance began to carry things from the cabin to the railing, Charlie entered the stateroom again. He lighted a second cigarette from the first and then put them both very carefully on top of the paper in the hole in the mattress. He pulled the sheet over it, and the bedspread, with ripples in it for air to pass through easily. For years, he had known how easy it would be, how well he would be able to do it. He put the extra life jackets on that bed, and then he was through. He left the stateroom door open when he went into the cabin. One last thing he had to get, he thought, almost leisurely, and he went to the drawer where he had seen an assortment of thread and needles. He chose the largest needle, a darning needle, or a sail-mending needle; it was four inches long and only slightly less thick than an ice pick. He stuck it through his shirt. Constance returned for the last of the items she had put aside, the bag of sandwiches.

"Listen," he said to her softly. "We'll put the raft out, make sure the paddles are in it, and then load. While you're putting the flashlight on the flybridge, I'm going to swim around the boat. The last thing you do is hang the ladder over the side, make sure it's secure and everything. We don't want her to get suspicious now. Then you get in the raft and start paddling to the front end of the boat. You pick me up there and we paddle like hell."

"What are you going to do?"

He pointed to the needle. "Puncture her escape route."

Constance shook her head and began to strip. "That's my department," she said. "You'd never make it in time, and you splash like a puppy. Same plan, different performers."

"No!" He saw her, arms crossed over her chest, sinking, sinking. . . .

"Yes! Let's move!" She was making a bundle of her

clothes. She had on only her bra. Now she reached out and took the needle and put it through the top of the bra. "You know the only way it'll work is if I do that part. You know that. We don't dare have her out in the water alive. We have no idea how far she can reach."

He pulled her to him and kissed her hard, and then they hurried to get the raft into the water, get it loaded. Only one quadrant of the sky was still light now; to the east, the sky and sea merged in blackness.

"Arrange it any way you can," Charlie said, nodding to her, when they were through. She slipped from the raft soundlessly and vanished into the dark water. "That looks good enough for now. When I get in, we can shift things around some. I'll put the flashlight up there and then give her the ladder. You okay?"

It was all taking much longer than he had realized it would, he thought bleakly. What if smoke began to pour from the cabin? What if she got suspicious, caught Constance down there in the water? What if she took this as her last chance to get them both? He climbed to the flybridge and put the flashlight down, shining toward the stern, away from where Constance might be surfacing. What if there really had been a shark? He felt weak with fear; his hands were trembling so hard, he could scarcely hold the rail as he left the flybridge to get the ladder.

Constance surfaced at the prow of the boat and waited. There was the ladder, and Charlie was running away to the other side. June Oliveira had to haul herself in hand over hand to reach the ladder; she started to climb. As soon as she started up, Constance sank below the surface again and swam to the raft. She lifted her face only enough to get air, then went under and pulled out the needle and stuck it into the raft. The raft bobbed and she stopped moving, afraid the woman would be alarmed, turn around. She stuck the needle in three more times before she had to surface for air. The next time she went under, she began to swim toward the prow of the boat, praying that Charlie would be there by now.

When Charlie first started to paddle, he found himself moving away from the boat at right angles. Frantically, he pulled with one paddle until he bumped the boat. Keeping against the hull, using one paddle only, he finally got to the front end. Where was she? She should be here by now, he thought with despair, and she appeared at the side of the raft. He grabbed her arm and hauled her in, and she began to pull on her clothes as fast as she could. She was shivering hard from the cold water, the chill night air. Before she got her shirt buttoned, Charlie was putting the life jacket on her. He was wearing his already. As soon as she had the life jacket tied, she took her place by him, took up the paddle, and they both began to row hard. The raft did not move through the water easily; it seemed to be mired in tar. But gradually, they pulled away from the boat, and now Charlie could see the light from the flash bobbing in the windows of the cabin, then the pilot's cabin, stern. She was checking it out, as he had thought she might. She went to the fly-bridge and in a minute or two the boat's engines started up.

Constance groaned and pulled harder on her paddle. It was no use, she thought dully. She would run them down, watch them die anyway, feel them die.

"We have to stay behind the boat," Charlie said. "You know how to turn these things?"

"You push; I pull," Constance said, knowing it was no use. They could dodge for a while, but eventually they would tire, or she would make one of them stop paddling, or something.

Slowly, they made the raft go astern. The boat was not moving yet; the engines were idling. Now the lights came on. Constance blinked as the light hit them. "Charlie, she can back up!" she whispered.

"Christ!" He had forgotten.

The boat began to move forward, not very fast; the wake shook the small raft, tilting it high to one side. The boat left them behind, then started to turn. Like steering a car, Charlie remembered. It was just like steering a car, except you need more room. She turned too wide and came out of it far to the right of the raft. She had switched on a searchlight now, was playing it back and forth, looking for them. She seemed not to realize how wide her turn had been; the light came nowhere near them. It stopped moving.

Constance watched fearfully. The boat looked so close. The engines were so loud. She felt herself go blank, felt sleep-heavy, immobilized. When it passed, in a second or two, the light began to move again, this time swinging around to focus on them.

"She reached me," Constance said tonelessly. "We can't hide from her."

Why didn't the damn boat start burning? He knew it had to burn. He visualized the fire that had to be smoldering along the bed board, in the cabinet under the bed. The towels should be blazing by now. The boat was turning slowly; she was being careful. She had all the time in the world, she seemed to be telling them, keeping them pinned by the blinding light, keeping them waiting for her next move. Charlie wondered if she laughed. If she ever laughed.

She was steering with one hand, holding the light with the other, not letting either go to increase her speed. The throb of the engines did not change, only grew louder.

Constance began to pull on her paddle. "At least let's

make her work for it," she said grimly. Charlie pulled hard, sending them on the beginning of another circle. Then suddenly, the light made an arc, swung wildly away, up, down, off to the other side.

"I'll be damned," he said, pleased. Smoke was rolling from the cabin windows. He began to pull on the paddle again, harder now. "We should try to get some more distance from it," he said.

Silently, they rowed, not making very much gain, and they watched the boat. The smoke had lessened. Constance was afraid June Oliveira had put the fire out already. Charlie felt almost smug; he knew the smoldering had turned into blazing; there would be less smoke, more heat, more fire. When the first flame showed on the side of the boat, he said, "I think we should get down in the bottom of this thing, as flat as we can." It would blow, he knew, and he did not know how much of an explosion there would be, what kind of shock there would be, if they were too close. He hoped June Oliveira was tossing water on the flames, that she had not thought of the beautiful fire equipment on board, or of abandoning the boat. He had not seen her since the powerful spotlight had come on.

He and Constance curled up in the bottom of the raft. "Try to keep your ears covered," he said. He raised himself enough to continue to watch, his hands cupped over his ears. Flames were shooting out every window now, licking up around the flybridge. When the explosion came, it was not as loud or as violent as he had thought it would be. A fireball formed, then vanished almost instantly, and the boat erupted in a shower of fiery objects; the lights went off, and now there was only a low fire that was being extinguished very fast as the boat settled, began to slide under the water.

They could hear a furious bubbling, then nothing, and the fire was gone. The sea was inky black.

Constance was on her knees, clutching the side of the raft. She shuddered and Charlie put his arm about her, held her close. "Did she get off?" she whispered.

"I don't know yet."

They waited in silence as their eyes adapted to the darkness. Charlie could see nothing out there; he could hardly even see Constance. She was little more than a pale shadow. He strained to hear.

When it came, it sounded so close, he felt he could reach out and touch the woman. She sounded as if she was weeping. "Why do you do that? Why? Now we all die in the sea!"

He could not tell her direction, distance, anything at all. The voice seemed close, all around him.

Constance put her head down, pressing her forehead against the rounded side of the raft. "We should have slashed the other raft, scuttled it."

He had been afraid that if she had not believed she had an escape at hand, she might have used the impressive fire-fighting equipment. She might have been able to put out the fire with it. She might have known about the emergency hatch in the tiny engine room with the simple instructions: *Open in case of fire.* It would have flooded the engines and the fuel tanks with seawater; the boat would have been immobilized, but it would be afloat. Worse, he had feared that if she had been trapped, she might have reached out and killed them both instantly. She had been in the raft, knew it was comparatively safe; she had to trust it again. How long would it take for the air to leak out enough? He did not know. He could hear a paddle splashing awkwardly.

"Do you remember where we put the flare gun?" he

asked in a whisper. One to light up the scene, he thought; the next one aimed at her.

Constance began to grope for the gun. There was a loud splash close by. June Oliveira screamed shrilly.

"Sharks!" Constance yelled. She knew sharks did not make splashes, did not leap from the water. Perhaps the porpoises had come to investigate the explosion. Maybe a seabird had dived. Her hand closed on the gun and she handed it to Charlie.

"First, Charlie," the woman called out. "Constance stay with me until morning. You are good swimmer. I saw you in water. Is possible I need you to swim for me."

She was talking to still her terror of the water, the sharks she believed to be circling her, to break the silence. Constance recognized that shrillness, the clipped words; Oliveira was panic-stricken.

"Sometimes they come up under you and graze the boat," Constance yelled. "They're so rough, they puncture the rubber, and you don't even know it until too late. You can feel the sides of the raft getting soft, the top sinking in a little. . . ."

Charlie was searching for the extra packet of flares. One was in the gun; he wanted a second to jam in and fire quickly before the light faded, while she was still dazed from the sudden glare.

"I've got it," he whispered finally. "Shield your eyes."

He fired straight up, then scanned the water. She was several hundred feet away, kneeling in the other raft, holding the paddle with both hands, stilled by the unexpected light. He rammed the second flare into the gun, then pitched forward, dropping the gun, not unconscious, but without muscle tone, unable to move.

Constance snatched up the paddle and started to row as

hard as she could. She was stronger than the other woman; at least she could outdistance her.

"Stop!" Oliveira called. "Stop or I kill him now. I do not like it at this distance, but I do it."

Constance put the paddle down. The light had faded already; again there was only darkness, now even deeper, blacker. Charlie lay huddled in the bottom of the raft, unmoving.

"Stay very still," the woman said. "I come to your little boat. You are right about many things. During the night you explain to me how you know, what makes you guess, so I tell my people."

"Why Bramley? People are dying all the time. Why him?"

"Because I know him. We seldom know them, the people who are dying. It is more interesting to know him."

The water remained quiet around them; there were only the splashes of her paddle. She was so inept, it would take her a long time to cross the distance separating them. Constance nudged Charlie with her toe. He did not respond.

"Why don't you just hang around hospitals? People die there every hour, every day."

"They are drugged. Sometimes it is good." Her voice was getting firmer, losing its fearful note, as she narrowed the space between them, and the water remained still.

Constance nudged Charlie again. Move, she thought at him, please move, get up. "You come here and murder, kill people. Watch them suffer for your own amusement. Do you torture them to death to drag it out?"

"We are not uncivilized," the woman said sharply. "We do not kill; we participate. It does no harm."

"You killed Dino!"

There was silence; her paddle slapped the water, then

again. "I expect the other one. I have only until Sunday. I will be forgiven."

Constance shuddered. She reached out and touched Charlie's face. She wanted to lie down by him, gather him in her arms, just hold him.

The paddle hit, lifted, hit. And then it suddenly splashed very hard, and the woman screamed hoarsely. "My raft getting soft! It is punctured!"

Charlie stiffened even more under Constance's hand. *She* was using him as a beacon, homing in on him.

Constance picked up one of the water jugs and heaved it out toward the other raft. It made a loud noise when it hit the water.

"Sharks are all around us!" she yelled. The other paddle stopped and there was no sound. Constance groped for something else to throw, something heavy enough to make a noise, light enough to lift and heave. Her hand closed over the paddle. She lifted it silently and brought it down hard on the water. She screamed. "They're hitting our raft! Charlie, do something!"

Charlie began to stir; he pulled himself to his knees cautiously; the woman was letting go. Her terror was so great, she could no longer hold him. From the other raft, there were sounds of panicky rowing; she was simply beating the water with the paddle. Charlie and Constance began to row, saying nothing, trying to slip the plastic paddles into the water without a sound, pulling hard.

"It is sinking!" the woman screamed. "Help me!"

Constance screamed also, trying for the same note of terror. She screamed again, then listened. The other woman was incoherent, screaming, screeching words that were not human language. Soon it all stopped.

* * *

For a long time, they sat holding each other without speaking. Now and then, something splashed, now close to them, now farther away. They could see nothing.

In a little while, Charlie thought, he would fire the flare gun again, then periodically repeat it through the night. Someone would see. Maybe someone had seen the fire, was on the way already. He would have to think of a story to tell them—a fire at sea, Dino's going back after getting them into the raft.... He could handle that part. He had heard enough stories essentially like his, lies, excuses, reasonably enough put together to fool most people. He could do that.

And Constance was thinking: There would come a day when one or the other of them would start to doubt what had happened. What that one would remember was that they, together, had killed a crazy woman.

"She wasn't human," Charlie said, breaking the silence. And Constance knew he would be the one who would come awake at night and stare at the ceiling and wonder about what they had done. She would have to be watchful for the signs, make him remember it exactly the way it had happened. And one day, she thought, one of them would say what neither had voiced yet: That woman had not been alone. There were others.

Now Charlie thought: They would live with this, knowing what they had done, that there were others out there, maybe not as murderous as this one had been, or maybe just like her. They could tell no one; no one would ever believe. Constance had her proof of that uncharted part of the psyche and could not even use it.

"I think I dislocated my shoulder when I threw that jug out," Constance said, shifting in his arms. "I'm aching all over."

And he knew his hand was bleeding through the bandage; it was throbbing painfully suddenly. He had forgotten about it. "In just a minute, I'll see if there's a sling in the first-aid kit. I need a new bandage, too." He felt her nod against his shoulder.

"Poor, little, miserable, helpless, vulnerable, hurt people," she sighed. "That's us. Adrift on an endless ocean as dark as hell. With a terminal case of life. But I wouldn't trade with them." Knowing you were gambling eternity, you wouldn't dare risk your life for someone you loved, she thought, trying to ignore the pain in her shoulder, down into her arm. You wouldn't dare love, she thought. You wouldn't dare. Period. Not far away, something splashed.

Neither of them moved yet. It was enough for now to rest, to feel the solidity of the other, to renew the strength the last several hours had taken from them. Quietly, they drifted on the dark sea.

SISTER ANGEL

DINNER HAD BEEN extraordinarily good, Charlie thought with contentment, even if he had cooked it himself. From the kitchen there now came the soft chugging of the dishwasher at work; closer, the clink of cup on saucer, a pop from the fireplace or a hiss; even closer, the nearly inaudible purr of Ashcan, who had settled on his lap instantly when he sat down. Outside, silently, the snow was piling up. He sighed again and opened his eyes.

Candy was sneaking up on the cream pitcher on the coffee table. Her forequarters were low to the floor, her rear up high, and the white tip of her tail twitched like a semaphore flag.

"Ridiculous cat," Constance said. "That's how she hunts, signaling, Here I am!" The cat reached the table. "Candy!" Constance said, not raising her voice. Candy now discovered that her right-hind leg was filthy and started to wash it.

Gretchen laughed. "It was so strange to think of you and Charlie stuck way out in the country, but it's kind of nice. I like it." She glanced at her husband and added quickly, "Not for myself, of course."

"We're two hours out of New York," Constance said.

63

"And the village is lovely. The people, now that the tourists have gone, are very nice to us. They still don't trust us, or include us when *they* say 'us,' but it will come."

"Maybe," Gretchen said. She lifted her cognac and swirled it. "Is Charlie going to sleep now?"

"Probably. Are you, Charlie?"

He opened his eyes again and winked at Constance. "Tough day down at the south forty," he drawled.

How good it was, Constance thought then, to see him so relaxed, so content. During the year since his retirement, he had become younger-looking; the lines were melting away, the mask dissolving. The real difference was in his eyes, she thought, considering him; they had been turning hard, impenetrable, and now the deep brown was softening again, reverting to how his eyes had been when they first met at college over twenty-five years ago, before he had become a New York City cop. He was watching her watch him, she realized. She tried not to smile, shook her head almost imperceptibly, and turned to Gretchen, but not before Charlie raised an eyebrow and practically leered at her.

She heard the hint of laughter in her own voice now. "Okay, we've wined you and dined you and later we'll even bed you down. Can't go out into the storm, my dears. Your turn. You said there was an urgent problem you had to discuss. Give."

"Do you believe in ghosts?" Dutch asked suddenly before Gretchen had a chance to speak. He ignored her stiff glance of reproof. Dutch was in his late forties, a very tall, heavy man who had been an athlete in school and had kept in shape since. He was an engineering consultant, with clients throughout the world. He was leaving again the following day, Gretchen had mentioned when she called.

Gretchen was trying to contain her anger by studiously pouring herself more coffee, looking at her cup, the coffee carafe, anything but her husband. It bemused Constance to find that she had slid from her country hostess role into her professional psychologist role effortlessly, against her will even. Here she was observing, taking mental notes.

Dutch scowled at the cat in the middle of the room, still grooming itself. "It started back last summer," he said. "At her cousin Wanda's house in Connecticut. Vernon and Wanda Garrity. Only Vernon is dead now, and Wanda thinks he's haunting her. And *she*"—he poked his thumb in the direction of his wife—"thinks I'm to blame."

"I never said that."

"You all but said it a hundred times."

"Wasn't Vernon Garrity the inventor?" Charlie asked lazily. "I didn't know he was dead."

"That's the one," Dutch said. "He showed us some cats he was working on last summer." He chuckled and shook his head. "Here's a guy who invents million-dollar gadgets for the government, for industry, and in his spare time he plays with mechanical cats."

"What happened last summer?" Charlie wished he could close his eyes again and take just a small nap. He had spent the morning splitting firewood and now it felt good to be tired, full, and warm before the fire, too good to ruin by talking about ghosts. Still, trying to connect a man like Vernon Garrity with ghosts had turned on a switch in his head and sleep switches had been shut down.

"You know how many times someone asks if you believe in ghosts and everyone says no and then they all spend the evening telling one improbable story after another without ever giving you anything you can hold on to. Noises, feelings, precognitions, fears. Bullshit!" He glanced apologetically at Constance. "Sorry. But that night, it got to me. I'd only met Vernon a couple of times, and there were things I really wanted to talk to him about. Anyway, at dinner he says, 'Do you believe in ghosts?' And I said something or other that squelched the topic."

"What you said," Gretchen remarked, almost casually, as she studied the design on her coffee cup, "was that only idiots take seriously the superstitious fears of women, children, savages, and lunatics."

He flushed. "I don't know exactly what I said, but whatever it was, the topic was dropped and wasn't brought up again. And now his widow is haunted, and *she* thinks it's my fault."

"Wanda didn't get a chance to talk to Vernon again about what was on his mind," Gretchen went on when Dutch stopped. "The next day, she drove back to New York with us, and the day after that, before she returned, he was killed. And now, six months later, she is getting messages from him, she says."

"How was he killed?" Charlie asked.

"He was walking on the beach and someone hit him in the head with a rock and robbed him. No one was ever arrested."

"Didn't I meet Wanda years ago? She was a little girl," Constance said then.

"She's thirty-five now. Maybe at a slumber party at my place? She was at our house a lot."

Constance and Gretchen had been in college together, had been friends, had parted and lost track of each other for many years. Gretchen's call had been a surprise to Constance and, she admitted to herself ruefully, she had looked forward to gossip about mutual friends and enemies from the past. What she was hearing now was not at all what she had had in mind.

"Don't forget Brother Amos," Dutch said. "And Sister Angel."

"Please. I'm getting to that. Brother Amos calls himself an evangelist. He claims that Vernon is in touch with him, and he tells Wanda what Vernon says. Angel is his daughter, a teenager. He calls her Sister Angel."

"Nasty can of worms," Charlie commented, shaking his head. "People who want to hear from the dead always find a way. Not much you can do about it."

"I said she should see a shrink."

"Well, she won't," Gretchen snapped. "She claims that Brother Amos has told her things that no one on God's earth but she and Vernon could have known. She isn't hysterical or crazy or disturbed in any other way."

"So you want Constance to go talk to her." Charlie glanced at Constance with what was almost an evil grin. She understood the message: Now it was her turn to explain that she was retired, not taking private cases, busy writing a book and being a country housewife.

"Aunt Louise," Gretchen said carefully, "asked me to get in touch with both of you. She wants someone to investigate Amos. And she wants Constance to talk sense into Wanda."

"For the first time in her life, Aunt Louise has money in the family," Dutch added dryly. "And she wants to keep it there."

Gretchen nodded. "That's part of it, of course. The way things are going, Brother Amos is likely to be the main beneficiary of Vernon's death. And, of course, Brother Amos is a fraud." She took a deep breath. "I have a letter from Wanda agreeing to cooperate with both of you, agreeing to pay your fees. She isn't any happier about this than the rest of us. But neither can she deny that what Amos is telling her is authentic."

Later, propped up on pillows in their king-sized water bed, Constance said thoughtfully, "It's so weird that no one even thought of investigating Amos MacHugh until Gretchen mentioned it." Charlie was undressing slowly, methodically, as he always did. She laughed. "What a pair they are, Gretchen and Dutch."

He shook his head. That was not the way to live, forever snapping at each other's heels. Looking at Constance now, he saw the woman in her forties, but he also saw the girl he had fallen in love with, had married twenty-five years ago, and he could not decide which woman he was more attracted to, and, unable to decide, he thanked his good luck in having both in one package.

"You know we won't be able to convince Wanda that Amos is out to get her money, don't you?" He got into bed, making waves that bounced her up and down.

"Probably not. But you may turn up something to shake her faith in what he's telling her. Maybe that's all we can hope for."

Charlie groped for her under the covers, grinning his most wicked grin. "That's not all that I'm hoping for, cutie. Make eyes at me in front of company, will you, shameless blond hussy?"

The Garrity house was immense. The entrance was out-thrust like the prow of a ship, with a wing angled off on each side. There was a wide, covered portico outside a spacious foyer that extended upward the two flights of the house. On the upper level, a balcony was bathed in light from windows on the north and south, with the bedroom wings on either side. From the foyer, the living room was down several steps; its southern exposure was glass, overlooking a red-tiled terrace, the lawn, and, beyond it all, a lake. Family room, TV room, dining room, library, studies, all were large, brightly lighted with wide, tall windows, all furnished in warm colors, decorated with American Indian artwork, wall hangings, rugs.

Wanda was an interior decorator; her own house was proof that she was a very good one. She had not given up her work after marrying Vernon, Gretchen had said, rolling her eyes in exasperation.

"This is all very lovely." Constance waved her hand at the house generally.

"Thank you," Wanda said. "When Vernon's first wife lived here, it was white and a deep blue—ice-cold. We met at my shop, actually. He wasn't sure what he wanted, just some color. We ended up with this." She laughed, stopped abruptly, and looked past Constance at the fireplace wall where a Navajo rug glowed in the light of the low afternoon sun.

Slender, dark-haired, she looked as if she had been ill, had not recovered fully; there were circles under her eyes and she had the absent expression of someone still paying more attention to her body than most people did. She was chain-smoking.

"Please call me Wanda," she had said almost instantly. "I'm sorry Gretchen is out. She's told me so much about you and Charlie, your careers, I feel as if I almost remember meeting you at her mother's house, not once, but several times. And it will make it easier to explain to Brother Amos. You know, friends from our childhood come to visit."

"You have to explain us to him?"

"Not really, but . . . One does, you know." A flush colored her cheeks and left again.

"Wanda," Charlie said then, "I'll want his fingerprints—a glass he handles, a picture, almost anything will do. That's where we'll start."

She nodded, then with a swift motion she stubbed out the cigarette and took a deep breath. "I don't know what to say, how to treat you, how to expect you to treat me. Do you want to ask questions?"

"Not yet," Constance said. "Let us be houseguests for the time being, get acquainted. Let questions come up naturally. How does anyone manage to gather all these artifacts? Are they all for sale somewhere, like a sublime supermarket?"

Wanda laughed, this time a genuine laugh, and stood up. "I'll show you the rest of the house. It took me nearly a year to gather the stuff. I made a dozen trips out to Arizona, New Mexico, Montana. . . ." She looked inquiringly at Charlie; he shook his head.

When they were out of sight, he started his own tour of the house and yard. He met Mrs. Riley, the housekeeper, and Jefferson Smith, the yardman, and ended up at the lakefront, on the narrow strip of beach. The lake was about three miles long, two miles across at the widest point. Straight across it, there was a bluff, and on that a trailer court where Brother Amos and his daughter lived. With a good telescope, anyone over there could look right into the Garrity living room, he realized. He turned to look back at the house, even more imposing here than from the front, because from here he could see the mammoth living room, the terrace, sun glinting off the upper-floor windows, turning them all gold. From across the lake, the whole house must look like a gold mine, he thought.

Inside the house, Wanda pointed to him on the beach. She and Constance were on the upper balcony. "You're yin and yang," she said. "He's so dark and mysterious-looking and you're like a Nordic queen, tall, fair, splendid."

Constance smiled. "Tell me something about Vernon," she said, looking out at Charlie on the beach.

"Charlie reminds me of him," Wanda said slowly. "Not the way he looks, but the way he listens, the way he accepts what he hears, maybe. Vernon was like that. Quiet, steady, so loyal that when his first wife left him, he waited for her for more than a year, really believing she'd come back. She left him for a ballet dancer," she added wryly. "We were both so cautious. I had been married before, too—my childhood sweetheart. We used to fight all the time; he beat me up regularly when we were children. After we got married, he reverted to his childhood behavior." She stopped. When she went on, her voice was crisp. "People thought I married Vernon for his money, of course. And I suppose there was something to that in the beginning, but not later. We were married five years. Each of us needed something the other had. We were happy together."

They started to walk down the wide stairs that led to the foyer. Indian masks lined the wall here. "This is for the peyote ceremony," she said, pointing to a ceramic mask grotesquely contorted, brilliantly painted. "And that one was used for the buffalo hunt. The medicine man wore it and danced for eighteen hours to call the buffalo. . . . He was going to leave me. He had fallen in love with someone else."

Constance could feel the presence of staring eyes from

the empty holes of the masks, could feel the presence of the ancient shamans. "Did he tell you that?"

Wanda looked up at her. "He didn't have to. He said he was haunted by her, obsessed by her, that he couldn't stop thinking of her. I told him I had to go away to think, and I went home with Gretchen and Dutch, and he was killed."

Her face was so white, it could have been one of the masks.

"You hadn't suspected before he told you?"

She shook her head. "Naturally, I knew there was something preying on him, but not that. I was as naïve as he had been with his first wife. I don't know when it could have happened. We were never apart. I don't even know who she is." Her voice was faint, unbelieving. "I never told anyone, not Gretchen, not my mother, no one! And that's one of the things Brother Amos told me. There's no way he could have found out, no way. No one suspected." She started to walk again, this time holding tightly to the balustrade.

"What did Vernon mean when he brought up ghosts that last night?" Constance thought at first that she would not answer. She kept taking one step after another as if she had not heard. At the foot of the stairs, she stopped.

"I think it was a premonition, that he was telling me he would come back when he died."

"Maybe you think that now, but what did you think then?"

"Nothing. We never had talked about ghosts. It was an incredible thing for him to bring up like that, and of course Dutch behaved so badly. I didn't know what he meant."

"Wanda, why did you agree to have Charlie and me come? What do you want?"

"I read your book. You have an open mind, don't automatically reject things. I agreed more than a week ago.

Since then, every day there's something new, something that only Vernon could be saying to me. Brother Amos says *ghost* is the wrong word. It's a spirit, a soul, something else. Vernon isn't able to leave because there were things he didn't finish, things he has to tell me. I just don't know what to think, what to do. I'm sorry I can't answer your questions better. Every time I see him, I find out more. Perhaps in time I'll have better answers."

"You mean from Amos."

She shook her head. "From Vernon. Through Brother Amos."

Brother Amos was tall and blond, broad-shouldered, trim. He could have been a car salesman, an insurance agent, a government undersecretary, anything that called for a smooth exterior, good manners. He shook hands heartily, like a good bureaucrat, and when he took Wanda's hand, he used both of his and pressed hers between them as he gazed into her eyes and murmured something inaudible.

His daughter, Angel, was very thin, still gangly, with long, pale hair that was baby-fine and very beautiful eyes a deep violet color. Give her a few years, Charlie thought, and she'd have Daddy pacing the floor every night.

"It was good of you, Gretchen, to bring company to help enliven the atmosphere in this house. Wanda needs company, needs companions, conversation. Too much grieving is a bad thing for anyone. Life is to be lived fully if we are to rob death of its fears."

"I'm acting bartender," Charlie said rather briskly. "Martini mixings, scotch, let's see. . . ." He looked over the bottles, found the shaker, and started to mix martinis. "And for the young lady, we have Coke, Pepsi, juice. . . ." He looked at her as he continued to shake the gin and ice.

When they had been introduced, she had ducked her head quickly, shyly, but now she looked at him, and again he was struck by the loveliness of her eyes.

"Coke," she said in a low voice.

"And juice for me," Amos said. "I don't condemn moderate alcohol, you understand, but I prefer to be abstemious. The training of a lifetime is hard to put aside."

"Where do you preach?" Constance asked.

"Nowhere at the moment. My calling was late, too late for divinity school, too urgent for years of education. My church is the world, wherever there are human souls yearning for the Word, for Truth, for Guidance."

Constance knew he capitalized the words in his head. Mildly, she said, "A tent revivalist? Really?"

"My dear lady, the Word of God is valid wherever it is uttered, be it in an alleyway or a tent or the finest cathedral. Wherever there is an open heart, the Word of God can enter."

"Here you go," Charlie said cheerfully. "Juice, Coke, and for the rest of us, good old booze." He handed out the drinks. "Do you heal at your meetings, Brother Amos? The laying on of hands, all that?"

"Enough about me," Amos protested, putting his glass on the table at his elbow. "What is your trade, Mr. Meiklejohn?"

"Retired. Out to pasture. Used to be a building inspector of sorts."

Constance looked at him admiringly, wondering if he had rehearsed that answer. In the arson squad for years, he had indeed inspected many buildings for the New York City Fire Department. Now Brother Amos turned to her.

"And Mrs. Meiklejohn? Do you have a profession?"

"I'm thinking of writing a book," she said seriously. "As soon as I have enough time."

"A writer! How exciting." He dismissed them both and turned his attention to Wanda. "And you, my dear, are you feeling better today?"

"I'm fine, really," she said. She looked at her martini, tasted it, put it down, and picked up her cigarette instead.

"Amos wants to build a church in town," Gretchen said then.

"Perhaps," he said. "Perhaps. I am awaiting guidance, as we all must."

Charlie poured more martinis, refilled Angel's glass with Coke, and then knocked Amos's glass off the table when he started to refill it. He put it aside, brought out a fresh glass and filled that one, and went on to pass the tray of cheese and shrimp pastries. He managed to spill one of them on Amos's knee.

"Keep falling over my own feet," he said. "One of those days. . . ."

Amos was wiping away the stain of shrimp.

"Needs a little water," Charlie said, dipping a napkin into the pitcher of water; he returned to Amos, began to sponge off the spot.

"Thank you," Amos said stiffly. "I can manage. If you don't mind."

Charlie was practically on his lap, close enough to see that Brother Amos dyed his hair. He backed off with an apologetic grin and took his own seat, drained his martini. When he looked up, he found Angel's gaze fixed on him, her violet eyes unblinking, an unfathomable expression on her face, the kind of look children sometimes assume. After what seemed an uncomfortable time, he asked, "Do you go to school here?"

She shook her head.

"I tutor her at home," Amos said. "I don't approve of the moral values the school systems teach."

Dinner was interminable. Everyone waited for Brother Amos to lead the conversation, and this he did willingly at first, then with more and more reluctance. His store of small talk ran out before the entrée was served.

When he began to discuss weather, even Wanda looked desperate. Gretchen maliciously kept silent and allowed Constance to feed him enough response for him to keep floundering.

"Have you been through a tornado?" Constance asked, eating her scallopine.

Charlie ate with pleasure, listening to everything, seeing every gesture. Angel was yawning.

Amos tried baseball. No one else was a sports addict. With dessert, the talk moved on to television, and again Amos had to carry it alone. None of the others watched much television.

"There are a lot of good programs," Amos said. "Good educational programs for children, spiritual programs, some fine old movies. . . ."

Charlie thought he could see a glaze forming over Constance's eyes and he suppressed a grin. Brother Amos was wearing out his welcome. As soon as there was a pause in the monologue, he said, "Wanda, any chance of seeing those mechanical cats Gretchen told us about?"

She looked relieved. Without even making certain they were all through with the mousse, she stood up, moved to the door. "Why don't you go into the living room for coffee. I'll bring in one of the cats."

The others left the dining room at a more leisurely pace and had not seated themselves yet when she reappeared, holding a furry white cat. At first glance, it appeared to be a live cat, its tail full and limp, its forepaws dangling, but then, looking at its too-bright emerald eyes, one could see that it was a toy, a stuffed animal. Wanda put it down in the center of the room and they formed a circle around it.

"This one's set to respond to my voice. They're all voice-activated. They're covered with mink, or vicuña, or even silk. There are still problems with them. They're heat-seeking, but they're so dumb that they can't tell one heat source from another. They'll approach the fireplace and stop at a certain temperature and curl up and purr. Or maybe go to a lightbulb, or a toaster, anything that's the right temperature. He was trying to get them to go to people only, but all they know is temperature."

Angel moved in front of the toy, bending slightly to peer at its face.

"Kitty, kitty," Wanda said then.

The cat moved, slowly rose from the sleeping position to stand on four feet; its tail went straight up in a realistic way, and it turned its head from side to side and then started to walk a bit stiffly, but catlike.

Constance was watching the cat with amusement when she felt a wave of revulsion and fear, then another even stronger, and something else. Angel screamed.

The next several seconds were confused; Angel was screaming, backing away from the cat that was homing in on her. Wanda had thrown her hands over her face and was swaying, moaning. Charlie caught Angel and half-carried her out of the path of the advancing cat, held her pressed against his chest as she screamed again and again and finally started to sob. Amos grabbed the cat and held it at arm's length, like something dangerous. Constance backed Wanda into a chair, forced her down. The revulsion, horror,

terror had faded, leaving her spent and weak. She saw that
Gretchen had gone white also, and she groaned, left Wanda,
and took Gretchen by the arm, sat her down, too.

"For heaven's sake!" she exclaimed, and took the cat
from Amos, who was staring at it as if entranced. She
started toward the workroom with it.

The spell was broken. Amos shook himself and ran over
to Angel. "Baby, baby, it's just a toy! It's all right, sweetheart."

Angel clung to Charlie, burying her face against him, no
longer crying. He tried to loosen her grasp, but she shook
her head, held on.

"Come on, honey. I'll take you home. It's all right now."
Amos pried her loose and held her, stroked her fine hair, all
the while making soothing noises.

"I need a drink," Constance said, rejoining them.

"Amen," Charlie said, already at the long table where the
bottles were lined up. He filled a glass with brandy and
downed it.

Wanda stared fixedly at Brother Amos. "He was here,
wasn't he? What did he want?"

He nodded gravely. "Yes. Tomorrow we'll talk. I have to
take my girl home now. She's had a shock. She's very sensitive to this kind of thing, very sensitive."

"In the morning? At ten?"

"After lunch," he said. "I'll come at two."

Charlie handed Angel a glass of water. "You need this,
too," he said gently. Her face was swollen, hurt-looking. He
patted her shoulder, then took brandy to Wanda. And she,
he thought, looked like staring death.

Amos took the glass from his daughter, put it down, and
left with her, holding her around the shoulders as they
walked out.

Now Wanda stood up shakily. "If you'll excuse me," she said in a low voice. "I don't think I can stand to talk about anything tonight."

Gretchen left with her. "I'll be back," she said at the doorway.

Constance drank her brandy almost as fast as Charlie had done earlier. "Another."

They both had another. They sat in facing chairs, not talking yet. Finally, he said, "You were swell."

"And you had your hands full. What happened, Charlie?"

"Damned if I know. Did you feel . . . ?"

She nodded. "Like being at one of those awful horror movies, and you're the victim."

"Yeah. Maybe another brandy. And I've got to retrieve that glass." He went behind the table and stopped, then cursed. "Mrs. Riley found it first. I thought I had it hidden."

Constance pointed to the water glass. "He handled that."

He picked up the glass carefully, holding it at the bottom, and dumped the remaining water back into the pitcher. He started to leave with it, then hesitated, a curious look on his face, as if he was surprised at himself for the question he had framed even as he asked, "Will you be all right alone for a couple of minutes?"

"Fine," she said, glad that he had asked, startled that he had asked.

Gretchen joined them while they were having coffee. Wanda had agreed to take a sleeping pill, something she generally refused to do, afraid of addiction. She was sleeping already. Lucky Wanda.

"I don't dare close my eyes," Gretchen said. Then darkly, she added, "I sure wish Dutch had been here, the bastard, laughing at ghosts."

"Gretchen, that's the last kind of thing you should say now," Constance said severely. "All Wanda needs is any sort of confirmation and she'll be over that edge so deep, we may not be able to pull her out again."

Gretchen looked at her with amazement. "What else do you think it could have been? It was Vernon, mad as hell at us for playing with his toys! She knows that."

Before Constance could respond, Charlie asked, "Is Amos always that solicitous with Angel?"

"Always. He won't leave her alone at all. That's why she isn't in school. He hinted of bad things that happened years ago. I guess we all know what that means. She may be a bit retarded. She looks and acts like a twelve-year-old, but she's sixteen or seventeen."

"Does she sit in on his talks with Wanda?" Constance asked.

"No. But she isn't very far away, the next room, maybe. No more than that."

Before midnight, they were all in their rooms, the house quiet. Constance and Charlie had twin beds, each with its own headboard lamp. Charlie's was turned off; he was lying on his back, his hands under his head, staring at the ceiling, now and then grunting softly, thinking.

In the other bed, Constance was writing in her notebook. *What happened?* headed the page. *Had Angel felt* it *first, stronger than the rest of them? Why had she screamed so? Why had she stopped screaming?* Constance examined that question thoughtfully and then underlined it.

"Honey, you want to go to town with me when I take the glass?"

"I guess I'd better stay here, don't you think?"

"Yeah, but I don't want you to."

"Charlie! Stop that. You'll scare me!"

"Wasn't thinking of ghosts," he said soberly. "Poor old Vernon didn't get bopped on the head by a ghost."

She had forgotten Vernon. "You think all this is connected?"

"Oh sure." He bridged the space between them and kissed her. "I want to scare you a little. I want you to be damn careful."

He dreamed: He was dancing with a woman. His eyes were closed, his cheek against her hair, his hands moving down her soft, silky body, warm and yielding to his touch, so responsive that her body and his were not really separate, but moved together as if joined at a common nerve center. Her hands were like warm kisses on his skin; where they touched, he came alive. *Now*, he whispered into her hair. *Now!* They sank into a cloudlike softness.

He came wide awake and sat upright. "Good Christ!" he whispered, wet with sweat, shivering. He got out of bed and pulled on his robe, stumbled from the bedroom. Behind him, Constance made a slight noise, and he saw her, an old woman with graying hair, lines at her eyes, old, old.

Moments later, she sat up, looking at the other bed, sure he had said something. She reached over to touch him and found the bed empty. Slowly, she got up and put on her robe and slippers, troubled without cause, wanting to find him. The bathroom door stood open. She went into the hall, where there was a dim light. Going down the stairs, she felt again the presence of the masks, the staring eyeholes, and she drew her robe tighter about her. He was standing at the broad expanse of glass in the living room, outlined against the pale dawn light. He was smoking.

"Charlie! What's wrong?" He had not smoked a cigarette in over ten years.

He stiffened, then turned to look at her, and again he saw an aging woman with tousled hair, sleep-heavy features. The image faded and he saw Constance.

"I thought I heard something." Deliberately, he stubbed out his cigarette and turned again to look out over the lake, which was like a silver skin over an abyss.

She went to stand at his side but did not touch him. In profile, he looked hard, unknowable. "Char—"

"Go back to bed. I have to think and I have to be alone for a while." He looked at her; his eyes were like obsidian disks.

She left him standing before the sliding glass door to the terrace.

Why didn't it fade? he thought almost savagely. Dreams always fade on awakening; the most frightening dream loses its power after you're fully awake; the edges begin to crumble, details sink back to the pit. He was still there an hour later when rain fractured the surface of the lake. He went back to bed then. Constance was awake, he knew, but he did not speak, nor did she. He was so tense, he knew he would not go back to sleep, was afraid to go back to sleep, afraid he would slip into that other reality that was more compelling than anything he had ever known.

Gretchen and Constance had breakfast together in a pleasant little room off the kitchen. Charlie had gone into town, and Wanda was not feeling very well.

"What was the routine here?" Constance asked. "They were both home most of the time—doing what?"

"I don't know what Vernon was up to. We never did until he showed us, like with those damn cats. That was a complete surprise. Wanda's allergic to cats, you see, and he wanted to give her a present. Spent over a year working on the fool things. And Wanda could afford to be a consultant when it pleased her. The last job she did was two years ago, a remodeled opera house in Bridgeport. They wanted to recreate a turn-of-the-century ambience, and she flew into it like a whirlwind. It's gorgeous. He walked every day for a couple of hours. Sometimes she went with him, sometimes not. She was busy off and on with her pet charity, a crippled children's hospital in Bridgeport. And they played games—word games, chess, even television games. He loved games."

Constance finished her toast and sighed. Nothing there. "Did they entertain much, go to other people's houses, that sort of thing?"

Gretchen shook her head. "When he married Wanda, it was evidently the last thing this nice old community could tolerate. Someone snubbed them both early on, and that was the end of that."

"Did Amos live over there last summer?"

Gretchen frowned. "I just wish," she said. "But no. They moved in two and a half months ago. That's when Wanda began hearing from Vernon. She was doing okay until then. There was the shock, of course, and she was grief-stricken, but she was pulling out of it, and then he came along and threw her into a tailspin."

Outside, the rain was splashing on the red tiles and the lake was churned by a brisk wind, and Charlie did not have a raincoat with him. Constance knew exactly where it was, in their hall closet at home. She wondered if the snow was getting too deep to dig out again without a tractor, wondered if their house sitter was burning wood and not turning the thermostat up, using oil that was fantastically expensive,

when the wood was free. Charlie would be soaked. She
had not even seen him before he left that morning. She had
been in the bathroom showering and when she got out, he
was gone. The rain began slanting in against the glass.

Gretchen had shopping to do. Constance read for a while,
then prowled the silent house restlessly, finally settling
down to look through scrapbooks she found in the television room. Many of the pictures were of Vernon, a
gray-haired, slender man with a straight carriage, squared
shoulders. There were also many pictures of children, most
of them in braces, or in wheelchairs. There were several
of Vernon holding one child or another up at a game of
chance, a ball toss, or dartboard; then one of Wanda at a
booth, with a child on a counter, eating cotton candy. There
were no more pictures after that series.

Charlie called shortly before noon. "I won't be back for
a couple more hours. Everything quiet?"

"You wouldn't believe how quiet. What are you doing?"

"I don't want to talk now. Okay? Guess who's chief of
police in Bridgeport these days. Tony Francello! We're having lunch, and I'll hang around to get some information
when it comes in."

Constance stared at the phone for a long time after replac-
ing it. She shivered with a sudden chill. What in God's name
was wrong with Charlie? He had talked like a stranger.
Thank heaven Tony was at hand, she thought then. He would
speed things along. He and Charlie had worked together for
several years before Charlie transferred out of the arson
squad. She wanted this finished, wanted to take Charlie and
run home as fast as they could get there.

Amos and Angel arrived shortly before two. Constance
admitted them, prepared to take Angel somewhere to talk.

"Hello," she said cheerfully.

Amos nodded at her. "I told Sister Angel that she could watch television while I talk to Mrs. Garrity. I'll hang up your coat, honey." He hung both coats in the closet, and Angel went down the hallway toward the television room. Constance started to follow her.

"Mrs. Meiklejohn," Amos said urgently, stopping her, "your husband is in danger. I see him surrounded by flames and he is desperately afraid. Take him away from here!"

"What are you talking about? What do you mean?"

"He is in mortal danger! He fears the flames as he fears hellfire! Take him home! If you want to save his sanity and his life, take him away from here!"

"Brother Amos! Come up, please!" Wanda stood on the balcony, looking down at them. Amos turned away from Constance and ran up the stairs.

With great effort, Constance released the railing she had grasped. Flames! She had known when Charlie began having nightmares about arson. She remembered too vividly the things he had muttered, thrashing about in his sleep. *Here! Not like that for Christ sake! It won't catch like that. Let me do it!* They had talked about it then, but not since, never since. He had asked for a transfer, had changed his job, and, she had thought, it ended. The nightmares stopped gradually. Was that what had troubled him so terribly last night? One of those nightmares? Her palms were wet. She wiped them on the legs of her pants. How had Amos known that?

The masks stared down at her. They saw everything with those empty eyes, heard everything, knew everything. And Amos? How had he found out that?

She knew she was not ready just yet to question Angel.

She wished Charlie would come back. More than anything, she wanted to talk to him.

Half an hour later, she joined Angel in the television room. "Mind if I watch with you?" she asked. "It sure is quiet in this house today."

Angel glanced up at her and shrugged, turned her attention back to the set. She was watching a game show.

"Our daughter is in college," Constance said, settling herself into a chair near Angel's. "She wants to be a biologist. What will you major in?"

Angel continued to watch the show. "I don't know."

"That's the best way to enter, I think. Leave it open until you've tried out various fields. Where will you go?"

"I don't know."

"Well, I don't think it hurts to wait until you're older. Have you always been afraid of cats?"

"I'm not afraid of cats."

"Mechanical ones, I meant. It was rather cute, like a stuffed toy that can move."

Angel pushed a button on the remote control, got a black-and-white movie with Myrna Loy.

"It really isn't very different from the windup toys that kids play with when they're young."

Angel pushed the button again, then again.

"Actually, what you're doing now with that control is pretty much how the cat works, I think. You give a signal and it does something that it's been programmed to do."

The stations were flicking past faster and faster.

"It wasn't aiming at you, you know. You just happened to be closest to it."

Flick, flick. They were back to the original game show. Angel turned up the volume.

"Angel, there are people who can help you. These things don't usually get better by themselves. You don't have to be so afraid."

Angel jumped up and glared at Constance. "Leave me alone! I'm not afraid of a stupid cat!" She ran from the room.

Gloomily, Constance turned off the set and followed the girl. When she reached the foyer, it was in time to see Charlie leading Angel back into the house, his arm about her protectively.

"Take it easy," he was saying. "No one's going to hurt you. I won't let anyone hurt you. Come on, let's have something to drink. Who was chasing you, anyway?"

"She wants to hurt me," Angel said breathlessly, her face pressed against his side. "She won't leave me alone."

"Who, honey? Just tell me who."

Angel nodded at Constance, who was standing at the hallway entrance, and pointed. "Her," she said.

When Charlie looked at Constance, his face was set in hard lines. This is how *they* must have felt, Constance thought distantly. By *they*, she meant the ones he interrogated, the ones he suspected, the ones he intended to stop one way or another, the ones he hated.

Before either could say anything, Amos came running down the stairs. "Time to go home, Sister Angel," he said cheerfully. "Lessons to do. Sister Wanda is resting now. We'll come back later."

There was a glint in his eyes that looked like satisfaction, or possibly even contempt.

In their room a few minutes later, Charlie told her what he had found out. "His name is Andrew Donovan, half a dozen pinches but never a conviction. Petty stuff. Con games, most of them, the chicken-drop switch, stuff like that. And for the last few years, he's been with a carnival, a magic act. Long black hair, full black beard. It played in Bridgeport last summer, but no one would recognize him now."

She shook her head. It made no sense at all. This was not like any con game she had heard of. And why had he warned her to get Charlie out of here?

"Don't shake your head," Charlie said brusquely. "It all fits. He killed Vernon, split, came back when things quieted down. And now he's working his way into the house. What more could you ask for?"

She told him about the picture album. Vernon could have met him at the carnival. "But why did he kill Vernon? Petty con men don't murder as a rule."

"So Vernon found out something about him. What difference does it make? Even if he didn't do it, he's a con artist, and with the background of a magic show, mind reading and all, the rest of it's easy. This is what Wanda needs to help her give him the bum's rush."

"She won't be convinced."

"I've got what they wanted. We're finished here. I want you to take the car back home this afternoon. I'll be along in a few days."

He was looking out their window at the lake, his back to her. The rain had stopped and a feeble sun was lighting the clouds that lingered.

"Charlie, this is what we have to talk about. What's wrong with you? What's happened to you?"

He looked at her with an expression so miserable that she wanted to go to him, hold him hard. "I don't know. I have to be alone for a while. I have to be alone so I can think something through."

"Vernon became obsessed with someone else all at once," she said slowly. "I think that was the ghost he wanted to talk about that night. Who is it, Charlie?"

He had averted his face, did not answer.

"You don't know, do you?"

"I'll find her. That's why I have to stay after you go home. I have to find her, find out how real this is, what I can do about it." His voice was strained and harsh.

Like Vernon, she thought. Just like Vernon. "You didn't get any sleep last night," she said. "Why don't you nap now before dinner?"

Outside their room, she looked up and down the hallway and said under her breath, "You can't have him! Ghost, ghoul, whatever you are, you can't have him!"

Gretchen met her in the lower hallway. "Telephone for Charlie. Is he in your room?"

"He's sleeping. I'll take it." She took it in the living room.

"Constance? Hey, how're you? It's Tony."

"Fine, Tony. What a nice surprise to have you here. How is Frances?" They chatted another moment or two before he came to the point.

"You want to give Charlie a message? It's about that other set of prints on the glass. She's Angela Schnabel, a runaway from Philadelphia juvenile court, but hell, she's going to be eighteen in a few months, and she's clean. No one's going to haul her back now."

"Juvenile court? For what?"

"Nothing. Abandoned by her mother. She was a ward of the court in a disturbed children's home and split."

She paced the living room for several minutes, then sat down and called Philadelphia information and got two numbers—one of a colleague who had worked with her several times and another of a child psychologist she knew by reputation.

At first, her friend protested that the information she wanted was not available. Constance talked hard for the next few minutes, hung up, called the child psychologist and talked even harder to her, then called her friend back.

"Dr. Walker will intercede for you," she said forcefully. "She has influence at the detention center. Just get over there, Vanessa, will you, for crying out loud?"

Vanessa grumbled, but she would do it and call back as soon as she had anything to tell.

Constance was still waiting when Gretchen joined her for a drink. Close on her heels was Charlie, who looked as if he had not slept.

"Cheers," Gretchen said, and upended her martini glass. "She's giving us all the old heave-ho, I'm afraid. She'll be down to tell us officially that we're invited to leave at the first opportunity. That cat/ghost act last night was the last straw."

"Amos called her Sister Wanda today. I was afraid he had won," Constance said morosely.

"Maybe what I have to tell her will change her mind," Charlie said.

"I doubt it." Wanda entered the room. She looked poised and calm, as if making up her mind had been a panacea. "Brother Amos already told me about his past. He went through a conversion last fall as real as that which changed the life of Saul of Tarsus."

"You know about his little mind-reading act with the carnival?"

She nodded. "Everything. And he really does communicate in ways not available to the rest of us. He said Con-

stance knows that now." She looked inquiringly at
Constance, who nodded.

"He knows things he shouldn't."

"See? I've invited him and Sister Angel to come stay
here, but not until my other guests have departed," she said
without a trace of embarrassment. "They will join us tonight for a short while, then move in to keep me company
tomorrow. Will that be convenient?"

Charlie poured a martini for her. She accepted it and
sank into one of the overstuffed chairs, picked up her cigarettes, and lighted one. "He also said that you, Charlie,
should leave here tonight. Whatever it was that haunted
Vernon has now transferred its attention to you. You're in
danger."

"Vernon hasn't told you anything about that ghost yet?"
Charlie's voice held a trace of mockery and there was the
hard surface over his eyes that Constance had hoped would
never reappear.

"Not yet," Wanda admitted. "But he will eventually. Last
night was the first time he has shown such displeasure.
That was directed primarily at you, Charlie, because you're
here under false pretenses. You're the one who wanted to
play with the cat, and you threaten Amos."

Charlie laughed. "You told him about us?"

"No. I don't break my word. I've told him nothing." She
stubbed out the cigarette and lighted another. "There's no
need to tell him anything. He knows."

Why didn't Vanessa call back? Constance looked again
at her watch.

"Come down to my place in New York for just a few
days," Gretchen was urging Wanda. "There's nothing you
have to do here all that fast."

"I can't."

Gretchen turned to Constance. "You aren't even trying to talk reason to her!"

Call, damn you, Constance thought at Vanessa in Philadelphia. "When do you expect Amos and Angel tonight?"

"Around nine-thirty. I asked him if he would drop in for just a few minutes. Maybe I won't need a pill if he talks to me soon before I go to bed."

When dinner was ready, they all poked at their food without real interest. The call for Constance came midway through the meal.

When she returned to the dining room, Wanda was regarding Charlie. "That's exactly how Vernon acted," she said. "That same kind of absent look, pale, taut . . ."

Charlie stood up, stalked from the room, with Constance right behind him.

She nearly pushed him into the television room and closed the door. It was almost nine-thirty.

"I know who it is," Charlie said grimly. "She's scared to death. She needs help desperately."

"I know she does. There's no time now, Charlie. Please trust me. Go along with me for the next hour. Whatever you start to think, please trust me!"

"If you do anything to hurt her . . ."

"You know I won't hurt her."

He rubbed his eyes and took a deep breath. "What are you up to? Who called?"

"I can't tell you. You're too open to her."

"We shouldn't have come here. We can leave now, forget all this. Maybe that's what we should do, just get the hell out of here."

"We can't. You can't. It's too late for that." She looked at her watch. "It's time. He'll go upstairs with Wanda. Angel is going to have dessert with us. Let's go back now. And, Charlie, don't interfere. Promise!"

He shook his head. "I can't promise that."

"All right. But you do trust me, you know. You can't stop trusting me now."

Almost all day, *she* had been with him, gone briefly now and again, but then back even stronger—whispering in his ear, sitting on his lap, lying with him, moving with him, caressing him with her warm hands that were touches of electricity. When he paused at the dining room door, she was seated at the table with cake before her, her fork halted in midair. She looked directly at him. He saw her across the room and he felt her in his arms, her warm breath on his neck, her laughter in his ear. Her incredible violet eyes, he thought, unable to look away until she lowered her gaze. Then he moved, resumed his seat, stared at her. Wanda had left.

"Good evening, Angel," Constance said briskly. "It's time that we all began telling the truth around here, don't you think? First of all, Charlie is a detective. He used to work for the police in New York; now he's freelance."

He started to rise, relaxed again. *She* didn't care. In his mind, he was holding her, the way he had held her when the cat moved, hard, tightly, securely, with her face pressed against him.

Gretchen was regarding Constance as if she had gone mad.

"We were hired," Constance went on, very businesslike, almost brusque in her speech, "to investigate Amos and his claim that there are ghosts in this house."

Charlie closed his eyes. Again it was all right. He moved in a slow waltz with her, both of them naked, warm against each other. If he looked at Constance, he would see an old, rather ugly woman, he knew. He did not want to see that. He kept his eyes closed and felt the lithe body against him.

"I'm sure you know that what I'm telling you is true," Constance said. "And this is true also. I'm a doctor, a psychologist. . . ."

There was a wave of hatred, loathing, terror. Charlie jerked his eyes wide open, grasped the table hard. The emotional wave was gathering momentum, hitting him like surges of power. Gretchen screamed and pushed herself away from the table, stumbled when she stood up, fell back into her chair. Charlie tried to yell, tried to call out Constance's name, but he could make no sound. *Stop it*, he tried to whisper. *Stop it!*

Constance had been prepared for something, but not this. She was the target; she knew that as she felt nausea and vertigo. She felt as if she were falling from a terrible height, falling faster and faster, and knew that when she hit, she would die. She wanted to fling out her hands, to catch herself, to stop the fall; if she did that, she would be lost. There were words in her head, words she had to say now. She tried to speak; her throat was paralyzed, her tongue paralyzed. Angel leaned forward, her eyes wide and staring, her face as pale as death. And in her mind, Constance cried, *No!*

"Angela," she said in a hoarse whisper, "close your eyes. Go to sleep."

Angel blinked. For a moment, Constance was afraid it was not going to work, but then the childish face relaxed, her eyes closed, and she took a deep breath and let it out slowly.

It was over. Charlie's hand shook when he reached for his water and took a drink. It was *all* over, he thought, and he looked at Constance, who was very pale, breathing deeply.

"You were swell," he said huskily.

She nodded thankfully but kept her attention on the girl across the table from her. Slowly, softly, she said, "Angela, go into your deepest trance. Very relaxed, comfortable, down, down."

In a few minutes, Constance asked, "Angela, does Amos hypnotize you?"

"Yes."

"You won't allow him to ever again, Angela. Do you understand?"

"Yes."

"When he tries to hypnotize you again, you will remember what I'm telling you now and he won't be able to control you ever again." Constance repeated this several more times before she was satisfied, then said, "I am not your enemy, Angela. I won't send you back to the home. You don't have to hate me. You don't have to be afraid of me. Do you understand?"

Charlie watched in fascination, but time was running out, he thought, and he caught Constance's eye, tapped his watch. She nodded.

"When you wake up, Angela, you will remember what we've talked about, all of it. You won't be afraid or nervous, but very relaxed and peaceful. You'll know that Charlie is not your father, Angela. You'll want to stay here with us tonight so we can take care of you. You don't have to go with Amos. You can stay here with us." As before, she repeated each part of her message several times.

At her command, Angel opened her eyes. She blinked rapidly a few times and started to eat her cake.

"Do you remember what happened?" Constance asked.

"Nothing happened." Angela did not look up at her.

Gretchen had not said a word throughout. Now she got up and started for the door. "I want coffee, in here, not later in the living room. Maybe I want a drink, too. Charlie? Constance?"

They both nodded and she left.

Charlie looked from Constance to Angel and back helplessly. Had it taken? He could not tell. Constance raised her eyebrow in a "let's wait and see" manner and he dug his fork into his cake, then put it down.

Angel looked at him and said scornfully, "I knew you were a cop from the beginning. You look like a cop, walk like a cop, smell like a cop."

Charlie grinned at his cake and started to eat it. "That's more like it, kid," he said under his breath. Aloud, he asked, "You had that much experience with cops?"

"Yeah." She looked past him. He turned, to see Amos in the doorway.

"Come along, Sister Angel. Time to go study."

She started to rise, then sat down again. A puzzled look crossed her face. She shook her head.

"Sister Angel, it's late. Time to go home."

Again she shook her head. "They said I can stay here."

"We'll come tomorrow, move in tomorrow with all our stuff. You can wait one more day."

She was pushing crumbs around her plate with her fork, not looking at him. She shook her head.

Now Amos walked around the table and put his hand on her shoulder lightly. "Be a good girl, Sister Angel. You hear me? Get up and come along home with me."

Gretchen entered, carrying the coffee tray, to which she had added brandy and glasses.

"Hi, Amos. Just in time. Join us?"

He was watching Angel closely, his hand tight on her shoulder now. "Be a good girl, Sister Angel," he repeated clearly.

She stood up. "Is it okay if I go watch TV awhile?"

"Run along," Constance said. "We'll be in here if you want anything. You sure you don't want coffee, Amos?"

Angel nearly ran from the room.

"You can't keep her," Amos said harshly. "She's going home with me now."

"You'll have to get a warrant, I'm afraid," Charlie said. "The kid wants to stay."

Amos looked at him, his eyes narrowed, his face mean and rigid. "You'll regret this," he said. "You don't know what you're doing." He stalked from the room and Charlie followed him through the hallway, watched until he went out the front door, which Charlie then locked.

He returned to the dining room, where Gretchen was drinking brandy as if it was going out of style. "Now tell us what that was all about," she demanded of Constance.

"I don't want her to overhear," Constance said, and Charlie took his glass and stood by the open door, where he could see the length of the living room, the hallway to the television room beyond it.

"I found out that she's a runaway," Constance said then. "She was in a home for disturbed youngsters in Philadelphia up until two and a half years ago, when she ran off. There was a scandal; the director apparently helped her, gave her money, took her out with him, then she vanished and he had a nervous breakdown, resigned. She was classified schizophrenic. Her father abandoned her and her mother when she was three. When she was six, she landed in a hospital with multiple bruises, abrasions, a concussion, and she had been sexually molested. She had amnesia about

the incident. The mother said it was an attack by an unknown. Case closed. Two years later, it was repeated, but
this time the mother was implicated in the beating—by a
neighbor who testified that she often beat the girl. Now the
mother came under investigation. A series of live-in boyfriends, abandonment, the usual story. The mother was ordered into therapy. When Angel was twelve, her mother
had her committed, called her sexually promiscuous and in-
corrigible. She authorized a series of shock treatments."

Gretchen looked pale and sick and Charlie's face was a
mask.

"They started her on hypnoanalysis. And they got the
story about her father, about the boyfriends she wanted to
be her father, her mother's reaction each time. And they got
a dose of what we've had from her, the projections she's
capable of. Easier to call her schizophrenic than try to deal
with that. Delusions of grandeur, nymphomania, schizo . . .
she's had it all pinned on her."

"They gave you the key words to induce trance?" Charlie asked after the silence had persisted many minutes.

"Yes. First, she had to know that I was a doctor. That
was the kind of cue they left with her, that she would respond to a doctor using those words." She glanced at
Gretchen and added, "It's a posthypnotic suggestion to return to trance instantly on cue. Obviously, Amos planted
one also, but he's an amateur. He didn't know enough to
protect his power over her. Probably never even occurred to
him that anyone else could step in so easily."

"He isn't even her father," Gretchen said in disbelief.
"He's living with her, that poor little kid, using her."

And they were in the area last summer, Constance
thought, when Vernon became obsessed with a mysterious
woman and then was killed. She looked at Charlie and he

shook his head slightly. She had told enough for now. She nodded just as slightly.

"I'm going to go keep her company," Gretchen said then. "She may be lonesome tonight, and afraid. Poor little kid."

Charlie nodded. "I want to go over the security system."

It wasn't over, he thought. Not with Amos out there in a rage, not with that strange girl in the house with powers she seemed to have little control over. They separated then and Constance went upstairs to get her notebook. As she passed the masks on the stairway wall, she scolded them. "You knew all the time," she muttered. "Damn enigmatic Indians."

When she returned to the living room, Charlie was closing the drapes; beyond the glass, the floodlights were on, lighting the entire yard down to the lake.

"No targets," Charlie said. "Anyone tries to open a door or window, the system goes off. Sort of like locking up a wide-open field, but it's all we can do."

"You think he'll try to get in tonight?"

"Not if he's got half the brains he should have, but I'm spending the night on the couch there, just in case I overestimate his intelligence."

And she would keep him company, she thought, eyeing the chairs, the other couch. The upstairs bedroom seemed very far away, inaccessible, out of earshot even.

"Vernon and Wanda used to play games," she said. "Chess?"

He nodded. She went to the television room and asked Gretchen for the set and presently they were at play. Shortly after twelve, Gretchen and Angel went upstairs, and soon after that Charlie made his first check of the house. From the dark television room, he looked out at the yard. It was raining, and the wind was blowing fitfully. A freeze was predicted for overnight. The roads were going to be bad for going home, he found himself thinking, and he longed to be there in front of the fireplace, the silly cats trying to filch anything edible, Constance in her chair, reading or writing away. Maybe tomorrow they would wrap it up here and go home, ice or no ice, he decided, then finished his tour of the house.

Amos would not be able to give her up, Charlie was thinking later, staring morosely at the game, where he was going to be mated in another move or two. In some ways, he pitied Amos, who had tangled with something he could not control or understand or resist.

"Vernon must have seemed a real threat," Constance said, finishing his thought as she so often did.

"Yeah. But why does Angel keep on looking if she's found someone?"

"The three-year-old in her is still looking, remember. When the father turns out to be a lover, the three-year-old knows something is wrong, and the search is on."

"And it'll never end for her."

"I don't know. I want her, Charlie. I want to help her, to work with her, find out what she's capable of, help her learn to control it."

Charlie thought of the images of Constance that Angel had put in his head—old, ugly, fearsome even. He doubted that Angel would let Constance anywhere near her, if she had a choice. Yet, they couldn't just turn her loose. And they sure couldn't send her back to the institution. She isn't our problem, he wanted to say, but obviously Constance thought she was, or was willing to take her on as a problem.

"I concede," he said then. "Want to break the tie?"

"Sure." She started to set up the pieces again, then

stopped when Wanda appeared in the doorway from the kitchen area.

"Why are you both still up?"

"How did you get down here?" Charlie asked.

"The back stairs. It's after two."

"Is anything wrong?" Constance asked sharply. Wanda had on a long robe that looked warm, but she was shivering and very pale.

"Please, both of you, please go to bed. This is terrible, staying up all night, not sleeping. I have to be alone sometime! There's always someone. . . ." She fled into the darkened hall.

Constance followed her to the kitchen. "What happened?" She asked again, sharper this time.

Wanda put a teakettle on the stove and turned on the burner. "I want a cup of tea."

Constance looked at her helplessly. "Were you dreaming? Is that it?"

"Just leave me alone."

"Listen to me, Wanda. There are things about him and Angel that you have to know. She isn't his daughter, and she's the one with telepathic powers. He never knows anything until they go away and he gets it out of her. She's the one giving him information, not Vernon. And it's information right out of your head, our heads, not from beyond the grave."

Wearily, Wanda turned off the stove, then faced Constance. "I called Amos. There are things moving in the house, unquiet things. I want to see him alone. You and Charlie have to go upstairs, mind your own business. I don't want you here any longer. Isn't that clear enough? I don't want either of you here now. If Vernon tries to tell me something, Charlie just gets in the way." She moved toward the hall, this time resolutely.

In defeat, Constance walked with her. They could not order her not to see Amos, order her to keep her house locked up all night, order her to do anything. They were nearing the end of the hall, the bright living room open before them, when she stopped abruptly, her fingers digging into Wanda's arm, pulling her back, her other hand on Wanda's mouth. Amos was standing in the living room, holding a small gun, looking at Charlie on the couch.

"Just don't forget it's here," Amos was saying, putting the gun in his raincoat pocket, keeping his hand on it. "When she comes out with her nice tea, then we'll talk."

Wanda pulled hard against Constance, and Constance tightened her grasp, held her without difficulty. She pulled her back farther into the shadows.

"You don't think people might talk if you come in and shoot up the company?" Charlie said pleasantly. His voice was so mild, so easy, he might have been asking about ball scores.

"You're a firebug. Angel told me. Wanda and Angel and I are leaving and you can play with fire." He had turned so that he could see the hallway to the kitchen. "Just sit still until your wife joins us with her tea."

"Were you afraid Vernon was going to take her away from you?"

Amos moved out of range; they no longer could see him. Constance let go of Wanda and ran to the living room.

He was standing close to Charlie, speaking in a low, intense voice. ". . . her fault. She can't help it. He was going to investigate us, investigate her, take her away."

"And you killed him. He just wanted to do something decent for the kid."

"Decent! You know what she does! She told me about you, how she wanted you. I know what that means."

"What does it mean?" Wanda asked, holding on to the door frame. "What exactly is it she does?"

For a moment, Amos looked too stunned to speak. He recovered quickly. "She's sick. I've known it for a long time, but I thought I could cure her. I thought my love would be enough to make her well. It was a mistake. I was misguided. I know that now. She needs medical treatment, a hospital, help—"

Suddenly, Constance felt as if she had been punched in the stomach. She doubled over in pain, unable to breathe, and at the same time a red hatred poured through her, wrenching her, numbing her. Things were flying through the air; the masks were flying. She tried to dodge, but something caught her on the side of the head and she fell, dazed, far removed from the room.

Charlie threw his arm up before his face to ward off the masks, caught one on his elbow and felt his entire arm go numb. Hatred and fury blinded him. He grunted and fell to his knees when something smashed into his midsection. The chessboard flew from the table, scattering pieces, and hit Amos in the back. Amos was screaming hoarsely. "Angel! For God's sake, stop it! Sister Angel, be a good girl. Stop!" It was cut off by a scream, and Charlie could not tell whose scream it was. Wanda crumpled to the floor.

Constance pulled herself up, got to her knees. Angel was on the top step, barefoot, dressed in a man's pajama shirt that reached down to her midthighs. She was crying the way a child cries, like a three-year-old, openmouthed, her eyes tightly closed, screaming.

She had to make the child hear her, had to say the right words, make her hear. . . . Her words were drowned in screams. An end table flew across the room, hit Amos on the leg. She said the words again and could not even hear them herself. The entire room was alive, moving, crashing. She would kill them all, Constance thought distantly.

"I'm coming!" Charlie whispered. "Hold on, baby. I'm coming!" He tried to move, tripped over the chess table and felt it jerk out from under his body, saw it fly across the room, crash into the wall. He pulled himself on the carpet, clutching it, trying to drag himself to her. *I'm coming. Honey, don't scream! Stop screaming! I won't let him send you back, Angel! I swear it!*

Amos was dragging one leg, holding on to the back of a chair, unable to stand upright, yelling hoarsely to her, calling her name over and over. The chair tilted and he crashed to the floor again. The gun was shaken from his pocket to the floor. Angel kept screaming.

Amos flung up his hand to ward off something; he rolled and doubled up in pain and his hand closed on the gun. He was moaning. "Stop it, Angel! My God, Angel—" He convulsed with pain again, and this time he lifted the gun and fired.

"Angel!" he screamed. He dragged himself to the steps, and she fell down on top of him. Her eyes had opened; she stared unblinking at the ceiling; her long white hair swung when he lifted her. "Angel!" he cried out again, and pressed her body to him, cradled her like an infant, rocking back and forth with her, crying out her name over and over.

Constance buried her face in her hands and shook with weeping. She felt Charlie's arms around her and leaned against him blindly.

His eyes were closed tight, his face against her neck. He stirred first. Wanda, he thought. Someone had to see how badly Wanda was injured. He lifted his head. "I'll be damned! Constance, look!"

Nothing in the room was disturbed, nothing broken, nothing out of place. Constance raised her head, reached up to feel her temple, expecting a lump, a cut, blood. There was nothing. Amos rocked back and forth, sobbing, holding Angel in his arms. Wanda was starting to move.

The police had come and gone, and now the sky was lightening. Charlie and Constance stood before the wide expanse of glass and looked at the lake, unbroken by a ripple. He had told the police that Amos had come for his daughter, then shot her when she appeared on the top step. Constance and Wanda had repeated the story, adding nothing at all to it.

"That poor kid," one of the policemen had said over and over. Poor kid, Constance echoed in her mind. She never had a chance. She remembered the toy cat, how it had thrown Angel into a panic as she equated herself with it—soulless, will-less, an automaton, taking orders, never free. And with powers that never would be studied, never understood, never used for something other than deception and destruction. Powers that finally killed her, after making her life hellish. "She never had a chance," she whispered.

Charlie tightened his grip on her hand. And Amos, he never had a chance, either, he thought, but did not say it. He would have had to kill father figures for an awfully long time. Constance had not asked what Angel had made him feel, what she had made him see. She never would ask, and he never would bring it up, either.

"I wish we were home," he murmured, yearning for their comfortable living room, the three raunchy cats, the quiet fire, the silent snow accumulating under the windows.

She leaned against him and sighed. "Let's not go anywhere again for a long, long time."

They went upstairs then, and when they got to their room, they shared one of the twin beds, just to hold each other, just to be close.

ALL FOR ONE

IT WASN'T THAT Charlie didn't like young people. He believed firmly that they should wear their hair any way that pleased them, that they had the right to adorn their bodies however they chose, that their music was their business, as were the movies they watched, the videos they memorized. Their vigor and passion, their frontal approach to problems, all that he could appreciate and applaud, but he really didn't want to work for them, he was thinking that afternoon in May as he watched a young trio in his driveway. It was obvious that they were arguing even if their words didn't carry to him at the window in his living room.

A young woman, Teresa Coultier, he assumed, since she had called earlier, and two younger men had emerged from a Land Rover and started to approach the house, then stopped when she turned on them both, apparently to lay down the law. The younger of the two men nodded meekly enough, but the other one was showing an attitude. Charlie didn't care much for young people with an attitude. The trio seemed to come to an agreement and the procession resumed. He went to the door to admit them. "Ms. Coultier?" he said. "Come on in. I'm Meiklejohn."

She shook hands with him and then pointed to one of the

young men and said, "This is my half brother Michael
Andreson. And this is my half brother Nathan Coultier."

She was in her twenties, and very pretty, slender, small-
boned, with deep-set blue eyes and long black hair. He
could see the resemblance between her and each of the
brothers, both apparently younger than she was; Nathan had
her lovely eyes, and Michael had her peaked eyebrows and
black hair.

He ushered them to the living room; Constance walked
in from the kitchen to be introduced, and they all sat down,
the three young people in a line on the sofa, Constance
in the wing chair, and Charlie in his morris chair, from
which he regarded them without much enthusiasm. It was a
warm day, and they were flushed and sweaty, dressed in
jeans, running shoes, T-shirts.

"All right," he said. "What's the problem?"

"It's very complicated," Teresa Coultier said. "Will you
just listen to the whole story before you ask anything?"

"Can you tell it in half an hour?" he asked.

Teresa flushed. Michael started to speak and she jabbed
him with her elbow. "Yes. My stepfather is trying to kill
me."

Charlie didn't groan out loud; he knew he didn't make a
sound, or change his expression, any more than Constance
did, but he groaned inwardly. "Go on," he said.

Teresa looked from him to Constance, to him again, apparently startled at their lack of response. Nathan glared at
Charlie, and Michael drew in a deep breath but did not interrupt when Teresa continued. "My grandmother is very
old, ninety-two, and she is very ill, in a hospital in Paris.
When she dies, a large estate will be distributed to her
heirs. I'm one of them, and Michael is another. I believe
my stepfather killed my brother and my sister, and tried to

kill me last summer, and again two weeks ago. So my part of the inheritance will pass on to my mother and to Michael, and my stepfather will control it."

"She's talking about your father?" Charlie murmured to Michael when Teresa paused.

Michael nodded; he looked belligerent and eager to talk but maintained silence, probably under orders.

"What happened last summer?" Charlie asked.

"There was a fire in the guest house where I was staying. I had to jump out of a second-floor window, and I broke my arm and my leg in two places."

"You think it was an arson fire? Where is the guest house?"

"It's on his property, and yes, of course it was arson!"

"Was there an investigation? Do the police think it was arson? Does the fire department?"

Her face tightened and she shook her head. "They seem to think I left a fire screen open, sparks flew out, something like that. But I didn't."

"Okay," Charlie said. "What happened two weeks ago?"

"I was shot at in my car. And the police call that a random shooting, but it wasn't. He did it."

"Why?" Charlie asked bluntly. "If he wanted you out of the way, why wait almost a year to try again?"

"It's complicated," she said.

"Let me tell this part," Michael said.

"Is that what you were arguing about in the driveway? Who would tell which part?"

Teresa nodded unhappily. "I didn't want Michael to have anything to do with calling his father a murderer."

Charlie was watching Michael. He was a long boy, with long legs and arms, not yet filled out, as if he hadn't quite stopped adding height. His legs were stretched out before him and he seemed to be fascinated with his shoelaces, but there was a telltale tendon in his neck, and tendons showing on the backs of his hands. As relaxed as a guy facing a firing squad.

"Someone should tell us," Charlie said when the pause seemed to extend long enough.

"Trying to decide where to begin," Michael said, and drew in his legs, sat up straighter. "Okay. Her father is Jeffrey Coultier, and my dad is Sam Andreson. They were in the army together in Berlin back in the fifties, where they met Marie Lanier. She was working for the French government. They all became friends, and both of them wanted to marry her, but she picked Jeffrey."

He spoke with few pauses, no backtracking, as he covered the brief history. Marie and Jeffrey had come to the States, settled in his hometown, near Oyster Bay, and he returned to school to finish his education. They had Gary, Suzette, and Trish—she poked him with her elbow again, and he corrected himself—Teresa. When Trish was two years old, Marie divorced Jeffrey and married Sam, and a year later he, Michael, was born. Both families lived just outside of Oyster Bay.

"Grandmother was pretty sore over her daughter marrying an American," he went on, more slowly now. "She had lost her husband and three sons during World War Two, and her only surviving child was leaving the country. She set up a trust fund for the grandchildren, twenty thousand dollars a year when they reached twenty-one, and at twenty-five they would receive a very large settlement, and eventually, when she died, split the estate, half for the grandchildren, half for Marie."

"What kind of money are you talking about?" Charlie asked when Michael stopped.

"A million dollars, what Trish will get next August and I'll get in a few years. I'm twenty-one. When Grandmother dies, there will be a lot more."

Charlie whistled, then glanced at Nathan, who shrugged.

"She doesn't care if my dad is alive or dead," Nathan said. "She probably never even heard of me. I have zilch coming."

"I'm twenty-four," Trish said then in a low voice. "I want to live to see twenty-five." She sounded like a frightened child.

Nathan took one of her hands, and on the other side, Michael took the other. They looked very young, lined up on the sofa, holding hands.

After a moment, Charlie said brusquely, "You've made some drastic accusations; let's have some facts. Tell us about Gary. How did he die?"

Trish nodded and drew in a breath. "Seven years ago, he brought a girl home to celebrate his engagement. They were going to be married on his twenty-fifth birthday in July. There was a dinner party. Later on, he decided to go see Dad, our father, Jeffrey, and he ran off the road and was killed." She said this rapidly with no inflection, as if she were reciting a boring history lesson.

"He had been drinking?"

"Not that much!" she cried. "He never drank much. But they said the autopsy showed a high level of alcohol, anyway. Legally, he was drunk. I didn't believe it then and I don't now!" She pulled her hands loose from her brothers', and clasped them together tightly.

"Okay. Suzette. How and where?"

"Two years later," Trish said, but this time her voice broke. Michael put his arm about her shoulders, and Nathan looked at her uncertainly, as if he wanted to pat her or put his arm around her, too, but wasn't quite sure just how to do it.

"She was really upset by Gary's death," Trish said after a second or two. "They were close; I was five years younger than Suzette, but it was never the same. She missed Gary. Anyway, she had an apartment in New York and a job with a magazine, and she was getting better. When she didn't turn up at work on Monday and didn't answer the phone, one of her friends went to see what was wrong. She had died on Saturday night, they said. Overdose. Possibly suicide. She was twenty-four." Trish ducked her head, opened her clenched hands, closed them again harder.

Michael looked at Charlie. "Last June, Trish was home, my dad's home, Sam's. She had got her master's from Johns Hopkins, and we had a little party for her, just family and a couple of friends. There was a problem with the plumbing upstairs, and Dad suggested she might want to stay in the guest house because plumbers would be there early the next morning. You have to understand," he added quickly, "that wasn't punishment, but more like an honor. We all used to sneak in there and play when we were kids. I was a little jealous, to tell the truth, that he was letting her use it. After dinner, we sat around and talked awhile, and Mother went to bed." His voice faltered. "She hasn't been very well these past few years." Then he continued: "Trish, I, and a friend, Rita Glenwood, went on to the guest house. We made a fire in the fireplace and talked for a couple of hours, listened to music, and around midnight Rita said she had to be on her way, so we left and I drove her home. At four in the morning, the yardman woke up smelling smoke, and he yelled and got everyone up. When I got downstairs, I saw the guest house burning. The fire department got there about five minutes later, and one of them found Trish unconscious on the ground."

Charlie felt the cold knot that paradoxically came with fire. Trish looked frozen in place, hardly even breathing. Michael's arm was still around her shoulders; he had drawn her closer, and Nathan had moved in closer on the other side. "No smoke alarm?" Charlie asked.

"They said it had a bad battery," Michael said flatly.

"Okay. Trish, had you been drinking that night?"

"Hot chocolate," she said.

"When I heard she was going to stay in the guest house, I brought chocolate and milk and cookies, stuff we always liked when we were kids," Michael said.

Charlie nodded and asked Trish, "You went on to bed when your brother and his friend left?"

"Within a few minutes. Later, I woke up coughing and choking. My room was filling with smoke. When I touched the doorknob, it burned my hand, and I ran to the window. I couldn't get it open. The lights were out, and there was a glow from the bathroom, but it was too smoky to really see anything. Then I stumbled over my suitcase. I grabbed it and swung as hard as I could and the window broke. Flames came through the door and one of the walls then, and when I looked down, flames were coming from the windows on the first floor, and I just jumped."

And damn lucky you didn't kill yourself doing it, Charlie thought. He nodded. "Okay, two weeks ago. What happened?"

"I was driving from the train station to my father's house. I stayed there after I got out of the hospital—"

Suddenly, Nathan blurted, "He was afraid for her to go back up there. We all were. No one said anything, or why, or what we were afraid of, but we were. Dad had a fit when she said they were expecting her to come back. They stayed home; I changed my plans. I was supposed to go to Michigan State; I went to Stony Brook instead. No one argued. We all knew we didn't want to go away, be away. We wanted her home with us." He was flushed, very red.

Trish put her hand on his arm. "Take it easy," she murmured, and turned to Charlie. "They had planned to take their sabbaticals together and go to England, but they stayed home with me instead, Dad and Lorraine, I mean. And Nathan went to school every day and was home every night. And no one ever said anything, never raised a suspicion, pointed a finger. It was just a feeling of uneasiness. Anyway, the shooting. I went to New York City that day and left my car at the station. It was dark and raining when I got back, so I was driving pretty slowly." She looked down at her hands again and spoke very fast now. "Then he shot at me; I didn't know what it was at first. The rear window shattered, and the windshield cracked all over. I could hardly see through it, and I realized it was a shot. I sped up and drove the rest of the way home as fast as I could. Dad called the police."

Charlie gazed at her unhappily. "Did you see any lights following you?"

She shook her head, not looking up.

"And no one followed you home, or shot at you again?"

She shook her head again.

"Ms. Coultier, exactly what do you want me to do?"

"Are you kidding?" Michael demanded. "Look into it. Investigate the doctor who's treating my mother! He's keeping her so doped, she doesn't know if it's day or night!"

"Investigate Sam Andreson's finances," Nathan chimed in. "I think he's in deep shit and needs the money."

"See if there was a real investigation of Suzette's death!" Trish cried. "She didn't kill herself, and she didn't take drugs by accident!"

Charlie held up his hand for silence. "What about your mother?" he asked Michael.

"She took Gary's death hard, and she was just beginning to recover when Suzette died. She went into a tailspin then, but she was coming out of it again finally when Trish was nearly killed in the fire. She thinks Trish is dead, or she thought that for a long time. I don't know what she thinks now. He's keeping her doped all the time."

"She's under a doctor's care?"

"Yes! But he picked the doctor and he pays the bills and he hired a nurse and tells her what to do and when to do it."

"Have you told the police what you've just told us?"

"I tried. What's the use?" Michael muttered. "You don't understand the politics of a place like Oyster Bay. The police have it all figured out. Gary was drunk. Suzette took drugs. Trish was careless with fire. Coincidence, bad luck."

Charlie looked at Trish. "Have you told your father what you suspect?"

"No," she said in a low voice. "He's afraid all right, just as Nathan said, but there's nothing to name, to be afraid of. It's formless. But if he believed me, if we put this name on it, he would kill Sam Andreson."

"Ms. Coultier, why are you still hanging around if you really believe what you claim?" Charlie asked then. "You have some money, go visit your grandmother, or go to Hawaii for a vacation."

"I just came to understand this after he shot at me," Trish said slowly. "Two weeks ago. And we talked it over," she went on, looking first at Nathan and then Michael. "Maybe

I've really believed it for a week or even less. But I can't leave Mother with him. I'm afraid that when Grandmother dies and my mother inherits, he'll kill her and get her out of the way. Then he'll inherit her estate."

Michael nodded.

Before Charlie could ask anything else, Constance got in a question. "Why did you come here? How did you know about us?"

Trish glanced at Michael. "He read about you."

Constance turned her gaze to Michael and waited. After a moment, he said, "In a true-crime magazine, they ran some articles about private investigators, how they work, what they do. When we were talking last week, I suddenly remembered your names. The article said Mr. Meiklejohn used to be an arson investigator."

"And I looked you up," Nathan added. "You checked out okay."

"Looked us up where?" Charlie asked with interest.

"Chamber of commerce," Nathan muttered. "They didn't have any complaints filed against you."

Charlie regarded him, trying hard to conceal his disbelief. Nathan flushed very red again and averted his face.

Constance stood up then. "Charlie, why don't you take our guests out to the patio. It's such a lovely day. I'll bring some lemonade. Or would you prefer soft drinks; Cokes?"

The trio exchanged glances and got up uncertainly.

"Come on," Charlie said, ushering them from the living room. "I'll be waiter, take orders on the patio. That way." He took them through the living room and into the hall, out past the dinette space, through the sliding glass doors to the patio. Ashcan, the gray cat, streaked away in terror.

Constance watched them thoughtfully and then went to the kitchen, where she waited for Charlie to return.

"Cokes," he said. "I want a shot of whiskey." At her look, he added, "Later, when we get rid of them."

"You know what they're doing?"

He knew, but he shook his head. "You first."

"Setting us up for the defense?"

He grinned fleetingly. "Tell you one thing, I would not want to be in Sam Andreson's shoes. Now, for the Cokes, and then the bum's rush."

He gathered glasses and added ice cubes, got drinks from the pantry, and put everything on a tray while Constance stood facing out the window with unfocused eyes. She was hardly aware when he left, and then he was back at her side.

"I can imagine the courtroom pounding," she said in a low voice. "From both sides."

He nodded. "I noticed that you didn't bring up the question of abuse, or why Michael is going along with condemning his father as a killer, why Nathan is involved."

"They're being very clever, aren't they?"

"Michael just happened to remember our names," he murmured. "No doubt the fact that you're a psychologist escaped his memory." A fleeting grin softened his face. "Chamber of commerce!"

"Charlie," she said, hating what she was thinking, "the real fact is, they've involved us in whatever they're planning. We can't just turn them out and let things happen, then plead ignorance. The deaths of her brother and sister must be true, on record; Trish's suspicions may even be correct. She may actually have reason to be afraid she will be killed before August."

"And none of it provable. If there was anything to it, the cops would have been all over the place," he said sourly.

"But if they kill Sam Andreson, that will be murder, no matter how you cut it, and if they're caught, and they will be, we'll be dragged in. But we don't have to walk in with open eyes." He put his arm about her shoulders; she was stiff, unyielding. "Honey, those kids are bad news. Real bad news."

She nodded absently. "They expect us to turn them down. Then they can say they tried the police, and a private investigator, and a psychologist, but to no avail. In desperation, they acted on their own. The defense will say, What would your child do if she knew her life was in danger and no one would help her? They'll bring in a lifetime of abuse of one sort or another, and they'll get away with it, won't they?" A shudder passed through her. "And they'll be destroyed, all of them."

"Our three brave knights will slay the dragon, rescue the endangered mother, move to France, and live like royalty for the rest of their lives," he said. He pulled his arm away and said, "I don't want them, Constance."

"Neither do I," she said in a very low voice, "but I think we have them, anyway."

She turned to face him, her pale blue eyes very remote and cool, like twin frozen lakes viewed from a great distance. He knew from the way her mouth was set, the way she met his gaze levelly, from her whole body stance that she intended to save those kids if she could. The question she had posed hung there between them: What would your child do . . . ? He added silently, What would you have your child do if her life was in danger? After a second, he shrugged.

"Maybe we've become too cynical," she said then. "Maybe they're telling the exact truth as they see it."

"Right. No lemonade. Iced coffee with a slug of rum."

He glanced at his watch; it was 2:30. "I intend to give them a dose of what it's going to be like if they try anything."

She nodded, still absent, distracted. When he stamped back out to the patio, she followed him.

"I'm sorry we intruded," Trish said as they drew near the table where the three youngsters had been whispering with their heads close together. "It was a mistake. We'll pay you for your time, of course, and just be on our way now."

"Nonsense," Constance said serenely. "I couldn't find any lemons, so I'm making iced coffee. It will be ready in a minute or two. Meanwhile, Charlie has a lot of questions to ask. I'll be right back."

Trish and Michael exchanged looks. "You mean you'll take our case?" Trish asked. It was hard to tell if she looked more disbelieving or alarmed.

"Of course," Constance said. "Excuse me for a minute."

Couldn't find lemons, Charlie thought at her darkly. Not in the sink, or out back. He glowered at Trish. "You might as well try to relax. You hired us; you put up with questions. Right?" He pulled out a notebook and sat down at the glass-topped table.

As Charlie probed and pushed that afternoon, Constance formed a narrative of life with the Coultiers and the Andresons throughout the past twenty-five years. Jeffrey Coultier had supported his three children until they reached twenty-one and came into their trust funds, and he had stayed on the edge of bankruptcy for most of that time. Sam was niggardly, Trish said at one point, and Michael had agreed. With him, too, he had added. His mother had not been any help financially, since she had no money of her own, despite the fact that any day she would become a millionaire.

The Coultier children had spent their weekends and most of their vacations with their father, and later with him and his second wife, Lorraine, Nathan's mother. Michael had never been allowed to go to the Coultier house, and he had been jealous and lonely when the three stepchildren left for holidays and weekends. When Nathan was born, he had been afraid the love Trish had for him would be diverted to her new half brother, but it hadn't happened. Trish simply had two younger brothers to love after that. And they both adored her. Nathan had been as lonely as Michael when the three children were at Sam's house. He never had been invited up there, and he used to fantasize about the parties they were having, the good things they were eating, the fun they had swimming in their own pool.

"In fact," Michael said during that grueling afternoon, "I'm not supposed to be spending time with Trish or Nathan even now. When she went to Jeffrey's house to recuperate, Dad was furious. He had promised to hire a nurse, to arrange therapy, everything, and she turned to her father instead. But I was over there just about every day this past year," he added defiantly.

The three knights, Constance thought, watching them.

"Why aren't you supposed to see Trish or Nathan?" Charlie asked.

"Dad says the Coultier kids are unlucky, that they have a death wish or something. He's afraid it'll rub off."

"Yet, here you are with them," Charlie commented.

"Dad's out of town, in Chicago. He arranges sales of buildings," he added with a shrug. "Big buildings, skyscrapers, that kind of thing. He'll be back Sunday."

"Were you at home all this past year?" Constance asked then.

"Yeah," he said. "After Mother came home from the

hospital, she was ... I don't know, afraid maybe. She wanted me there, so I dropped out of school for a year and stayed."

Trish put her hand on Michael's on the table. "Tell the rest of it," she said.

He looked at her miserably, then gazed out over the yard in full bloom. "She'd start like, 'Where's Gary? Where's Suzette? Where's Trish?' And by then, she'd be crying and screaming, 'Where's Michael?' Sometimes, if I was around, she'd calm down again. If I wasn't there, they'd give her a shot, and she'd be out for a week or more."

Constance could imagine how close they must have become, how much they had depended on each other. And now he was feeling the responsibility of keeping her sane.

"Finish it," Trish demanded.

"Yeah. I heard him, my father, tell her to just shut up, they were all gone, and that time she kept screaming even though I was there. It was like she couldn't see me." He stared out past them all, and the tendon in his neck grew taut. His hand must have tightened painfully on Trish's; she grimaced, but she didn't pull free.

Constance called for a break then. Michael strode off for a walk, his hands jammed in his pockets. Charlie vanished. Nathan and Trish tried to lure Candy from her perch on a deck rail. Her tail twitched a few times, signifying displeasure at being disturbed, the only indication that she was aware of their chirping and clucking.

"Okay," Charlie said when they all reseated themselves at the patio table. "This is our standard contract. It's in your name, Trish, not the consortium of three. We agree to look into the deaths of Gary and Suzette; we will see what the fire marshal had to say about the fire; we will check out the police report on the shooting; we will look into Sam

Andreson's finances. And I can find out if the doctor who is treating Marie Andreson is reputable. Aren't those the items you mentioned in the beginning?"

"What's the point of that?" Nathan demanded. "We know what the police say, and why not have all our names on a contract?"

"Do you have any money?" Charlie asked.

He shook his head.

"How old are you?"

"What's that got to do with it? I'm almost nineteen, old enough to sign a stupid contract."

"But you wouldn't have anything to do with the financial responsibility," Charlie said blandly. "You see, I believe those who pay the bills should be allowed to give the orders and receive the reports. And that brings up a point I'd like to clear up. What's your role in all this? You don't come into any money; Sam Andreson has nothing to do with you."

"She's my sister! If he hurts her again, I'll kill the son of a bitch!"

Charlie regarded him silently for several moments until Nathan looked away.

"Actually," Trish said, "he will come into money. I've always told him that when I inherit, I'll share it with him. At first, that's all it was, share it, but after I nearly died, too . . . I intend to split whatever I get with Nathan. He's my brother." She said this in a vehement rush. She turned to Nathan and continued. "It doesn't matter whose name is on the contract. We know we're in this together; that's the important part."

My yes, Charlie thought, you're in it together. He said, "As far as your knowing what the police reports contain, forget it. You know what they told you, not the extent of their investigations. I can find that out. After I do this preliminary work, we'll have another conference."

"When?" Michael asked.

Charlie shrugged. "Obviously, I can't go to your father and question him directly. I can't tell you when. That's just the way it is."

Michael and Trish passed a silent message, and she nodded. "I'll sign it and give you a check. Do I call you or something?"

"Nope. You don't do a thing until I get in touch with you. Do you visit your mother?"

She nodded. "Several times a week, at least."

"Can you visit her and stay away from Sam?"

She looked uncertain, and Michael said, "I can let you know when he's out. He's gone a lot," he added, glancing at Charlie.

"Okay," Charlie said. "Trish, will you promise to keep away from Sam Andreson until this is over?"

"You do believe me!" Trish exclaimed. Her eyes sparkled and both cheeks flared with color.

Soberly, Charlie shook his head. "I believe the sun is shining because I can see it; I believe our cat is over there. What I'm saying, Trish, is that I believe the evidence of my eyes, my senses. If you're not mistaken in how you've interpreted events, that's simple good sense: Keep away from Sam. Don't go out driving alone at night. Be cautious. If you are mistaken in what you believe, it can't hurt anything to keep away from him. Okay? Will you do that?"

For a moment, she stared at him, then she sighed and nodded, drew the contract across the table, and pretended to read it. Constance and Charlie were both aware that her eyes were not tracking the words, that she was hiding the way a child hides, by not seeing them.

* * *

It was 5:30 when Constance returned to the patio after showing them out. Charlie had not moved.

"What are those spiky blue flowers?" he asked.

"Delphiniums."

"And the yellow mounded things?"

"Euphorbia polychrome."

He knew the red tulips that completed the grouping. "Nice," he said.

The sun was still high and it was quite warm. Now Candy flowed off the rail and began to sniff the chairs the kids had occupied, taking her time about it, being thorough. Ashcan appeared, apprehensive, ready to flee again, and Brutus swaggered in from under the lilac bush. Ashcan tensed, preparing to stalk a butterfly table-hopping among the pansies.

"Long Island," Charlie muttered.

"I know." She stood up. "Of course, the doctor, Sam's affairs, the two deaths will turn out to be exactly what they seem. As for the shooting, it just won't work as a murder attempt, will it? I'm going to pick peas and asparagus and salad greens."

Charlie nodded, to all appearances fascinated by the colorful flowers. In a low voice, he said, "But someone probably did set an arson fire and try to kill Trish."

Constance sat down again. "Why do you think that?"

"She wakes up in a smoky room, no lights. The door is hot, fire in the hall outside. And there was a glow in the bathroom. Why couldn't she open the window? I need to see a floor plan." Suddenly, he stood up. "I never did get my rum."

Constance watched him reenter the house, and after a few minutes, she went out to pick vegetables for dinner. A mistake, she kept thinking. She should have let him get rid of those kids when he wanted to.

That was Thursday. On Friday, they both put in time on the telephone and computer modem and later exchanged notes glumly. Sam Andreson was a dragon all right, Charlie said, mean, inflexible, tight, never lost a battle in his life that anyone knew about, but if he was in financial trouble, it would take more than a dozen phone calls to find out. A herd of auditors and accountants, maybe.

She said Marie's doctor not only was above reproach but was rated one of the best psychiatrists in Manhattan.

"Okay," Charlie said. "Monday, Manhattan and Suzette's files. And then Oyster Bay."

They wouldn't need a house sitter for a few days, she decided. One of the Mitchum boys would come to feed the cats, have a look around. She said, "It doesn't make much sense, does it? Sam is sixty-five. He has plenty of money, no need to murder for more."

"Honey," Charlie said gravely, "you can't be too rich, ever. A million here, a million there, every little bit helps."

"I wish we could think of an excuse to go talk to him," she said. "Maybe we should have asked more indelicate questions of those kids."

Charlie snorted. "They told us exactly what they planned from the start. If they'd wanted to talk about child abuse, we would have gotten an earful. Right?"

"Right."

"Now I'm going to fire up the grill, thaw out some of those trout in the freezer, and, in a couple of hours, eat. No more talk about the three knights for today."

She eyed the sky. "It's going to rain."

"Later it will rain. Much later."

Later he dragged the grill under the overhang of the

house and shivered as the wind drove rain into his face
when he turned the fish. Even the cats were indoors instead
of prowling underfoot hoping for a handout.

He scowled at her when he reentered the house, shaking
water from his hair. "The damn rain's putting the fire out."

"We could wrap the fish in rice and call it sushi," she
said.

"Funny, very funny."

Later they fed the nearly cooked fish to the cats and went
to their favorite Mexican restaurant, where the margaritas
were always extraordinarily good.

"What would you do with a million dollars?" she asked,
holding her glass up to admire the light through the pale
green drink. Salt on the rim sparkled like diamond chips.

"I'd think of something," he said. "You?"

"I don't know. Travel a little more maybe. I wouldn't
change anything much, I don't think."

Looking at her across the table, he knew he wouldn't
change much, either.

On Sunday night, they watched the midnight news brief on
television. Constance was paying scant attention, her
thoughts on several pop psychology books she was going to
review, and Charlie was thinking of the coming drive down
to New York, the hassle of traffic, windshield wipers, mug-
gers. . . . Then they both came to full attention. The news-
caster was saying, "Police are investigating the brutal
murder of Samuel Andreson, who minutes ago was found
shot to death in his burning car on a lonely road near his
home at Oyster Bay."

"Oh dear God," Constance breathed.

"Those goddamn kids!" Charlie said furiously. The
newsman was talking about some of Sam Andreson's most

notable accomplishments, the sales he had negotiated. At the commercial break, Charlie turned off the television.

"What are we going to do?" she asked.

"Not a goddamn thing! They'll come here soon enough. I'm going to bed." He turned off his lamp, stamped out to the hallway, paused, and came back. "We did what we could," he said. "I thought there'd be a little time, for God's sake. I thought they'd give us a week or so to start poking into things, and we'd have time to come up with a way to head them off."

"Charlie," she said sharply, "it's not our fault. I thought that, too."

"I didn't know they were *this* dumb. For God's sake, they've cooked their own goose. Can't you see it? The prosecutor yells, You hired a detective and didn't wait for him to detect! Why not? Because you knew there wasn't anything for him to find, isn't that why? What's their answer? Those dumb-ass kids don't have an answer!"

Constance got up and went to him, took him by the arm. "Hey, come on. You did what you could. So did I. We granted them more sense than they have perhaps, but no one could have guessed something like this would happen right now. Charlie, maybe they didn't do anything; maybe it was someone else we don't know anything about."

"Hah!" He took a deep breath. "Bed. I was on my way to bed."

She kissed his cheek. "Thank you, Charlie."

"For?"

"For not saying you didn't want them in the first place."

He looked at her, puzzled. He had not even thought of saying that.

"Go on," she said. "I'll close up, do lights and things, be along in a minute." But when he went up the stairs, she sat on the sofa again, frowning into space. They should have done something to prevent this, should have anticipated something like this, should have warned the youngsters of the danger, let them know they were suspect from the beginning. . . . It was more than a few minutes before she was ready to go upstairs.

Charlie always got up first, and he almost always made breakfast. *She* didn't care if she ate or not when she got up, but he did, and he liked a variety—pancakes, omelettes, bacon and eggs, French toast. . . . If she actually made breakfast, it usually was something weird, like oatmeal, or some other cereal that looked like baby food. No, it was better if he did it, he was telling himself as he rummaged in the refrigerator for eggs and scallions, considered a hot pepper and decided not this time. The answering machine across the kitchen was blinking, but he ignored it. He liked a certain decorum in the early hours: coffee, food at a leisurely pace, and then business.

By the time Constance came down, he had everything ready to scramble the eggs and make the toast. *She* went straight to the answering machine and pushed the button. Before coffee, even.

Trish's voice came on: "Mr. Meiklejohn, this is to inform you that we—that is, I—have terminated your services. I will send you a registered letter to this effect. Please send me an itemized accounting and a refund."

"Well," Constance said.

"And good morning to you, too."

"That, too." Now she poured herself coffee and sniffed at his eggs and scallions. If he made breakfast, he had always noted, she ate it appreciatively. She tilted her chair to pour off Candy, who complained in a loud voice and stalked to the back door with her tail up like a standard. Constance let her out. "I'll go do my aikido class and then a little shopping for dinner. What are you up to for the day?"

He shrugged, paying attention to the eggs in the skillet. The last thirty seconds of cooking should be done on the plate, and it took concentration. Actually, he had decided to overhaul the tractor; he always decided that when he was grumpy, and he had not quite gotten around to it yet. He brought the perfect eggs to the table and said, "I know how we can get a million bucks; maybe I'll work out a few of the details."

She gave him a skeptical look and got up to fetch the toast.

"See, when they arrest the kids, our names will come up, and every tabloid in the country will be hot for our stories. You'll have the psychological dope for them, and I'll be the hard-boiled detective and give them clues we gleaned from the knights. We'll charge what the market will bear, get them bidding, have an auction maybe. More for TV appearances. You'll need a few new things. More cleavage maybe." He paused with a thoughtful look. "Think I should have my hair styled?"

"I'll stop in at the travel agent and get some brochures," she said, handing him a piece of buttered toast.

Abruptly, they both dropped the subject. Constance knew he had been restless throughout the night, and while Charlie couldn't have said the same of her with certainty, he thought she looked tired that morning.

It was not a good week. Charlie wrote "Void" across the face of Trish's check, wrote a brief note, and mailed both to her by registered mail, return receipt requested. They received her letter of dismissal. He took a wrench out to the

barn and banged on the tractor a bit. They read the newspapers, which reported on Suzette's death, on Gary's, on the
fire. A tabloid headline screamed: MARIE ANTOINETTE RE-
INCARNATED AS MARIE ANDRESON. STILL PAYING FOR HER
SINS. . . .

On Friday when Constance arrived home shortly after
twelve, Charlie was at the back door. He jerked his thumb
toward the answering machine, and she pushed the message
button.

"Mr. Meiklejohn, Dr. Leidl, this is Lorraine Coultier. I
have to talk to you. I'll call back at one."

Her voice was very clear, the words crisp, a teacher's
voice. And she had addressed them both, Constance added
to herself; Lorraine Coultier knew who Constance was,
what her title was.

"Well," she said. "Well, I guess things are moving."

He grunted. "Right down the slippery slope."

The second call came promptly at one. Charlie answered,
and Constance listened on the extension in his office. Lorraine Coultier did not waste words, did not pretend anything. They were in desperate trouble. She knew the
youngsters had been to see Charlie and Constance. They
needed help.

"If you can come today," she finished, "I'll make a reservation for you at the Oyster Bay Inn, either a room or a
cottage, whichever you prefer."

Charlie waited a second for Constance to object if she intended to, then said okay. A cottage.

Lorraine Coultier gave them directions, her telephone
number, the number for the inn, and they hung up. Already
he was thinking of the traffic leaving New York City on a
Friday afternoon. He would have to drive; Constance re-

fused to drive in or through New York City. She had done that, she said.

Actually, Charlie felt pretty good when they began to smell the sea air a few miles outside of Oyster Bay. The road was blacktop, narrow, and there was little other traffic. After the fumes of the city and then the Long Island Expressway, the air was refreshing and pleasantly cool.

"There's the fork," Constance said.

"Yep." He slowed down just to make sure; at the sign— OYSTER BAY INN 1 MILE—he swung to the left, onto an even narrower road with a high crown. They glimpsed big houses set back among wind-sculpted pine trees. Now and then, a landscaped yard came all the way down to the road, but for the most part, the pines, scrub brush, and straggly grass made up the only visible greenery. The ground was rocky here, the woods sparse—coastal scenery.

They rounded a curve and a mammoth white building came into view on the bay side. The building was from the turn of the century or earlier and had sprouted growths in all directions: wings, ells, dormers over additions, balconies jutting out here and there. As a gravel drive came into sight, Charlie slowed to a crawl and then made the turn to the inn.

"I love it!" Constance said when he stopped at an entrance with a wide porch. "In season, I bet that porch is thick with chairs and people taking their ease."

Now it was empty. A sharp wind came in from the bay some fifty feet below; it was pretty out there, with a few sailboats leaning precariously. The water was deep blue.

A man was standing at the entrance door, watching when they got out of the Volvo. He was scowling, in his fifties or sixties, jaundiced, stooped, with a mean look in his eye. "You're Meiklejohns?" he snapped.

"Yep," Charlie said. "You have a cottage for us?"

"Not in season, you know. Not until Memorial Day. Won't have any food here until after Memorial Day."

"Fine," Constance said. "This is a wonderful building. How old is it?"

He looked at her suspiciously and turned his back. "You have to sign the book," he said. "Inside." He entered without another look at them. Charlie shrugged, and Constance fought the twitching of her lips as they followed their host.

Charlie signed the book; the yellow man studied his signature, then compared it to the ones on his driver's license and credit card.

"Third cottage across the road and up the hill," the man said finally, handing Charlie a key. "Park next to the back door."

Charlie saluted and walked out with Constance, got back in the car. At the road, he began to search for the next driveway. It was another gravel drive that climbed upward, narrower, with potholes; he passed two cottages and pulled in at the third, close to the door.

"Home," he said.

The cottage had been aired; it was clean, and over fifty years old. Constance loved it, too. "Look," she said, "we have a front porch." There was a living room area with a table and chairs for meals, as well as four rattan chairs and another table. The woodwork was blue, the walls white; blue-and-white-striped curtains and blue drapes hung at the windows. A tiny kitchen looked like a galley on a small boat, and the bedroom had twin beds pushed together.

"Home," Charlie said again, more glumly this time, looking for the bathroom, hoping for a modern shower.

There was a bathtub with a handheld shower hose but no shower curtain.

Constance was standing in the open door, gazing at the bay. "Come look."

She was letting in a lot of cold air and the cottage had no heater that he could find. Of course, no one needed heat in season, he thought as he went to stand by her, intending to pull the door closed, get on with unpacking the car. He had a bottle stashed away, and he wanted it very much at that moment.

Beyond the porch, the rocky ground sloped downward for twenty feet or so, then apparently dropped steeper; the road was not visible, but the other side of it was, more rocky ground and then a drop-off to the bay. The water sparkled and tiny whitecaps raced erratically. He started to close the door, then paused as a woman rose into sight before him. First her head appeared, then shoulders; evidently, she was climbing stairs. She reached the top and waved.

"Meiklejohn? How do you do? I'm Beverly Kratz." She was huffing from her exertion. She had red hair and freckles, was heavyset, dressed in a black skirt that was too short and a red sweater that was too big.

She examined Constance as she drew near and then looked Charlie over. "I paid old sourpuss a ten spot to let me know when you arrived. Wanted to have a little talk before you get in the middle of the Coultiers and Andresons."

She thrust out her hand to Constance first and then to Charlie. It was like shaking hands with a stevedore.

"You're the family cook, come to find out what we will or won't eat," Charlie said.

She shook her head. "Attorney. Can we go in? Worked up a sweat that's cooling pretty fast."

Constance and Charlie moved aside and she entered the cottage; Charlie closed the door at last.

"I want to know how far you got with the stuff the kids hired you to do," Beverly Kratz said. She sat in one of the rattan chairs.

"I'll bring in the other suitcase," Charlie said. "Anything else?"

"I think that's all," Constance said.

"Hey, you guys, knock it off," Beverly Kratz said. "I know they hired you, and why, and that they fired you. I'm going to represent Trish."

"If you do take menu orders, Ms. Kratz," Charlie said thoughtfully, "you might mention that I eat just about anything. The exceptions are items you have to go scour the gourmet shops for, so they don't come up too often."

Beverly Kratz reddened. She fished in a pocket and pulled out a card, stood up, and handed it to Charlie. "Call me Bev. See, a real card."

"So it is," he said, and handed it back. "Excuse me." He walked past her to the door and out to get the other suitcase and the bag with his bottle. The bag was heavier than he had thought it would be, and it clanked. He grinned. Constance had added something.

Inside, Beverly Kratz said to Constance, "I shouldn't have come on like that. Manners of a hog. Did Trish go into the child abuse, sex abuse, any of that?"

"I think we may have some glasses, with any luck," Constance said, and went to check in the tiny kitchen. There was one cabinet, and it did have glasses. She brought out three. They were as thick and heavy as jelly jars.

Charlie put the suitcase in the bedroom and opened the grocery bag, to find three bottles, the bourbon he had put in and two bottles of wine. There were peanuts and crackers, cheese, and a tin of smoked oysters. "Well, well," he said, pleased. "Honey, you travel in style." He got a tray of ice cubes from the minuscule freezer compartment of the refrigerator and worked at liberating them. Then he asked, "Bourbon, with or without ice, with or without water, chardonnay, or pinot noir?"

He put the white wine in the refrigerator and opened and poured red wine for Constance, handed her the glass, and turned to Beverly Kratz.

"Bourbon, on the rocks," she snapped.

"My drink exactly," he said. After he finished being host, he looked at her pleasantly. "You still don't quite get it, do you, Bev?"

"I get it." She glanced around. "This is a real dump. Jeff talked old sourpuss into opening a cabin for you. Reporters down in Oyster Bay. I'd go with the reporters, personally, if I didn't have a room over at their house."

Charlie motioned her toward a chair, and he sat down in another one and stretched out his legs. Constance sat at the table, and after a moment Bev sat opposite her. She sipped her drink and put it down.

"Look, everything on the table," she said, and shrugged. "The kids told us what they hired you to do. Lorraine and Jeff will hire you to do the same things. Okay, you don't tell me anything until you talk to them. Fair enough. But let me lay it out for you, anyway." She went on before either of them had a chance to interrupt. "Sunday evening, Sam and his secretary, Ellen Hosty, came home around four. They had something going, those two," she added with a knowing look that was not quite a leer. "So, at seven they had dinner, Marie, Michael, Sam, and Ellen. They got into a real fight, with Sam and Michael yelling at each other. Sam yelled that he'd go see Jeff and put a stop to it. Sam went back to his office and Michael ran upstairs to his room. A couple of minutes later, Sam left in the Caddy. Michael called Trish to warn her that Sam was on his way. Nathan took the call."

She began to make rings with the wet glass. "Trish went to her room to watch out the window for him, and Nathan hung around downstairs to make sure Sam didn't walk in on Jeff and start anything. Sam never showed up. They gave it up around ten; Nathan went to his room and listened to music or something, and Trish stayed in her room, reading. End of their story. At ten-thirty or thereabouts, Michael knocked on Ellen Hosty's office door and asked her if Sam had come back. They decided he must be out driving around to cool off. He did that sometimes. They went to the kitchen for a sandwich. At quarter after eleven, a neighbor saw the glow from a fire off the road and called the cops. Then at twenty-five after eleven, there was the explosion and the car blew to hell and gone."

"He was shot," Charlie said. "Fatal shot?"

Bev shook her head. "His death officially was due to fire-related injuries. The head wound would have done him in, though—massive brain damage. They recovered the gun. It was Sam's."

"Where was he shot?"

She put her finger on her right temple. "Close range, real close, as if someone had been sitting right next to him in the car."

She finished her drink then, glanced at her watch, and stood up. "You want to see the place Sam got it?"

"Yep," Charlie said. He pulled on his jacket, Constance got her sweater, and they left. Constance drove, Charlie beside her, and Beverly Kratz sat in the back.

She directed Constance. "First house on the right is the

Coultier place." It was less than a quarter mile away, a big gray boxy house with white trim and a porch that seemed to encircle it completely. The yard was untended, unkempt. Constance drove on.

After a short distance, Bev said, "There's the road on the left. Keep going and you'll see the Andreson place. That's the neighbor who spotted the fire, Edward Blachley." That house was on the bay side.

The road was not very steep, but in bad weather, in fog, for anyone speeding, it would become a very dangerous road. Then the Andreson house came into view. They didn't go farther into the driveway than Constance needed in order to turn around, but even from here it was apparent that Sam had built a spectacular house for his wife and family. There was a frosted-looking dome behind it—a covered swimming pool. Constance drove more slowly going back down the winding road. The road curved again, then a straightaway, followed by another curve.

"Where Gary went off," Bev said.

Constance stopped. The curve here was no worse than the others; the edge of the road was ten or twelve feet from the edge of the cliff. He shouldn't have run off the road here. She started again.

"It's two miles from Sam's house to the spot where he died," Bev said. "One mile from Jeff's house. The turn's coming up around the next curve."

Constance turned onto a very narrow road that had been gravel but was mostly dirt now.

"Used to be a cabin back there," Bev said. "Gone. And the road's going fast."

The road wound among stunted trees and boulders for less than a quarter of a mile and then came to an opening where obviously there had been a recent fire. She stopped and glanced at Charlie. He shook his head, meaning later they would come back and examine it, but not now. She drove back out.

"You can see the fix," Beverly Kratz said when Constance stopped in the Coultier driveway. "How likely is it that a stranger happened back that road? No one knew Sam would be going out that night. He wouldn't have picked up a hitchhiker. He had no enemies in these parts. No friends, either. Not popular, not a third- or fourth-generation resident the way Jeff is, but he was respected. His car was noticeable, a big black Caddy with dark windows. If he'd been out prowling, he would have been seen."

"How close are the cops to Trish and Nathan?" Charlie asked.

"Close. Asking too damn many questions, hanging out in Oyster Bay and asking questions. Meiklejohn, we need you to prove Sam Andreson tried to kill Trish, and to prove that he did kill her brother and sister. That's all we need. I'll take care of Trish." She opened her door, then added, "Everyone reads the papers, watches TV. The abused wife, abused kid, hell, an abused goat would get a sympathetic jury these days. I'm not too worried about Trish, or I won't be when she comes clean. What she can't do is stick to her story." She got out of the car, strode toward the big gray house.

Charlie glanced at Constance, who raised her eyebrows in such a noncommittal way that he grinned. "Onward," he said, and they left the car and followed Bev.

Lorraine and Jeffrey Coultier met them at the door. She was a large woman, taller than Constance, and big through the shoulders, almost masculine-looking in her body, but with a pretty face and curly brown hair. Jeffrey had the deep-set blue eyes that Trish and Nathan had inherited, thinning gray hair, and was inches shorter than his wife, not frail, but delicate in appearance. His handshake was surprisingly firm; his slight build concealed a wiry body. Nathan's resemblance to him was startling.

After a quick scrutiny of Constance and Charlie, Lorraine said, "Let's go into the plant room. It's more comfortable."

In the wide foyer they had entered, there were side tables, chairs, the wall space covered with overlapping pictures—portraits, photographs, even a New York State map. Constance glimpsed the living room they passed; it looked like a museum managed by an insane curator, with every period represented, every inch of space occupied with furniture, book stands, lamps, rugs on top of rugs. . . .

"We always figured if there are ghosts and they come back home," Jeff said, "they should feel comfortable, surrounded by familiar things."

Constance caught a gleam in his eye, although his voice was dry, his demeanor quite sober. Charlie was thinking, What a sensible house. You built a box, divided it into rooms with a central hall and central stairs, and then filled it. They had filled it admirably.

The room they were led to used to be a dining room, Lorraine said as they entered double doors. "Jeff's mother," she continued, "was a Virginia girl who couldn't abide the northern winters, so Jeff's father knocked out the south wall, added a lot of glass to the porch, ceiling, and walls, and turned the whole thing into a conservatory for her."

The room was very large, an indoor garden with a lemon tree, raised beds of vegetables, a hydroponics tank, and a pair of tomato plants that reached the ceiling and were laden with fruits. Pots of blooming plants were everywhere, hanging from the ceiling, in planters, on the floor. . . . There were redwood chairs with print cushions, glass-topped

tables, a long dining table. The room was bright with sunshine and smelled fresh and good.

"It's wonderful," Constance said. "Lovely!"

"We like it," Jeff said. "We garden at strange hours in
this house."

"He gardens," Lorraine said complacently. "I come in to
smell the roses." She gestured toward the end of the room.
"Let's sit over there." The area she indicated was like a
separate little sitting room within the bigger room; there
was a television, the redwood furniture, tables covered with
books, good reading lamps. "Can I get you something?
Coffee, wine, a drink?" Constance and Charlie both said
coffee and sat down; she excused herself.

Bev sat down with a grunt, and Jeff sank into the cushions on the sofa. He regarded them evenly, the gleam gone
from his eyes now. "You know why we called you," he
said finally. "Will you continue your investigations?"

Charlie shook his head. "Mr. Coultier, or is it Dr.
Coultier?"

"Jeff," he said impatiently.

"Okay, Jeff. You see, the problem is that I consider everything your daughter said to me as confidential. We terminated our relationship. If you want to hire us now, you
should tell us what you want us to do, and we'll start fresh.
And we have to know up front who is offering to hire us.
You or your attorney?" He glanced at Bev, who was scowling at him fiercely.

"I want to hire you. Whatever you say can be said in
front of Bev. I want you to investigate the deaths of my el-
der son, Gary, and my daughter Suzette, the fire that very
nearly killed Teresa, and the shooting at her a few weeks
ago."

Charlie nodded thoughtfully. Lorraine returned, pushing a

cart with coffee and cups. Charlie waited out the confusion of serving everyone before he spoke. "Let me tell you the usual procedure. The cops find a murder victim. First they look into the domestic situation, because usually that's where they find the murderer. But at the same time, they'll be looking into possible business enemies, transients, a neighbor with a grudge, a madman on the loose, an Iranian terrorist, you name it. They'll be looking into this family, of course. All of this is routine for them, and it takes time. Weeks, sometimes a lot of weeks. But as soon as they know you've hired someone to look into the other deaths, the fire and the shooting, they'll home in on this house. And once they decide they know who's guilty, the other investigations tend to get less attention, or even get dropped. That's just how it is. Are you sure you want that?"

Bev had been following this closely. Now she snapped, "Don't tell me you didn't know what those kids were up to when they came to see you!"

"All right, I won't," Charlie said, but he kept his gaze on Jeff, who had gone paler and paler, until now he was chalky.

"Is that true?" Jeff asked Bev.

She shrugged. "He's the cop expert. If he says so."

Jeff turned to Lorraine as if asking what he should do. She was sitting next to him and took his hand.

Charlie said, "I suspect they already have started to consider this household simply because you've brought in an attorney."

"I've known Bev all my life," Lorraine protested. "She comes here to visit a lot." She glanced at Bev, then said, "In fact, after the fire, I asked her how I could get a look at the police files on Gary's and Suzette's deaths. It just didn't seem reasonable to have three children either dead or nearly dead so violently."

Jeff jerked around in surprise, stared at her, then at Bev.

"You didn't know?" Charlie asked.

He shook his head.

"And?" Charlie asked the attorney.

She shrugged. "I have the police reports."

"I want what you have," Charlie said.

She nodded. "But you'll have to go farther than those reports; they won't help."

"Were any of you at the party they had for Gary?" They shook their heads. "See the problem?" he said. "As soon as I start asking questions, it's going to be out, what I'm digging for. How about the secretary, Ellen Hosty? Was she there? Can she be questioned without having everything turn up the next day in the *National Enquirer*?"

Bev snorted. "She's so closemouthed that if her nose got stopped up, she'd suffocate. If she'll talk to you? Who knows? She was there."

"How about the fire? Who investigated that?"

Jeff told him two names, men he had grown up with, went fishing with. They could both be questioned, he said without hesitation. He turned to Lorraine and added, "In fact, last year I talked to Pete Belasco about the accidents and the fire, had him look into the reports, exactly as you did." He looked at Charlie again, a haunted expression on his face. "It's hard to accept coincidence when it's your children's deaths you're talking about."

Before Charlie could ask anything else or vent his frustration with this secretive family, he felt as if Constance's fingers were tickling his back. She had not moved, and he knew she had not, but she had a way of signaling that was unmistakable. He glanced at her, waiting.

"Jeff, Lorraine," she asked, "didn't you talk about this? The two of you?"

They both shook their heads. "I started to a dozen times," Jeff said, "but what was the use? Pete couldn't find anything to suggest. . . . He couldn't find anything."

"Did you believe Sam Andreson was responsible?"

He hesitated, then said, "I'd known him for forty years. After Marie . . . There wasn't any reason for him to do anything like that."

Bev suddenly yelled, "For God's sake, Jeff, just shut up!"

Constance ignored her. "What about the shooting? Did you think someone tried to kill Trish that night?"

He looked miserable. "Pete and I talked it over. If anyone had wanted to kill her, he could have done it out there."

"Yet a year ago, you canceled your travel plans for your sabbatical, stayed home with your daughter," Constance said.

He nodded and cleared his throat, then said raggedly, "There wasn't anything to point to, nothing concrete, but I wanted to stay close to her."

"Did you talk to her about any of this?"

"No. We talked about using caution, not being out alone at night, general precautions, nothing specific." He looked desperate, near tears. "I was a fool. I had no idea she had grown suspicious of Sam, that she was terrified of him."

Constance studied him, finished. Charlie knew she was finished just as he had known she wanted to ask questions, without being able to say how he knew.

"You haven't answered the question I asked awhile back," Charlie said then.

"I don't want you to bring the police here. Maybe they'll never come here."

Bev made an indignant noise and straightened in her chair. They both ignored her. Charlie said, "You understand that I may come up with no more than you already have learned? Maybe there's nothing to find?"

Jeff nodded. "I know that. Pete's good, he's our chief of police here, retired from a long-time position with the state police. But he might have missed something."

"Right," Charlie said. "I can start with those people who won't blab about it. In this house, for openers. And I want to be brought up to date about Sunday night."

"For God's sake!" Bev snapped. "What for?"

At last, Charlie turned to her. "I don't tell you how to run your law office; you don't tell me how to conduct my business. Okay?"

She flushed a deep red and her mouth tightened until her lips all but disappeared.

Charlie glanced at his watch; it was close to seven. "We have to discuss fees, and I have to ask you a number of questions that might become pretty personal. For example, why did Sam Andreson forbid his son to hang around here?"

Lorraine stood up. "Please, will you both stay and have dinner with us? I made enough. I'll just go see how it's coming along." Charlie glanced at Constance, who nodded. Lorraine walked behind Jeff and laid her hand on his head for a moment. "I can tell you why Sam was so determined to keep Michael away," she said. "He was insanely jealous of Jeff." She moved on.

Constance stood up. "Can I help?" she said, and trailed after Lorraine toward the door to the kitchen. Watching, Charlie knew she would be as hard at work in the kitchen as he would be in the garden room, and her work would not be culinary.

"You want me to beat it, too?" Bev asked meanly.

Jeff shrugged. "I don't guess we have a single secret you haven't known about for years." The glint was back in his eyes when he said this. Then he asked Charlie. "Fees first?" He stood up. "We should move to my study. They'll be setting the table in here." He led the way across the hall to a study that looked like a library that had long ago run out of shelf space. Books were everywhere—on tables, the floor, every shelf, on a chair.

Trish and Nathan set the table in the garden room, and at a quarter to eight they all sat down to dinner. The young people were subdued, even embarrassed. Trish played with her food and kept her gaze on her plate. Nathan fidgeted, but he had an appetite. They talked about fishing, about baseball, about colleges, about everything except what they were all thinking about.

The dinner was okay, Charlie decided, the sort of meal Constance might turn out on one of her infrequent bad days in the kitchen. Roast beef too well done, oven-roasted potatoes, green beans, salad . . . all okay and very plain. Wholesome, he thought, plain wholesome chow.

"We'll clean up," Trish said after they all had strawberries with cream.

"Ah, I have a favor to ask," Charlie said. "How are you at drawing? Ever make a floor plan? Do any drafting?"

"No."

"Try," he said. "Maybe Nathan can help. A drawing of the guest house. Upper and lower floors, everything you can think of, like where the fridge was, the outside entrances, bathroom, the window you jumped out of, everything. Can do?"

She glanced at Nathan and said faintly, "I'll try." They left together.

Charlie turned back to Jeff. "You up for any more tonight?"

Jeff sighed and nodded.

In half an hour, Trish and Nathan came back with the sketch, and Charlie sat down by Trish at the dining table and began asking questions about it, redrawing parts of it as she answered.

"Circular stairs?" Charlie asked, pointing at a squiggle.

She nodded and watched him redraw them.

"Okay. The fireplace. Was there a pull screen, or a screen that had to be lifted out of the way and put back?"

"A pull screen with a chain."

He studied the drawing some more and kept asking questions until he had a pretty good idea of the cottage. About twenty by twenty-five feet, a cathedral ceiling in the living room, the upstairs bedroom over the kitchen, in the back. Circular stairs, near the wall opposite the fireplace, went to an open, railed landing, where a bathroom door was at the head of the stairs and the door to the bedroom down farther.

"Was there another door to the bathroom?"

She blushed and said yes, she had forgotten. She pointed and he added a door from the bedroom.

"Uh-huh," he said. "Describe the bathroom. Tiled?"

She nodded. "A tub here, and a shower stall next to it. I used the shower before I went to bed. Toilet, double sink at the vanity, here." He filled in the space as she pointed.

"Good," he said finally. "See, you can do drafting, draw floor plans."

She gave him a look of such skeptical derision, he wanted to pat her, the way he would have done his own daughter. Instead, he leaned back and said, "I know this is hard; sometimes you just don't remember a lot both before and after a severe trauma, but can you remember that evening in the guest house?"

"Yes. I know what I did, and I did close the screen." She sounded defiant now, for the first time.

"Okay," Charlie said. "But I want you to back up a little. Where were you guys sitting, where did you drink your chocolate? That kind of stuff. Can you remember that?"

She was eyeing him doubtfully. "Sure. We sat on the floor on cushions."

"From the beginning," he said. "Consider it a memory test. First you entered the house. Was the door locked when you got there?"

Step by step, he took her through the evening. The door had not been locked; they went inside and Michael made the fire while she heated milk for the chocolate. She used two packets of cocoa mix, made four cups. The milk, cocoa mix, cookies had all been unopened. She took the hot chocolate and cookies to the living room and they sat on the floor on the cushions and listened to music on Michael's CD player.

"It just wasn't working, having the party, I mean. We were all tired and sleepy. It wasn't the same, being allowed to be in the cottage. It used to be fun when we sneaked in, but too much had changed."

"I understand," Charlie said. "Did people go up to use the bathroom?"

"I think we all did. Oh, I took Rita up and showed her the bedroom and bathroom."

"Were there locks on the bathroom doors?"

She frowned. "Probably, but I don't know for sure."

"Okay. You were all tired and Michael's friend had to leave. What then?"

"We took our mugs out to rinse them and left them and the pan in the sink to soak. We pushed the cushions back against the wall, and they left. I closed the fire screen and turned off lights and went upstairs. Then I took a shower and went to bed."

Charlie nodded, but he had her back up again. "Did you lock the door when they left?"

"It had one of those push-button locks. I pushed it in."

"Okay. Upstairs. You went to the bedroom and undressed there to shower?"

"Yes," she said tiredly. "I got my nightshirt out, undressed, and took a shower."

"You entered the bathroom by the door to the bedroom? Not the hall door?"

She was looking exasperated now. "Yes. Do you want to know what kind of soap I used?"

Charlie grinned. "Maybe. Was the door to the landing open?"

"No. You couldn't have both doors open. They hit each other. Oh." She looked at her sketch, pointed. "That's not quite right. The door's down farther."

Charlie erased the door and put it closer to the landing so that if both were opened, they would hit each other. He nodded, satisfied. "Just a couple more questions," he said. "Did you leave the bathroom door open to the bedroom when you went to bed?"

She looked at him as if she thought he was crazy, but she nodded. "Yes. Mr. Meiklejohn, is all this important?"

"Well," he said. "Let's pretend we know an arsonist entered the guest house. We don't know for sure at this point, but we'll pretend we do. See, he has to open the fire screen, and then he has to go upstairs and open the bathroom door to the hall. You saw a glow, and that means either the bathroom was burning or else both bathroom doors were open, the one to the bedroom and the one to the landing. A tiled bathroom that's been used recently for a shower holds a lot of moisture in the air. That would have slowed the fire. And tile isn't good combustible material; that would have slowed it down. Fire was burning throughout the lower building, all the way into the kitchen, flaming out the window over the sink. It was on the landing; you said the doorknob was hot, but no fire had come into the bedroom yet. But if the bathroom had been in flames, so would the bedroom have been. You would have seen fire, not just a glow."

"Someone sneaked in and opened the door?" She stared at him, then added in a whisper, "To make sure the smoke went to the bedroom?" She looked bloodless, as if only now did she realize what her accusation about arson meant.

Charlie nodded.

Bev let out a long, loud breath, and Jeff moved to his daughter and put his arms around her; he was nearly as colorless as she was.

Charlie folded the sheet of paper with the sketch of the house plan and put it in his pocket. When he turned away from Trish, he saw Nathan staring at him with what he hoped was awe, not terror. It was hard to tell.

It was after eleven when they left the exhausted Coultiers and drove the short distance back to their own cabin, which was like a refrigerator.

"What did you think?" Constance asked. She was moving about, putting things away, pulling the bedspread off the bed exactly as if the cabin was livable. His teeth were chattering.

"Tomorrow," he said.

She went into the bathroom and he could hear water running. Then, after a few minutes, she called, "Charlie, come here!"

He had taken his shoes off; the floor was icy. He hurried across the room to the bathroom door and flung it open, to be enveloped in a cloud of steam.

"Have you looked at this tub? It's gigantic! Come on in, the water's fine."

He stood for a moment and then laughed and began to strip off his clothes.

The tub was gigantic, and the water was very fine. He soaped her back, as muscular as a boy's, with skin as soft as a baby's, and he thought contentedly how one thing usually led to another, and another.

Constance heard Charlie get up the next morning, and she snuggled down lower in the warm bed; she heard him leave, and she drifted off to sleep again, and then she was dreaming of coffee and cinnamon. Cinnamon? She sat up and stretched.

When she got to the kitchen, coffee was ready, cinnamon rolls were hot, and Charlie was sorting through a pile of papers. She kissed him. "You are one good provider," she said, pouring coffee.

He grinned at her. He had gone to town, nothing open but a little café, and he had done the sensible thing, he told her; he had eaten breakfast and waited for the grocery to open. "Juice in the fridge, and eggs, bacon. Want me to rustle up something?"

"This is fine," she said, tearing a cinnamon roll apart. "What's all that?"

"Bev Kratz's reports on Gary and Suzette. Fire report in here somewhere. Nothing new so far."

She nodded. "According to Lorraine, Sam came sneaking

around to woo and win Marie while Jeff was tied up teaching and getting his Ph.D. Marie didn't put up any roadblocks. She was not happy," she added.

"And after Sam? Was she happy then?"

"Lorraine suspects it was frying pan to fire, but she has nothing definite. In the last few years, Marie has pretty much dropped everything."

She poured more coffee. "Your turn."

"One reason Jeff didn't pursue the idea of arson, aside from the fire report," he said, "is that the secretary, Ellen Hosty, and Sam both swore they spent the night together." He frowned. "You think Jeff is as naïve as he comes on, trusting police reports instead of his own suspicions?"

She nodded. "Experts tend to trust other experts, and he's an expert in history. Lorraine trusted the reports. Only Trish trusted her own senses and intuition. She's too young and fresh out of school to have faith in experts yet."

She cocked her head, listening, and now Charlie heard it, too. Tires grated on the gravel outside their door, then stopped. He went to the door to look out. A man was climbing down from a beat-up pickup truck. The man was tall and thin, with a few white hairs and a very pink scalp. His face was brown from weather, as lined and wrinkled as a sun-dried peach.

"Meiklejohn? I'm Pete Belasco," he said at the door. He looked about eighty, but his handshake was firm and his eyes were clear and steady as he examined Charlie and then looked past him to Constance.

"Well, come on in, Chief," Charlie said. "We're having coffee. Want some?" He introduced Constance.

"You bet. Never turn down a free anything, that's my motto," Belasco said, watching Constance gather up the papers on the table and take them into the bedroom. New lines appeared on his face, at his eyes, his mouth; he could have been smiling.

Charlie put a plate down, poured coffee, and pushed the cinnamon rolls toward Belasco, who helped himself.

"Jeff told me about you," Belasco said. "Thought we might have a chat. You've seen the reports, not much to add."

"You knew Gary pretty well?"

"Knew them all pretty well. Jeff's kids, I mean. Gary was as straight as a young guy could be, a real surprise to find so much alcohol in him, but it was there."

"You don't know Michael well?" Constance asked.

He shrugged. "Sam had his own ideas about child raising. Private school when he was little, boarding school at thirteen, Princeton at eighteen, flunked out, dropped out, something, and went to Columbia. He didn't let Michael associate much with us common folk. The others went to the public school here, same as my kids."

"Tell us about the shooting a couple of weeks ago," Charlie said then.

"Got a piece of paper?"

Constance got up to bring paper. Belasco fumbled in his pockets, and she handed him a pen.

"Thanks. You know that fork back on One-oh-six where you turn off to come to the inn?" He drew the road and then a little rectangle. "Okay, here's her car, making the turn, where she says it happened. See, the bullet went through the left-rear window, out through the front-right windshield. A perfect diagonal. Only problem is where did he stand, or sit, or whatever he was doing?" He drew in the straight-line trajectory of the bullet. It would have been fired from the center of the road. He frowned at the drawing. "And why wait until she was turning if she was the target? Either he knew her car or he didn't, and if he did, why wait? And why not follow up?"

"Find the shell, anything?"

"Nope. And we searched."

"What kind of car?"

"Hers? Honda, two-door."

Charlie frowned at the drawing with him.

"Maybe he thought she was going to Oyster Bay," Constance said.

"Maybe," Belasco said. "Still the same problem—why wait until she was turning? But why didn't he follow up?"

"How high up did the bullet go through?" Charlie asked.

Belasco held his fingers about three inches apart. "That far down the windshield."

Charlie pushed the drawing aside. "Okay. What about Suzette?"

Belasco drank his coffee. His lined face grew even more lines, deeper lines. "She had a boyfriend in," he said. "They ate pizza, drank wine, went to bed, and afterward she did heroin, quaaludes, and sleeping pills."

Charlie gazed at him unhappily. "They're sure it was consensual?"

"No signs of roughhousing. He used a condom; she had lubricant in her vagina, a hickey on her neck. The sleeping pills were some Marie gave her when Gary died. Where she got the other junk, no one knows. She was wearing a nightgown, in her bed when they found her. Needle in the bathroom, her prints. No other prints that told them anything, a few unidentified, some smudges." He looked at Charlie and said, "I thought it stunk. She'd been a good kid, and to end like that ... Anyway, I asked questions. Whoever was with her spent time there, and Sam didn't have that kind of time that night. He had people around, some kind of emergency meeting. He could have left for a little bit, from fifteen or twenty minutes after seven until about eight, but his apartment is on Park Avenue South and she was in SoHo. He couldn't have gotten there, had a party, bed, and then the junk. His prints are on army files, no matches. I had to go along with them, Meiklejohn. Another good kid—drink, drugs, sex . . ."

Constance got up to pour more coffee for them all.

He nodded at her in thanks and held his mug in both hands. "The fire. I tried . . . God, I tried to find a way to prove arson. Even called in Ron Leicester. You know him?" Charlie nodded. "Yeah. He said it could have been, or not. No way to prove anything, no combustible fluids or oily rags. He said it's suspected that thousands of arson fires happen every year, all without any way to prove anything."

"Ninety-four thousand is the last number I heard," Charlie said tightly.

"Yeah. So we tried, but there wasn't anything, not a damn thing. Then the secretary swore that Sam spent the night with her. I thought he'd hit her for that, for saying it in front of Marie, but he went along with it. And that's how it was. No proof, no motive, and she was ready to alibi him." He drank his coffee and set the mug down hard. "If Trish had died, I would have taken him in anyway, proof or no proof."

"Did you tell Jeff Coultier that?"

He shook his head. "Look, Meiklejohn, I want to level with you. I don't come out smelling so good, but that's how it is. I was wrong about Gary; he really was drunk. I was wrong about Suzette; she really did have a boyfriend and really did the drugs. I think now that I was wrong about the fire. It just seemed too much at the time. One, two, three. Too goddamn much! Jeff's one of my oldest friends. I wanted to slam someone for hurting people I love. I should have talked it out with them all, Trish especially, because now they're in deep shit, and I might have prevented it." Abruptly, he stood up and made a motion toward the door.

"Sit down," Charlie said. "Pete, isn't it? Sit down and listen to me a minute." Belasco sat down again, and Charlie told him what he had gone through with Trish the night before. "Maybe Ron didn't ask her enough questions, or maybe she didn't think to mention seeing that glow in the bathroom, I don't know. But it was arson, Pete. It was an arson fire and attempted murder."

"But you can't prove it."

"Who do I have to prove it to? Why couldn't she get the window open?"

"We don't know. They got the fire out, but the place was falling down. They found the pieces of window, latch worked okay, what they could tell about it."

"Tell us about Sam Andreson."

"We all liked Marie when Jeff brought her home. Pretty little thing, with that great accent, a wonderful cook. She fit right in. But things were hard, three kids, not much money with him in school, then just starting to teach. So Sam began coming around, hanging around her. People tried to warn Jeff, but hell, Sam was an old army buddy. Way I figured, Sam was out to take what he thought was rightfully his. Folks here think he built that house on the hill to spite Jeff." He shrugged. "Then, later on, nothing good enough for Michael, and let Jeff do what he could for the others. Jeff never had an extra cent all those years, I can tell you. Sam broke Marie, turned her into a tight-mouthed, bitter woman, and he ran herd on Michael like a sergeant at boot camp."

Charlie sighed; Belasco's biases were showing, whether he knew it or not. "Sam's murder," he said.

Belasco didn't add a thing to what they already knew.

"What about the explosion? A bomb?"

He shook his head. "Gasoline. Fire burned the interior for a while, heat built up, the gas went. They had a pumper on the road, just about at the turn from One-oh-six when it blew. They put it out in a couple of minutes."

"Why a fire?" Charlie said. "Why not another shot if the first one didn't do him?"

"You can have the preliminary report," Belasco said. "State marshal toted the wreckage off to the lab. We'll know more maybe in a couple of weeks."

Charlie scowled at him. "Someone shot him in the temple, probably beside him talking or something, then got out, went to the backseat to arrange a fire. Jesus!"

"Maybe there were two of them," Belasco said quietly. "One in the front seat, one in the back."

After a moment, Charlie nodded.

Belasco didn't stay much longer and didn't add anything to what he had said. Charlie walked out with him, and Constance stood at the door, watching them go around the Volvo, pause at the truck, shake hands. She turned back to the table and studied the drawing of the fork in the road, visualizing the car on it, someone shooting at Trish.

When Charlie came back in, she said, "I keep hearing her tell Nathan they were all in it together, back at our house." He nodded. "She wouldn't have gotten in a car alone with Sam for anything," Constance said. She realized she was moving Belasco's sketch back and forth, and she removed her hand from it. "And the shooting . . ." When she looked at Charlie, he nodded again.

"Let's see if Marie is receiving," he said. He put his arm

around her shoulders and squeezed lightly, then went to the telephone.

The house was more impressive close up than it had been from the end of the driveway. Michael admitted them to a spacious foyer, with a lot of chrome, brass, and polished wood. There were open stairs with chrome trim, brass urns, a long hall carpeted with a thick black-and-white runner. He led them into the living room, two stories high, a mammoth L-shaped room, with floor-to-ceiling windows and a view of the bay. All the furnishings were sleek and modern; a fireplace was a brass and beveled-glass enclosure raised a foot above floor level. It was like walking into an illustration from an upscale women's magazine, Charlie thought.

"Mother will be down in a couple of minutes," Michael said. Like Trish and Nathan, he looked nervous and perhaps even embarrassed. "And Ellen said she'd come out whenever you want her to."

"Mind showing us around the house first?" Charlie asked.

Michael seemed relieved to have something to do. "There are people in the office, the lawyer sent them. Going over files with Ellen. This way."

Back in the foyer, he opened the door to the office, where several people were at desks and a table. No one looked up. Next to that was Ellen's office, Michael said, indicating the door. He didn't open it. Opposite the office was the dining room. Like the living room, it was spacious and sparkling clean. The table gleamed; sideboards had silver candleholders. The view was of a big garden terrace with red-tile flooring, and beyond it, the swimming pool dome. Michael showed the rest of the downstairs, a television/game room, the kitchen, another staircase in the rear.

"The master suite and four more bedrooms upstairs," he said. "You want to see them?"

Charlie shook his head. "Is there a housekeeper? A live-in?"

"Juana and Pablo. They have a little house behind the pool."

They were back at the dining room door. Matter-of-factly, Charlie said, "You were all at dinner when the fight started. What happened? What started it?"

Michael looked out the window, his shoulders hunched, hands deep in his pockets. "Dad said he and Ellen had more work to do, that they'd have coffee in his office, and Mother . . . she started to yell about being left alone all the time." He glanced miserably at Charlie. "She said I was gone, and when she tried to get Trish to come keep her company, she was gone. And he jumped to the conclusion we were out together. He began to yell at me, and she was still yelling, and I guess I was, too."

Charlie nodded, his gaze on the shining table. "So you were all yelling. Then what?"

Michael was staring down at his shoes. He mumbled, "He grabbed my arm and yelled at Ellen to get Mother up to her room. And he pulled me out into the hall. I . . . I could have hit him to get loose, maybe, but . . . Dad yanked me into his office and slammed the door. He was still yelling, saying if I wanted to stay in his house, I'd do what he said. Then he yelled that he'd stop it right now; he'd order Trish to keep out of his house. If Marie wanted to see her, they could meet somewhere else, and if I couldn't live by his rules, I could get out, too. . . . I ran out and up the stairs, and he followed me into the hall, yelling he'd put a stop to it, that he was going to have it out with Jeff and Trish. I didn't really think he'd go over to Trish's, but I was afraid he might, so I called when he left, to warn her. I got Nathan."

Charlie nodded when he'd finished. "You saw him leave?"

"Yes. Not from my room. It's on the wrong side. I went to the spare room and watched until he pulled out, then went back to my room to call."

"What time was that?"

"I don't know. Not nine-thirty yet."

"Okay. Then what?"

Michael shrugged. "Nothing. I hung out by the phone, hoping Trish would call. I didn't want to call them again, just in case they were having a fight or something. Then around ten-thirty, I began to wonder if he'd just driven around a while and had come home again. So I went down to see. Ellen was in her office working. We went out to the kitchen and had a snack together."

"Where was the nurse during all that?"

"She had Sundays off. Mother fired her on Monday."

"Michael," Charlie said slowly then, "you know it doesn't make much sense, having a fight like that because you'd spent time with your sister. What was it really about?"

Michael stared out the windows, hunched again. "I think he kept inventing new rules, hoping I'd finally get mad enough to walk out. He said if I left, I couldn't come back. He meant it. Then Mother would have been alone with him." He swung around and said vehemently, "You know what I kept wishing that night? I kept hoping he'd gone off the road where Gary did, that he was down in the bay just like Gary."

Charlie held up his hand. "Take it easy. In the office, what did he say?"

"He was yelling about me hanging out with Trish and Nathan. I was yelling, too. I mean, I'm twenty-one years old!"

"Where did he keep his gun?"

"In his office, locked up in his desk, or in the car. I think he carried it a lot."

"Know why? Was he threatened?"

"He just said he felt safer with a gun."

Charlie nodded. "Okay. When you were with him in the office, did you see the gun? Did he get it from somewhere?"

Michael shook his head. "We stood just inside the door. When I ran out and up the stairs, he followed me to the hall, still yelling. Then he went back inside his office and slammed the door."

"How long after that did he leave? Two minutes? Ten?"

"Not long, not even five minutes."

"So he had time to call someone?"

"Maybe. I guess so."

"Fine," Charlie said, and started to walk toward the living room. "You suppose your mother intends to come down?"

"Want me to get her?"

"Not yet. How about Ms. Hosty?"

Michael nodded and crossed the foyer to the office door and entered. He came out a second later along with a slender, fortyish woman with blond hair done in a chignon. Michael introduced them.

"Ms. Hosty, I know this is an imposition, but would you answer a few questions?"

She looked at him coolly, shrugged, and turned toward her office. She was trim in a pale blue linen suit, medium heels, no jewelry except for a watch, little makeup. She carried a pair of gold-rimmed glasses. When Michael started to accompany them, she regarded him even more coolly. "If you don't mind, this will be private," she said. Michael flushed. She opened her door, entered, stepped aside for Charlie and Constance, and then closed it.

"I agreed to see you," she said, going to her desk, "only to tell you that if there's anything I can do to make certain Trish and Nathan are convicted of killing Sam, I'll do it." She sat down, her back to the double windows, her face shadowed.

The office was as neat and efficient as she was—a chrome and teak desk, a computer station with a modem, fax, two telephones; a laptop computer, several file cabinets with locks; a door to the other office.

"They seemed to think he was trying to kill Trish," Constance said. She sat down in a low-slung chair. "Was he?"

"Don't be ridiculous! They are crazy. All Marie's children are or were crazy, just like her. Sam was good to those kids."

"We heard that he refused to give them a cent, that Jeff had to support them until they came into their own money," Constance said.

"Jeff and Marie had a divorce agreement; he accepted the terms, and if he had to cry poor, he should have thought of it sooner."

"Did Sam really get upset when Trish went to her father's house after the fire?"

"Yes. Of course he did. He tried to help her. That's how it always was—he tried to help, and they turned their backs on him. He tried to help Suzette in New York, and she . . . she preferred dope."

Constance nodded. Her eyes were adjusting now and she could see Ellen's face more clearly; the secretary's expression was grim; everything about her was stiff and unnatural. "What do you mean, he tried to help Suzette? Did he know she was into drugs?"

Ellen Hosty shrugged. "I don't know what she told him. They had lunch on Monday of that week, and he was upset, but when he called her a day or two later, she didn't take his call. Then she called him and agreed to have lunch again on the following Monday. She did drugs instead."

"And then the police asked embarrassing questions," Constance said in a low voice. "He must have understood the implications of their questions."

"Yes, he understood," she said bitterly. "He understood all too well." She looked at her watch. "I'm very busy and I have nothing to tell you."

"But you do," Constance said. "See, one way to interpret the history of these two families is to say that Sam came here and bought Marie with promises. He tried to ruin Jeff financially and extended his hatred for Jeff to his children. One by one, they were going to deplete Marie's inheritance, and Marie didn't stay bought. Did anyone weep for him?"

Ellen Hosty jumped up. "Please, leave. This is insane, trying to analyze a man you never even met!"

"Why didn't he divorce her, marry you? You were lovers for how many years? Ten, fifteen? Was it just good business to stay married, wait for the money to come along?"

"Everything he did was for her!" Ellen Hosty said in an intense low voice. "She was his dream for ten years and he came out here and saw how unhappy she was, her life a drudgery, living in that mausoleum. He still loved her, and she wanted what he had to offer. He gave her a dream house, and he thought she would be happy at last. Hah! He was in town all week and as soon as he got home, the children ran to their father, that pitiful little schoolteacher father, and she blamed Sam for separating her from her children. She blamed Sam! He was working eighteen-hour days, twenty-hour days, some nights he didn't sleep at all, and it was for her, all of it, Sam trying to make poor little Marie happy!"

Abruptly, she swiveled her chair around to face the windows. "He lost her, lost the stepchildren, lost his son, all because she's an emotional cripple, and he couldn't see it. He loved her for so many years, when he stopped loving her, he couldn't even see any other life for himself. She did that to him. Blinded him to life."

"Someone wept for him," Constance said softly.

Ellen Hosty didn't move.

"What do you mean, he lost his son, Michael?" Constance asked after a moment.

Ellen shrugged, still facing away from them. "She poisoned Michael against him. Sam tried to save him. At least, he could see what was happening to his son, but she won there, too. Sam sent him away to schools, tried to get him interested in sports, studies, anything, but the more he tried, the harder she held on." Her voice dropped to near inaudibility. "Eight years ago, he came to my apartment, and he cried. She despised him, he said, and Michael did, too. He cried, and I took him to my bed. We became lovers. He could have left her then. He admitted it that night, but he blamed Michael. If they could just get Michael past those awful teens, everything would work out. I felt sorry for the boy, taking the blame for his mother, but Sam was so sure it was only a matter of another year or two. He had to stay for Michael, had to try to straighten him out. Then, after Gary died, Marie's breakdown, his own frustration and unhappiness, the guilt he suffered over failing Marie, the trap had closed for good. The time for leaving had passed and wouldn't come back."

Throughout this, Charlie had pretended to be somewhere else, hardly even breathing. Ellen had made it clear at the start that she intended to stonewall him, and he had been afraid to remind her he was still around. Now Constance glanced at him, as if to say, Your turn. He shook his head slightly.

"Ms. Hosty," Constance said, "this has been helpful. Thank you. Can you tell us something about the party for Gary? Everyone was surprised by the high alcohol content in his blood. Do you know when he could have drunk enough to account for it?"

Ellen Hosty turned back around, reached for her glasses and put them on, probably turning Charlie and Constance into a blur. She shrugged. "If anyone gave him too much, it was Suzette, Trish, and Michael. They were making fruit punch, and they kept sampling it and passing out samples to Gary." She looked past Constance for a moment. "We had an early dinner party for about twenty people, with tables set on the terrace. After dinner, the kids started making the punch. There was to be a dance later on the terrace, with twenty or thirty more people expected. I know Trish and Michael took turns giving Gary and his girlfriend samples. Maybe Suzette did, too, but I didn't see her do it, and I did see them. Michael was only a kid, fourteen, and Trish was underage. They had no business getting involved with punch to start with." She thought for a moment. "The girlfriend went up to shower and change clothes, maybe lie down for half an hour. Gary tried the punch again, kidding around about it, pretending it was awful, and then he said he'd run down and say hello to his father. He left." She twined her fingers on the desktop and looked at them. "The police collected the punch when they came—about a cup of rum in nearly a gallon of juice. They decided he must have helped himself at the bar inside the living room. No one would have paid any attention if he'd wandered off for a minute or two. No one claimed to have seen him doing it." She spread her hands. "That's all I can tell you about it."

Constance nodded. "What about the night the guest house burned?"

Ellen Hosty looked at her over the top of her glasses, then looked down at her hands again. "I told the police I spent the night with Sam. I did. And he didn't leave."

"All right. But what about the plumbing problem? What was that?"

"When Juana went up to prepare the room for Trish, she found the bathroom floor soaking wet. Pablo tried to find a leak and couldn't, and they had to call the plumber. He was due the next morning. Pablo turned off the water to that bathroom and drained the toilet. So Sam said Trish should have the guest house and be done with it. The plumbers said later that it was a faulty gasket on the tank, where it joined the bowl."

"Why didn't Trish use the guest room in the house?"

Ellen Hosty looked at her coolly. "That room and my room share a bath. We thought she would be more comfortable all the way out."

Constance nodded, but before she could ask anything else, Ellen stood up. "One more thing about that night. We all thought Trish had died in the fire. We were shocked, stunned, and Marie turned on Sam and screamed that he had killed all her beautiful children. Then she fainted. But she said it in front of Michael, and no doubt during the next months she kept saying it. She's crazy, hysterical. But Michael is hers, and it would have been easy for her to convince him of her delusion, and for him to convince Trish and Nathan. Those three conspired to murder Sam Andreson. Michael called them, and they met Sam at the road and got in his car, and they killed him. And it's her doing!" Abruptly, she sat down again. "I have nothing more to say to either of you. Just go away."

In the sun-filled hallway again, Charlie took Constance's hand and held it. "I could have stayed home and read a book," he murmured.

Michael appeared at the living room door. "Mother said if you want to talk to her, she'll be in her room upstairs." He looked embarrassed again. "She's upset that you've been talking to Ellen."

"Oh, well, then upstairs it is," Charlie said, and gave Constance's hand a light squeeze. "Lead the way."

Michael nodded toward the wide stairs. "Sorry about this," he mumbled.

"It's okay. I sort of wanted to see the rest of the mansion. Quite impressive."

They followed him up and had to wait a second when he tapped on the door to his mother's room. Then he pushed the door open for them to enter. The rest of the house was sterile, decorator-perfect to the last detail, but here there were soft grayed blues and greens, terra-cotta colors in prints on a sofa and chairs, brilliant splashes of red and yellow on pillows, in prints on the walls. Mediterranean colors, Constance thought, Gauguin colors.

Marie stood in a doorway to a bedroom beyond, with more of the same warm colors visible behind her. She was wearing a simple gray silk dress with a green-and-violet scarf, and she was at least fifty pounds overweight. Her hair was black, streaked with gray, her eyebrows the same high peaks that Michael and Trish had inherited. Her brows were drawn close in a tight frown.

"You've talked to that woman, who, I imagine, has filled your heads with scurrilous lies. That can't be helped. Sit down."

She waited until they were all in chairs and then lowered herself onto a lounge and leaned back. "I know why you're here," she said then. "I know Jeff hired you, and the purpose. It's all a waste of your time and his money. That woman killed my husband. Michael, Trish, and Nathan had nothing whatever to do with it."

"How do you think she managed that?" Charlie asked with interest. "She was in the kitchen with your son when the fire started."

"She saw Sam arrive home; they argued and got in the car so no one would overhear them and drove to that place where she shot him and started the fire, and she came back on foot. If Michael had gone to her office five minutes earlier, he would not have found her."

Charlie nodded gravely. "The preliminary reports state the fire started at about eleven," he said. "She was here at eleven."

"The reports are mistaken."

"I'm afraid the police will go along with them," Charlie said. "Why would she have wanted to kill him?"

"Because he wouldn't divorce me and marry her. She waited and waited and he wouldn't do it. She was a leech, always hanging on him, taking trips with him, sleeping with him in my house, and she finally realized that he would never leave me and take her instead. So she killed him."

"Hm," Charlie said. She spoke with utter conviction, as if nothing she was saying was in any way disputable. "Why is she here now?"

"The attorney, the executor, said her presence is necessary to process the papers of my late husband's estate. I granted them three days, after which she will not be permitted on these premises ever again."

"I see." Charlie regarded her. Her face was smooth and calm, her expression benign, as if they were discussing the weather. "Mrs. Andreson, did you believe your late husband was trying to kill your daughter Trish?"

"Don't be ridiculous. Of course not. Trish had a ghastly accident."

"Or that he was responsible for the death of your son Gary, and your other daughter, Suzette?"

"That's absolute nonsense!"

"Would he have gained financially by their deaths?"

She shook her head. "My late husband did not believe in spoiling children by giving them more money than was good for them. He worked for his wealth and knew the value of doing so, and he expected them to take care of themselves. Many years ago, we both made our wills. In mine, I bequeathed my estate to my children, and in the event that I outlived them, I listed the various charities that would then benefit. I bequeathed only a token to Sam. His will did the same thing. We had a legal understanding about financial responsibility drawn up before we married so there would never be any misunderstanding years later."

Michael had been gazing impassively at a print on the wall, as if memorizing it, but he started at her words. "You never said anything like that to us."

"Of course we told you. You've simply forgotten. But you see the implications, I'm certain," she went on, addressing Charlie again. "There was no earthly reason for Sam to want to murder my children, and they certainly had no reason to fear him." She turned her calm gaze to Michael. "What kind of a monster would that make me, a mother who believes her husband is trying to murder her children and does nothing about it?"

She said that of course Gary had not been drunk; he never drank, and when a nondrinker has a little wine, a little punch, it is potent. Suzette reacted to sleeping pills and died. Trish forgot to close the fire screen and was afraid to admit it. Her expression remained placid. About the fight on the evening Sam died, she said, "That woman insisted on dragging him away when he obviously wanted to stay with me. He lost his temper and slammed out of the house. Michael tried to stop him and he nearly knocked him down, his own son, while that woman was forcing me upstairs. She seduced him, you know. Here in this house, in front of witnesses, she said they spent the night together, that they often spent the night together. But she was still only a secretary, someone to be used, and she wanted more. She wanted my place, to be chatelaine."

Abruptly, Constance rose, and Charlie got to his feet also. There was no point in hanging out here, he understood. They thanked Marie Andreson and left. Her calm expression never changed.

Downstairs again, on the way to the door, Michael said, "I can't make out my own mother. On Monday, she was so hysterical, we—I—called her doctor and he came and gave her some tranquilizers. Yesterday the house was full of flowers and she ordered Juana to get rid of them, everything. And now ... I've never seen her like this. I don't know what I should do, call the doctor back, wait it out?"

"She seemed calm enough," Charlie said after a pause that Constance made no effort to fill.

"Yeah, calm. Why does it make me feel like I'm in the eye of a hurricane?" He laughed unconvincingly and stopped at the massive door. "Can they really tell when a fire started?"

"Pretty much. They know how long it takes to burn through upholstery; they'll find out what kind that particular car had. They know how long it takes to blister paint, or to burn through it, and so on."

"But they could be wrong," Michael said. He sounded more hopeful than convinced, and very confused.

"Don't count on it," Charlie said. "Was that true about the prenuptial agreement, the wills?"

"I don't know what's true anymore," Michael muttered. "I found out about Dad's will from the lawyer yesterday, first I knew anything about it. Mother and I get the house, with a trust for upkeep, there's a pretty good bequest for Ellen, and I get the rest. No idea yet what that will amount to. They never said a thing about it to us—at least not to me. And I'd swear Trish doesn't know."

"Insurance?"

Michael nodded. "Two policies—one for the business, to let them liquidate in an orderly fashion, according to the lawyer; one personal, I'm the beneficiary, a hundred thousand, with a token amount for my mother."

"Whew!" Charlie said. "Well, take it easy, Michael. We'll be seeing you." He and Constance left.

Constance got in the passenger side and he drove back down the long driveway to the road. "Wait until Beverly Kratz hears her," he said. "She'll blow steam out of every orifice. There goes Trish's preemptive self-defense defense." When Constance made no response, he glanced at her and let it drop. She had gone into a place where she had to think about something. How long she might stay there, he never knew, but he knew enough to leave her alone until she came back. He drove slowly, and when he got to the turnoff to where Sam had been killed, he turned onto the narrow, crumbling road.

And he might as well have driven straight past, he decided a few minutes later. He could replay the action here almost minute by minute from the evidence still at hand, but what good that did, he couldn't tell. Sam had driven into the center of the clearing, an old homestead, the house gone for decades, with grasses and low straggly shrubs now reclaiming the land. Someone had shot him in the temple; then someone had arranged the newspapers for a nice little fire. *The New York Times*, picked up on the plane from Chicago, had been sufficient kindling. Then someone had doused things with brandy and lighted it. He scowled.

Why not a second shot if one hadn't been enough? Why brandy *and* papers? How flammable did the someone need it to be? Other bottles had been broken, but they had found the brandy bottle intact, the cap behind the backseat, and obviously brandy had burned. Champagne had spewed, tonic spilled, bourbon and gin bottles broken, but brandy had been splashed around. Why? Why the fire to start with?

Because he had tried to burn Trish?

Where had he been from nine-thirty or thereabouts until eleven, when he ended up here with a hole in his head in a burning car? Charlie gazed at the clearing unhappily.

Old sites like this had ghosts: irises in a line, a row of rosebushes, a path outlined with daylilies, plantings long since reverted to more natural forms and colors, plants that sprawled and violated their own boundaries and that told the story anyone could read. Here was where they'd sat, where they'd walked, where they'd planted their garden, burned their trash. . . . He prowled about the clearing, around the perimeter, examined places where burning debris had landed, the flames extinguished; he stopped and examined places where dirty water had flowed, swirled, puddled, evaporated. . . . The arson squad had been too damn thorough, he decided, heading back to the Volvo. There was nothing left for him here.

Constance was standing by the car, facing in his direction but seeing little, he knew.

"Ready?" he asked.

She nodded and got in the car.

"Is it Marie?" he asked then before he turned on the ignition.

She nodded again. "She intends to protect her children at any cost," she said.

He remembered Marie's words: *What kind of a monster would that make me, a mother who believes her husband is trying to murder her children and does nothing about it?* If she hadn't believed it then, she clearly saw the danger her daughter was in now. He turned on the key, glanced at Constance. "How far do you think she'd go toward implicating Ellen?"

"She was pushed into a corner, and a tiger came out. As far as necessary."

"And she'll do and say all the wrong things and turn this mess into pure hellish chaos," he muttered, and started to drive.

"I have to talk to Belasco and his fire chief," Charlie said after a moment. "If they can't answer a couple of questions, I'll go to the fire lab and poke around."

She nodded. "And I have to talk to Bev Kratz. If she believes the defense she was preparing can't stand, that Sam wanted to inherit a significant amount of money and killed in order to get it, all she has to fall back on is the child-abuse theory. There's simply no other reason for Sam to have killed Suzette and to have tried to kill Trish."

"Meaning?"

"They could have threatened to talk about it. That will be Bev's defense now, don't you think? And that would have ruined Sam Andreson; even the suspicion of sexually abusing his stepdaughters would have been enough. She'll have to use it."

He put his hand on her thigh. "Honey, isn't that exactly what we've both thought from the very beginning?"

"But it's different now," she said, giving him a surprised look. She patted his hand and then kept hers on it.

He sighed. She would explain and he would follow step by step and probably agree with her; he usually did. But he couldn't make the leaps.

"Michael's here," she said as they drew near the Coultier house. The Land Rover was in the driveway. "Why don't you go on and talk to the police and firemen, and I'll visit a little. I'll walk up to the cabin when I'm through. Meet you there."

He pulled into the driveway and watched her approach the house, feeling a bit irritated with her, but more pleased with the way she walked, the long, loose stride she had, the way her hair bounced. She was one gorgeous woman, he thought then, backing out of the driveway, and she was his. And he knew he could never say that out loud to her, never. He was grinning as he drove off toward Oyster Bay. But she was his, all his.

Lorraine opened the door for Constance. She looked frantic. "Do you know what's going on up at Marie's house?" she asked, and then she seemed to realize that Constance was alone. She glanced past her, and she appeared surprised that Charlie was driving away.

"Business to take care of," Constance said, motioning toward the Volvo. "What's going on is that Marie says she told the children there was a prenuptial agreement and wills that made it abundantly clear that Sam would never touch her money."

"Michael came running in saying he had to talk to Trish, and they went down to the beach. He looked desperate. Is that all it was?"

"As far as I know," Constance said.

Lorraine closed the door just as Bev came hurrying from the plant room. "I caught that," she said. "Marie told them about wills and stuff?"

"So she says."

"What else?"

"She thinks Ellen Hosty killed Sam," Constance said. For a moment, no one moved in the hallway; then Lorraine started to walk to the solarium. Constance followed.

Jeff Coultier rose to greet her, and they sat down where they had before, at the far end. Bev walked about the room jerkily, frowning, as Constance repeated what Marie had said.

"Cripes! She's a jealous bitch!" Bev cried when she finished. "She'll put a whammy on it all!" Then she stopped in the middle of the room and very slowly began to walk again. She looked intently at Jeff. "You realize what that means? If Sam didn't try to kill Trish for the money, then it was to keep her quiet. We have to get her to open up and tell us about it."

Jeff closed his eyes, as if they had gone through this too often already. "She's told us what she did that night," he said evenly.

"No one can pin it on Ellen Hosty," Bev said savagely. "They'll see through Marie in a second. Who's left?"

Constance said, "If I were conducting this investigation for the police, I would say there are several people left. There's Jeff, for example. Suppose he overheard Nathan on the phone. He could have met Sam at the end of the driveway, gone off with him. Or Lorraine could have met him, trying to intercede. Or Nathan himself. Or Sam could have called someone else whom we know nothing about."

Lorraine had gone bone white listening to her. "But they'll come here sooner or later, won't they? One of us. No one accepts a husband and wife alibiing one another, do they?"

Constance shook her head.

"Listen," Bev grated. She nearly threw herself into a chair. The rattan groaned at the impact. "The night of the fire, Trish was talking about a guy she'd been living with, talking about going off to California with him maybe. Sam got ugly, riding her about not being able to settle down, afraid she'd end up like her sister. Trish went white and gave him a look; for a minute, something was going on between them, and then she ran out. That's why Marie went all over sick that night and excused herself early. She damn well knows about it. That's why Sam had to act that night, for fear Trish was starting to remember. He was going out of town the next Monday; he had to act fast, or she might have escaped all the way to California, gotten in touch with a shrink, gotten it all back. That girl held his life in her hands and he knew it!"

Jeff was staring at her in wonder. "How do you know any of that? Who told you? Not Trish."

"Not Trish," she said impatiently. "I talk to people, get around. I heard." She shrugged. "Look, ask Trish about her childhood, you'll get great big blanks. There's nothing there. That's one of the signs. Ask why no boyfriend ever worked out. Same thing. They can't form a real relationship. My God, she's nearly twenty-five. Why the hell doesn't she settle down?"

"Have you asked her those things?" Jeff asked in a very quiet voice.

"Yes! What do you think I'm going on about?"

"And she didn't tell you anything?"

"She can't!"

"Bev, has it occurred to you that she probably thinks it's none of your business?" His voice was still very low and controlled, and ice-cold.

"Jeff!" Lorraine exclaimed. "It's Bev's business now."

"I wonder if Trish would agree," he said. "Let's put this off and ask her when she comes back in."

Faintly, Lorraine said, "Maybe it would be a good idea to have her talk to a . . . a professional." She looked out the window as she said this, her face strained; she was twisting her rings around and around.

Jeff's expression was sympathetic; he took her hands in his own. Then he turned to Constance. "What do you think?"

Slowly, she said, "We all know that many people who were desperately hurt as children suffer the consequences and bear the scars for a lifetime. But there are many people who, for whatever reason, are responsible for urging others to recount memories that sometimes turn out to be false. That can cause grave harm not only to the one accused but also to the one called 'the survivor.' Those consequences and scars can also be a life's burden. This is very dangerous ground, which must be approached with extreme caution. I wouldn't recommend such a course for anyone who is not personally compelled, overwhelmingly compelled to take such a step. Indeed, I would urge anyone without such an overwhelming need not to take such a step. The witches of Loudon were very real to those who encountered them, and present-day witches are easily roused."

She was very aware of Bev's blazing anger as she spoke, but she kept her gaze on Jeff, who was watching her without expression. "In this case, I would consider very carefully the implications of such urging. If the only reason is to suggest that Sam had a reason to silence Trish, and therefore she was in danger from him, aren't you in fact accepting that she actually did murder him? Wouldn't she interpret it that way? Wouldn't others? What kind of scar would that leave, abandonment by her family at this time, facing their disbelief in her? Is that what you believe?"

Jeff's face seemed frozen, it had become so still. Finally, he nodded. "She has to make that decision without any interference from anyone. From *anyone*!"

Bev threw up both hands. "Jesus Christ! Now we're on a high moral ground! Look at me, Jeff! Look hard, because I'm going to tell you the dirty truth. Those kids planned this a long time ago. Trish was scared, and with good reason, and they intended to set things right because no one else would. When they come for Trish, this is the only defense she has! I have a woman lined up, a damn good psychologist who has a lot of experience in these things, and the longer we put off starting, the harder it's going to get. Sam had a gun on her, it went off, and she panicked and ran—that's one thing. But there was the goddamn fire! That's not panic; that was planning. If the police decide it was a cold-blooded, premeditated murder, they'll play rough with your kid. If they know she's under a doctor's care, disturbed, seeking help, it's going to be a different story altogether. Those are the choices, my friend. I'm going out for a smoke." She stomped out.

Jeff held his composure until she was gone and then his face crumpled; he aged ten years in a second. He stood up. "Maybe I'll put on some coffee," he said. "She's good for us," he added. "She tells us what the rest of the world thinks. We need that."

Lorraine's gaze was on her hands in her lap, and he regarded her for a moment with an expression that was infinitely sad. Then he looked at Constance and said almost apologetically, "The problem is that I believe my daughter." He walked out.

Lorraine stood up, not facing Constance. "I think the kids are coming," she said. "I'll be back in a minute." She hurried from the room.

Constance watched the young people approach the house, their heads lowered, talking. They were dressed in jeans, sweatshirts, running shoes, and they were wind-blown, as if they had been on an outing that should have involved fun and games, not a discussion of murder.

"Hi," Constance said when they entered the solarium. "I think Jeff is making coffee, and Lorraine said she'd be down in a minute. I'm waiting." Michael looked resigned; Trish, apprehensive; and Nathan simply looked young and defenseless.

"I'll be going," Michael said.

"Can you wait a second?" Constance asked. "There are a few things we need more information about. Charlie's off talking to people, and I'm here to do the same." She smiled at them reassuringly and sat down, waving to nearby chairs. She could almost feel their reluctance as they seated themselves.

"Trish, on the night the guest house burned, did you

mention you were considering going to California? With a friend?"

Trish started and said, "How did you find out that?"

"Someone mentioned it. Will you tell me about it?"

"Sure. I said Barry Swanson wanted me to go to California while he attended law school in San Francisco. That's all."

Constance nodded, frowning slightly. "Did Sam make a fuss about it?"

Now Trish drew in a breath. "Okay. See, Barry and I had been together for about a year, but I had already decided to end it. I was trying to make up my mind about going for a doctorate, and it was tough. I mean, the world isn't exactly clamoring for any more Ph.D.'s in English. Not that I could tell. And I had come to wonder what I'd do with more degrees if I had them. I didn't want to talk about that—you know, you always get so much advice—so I brought up Barry instead." She glanced at Michael. "Remember? Mother wanted to know about him, his family, everything. And Sam made some kind of stupid remark about how girls didn't sleep around when he was in school, and maybe it was time to start behaving more responsibly. I was pretty mad about it. I mean, I'd had one other real boyfriend, and I was twenty-three. That's hardly sleeping around! The first one, Luke Wertheimer, was an English major, and after about six months I got tired of having to tell him how wonderful his poetry was, so we split." A gleam had come into her eyes as she spoke.

"What happened to Barry?" Constance asked.

The gleam shone more brightly, and now Nathan's eyes were gleaming, too—their father's eyes, right down to that rather unholy gleam.

"He came to the hospital to see me," Trish said gravely.

"I was pretty banged up, you know. Bruises, scratches, stitches, casts. Not a pretty sight. He was . . . unnerved. He questioned my doctors, the nurses, everyone, demanding to know if I'd recover, get back to normal. Later on, after I got home, he called and talked to Nathan. I coached Nathan on what to say." She looked at her younger brother and nodded. "Your turn."

"I told him the scars were hardly noticeable anymore, at least for us, because we knew Trish was still behind them." He couldn't control his demeanor the way she had; mirth was very near the surface and a grin kept forming as he talked. "I said I liked pushing her wheelchair, it was fun, and I'd be sorry when she got the brace and the special tripod cane. And we didn't care if she had to use it forever; she was still our own dear Trish." He laughed.

Trish was smiling. "It was cruel, I suppose. A couple of weeks later, I got a bouquet from him and a little note that said in view of the workload he had taken on, he thought it would be wise to postpone any plans for the time being. I wrote back and thanked him for understanding."

Constance laughed. "It was cruel all right. Poor Barry." Then she sobered again. "Trish, Michael, think back to that dinner party. Was any mention made of Suzette?"

Michael shook his head. "Not that I remember."

Trish said no. "If there had been, I would remember," she said. "Why?"

"Just a puzzling detail. Was your mother ill? Did she become ill at the party?"

Unhappily, Trish said, "You have to realize ours was not Ozzie and Harriet country. Mother and Sam tended to snipe at each other during meals, about the only time they spent together, I guess. If the sniping got bad, she got headaches."

"Do you remember what they said that night?"

Trish looked away, troubled. "I usually tuned them out. I'm not sure."

"I remember," Michael said. "After the talk about Barry, Rita changed the subject, something about always wanting to see the house. She said it was like a castle and Mother must have felt like a queen living there. And Mother said something about Anne Boleyn, but that at least her head was safe, since she had produced a son, but even a castle could serve as a prison." He spread his hands in a helpless gesture. "It was like that. Just sniping. Poor Rita didn't get much of it, I guess."

"Who is Rita?" Constance asked then.

"We went to high school together," Trish said. "We did things together, were camp counselors together one year. We weren't close friends; it just happened that we were together at events."

"And I didn't know that," Michael said with a contrite look toward Trish. "Rita cornered me in town a week or so before that night and said she'd heard Trish was coming home and that she couldn't wait to see her, and it suddenly struck me as a good idea to have an outsider, a guest, a longtime friend. Sometimes if we had guests, Mother and Dad were on good behavior. I invited her. A mistake. She gushed."

"Everyone leapt to the conclusion that she was chasing Michael," Trish said, the gleam in her eye again. "Both Sam and Mother were furious about that." Suddenly, she straightened and said, "I remember what set Mother off. Remember, Michael? After the Anne Boleyn bit, Rita said something dumb about people who didn't appreciate what they had probably didn't deserve it. Then Sam said gold diggers always deserved exactly what they got, and Mother said fathers deserved their sons and he said mothers deserved losing their daughters. That's when Mother left."

Abruptly, she became very still, hardly breathing. Then she said slowly, "I thought he was talking about Mother and her mother, or about me, considering going to California. Not Suzette. I don't think he meant Suzette," she said in a lower voice.

Definitely not Ozzie and Harriet country, Constance thought. At that moment, the door to the hallway opened and Jeff appeared, pushing the food cart.

"Sandwiches," he said. "Tuna, ham, or egg salad. Them's the choices, mates. Coffee, tea, or milk. Could rustle up some wine, if anyone insists," he added with a glance at Constance.

She shook her head and suddenly realized she was ravenous.

Michael jumped up. "Oh God! Lunchtime! I've got to go!" He rushed from the room. "I'll call, Trish."

Constance walked back to the cabin slowly. When she climbed the stairs from the road, someone yelled, "Dr. Leidl, were the children molested by Sam Andreson? Was Trish? Was Michael?" She kept moving toward the cabin; a photographer ducked in front of her, then ran to one side and then the other, snapping pictures, and the reporter, a bald, fat man, yelled questions.

Charlie opened the door for her and slammed it again. "I think they're on to us," he said gravely.

"I think it's time to go home," she said.

"My thought precisely. In fact, I already packed most of the gear."

Half an hour later, they were heading for the Long Island Expressway, Charlie driving.

* * *

They didn't talk much. Charlie passed a Day-Glo-painted bus and waved at the driver, who flipped him off. "Rita Glenwood gushes," he commented. The bus passed him. "Talk around town has it that Sam tried to kill Trish and that whatever she did was justified. Population about eight thousand, six thousand ready to be character witnesses."

Traffic picked up and he paid attention to driving. She filled him in on what she had heard and seen, and they became silent again until they were out of the city, heading north along the Hudson.

"Can she get off with the abuse defense?" he asked.

"I doubt it. At least not today. Hand her over to the right therapist, give them enough time, maybe."

He nodded moodily. "Every damn thing gets contradicted sooner or later, you notice that? Either she saw the glow in the bathroom or not; who knows? Not in her original report. Either they knew about the money matters or not. Mom says yes; kids say no. Rita said of course she wasn't chasing Michael; he was chasing her until she told him to get lost. God alone knows what all she told Bev; whatever Bev wanted to hear, I suspect. The night the guest house burned was the most boring evening Rita could remember; she couldn't keep her eyes open, it was so boring. She says they got there after ten-thirty and she wanted to go home before twelve. Trish and Michael said it was a couple of hours. Either Marie is hysterical, incapable of taking care of herself, in need of a nurse, or else she's a determined, cool woman who will lie until hell freezes. And Jeff? He didn't believe Sam was trying anything, but he decided to give up his year in England and stay home with Trish." He had been driving faster and faster as he spoke. He looked in surprise at her when she dug her fingers into his leg, and then he slowed down. She kept her hand on his leg.

They stopped for an early dinner; afterward she drove. Sam and Ellen, Charlie said, had driven from Kennedy; he had sat in the backseat and read the financial section, made some phone calls, and worked on the laptop computer. At the house, they had taken in a carry-on bag each, the computer, their coats, and had left the newspapers on the backseat. She had intended to go back out later and get them.

"Why splash paper with brandy?" he muttered. No one had been able to answer that one.

At home, they were greeted by the cats: Brutus glowered from atop the refrigerator, Ashcan whimpered and apologized, and Candy complained about the Mitchum boys, about the food, the water, the weather, about their lack of interest in her complaints.

On Sunday morning, Constance drank coffee on the patio and watched Charlie play with fire. He had put a stack of newspapers on the grill, crumpled one or two sheets and added them, and regarded it all with a match in his hand. He looked dissatisfied. He looked at his watch. "Ten-thirty," he said, and struck the match, lighted the crumpled paper, and sat down at the table by her. She had jotted down the time.

The top papers burned fiercely; the papers still in a stack began to char around the edges, to curl, and then one by one began to burn also. By eleven, the entire pile had burned to a stinking mass of crisp black ashes.

"So why the brandy?" he growled, poking the ashes with a long-handled fork.

"To make it all burn faster?"

"But why?"

She shrugged, then watched him clear the grill of the ashes and put a new stack of papers on it. This time, he doused an eight-ounce cup of grain alcohol on the paper and watched it burn even more fiercely and finish faster. He looked more dissatisfied. When he looked at Constance, she was holding the alcohol bottle, frowning at it.

"Wasn't purple-label rum listed on that inventory of Sam's bar in the Cadillac?"

"Yes. Why?"

"Isn't that one hundred and eighty proof?"

He sat down at the table. "Go on."

"If Sam always bought that purple-label rum, and if he had it on hand at Gary's party, that would have been a powerful drink, if someone spiked Gary's punch with it."

He nodded. "We can find out if Sam kept it on hand." He nodded toward the grill; the bottom part had filled with ashes. "I'll clean that out and try one more thing. See, the problem is that the newspapers didn't all burn up. Why not? If the fire started around eleven, the explosion twenty-five minutes later, and the fireman doused everything ten minutes after that, it seems to me the papers should have burned completely."

The ashes flew apart and onto the patio when he tried to collect them. "Sprinkle them with water," Constance suggested. "It will be messier, but at least you'll be able to scoop them up."

Charlie turned to look at her with a strange, distant expression. "That's it," he said after a moment. "My God, that's it!"

She watched wordlessly as he swung around and hurried to the door, went inside the house, and then reappeared with her watering can. She remained silent, watching, when he began to water papers in a stack on the table. He opened the stack in several places, poured water down between the pages, and then put the stack on the grill. He poured the rest of the water over it.

Then he crumpled up two sheets of dry paper, laid them on top of the rest, and lighted them. "Twelve-ten," he said. He closed the lid of the grill partway again and sat down opposite her, watching.

Several times, it appeared that the fire was going out altogether, it burned so feebly, with so much acrid black smoke; each time it revived without help, and finally at five minutes before one, it began to blaze in a meaningful way, as if it were done with playing around. By 1:15, the fire had burned itself out. There were many sections of newspapers stuck together, not wholly consumed.

Charlie nodded at the grill. "Right," he said.

"Why?" she asked after a moment. "An alibi?"

"Maybe."

Neither spoke for several minutes. A gust of wind lifted black ash from the grill and swirled it about, lofted it, and then let it fall in crumbling, ever-diminishing flakes.

"Why a damn fire?" Charlie muttered finally. "If he wasn't dead yet, why not another shot? The gun wasn't empty. A lovely piece of misdirection: brandy to make us think a fast fire was wanted, when actually brandy was probably the last thing to ignite and burn. It was on the upholstery, not on the papers. A slow fire. Alibi, maybe. If there hadn't been a fire, the car and body would have stayed hidden away all night, the following day, who knows how long."

He became silent again, pondering: What are fires good for? In arson, they served to get rid of the evidence of wrongdoing; the reason the number of unsolved cases was in the high thousands was because the evidence of the arson itself often went up in flames. Insurance, murder, revenge, malice. Way down on the list was a bevy of mental conditions that demanded spectacular events to keep the inner voice stilled, the inner person happy. They didn't apply here, he knew without doubt.

Alibi, insurance, revenge . . . He shook his head. To hide something. Another bit of misdirection?

Unhappily, he said, "I'll have to go snoop around the fire lab. What all was in that damn car?"

She nodded. "Who would know if the car phone was a cellular? If it was, all the calls made on that Sunday would be on record, wouldn't they? I wonder if anyone has found out yet."

"I'll give Pete a call," he said. He went inside, and when he returned, he was frowning. "A call at nine-twenty-eight to the Coultier number."

"Was it completed?" she asked.

"Yep. They don't keep a record otherwise." He sat down and tapped his fingers on the tabletop. "It must have been to Jeff," he said after a minute. "Goddamn it. No wonder Lorraine was concerned, asking if husbands and wives were credible alibis for one another." He slouched down in his chair, scowling darkly. "So Michael calls and gets Nathan and a minute later Sam calls and gets Jeff, or someone. And no one bothered to mention it." His anger was directed at Pete Belasco as much as at Jeff and Lorraine. He visualized the evening: Nathan and Trish upstairs doing whatever kids their age do; Lorraine watching television; Jeff in and out of his study. Probably heard the first call without paying much attention, but a second one following almost instantly, he might have noticed, picked it up without waiting for the machine.

A fire to get rid of fingerprints that didn't belong in the Caddy? Maybe, he thought. Maybe.

That evening, they went out for dinner and then a movie, which held their interest for over an hour, or at least kept them in their seats that long. When Constance stood up, he got up, too, and they left the theater, neither of them aware that the climactic scenes were yet to come.

"We've been trying to link everything," she said on the way to the car. "We should forget about the attempt on Trish's life and concentrate instead on Sam's murder. I think trying to link everything has complicated it so much, my head is spinning."

He grinned when they reached the Volvo and she opened the driver's side door and got behind the wheel. He got in the passenger seat without comment.

"Because," she continued as she turned on the key and gunned the engine, "if we keep the murder as a separate thing in and of itself, it's so clear. Isn't it?"

He laughed and leaned his head back against the head-rest. "I love you," he said, and laughed harder when she turned to give him a curious look.

"The problem will be proving anything," she said with a nod. She started to drive.

At home again, he realized she thought he knew what was on her mind, the conclusions she had reached. As soon as she began to talk about it, he realized he had known at the level he hadn't examined yet. But he had known. And she was right. The problem was going to be to prove any-thing. He watched her as she talked, how the lines of her face changed, how a slight frown came and vanished, the distant look in her eyes, and when she paused, he reached across the table and took her hand. She gave him another of her looks, and he kissed the hand and released it. Her face relaxed. And this time, he received a look that he knew was his alone.

And then they planned out the next day or two or three, the questions they needed answers to, the people who might have answers, who would use the car first. . . .

On Tuesday, Bev Kratz called Charlie. She sounded disheartened. "I don't know what you're messing with," she said, "but things are getting out of hand here. Trish is falling apart; her story's coming unglued faster than the tide moves in. They'll worry her about the shooting in her car and then spring the shooting in Sam's car, and she'll be in little pieces all over the floor. Jeff, Lorraine, Trish . . . they're waiting for you to do something, save the day, some goddamn thing! For God's sake, Meiklejohn, tell her to trust me!"

Charlie groaned. Too soon, he thought; there were things to be done, things to be looked into, but he didn't want to wait for the staties to make their move first. "We'll be there tomorrow," he said. "Early afternoon."

Bev wanted more, something concrete, but she had to settle for what little Charlie could give her, and after a few seconds, they hung up.

"Tomorrow," Constance said, looking unhappy.

He nodded.

Wednesday at 12:30, Charlie, Constance, and Chief Pete Belasco stood outside the door of the Andreson mansion. The housekeeper, Juana, opened the door and looked startled to see them.

"No appointment," Charlie said, "but maybe Mrs. Andreson and Michael can see us, anyway."

She hesitated, then admitted them. "I'll tell Mrs. Andreson," she said, and hurried away, up the stairs.

In a second or two, Michael came running down; he was in shorts and sandals, a tank top, and looked very muscular and tan.

"What's up?" he asked. "Has something happened?"

"Just a few things to clear up," Charlie said. "We need your mother's help."

"You want to go up?"

"Nope. We'd like for her to come down. I took the liberty of asking Jeff and his crew to come over at one. Hope no one minds. Seemed a good idea to have the whole family in on this at the same time, avoid misunderstandings later."

Michael glanced up the stairs, a worried frown on his forehead. "I don't know," he said. "She might not want to."

"Son," Chief Pete Belasco said firmly, "tell her I sort of think it's necessary. Okay?"

Michael nodded and trudged slowly up the stairs, as if he dreaded arriving.

Charlie grinned at Pete Belasco, who had not wanted to come here and had protested that the whole case was out of his hands, off limits. His face was set in so many lines that cut so deeply, he looked inhuman. He did not return Charlie's grin.

Michael came back down. "She said we should go to the den and she'll come down in a minute or two." He motioned toward the hall and the rear of the house. "She said I should tell Juana to bring us coffee, tea, something, if you want it."

Charlie shook his head.

"I didn't think so," Michael said. He led the way to the den, where Charlie began to arrange chairs in a semicircle.

"I'll tell Juana to bring the others back here," Michael said, and left.

When the others arrived, the family without exception looked frightened; Bev Kratz, who accompanied them, looked furious. "Goddamn it, Meiklejohn, when are you going to quit stalling? Have you got anything new on Suzette's death yet? On the fire out back here? What the hell have you been up to?"

Charlie regarded her for a second and then said very kindly, "Bev, just shut up. And stay shut up."

Marie Andreson came into the den and surveyed them all. She was in a silk dress the color of burgundy, her hair sleekly back off her face, wearing only a touch of makeup. She looked regal.

"Let's start," Charlie said without preamble. "Trish, do you realize that the state police are probably planning to arrest you within the next day or two?"

She was as pale as skim milk, with wide, staring eyes. She shook her head.

"If they question you seriously, they'll arrest you; and if they arrest you, you'll plea-bargain or stand trial. If you go to trial, no doubt you'll be found guilty."

"Just hold it a bloody second, mister!" Bev cried.

Without looking at her, Charlie said, "I told you to shut up. They know as well as you do, Trish, that no one tried to shoot you in your car. That's the first story that will fold. What did you do, park it somewhere, let Michael shoot a hole in it, and then drive on home? Was Nathan involved in that, too?"

Trish ducked her head as color flared on her white cheeks.

"Don't you say a word!" Bev yelled at her. "You want to get out of here, let's walk."

"They'll say you tried to manufacture an excuse to justify killing Sam Andreson, but in fact, Trish, they won't care too much about motive. Just what you did, what you said you did, and what they think you did. And they think you killed him."

Marie made a moaning sound deep in her throat. Charlie glanced at her without comment. He turned back to Trish. "He had no reason to kill you; they'll press that hard. If you go for a child-abuse defense, they'll make mincemeat of you."

Tears welled in her eyes and she shook her head. "I didn't do it," she whispered.

"I know that." He looked at Marie Andreson with a terrible pity then. "No one will make you choose," he said, "but you can see that they can't both be saved."

"What are you talking about? It was that woman! That Hosty woman!"

He shook his head and gazed at Michael, who had not moved for several minutes; it was as if he had become a wax model of himself.

"I kept asking myself, Why the damn fire?" Charlie said. "I came up with reasons: to make certain Sam actually died without having to touch him or shoot again. That gun must have sounded like a cannon in the closed car. Or to hide something: for instance, the cellular phone, but called numbers are automatically recorded, so that didn't seem likely. To provide an alibi: the most likely reason so far, and it did. But that seemed to suggest a greater familiarity with fire than anyone in this case had. Even wetting down the papers didn't determine exactly when the car would burn; it was a gamble if there would be enough time to get home before the fire was spotted. So much misdirection, and most of it awfully good, by the way. But if none of the above was the real reason for the fire, what was left? I kept coming back to the phone and the one call. The phone was in the backseat, out of reach for Sam at the wheel, but it could be argued that he used it and tossed it back there, or the killer tossed it back there. Then I called the fire lab and asked if there were any prints on the phone, and what do you know? No prints, it had been wiped. That and the gun gave it away."

Jeff looked completely bewildered. He clutched Trish's hand and stared at Charlie. "Just say it, whatever you're getting at!" he cried.

"You see, the gun presented another problem," Charlie said, not turning his gaze from Michael. The tendon was showing in his neck again and on the backs of both hands, which were holding tightly to the arms of his chair. "Sam wouldn't have left it in the car in a parking garage, and he wouldn't have tried to board a plane carrying it, and since he used a carry-on bag for his trips, the gun must have been here in the house. Someone from this house must have taken it to the car and used it to shoot him. It couldn't have been missing very long or he would have known."

"But Sam could have picked it up in his office," Jeff said.

Charlie shook his head. "Sam had no reason to carry a gun to your house," he said quietly. "I imagine he was on his way to warn you that Trish was in danger. I suspect he knew that the fire in the guest house really was arson and attempted murder, and he knew who had done it, and finally he was going to tell the truth about it, in an attempt to save Trish."

Marie buried her face in her hands; her body shook, but not a sound issued from her. There was total silence in the room. Suddenly, Trish wailed, "No! No! No!"

"He invited Rita Glenwood," Charlie said, "and she gave a statement about how innocent the evening was, hot chocolate, cookies, a nice little fire. Rita said she couldn't keep her eyes open; she fell asleep as soon as she got home and slept until after ten the next morning. You were supposed to sleep like that, Trish, but you didn't. You woke up."

"I didn't drink much chocolate," she whispered. "It was too sweet; I poured mine into Rita's cup when she wasn't looking."

Suddenly, Nathan launched himself across the room at Michael. They turned over the chair Michael was in and rolled on the floor, with Nathan trying to get his hands around Michael's throat, crying incoherently.

Pete Belasco separated them. He dragged Michael away.

Nathan was on the floor, crying, choking on words. "He kept going on about his father, how he was trying to kill Trish. We had to do something because he would kill her before her birthday. We faked the car shooting, just so people would pay attention. And we came to see you, to make someone pay attention." He looked at Charlie and then Constance; tears ran down his cheeks; he was oblivious. "I thought Sam would kill her. I wanted her to go away, anywhere. I would have gone, too, if she'd let me."

Pete Belasco had pushed Michael onto a straight chair and now stood with his hand on Michael's shoulder. Michael was pale, unmoving, his hands clenched on his legs. "You little creep," he said. "He's lying," he said to Pete Belasco calmly. "I don't know what anyone here is talking about."

"You had the fight," Charlie said, "and Sam said he would put a stop to it all. You ran to your room to get the gun and then ran down to the car, where you got into the backseat and made a call to Trish or Nathan, whoever answered. The call was recorded. Sam came out and started to drive, and you popped up with the gun and told him to turn off into that cul-de-sac. As soon as he stopped the car in the clearing and started to turn toward you, you shot him in the temple. Then you could have pressed his fingers onto the telephone, but you didn't. I imagine you couldn't bring yourself to touch him at that point. So the fire. So you could be somewhere with someone when the fire was spotted, and to get rid of the phone. But when you left the car and walked back to the road, you carried some peculiar dirt on your shoes—old homestead, flower gardens, a lot of fertilizer that's long since been incorporated into the soil, but also some ashes from an old fireplace or stove, ashes scattered around here and there, ashes that are still identifiable, maybe from coke, or coal. The lab will identify them."

Michael started up from the chair; Pete Belasco held him down firmly. "I've been down there a couple of times this past week," Michael said. "I wanted to see for myself where it happened."

Charlie shook his head. "Funny thing about ashes, Michael. Archaeologists can read a whole history in them, as I'm sure you know. See, the old ashes won't have any chemicals in them, chlorine, stuff that's in the city water. A good lab, good technicians, they can pretty much pinpoint where and when ashes were picked up on clothes, on shoes. Hard evidence, what they call 'physical evidence,' or sometimes 'circumstantial.' Like the prints they lifted from Suzette's apartment. They have them on file, you see; they will compare them with yours. No one did then, since you were only a kid. Now they will."

"I used to go see her," Michael said.

"Some of the prints will be hard to explain," Charlie said

coolly. "On things used that night. You were so young, no-where near as smart as you are now."

For a moment, no one moved or spoke. Then Michael whispered, "You don't know what it was like! He used to come into my room at night and do ... He made me do things, and he said if I told, he'd kill me, kill my mother. I was afraid. All my life, I was afraid of him, the things he did to me...." He buried his face in his hands and his body shook.

No one moved. Then very slowly, Marie rose to her feet and crossed the room to Trish, held out her hands to her daughter. Wordlessly, Trish stood up and they embraced.

Chief Belasco had produced a search warrant, and two men who had been outside entered the house and made the search. They all left, taking Michael with them.

Later, at Jeff's house, Constance and Charlie talked briefly to Jeff and Lorraine. Bev sat huddled in a deep chair. Trish was with her mother, and Nathan was out on the bay with his sailboard. No one had objected; he needed to be alone, to expend his emotions through physical exertion.

"I suspect he had no intention of really harming Gary," Constance said. "A rather childish prank, spiking his punch, hoping to make Gary look bad, foolish, at least drunk. But he died. And I imagine that Suzette knew what Michael had done. She was meeting with Sam; Michael probably was terrified she would tell. None of the past can be proven, of course, not unless he talks about it."

Jeff had gone very pale. "You know how they found Suzette? The details?"

Constance nodded. "Yes. We know. He was sixteen by then. If he doped the wine with his mother's sleeping pills, she would have been unconscious throughout the night. There was no sex," she added gently. "He made it appear there was, that's all."

"He cared for Trish," Lorraine said after a moment. "I'm sure he did."

Constance nodded. "I think you're right; he did. And she loved him, but she also loved Nathan and planned to share her wealth with him. And that would have left Michael on the outside. No money of his own, years to wait, Trish and Nathan rich, possibly traveling. All his life, he must have felt he was being left outside while the Coultier children were having fun with their father, one another. Finally, he saw a way to get rid of his own father, whom he hated, blame the death on Trish, and become extremely rich all at the same time."

"He'll try to use the child-abuse defense," Lorraine said after a few moments. "It's so patently fake!"

"More so than it would have been for Trish?"

"I don't know," Lorraine said. "God, I just don't know."

In her chair across the room, Bev did not look up or speak.

When they left, Charlie drove with his hand on Constance's thigh until he needed both hands at the wheel, and then she rested her hand on his leg.

"No one ever said there wasn't any sex that night at Suzette's apartment," he commented after a time.

"I know," she said.

Charlie put his hand on hers. No matter what came out now, Jeff would choose to believe that. Charlie thought of his own daughter; Jeff would choose to believe that Michael had not raped his unconscious daughter. Constance raised his hand to her lips and kissed it. *So sometimes you lie a little,* he thought, and she nodded. *Sometimes you do.*

THE GORGON FIELD

CONSTANCE TOOK THE call that morning; when she hung up, there was a puzzled expression on her face. "Why us?" she asked rhetorically.

"Why not us?" Charlie asked back.

She grinned at him and sat down at the breakfast table where he was finishing his French toast.

"That," she said, pouring more coffee, "was Deborah Rice, née Wyandot, heiress to one of the world's great fortunes. She wants to come talk to us this afternoon, and she lied to me."

His interest rose slightly, enough to make him look up from the newspaper. "About what?"

"She claims we know people in common and that we probably met in school. I knew she was there—it would be like trying to hide Prince Charles, I should think—but I never met her, and she knows it."

"So why did you tell her to come on out?"

"I'm not sure. She wanted us to come to her place in Bridgeport and when I said no, she practically pleaded for an appointment here. I guess that did it. I don't think she pleads for many things, or ever has."

It was April; the sun was warm already, the roses were budding, the daffodils had come and gone, and the apple trees were in bloom. Too pretty to leave right now, Constance thought almost absently, and pushed a cat away from under the table with her foot. It was the evil cat, Brutus, who didn't give a damn about the beauty of the country in April. He wanted toast, or bacon, anything that might land on the floor. The other two cats were out hunting, or sunning themselves, or doing something else catlike. He was scrounging for food. And Charlie, not yet showered and shaved, his black hair like a bush, a luxuriant overnight growth of bristly beard like a half mask on his swarthy face, making him look more like a hood than a country gentleman, cared just about as much for the beautiful fresh morning as did the cat. Constance admitted this to herself reluctantly.

He had been glad to leave the city after years on the police force, following as many years as a fire marshal, but she felt certain that he did not see what she saw when she looked out the window at their miniature farm. On the other hand, she continued the thought firmly, he slept well, and he looked and felt wonderful. But he did miss the city. She had been thinking for weeks that they should do something different, get away for a short time, almost anything. There had been several cases they could have taken, but nothing that seemed worth the effort of shattering the state of inertia they had drifted into. Maybe Deborah Rice would offer something different, she thought then, and that was really why she had told her to come on out.

"My father," Deborah Rice said that afternoon, "is your typical ignorant multimillionaire."

"Mother," Lori Rice cried, "stop it! It isn't fair!"

Constance glanced at Charlie, then back to their guests, mother and daughter. Deborah Rice was about fifty, wearing a fawn-colored cashmere suit with a silk blouse exactly the same shade. Lori was in jeans and sneakers; she was thirteen. Both had dusky skin tones, although their eyes were bright blue. The automobile they had arrived in, parked out in the driveway, was a baby blue Continental, so new that probably it never had been washed.

"All right," Deborah said to her daughter. "It isn't fair; nevertheless, it's true. He never went past the sixth grade, if that far. He doesn't know anything except business, his business." She turned to Constance. "He's ignorant, but he isn't crazy."

"Mrs. Rice," Charlie said then in his drawly voice that made him sound half-asleep, or bored, "exactly what is it you wanted to see us about?"

She nodded. "Do you know who my father is, Mr. Meiklejohn?"

"Carl Wyandot. I looked him up while we were waiting for you to arrive."

"He is worth many millions of dollars," she said, "and he has kept control of his companies, all of them, except what he got tired of. And now my brother is threatening to cause a scandal and accuse my father of senility."

Charlie was shaking his head slowly; he looked very unhappy now. "I'm afraid you need attorneys, not us."

He glanced at Constance. Her mouth had tightened slightly, probably not enough to be noticeable to anyone else, but he saw it. She would not be interested either, he knew. No court appearance as a tame witness, a prostitute, paid to offer testimony proving or disproving sanity, not for her. Besides, she was not qualified; she was a psychologist, retired, not a psychiatrist. For an instant, he had an eerie feeling that the second thought had been hers. He looked at her sharply; she was studying Deborah Rice with bright interest. A suggestion of a smile had eased the tightness of her mouth.

And Deborah seemed to settle deeper in her chair. "Hear me out," she said. Underlying the imperious tone was another tone that might have been fear. "Just let me tell you about it. Please."

Constance looked at Lori, who was teasing Brutus, tickling his ears, restoring his equanimity with gentle strokes, then tickling again. Lori was a beautiful child, and if having access to all the money in the world had spoiled her, it did not show. She was just beginning to curve with adolescence, although her eyes were very aware. She knew the danger in teasing a full-grown, strange cat.

"We'll listen, of course," Constance said to Deborah Rice, accepting for now the presence of the girl.

"Thank you. My father is eighty," she said, her voice becoming brisk and businesslike. "And he is in reasonably good health. Years ago, he bought a little valley west of Pueblo, Colorado, in the mountains. Over the last few years, he's stayed there more and more, and now he's there almost all the time. He has his secretary, and computers, modems, every convenience, and really there's no reason why he can't conduct business from the house. The home office is in Denver and there are offices in New York, California, England. But he's in control. You have to understand that. There are vice presidents and managers and God knows what to carry out his orders, and it's been like that for twenty-five years. Nothing has changed in that respect. My brother can't make a case that he's neglecting the business."

Charlie watched Brutus struggle with indecision and finally decide that he was being mistreated. He did not so much jump from Lori's lap as flow off to the floor; he stretched, hoisted his tail, and stalked out without a backward glance. Lori began to pick at a small scab on her elbow. The fragrance of apple blossoms drifted through the room. Charlie swallowed a yawn.

"I live in Bridgeport," Deborah was saying. "My husband is the conductor of the symphony orchestra, and we're busy with our own lives. Admittedly, I haven't spent a great deal of time with Father in the last years, but neither has Tony, my brother. Anyway, last month Tony called me to say Father was having psychological problems. I flew out to Colorado immediately. Lori went with me." She turned her gaze toward her daughter. She took a deep breath, then continued. "Father was surrounded by his associates, as usual. People are always in and out. They use the company helicopter to go back and forth. At first, I couldn't see anything at all different, but then ... There's a new man out there. He calls himself Ramón, claims he's a Mexican friend of a friend, or something, and he has a terrible influence over my father. This is what bothered Tony so much."

Constance and Charlie exchanged messages in a glance. Hers was, They'll go away pretty soon; be patient. His was, Let's give them the bum's rush. Deborah Rice was frowning slightly at nothing in particular. And now, Constance realized, Lori was putting on an act, pretending interest in a magazine she had picked up. She was unnaturally still, as if she was holding her breath.

Finally, Deborah went on. "Tony believes Ramón was responsible for the firing of two of his, Tony's, subordinates at the house. It's like a little monarchy," she said with some bitterness. "Everyone has spies, intrigues. The two people Father fired alerted Tony about Ramón. Tony's office is in New York, you see."

"That hardly seems like enough to cause your brother to assume your father's losing it," Charlie said bluntly.

"No, of course not. There are other things. Tony's convinced that Father is completely dominated by Ramón. He's trying to gather evidence. You see, Ramón is . . . strange."

"He's a shaman," Lori said, her face flushed. She ducked her head and mumbled, "He can do magic, and Grandpa knows it." She leafed through the magazine, turning pages rapidly.

"And do you know it, too?" Charlie asked.

"Sure. I saw him do magic."

Deborah sighed. "That's why I brought her," she said. "Go on and tell them."

It came out in a torrent; obviously this was what she had been waiting for. "I was at the end of the valley, where the stone formations are, and Ramón came on a horse and got off it and began to sing. Chant, not really sing. And then he was on top of one of the pillars and singing to the setting sun. Only you can't get up there. I mean, they just go straight up, hundreds of feet up. But he was up there until the sun went down, and I ran home and didn't even stop."

She turned another page of the magazine. Very gently, Charlie asked, "Did Ramón see you when he rode up on his horse?"

She continued to look at the pages. "I guess he saw me run. From up there, you could see the whole valley." Her face looked pinched when she raised her head and said to Charlie, "You think I'm lying? Or that I'm crazy? Like Uncle Tony thinks Grandpa is crazy?"

"No, I don't think you're crazy," he said soberly. "Of course, I'm not the expert in those matters. Are you crazy?"

"No! I saw it! I wasn't sleeping or dreaming or smoking dope or having an adolescent fantasy!" She shot a scornful look at her mother, then ducked her head again and became absorbed in the glossy advertising.

Deborah looked strained and older than her age. "Will you please go out and bring in the briefcase?" she asked quietly. "I brought pictures of the formations she's talking about," she added to Constance and Charlie.

Lori left them after a knowing look, as if very well aware that they wanted to talk about her.

"Is it possible that she was molested?" Constance asked as soon as she was out of the house.

"I thought of that. She ran in that day in a state of hysteria. I took her to her doctor, of course, but nothing like that happened."

"Mrs. Rice," Charlie said then, "that was a month ago. Why are you here now, today?"

She bit her lip and took a deep breath. "Lori is an accomplished musician—violin and flute, piano. She can play almost any instrument she handles. It's a real gift. Recently, last week, I kept hearing this weird—that's the only word I can think of—music. Over and over, first on one instrument, then another. I finally demanded that she tell me what she was up to, and she admitted she was trying to recreate the chant Ramón had sung. She's obsessed with it, with him, perhaps. It frightened me. If one encounter with him could affect her that much, what is he doing to my father? Maybe Tony's right. I don't know what I think anymore."

"Have you thought of counseling for her?" Constance asked.

"Yes. She didn't cooperate, became defensive, accused me of thinking she's crazy. It's so ridiculous and at the same time terrifying. We had a good relationship until this happened. She always was close to her father and me until this. Now . . . You saw the look she gave me."

And how much of that was due to adolescent string cutting, how much due to Ramón? Constance let it go when Lori returned with the briefcase.

"One last question," Charlie said a little later, after examining the photographs of the valley. Lori had gone outside to look for the cats; she had asked permission without prompting, apparently bored with the conversation now. "Why us? Your brother has hired detectives, presumably, to check on Ramón." She nodded. "And you could buy a hospital and staff it with psychiatrists, if you wanted that. What do you want us to do?"

She looked embarrassed suddenly. She twisted her watchband and did not look directly at them now. "Tony had a woman sent out, a detective," she said hesitantly. "Within a week, she left the valley and refused to go back. I think she was badly frightened." She glanced at Charlie, then away. "I may be asking you to do something dangerous. I just don't know. But I don't think the detectives looking for Ramón's past will come up with anything. They haven't yet. Whatever secret he has, whatever he can or can't do, is out there in the valley. Expose him, discredit him, or . . . or prove he is what he claims. Father named the valley. The Valley of Gorgons. I said he's ignorant, and he is. He didn't know who the Gorgons were. He named the valley after the formations, thinking, I suppose, the people turned to stone were the Gorgons. He hasn't read any of the literature about shamanism, either, none of the Don Juan books, nothing like that. But Ramón has studied them all, I'd be willing to bet. It will take someone as clever as he is to expose him, and I just don't think Tony's detectives will be capable of it."

"Specifically what do you want us to do?" Charlie asked in his sleepy voice. Constance felt a chill when she realized that he had taken on the case already, no matter what exactly Deborah was asking of them.

"Go out there and spend a week, two weeks, however long it takes, and find out what hold he has on my father. Find out how he fools so many people into believing in his magic. Prove he's a charlatan out for my father's money. I'll be there. You can be my guests. I've done that before— had guests at the house."

"Will you take Lori?" Charlie asked.

"No! She'll never see him again! This fascination will pass. She'll forget him. I'm concerned for my father."

Their tickets had arrived by special delivery the day following Deborah's visit, first-class to Denver, where, she had told them, they would be met. Their greeter at Stapleton had been a charming, dimpled young woman who had escorted them to a private lounge and introduced Captain Smollet, who was to fly them to Pueblo in the company plane as soon as their baggage was available. In Pueblo, they had been met again, by another lovely young woman who gave them keys to a Cadillac Seville and a map to the Valley of Gorgons and wished them luck in finding it.

And now Charlie was driving the last miles, according to the map, which had turned out to be much better than the road maps he was used to. Deborah had offered to have them met by the company helicopter, which could take them all the way to the house, but Constance had refused politely and adamantly. She would walk first. The scenery was breathtaking: sheer cliffs with high trees on the upper reaches, piñons and stunted desert growth at the lower elevations, and, watered by the runoff of spring, green everywhere. All the peaks gleamed with snow, melt water streams cascaded down the precipitous slopes, and it seemed that the world was covered with columbines in profuse bloom, more brilliant than Constance had dreamed they could be.

At the turn they came to next, they were warned by a neat sign that this was a dead-end road, private property, no admittance. The woods pressed closer here, made a canopy overhead. In the perpetual shadows, snow lingered in drifts that were only faintly discolored. They climbed briefly, made a sweeping turn, and Charlie braked.

"Holy Christ!" he exclaimed.

Constance gasped in disbelief as he brought the Cadillac to a stop on the side of the mountain road. Below was the Valley of Gorgons. It looked as if a giant had pulled the mountain apart to create a deep, green Eden with a tiny stream sparkling in the sunshine, groves of trees here and there, a small dam, and a lake that was the color of the best turquoise. A meadow was in the center of the valley, with horses that looked like toys. Slowly, Charlie began to drive again, but he stopped frequently, and the houses and outbuildings became more detailed, less doll-like. And finally, they had gone far enough to be able to turn and see for the first time the sandstone formations that had given the valley its name. It was late afternoon; the sunlight shafted through the pillars. They looked like frozen flames—red, red-gold, red with black streaks, yellow. . . . Frozen flames leaping toward the sky.

The valley, according to the map, was about six miles long, tapered at the east end to a blunt point, with two leg-like projections at the western end, one of them nearly two miles long, the other one and a half miles, both roughly fifty feet wide, and in many places much narrower. The lake and several buildings took up the first quarter of the valley, then the main house and more buildings, with a velvety lawn surrounding them all, ended at the halfway point. The meadow with the grazing horses made up the next quarter and the sandstone formations filled the rest. At its widest point, the valley was two miles across, but most of it was less than that. The stream was a flashing ribbon that clung close to the base of the cliffs. There was no natural inlet to the valley except for the tumbled rocks the stream had dislodged. A true hidden valley, Constance thought, awed by the beauty, the perfect containment of a small paradise.

Deborah met them at the car. Close behind her was a slender young Chicano. She spoke rapid Spanish to him and he nodded. "Come in," she said to Constance and Charlie then. "I hope your trip was comfortable, not too tiring. I'm glad you're here. This is Manuel. He'll be at your beck and call for the duration of your visit, and he speaks perfect English, so don't let him kid you about that." Manuel grinned sheepishly.

"How do you do?" Constance said to the youth. "Just Manuel?"

"Just Manuel, señora," he said. His voice was soft, the words not quite slurred, but easy.

Charlie spoke to him and went behind the car to open the trunk, get out their suitcases.

"Please, señor," he said, "permit me. I will place your things in your rooms."

"You might as well let him," Deborah said with a shrug. "Look." She was looking past them toward the end of the valley.

The golden globe of the sun was balanced on the highest peak of the formations. It began to roll off; the pillars turned midnight black, with streaks of light blazing between them too bright to bear. Their fire had been extinguished and the whole world flamed behind them. No one spoke or moved until the sun dropped behind the mountain peaks in the distance and the sky was awash in sunset colors of cerise and green and rose-gold; the pillars were simply dark forms against the gaudy backdrop.

Charlie was the first one to move. He had been holding the keys; now he extended them toward Manuel, and he realized that the boy was regarding Constance with a fixed gaze. When Charlie looked at her, there were tears in her eyes. He touched her arm. "Hey," he said gently. "You okay?"

She roused with a start. "I must be more tired than I realized."

"*Sí,*" Manuel said then, and took the keys.

Deborah led them into the house. The house kept changing, Charlie thought as they entered. From up on the cliff, it had not looked very large or imposing. The bottom half was finished in gray stone the color of the granite cliffs behind it. The upper floor had appeared to be mostly glass and pale wood. Above that, a steep roof had gleamed with skylights. It had grown as they approached, until it seemed to loom over everything else; none of the other buildings was two stories high. But as soon as they were inside, everything changed again. They were in a foyer with a red-tile floor; there were many immense clay pots with greenery; trees, bushes, flowering plants perfumed the air. Ahead, the foyer widened, became an indoor courtyard, and the light was suffused with the rose tints of sunset. The proportions were not inhuman here; the feeling was of comfort and simplicity and warmth. In the center of the courtyard was a pool with a fountain made of greenish quartz and granite.

"Father said it was to help humidify the air," Deborah said. "But actually, he just likes it."

"Me, too," Charlie agreed.

"It's all incredible," Constance said. They were moving toward a wide, curving staircase but stopped when a door opened across the courtyard and a man stepped out, leaning on a gnarly cane. He was wearing blue jeans and a chamois shirt and boots. His hair was silver.

"Father," Deborah said, and motioned for Charlie and Constance to come. "These are my friends I mentioned. They got here in time for the sunset."

"I know," he said. "I was upstairs watching, too." His eyes were on Constance. They were so dark, they looked black, and his skin was deeply sunburned.

Deborah introduced them. He did not offer to shake hands but bowed slightly. *"Mi casa es su casa,"* he said. "Please join me for supper." He bowed again and stepped back into what they could now see was an elevator. "And you, of course," he added to his daughter, and the door closed on him.

"Well," Deborah said with an undercurrent of unease, "aren't you the honored ones. Sometimes people are here a week before they even see him, much less have a meal with him." She gave Constance a searching look. "He was quite taken with you."

As they resumed their way toward the stairs and started up, Constance asked, "Does he have rheumatoid arthritis?"

"Yes. Most of the time it's under control, but it is painful. He says he feels better here than anywhere else. I guess the aridity helps."

The courtyard was open up to the skylights. On the second floor, a wide balcony overlooked it; there were Indian rugs on the walls between doors and on the floor. It was bright and informal and lovely, Constance thought again. It did not surprise her a bit that Carl Wyandot felt better here than anywhere else.

Deborah took them to two rooms at the southeast corner of the house. There was a spacious bathroom with a tub big enough to lie down in and float. If they wanted anything, she told them, please ring—she had not been joking about Manuel being at their disposal; he was their personal attendant for the duration of their visit. Dinner would be at seven. She would come for them shortly before that. "And don't dress up," she added at the door. "No one ever does here. I'll keep on what I'm wearing." She was dressed in chinos and a cowboy shirt with pointed flaps over the breast pockets, and a wide belt with a huge silver buckle.

As soon as she was gone and the door firmly closed, Charlie took Constance by the shoulders and studied her face intently. "What is it, honey? What's wrong?"

"Wrong? Nothing. That's what's wrong, nothing is. Does that make any sense?"

"No," he said bluntly, not releasing her.

"Didn't you feel it when we first got out of the car?" Her pale blue eyes were sparkling; there was high color on her fair cheeks, as if she had a fever. He touched her forehead and she laughed. "I felt something, and then when the sunset flared, it was like an electric jolt. Didn't you feel that?"

"I wish to hell we were home."

"Maybe we are. Maybe I'll never want to leave here." She spoke lightly, and now she moved away from his hands to go to the windows. "I wish we could have had a room on the west side. But I suppose he has that whole end of the house. I would if it were mine."

"It's just a big, expensive house on an expensive piece of real estate," he said. "All it takes is enough money."

She shook her head. "Oh, no. That's not it. All the money on earth wouldn't buy what's out there."

"And what's that?"

"Magic. This is a magic place."

They dined in Carl Wyandot's private sitting room. Here, too, were the decorative Indian and Mexican rugs, the wall hangings, the pots with lush plants. And here the windows were nearly floor to ceiling, with drapes that had been opened all the way. He had the entire western side of the second floor, as Constance had guessed he would. When she saw how he handled his silverware, she knew Deborah had been right; they were being honored. His hands were misshapen with arthritis, drawn into awkward angles, the knuckles enlarged and sore-looking. He was a proud man; he would not permit many strangers to gawk.

The fifth member of the party was Ramón. Thirty, forty, older? Constance could not tell. His eyes were a warm brown, his face smooth, his black hair moderately short and straight. He had a lithe, wiry build, slender hands. And, she thought, if she had to pick one word to use to describe him, it would be *stillness*. Not rigidity or strain, but a natural stillness. He did not fidget or make small talk or respond to rhetorical questions, and yet he did not give the impression of being bored or withdrawn. He was dressed in jeans and a long-sleeved plaid shirt; in this establishment, it appeared that only the servants dressed up. The two young men who waited on them wore black trousers, white dress shirts, and string ties. They treated Ramón with perhaps a shade more reverence than they showed Wyandot.

Charlie was telling about the day he had run into one of the arsonists he had put away, who was then out of prison. "He introduced me to his pals, told them who I was, what

I had done, all of it, as if he was proud. Then we sat down and had a beer and talked. He wasn't resentful, but rather pleased to see me again."

Carl Wyandot nodded. "Preserving the order of the cosmos is always a pleasing experience. He had his role; you had yours. But you can't really be retired after being so active, not at your age!"

He was too shrewd to lie to, Charlie decided, and he shook his head. "I do private investigations now and then. And Constance writes books and does workshops sometimes. We stay busy."

Deborah was the only one who seemed shocked by this disclosure.

"Actually, I'm planning a book now," Constance said. "It will deal with the various superstitions that continue to survive even in this superrational age, like throwing coins into a fountain. That goes so far back that no one knows for certain when it began. We assume that it was to propitiate the Earth Goddess for the water that the people took from her. It has variations throughout literature."

"To what end?" Carl Wyandot asked. "To debunk or explain or what?"

"I don't debunk things of that sort," she said. "They are part of our heritage. I accept the theory that the archetypes are patterns of possible behavior; they determine how we perceive and react to the world, and usually they can't be explained or described. They come to us as visions, or dream images, and they come to all of us in the same forms over and over. Civilized, educated Westerner; African native who has never seen a book—they have the same dream images, the same impulses in their responses to the archetypes. If we try to bury them, deny them, we are imperiling our own psyches."

"Are you not walking the same ground that Carl Jung plowed?" Ramón asked. He spoke with the polite formality of one whose English was a second language, learned in school.

"It's his field," Constance said. "But it's a very big field and he opened it to all. His intuition led him to America, you know, to study the dreams of the Hopi, but he did not pursue it very far. One lifetime was not long enough, although it was a very long and very productive lifetime."

"Did he not say that good sometimes begets evil? And that evil necessarily begets evil."

"Where did he say that? I don't recall it."

"Perhaps I am mistaken. However, he knew that this inner voyage of discovery can be most dangerous. Only the very brave dare risk it, or the very foolish."

Constance nodded soberly. "He did say the brighter the light, the darker the shadow. The risk may be in coming across the shadow that is not only darker than you expected but larger, large enough to swallow you."

Ramón bowed slightly. "We shall talk again, I hope, before your visit comes to an end. Now, please forgive me, Don Carlos, but it is late."

"Yes, it is," the old man said. "Our guests have had a very long day." One of the servants appeared behind his chair; others seemed to materialize, and the evening was over.

"Thank you, Mr. Wyandot," Constance said. "It was a good evening."

"For me, as well," he said, and he looked at Ramón. "You heard what he called me. Please, you also, call me that. It sounds less formal, don't you agree?"

Deborah walked to their room with them. At the door, she said abruptly, "May I come in and have a drink?"

Someone had been there. The beds were turned down in one room, and in the other a tray had been brought up with bottles, glasses, an ice bucket. Charlie went to examine the bottles and Constance said she wanted coffee. Deborah rang, and it seemed only an instant before there was a soft knock; she asked Manuel to bring coffee and then sat down and accepted the drink Charlie had poured for her.

"You just don't realize what happened tonight," she said after taking a long drink. "Father doesn't usually see strangers at all. He doesn't ask them to dinner. He doesn't introduce them to Ramón. And he doesn't take a backseat and watch others engage in conversation. Skoal!" She drank again, then added, "And Ramón was as gabby as a schoolgirl. Another first. He said more to you tonight than he's ever said to me."

Manuel came back with coffee and Deborah finished her drink and stood up. "Tomorrow when you wake up, just ring for breakfast. That's what we all do. No one but the managers and people like that eat in the dining room. Wander to your heart's content and I'll see you around noon and give you the grand tour. Okay?"

As soon as she was gone, Charlie turned to Constance. "He was warning you loud and clear," he said.

"I know."

"I don't like it."

"I think we're keeping order in the cosmos," she said thoughtfully. "And I think it's better that way. Now for those books."

They had asked Deborah for everything in the house about her father, the history of the area, geology, whatever there was available. Deborah had furnished a dozen books at least. Reluctantly Charlie put his drink aside and poured coffee for himself. It would be a while before they got to bed.

It was nearly two hours later when Constance closed her book with a snap and saw that Charlie was regarding her with brooding eyes.

"Wow," he said softly.

"The biography?"

"Yeah. Want me to paraphrase the early years?" At her nod, he took a deep breath and started. "Tom Wyandot had a falling-out with his family, a good, established English family of lawyers back in Virginia. He headed west, looked for gold in California and Mexico, got married to a Mexican woman, had a son, Carl. He heard there was a lot of gold still in Colorado and headed for the mountains with his wife, Carl, two Mexican men, an Indian guide, and the wife of one of the men. At some point, a gang of outlaws got on their trail and the Indian brought the party to the valley to hide. A few nights later, the outlaws made a sneak attack and killed everyone but Tom Wyandot and the child, Carl. Tom managed to hide them among the formations. The next day, he buried the rest of the group, including his wife, and he and the boy started out on foot, forty miles to Pueblo, with no supplies, horses, anything else. They got there almost dead. Carl was five."

Constance's eyes were distant, unfocused. He knew she was visualizing the scenes; he continued. "For the next eight years, Tom prowled the mountains, sometimes taking Carl, sometimes alone. Then he died, and it's a little unclear just how. Carl was with him on one of their rambles, and Carl returned alone. He said his father had fallen over a cliff. He led a search party to the location and they recovered the body, buried him in Pueblo, and Carl took off. He turns up next a year later in Texas, where he struck it rich in oil."

Constance pulled herself back with a sigh. "Oh, dear," she murmured. "Carl bought the valley in 1930. He started construction in 1940." She frowned. "I wonder just when he located the valley again."

"Me, too. But right now, what I'm thinking is that my body seems to believe it's way past bedtime. It won't have any truck with clocks."

"The idea is to bake yourself first and then jump into the lake," Constance said the next day, surveying the sauna with approval.

"No way. You have any idea of the temperature of the lake?"

"I know, but it'll have to do. There just isn't any snow around."

"That isn't exactly what I meant," he said acidly.

"Oh?" Her look of innocence was a parody; they both laughed. "I'm not kidding, you'll really be surprised. You'll love it."

They wandered on. Swimming pool, steam room, gymnasium, Jacuzzi, a boathouse with canoes and rowboats . . . One of the other buildings held offices; another was like a motel, with its own coffee shop. There were other outbuildings for machinery and maintenance equipment, garages, and a hangar. The helicopter, Charlie remembered. It was impossible to estimate the size of the staff. They kept catching glimpses of servants—the males in black trousers and white shirts, the females in gaily patterned dresses or skirts and blouses. They introduced themselves to several of the men Deborah had called the managers, all in sports clothes, all looking as if they were wearing invisible gray suits.

"It's a whole damn city," Charlie complained. They had left the main complex and were walking along a path that was leading them to a grove of cottonwood trees. Ahead were several cottages, well separated, very private. They stopped. Ramón was coming toward them.

"Good morning," Constance called to him. "What a lovely morning!"

He nodded. "Good morning. I intended to find you, to invite you to dinner in my house. It would give me honor."

Charlie felt a flash of irritation when Constance agreed without even glancing toward him. He would have said yes also, but usually they consulted silently, swiftly. And why was Ramón making it easy? he wondered glumly. He knew damn well they were there to investigate him. Ramón bowed slightly and went back the way he had come, and they turned to go the other way. Charlie's uneasiness increased when it occurred to him that Ramón had stalled their unannounced visit very neatly.

When Deborah met them at noon, she had a Jeep waiting to take them to the gorgons. The first stop was at a fenced area at the far end of the meadow. Inside the fence, smooth white river stones had been laid in a mound. A bronze plaque had been placed there. There were the names: Beatrix Wyandot, Pablo and Maria Marquesa, Juan Moreno, and Julio Tallchief. Under them was the inscription: MASSA-CRED JULY 12, 1906.

"Father left space for his grave," Deborah said. "He's to be buried there alongside his mother. Then no one else."

This was the widest part of the valley, two miles across. The mountains rose very steeply on both sides in unscalable cliffs at this end, exactly as if a solid mass of granite had been pulled open to reveal the sandstone formations. They started fifty yards from the graves.

Constance studied the columns and pillars; when Deborah started to talk again, Constance moved away from the sound of her voice. She had read about the formations. The largest of them was 180 feet high, with a diameter of 48 feet. The pillars soared into the brilliant blue sky with serene majesty. They appeared even redder than they had at a distance. The rubble around the bases was red sand, with silvery sagebrush here and there. Larger pieces had fallen off, had piled up in some places like roots pushing out of the ground. She had the feeling that the formations had not been left by the erosion of the surrounding land, but that they were growing out of the earth, rising of their own will, reaching for the sky. The silence was complete here. No wind stirred the sage or blew the sand; nothing moved.

There was a right way; there was a wrong way. She took a step, then another, another. She retreated, went a different way. She was thinking of nothing, not able to identify what it was she felt, something new, something compelling. Another step. The feeling grew stronger. For a moment, she held an image of a bird following a migratory pattern; it slipped away. Another step.

Suddenly, Charlie's hand was on her arm, shaking her. "For God's sake, Constance!"

Then the sun was beating down on her head, too hot in this airless place, and she glanced about almost indifferently. "I was just on my way back," she said.

"Did you hear me calling you?"

"I was thinking."

"You didn't hear a thing. You were like a sleepwalker." She took his hand and started to walk. "Well, I'm awake now, and starved. Is it lunchtime yet?"

Charlie's eyes remained troubled all afternoon and she did not know what to say, what to tell him, how to explain what she had done. She had wandered all the way back through the gorgons to the opposite side, a mile and a half at least, and if he had not actually seen her, she might still be wandering, because she had not heard him, had not even thought of him. She felt that she had entered a dream world where time was not allowed—that she had found a problem to solve, and the problem could not be stated; the solution, even if found, could never be explained.

Late in the afternoon, Constance coaxed Charlie into the sauna with her and then into the lake, and he was as surprised as she had known he would be, and as delighted. They discovered the immense tub in their suite was large enough for two people. They made love languorously and slept for nearly an hour. A good day, all things considered, he decided when they went to Ramón's cottage for dinner. It had not escaped his attention that Constance had timed things in order to be free to stand outside and watch the sunset flame the gorgons.

Tonight, Ramón told them, they would have peasant food. He had cooked dinner—a pork stew with cactus and tomatillos and plantains. It was delicious.

They sipped thick Mexican coffee in contentment. Throughout dinner, they had talked about food, Mexican food, how it differed from one section of the country to another, how it differed from Central and South American food. Ramón talked charmingly about childhood in Mexico, the festivals, the feasts.

Lazily, Charlie said, "You may know peasant food, but you're not a peasant. Where did you go to school?"

Ramón shrugged. "Many places. University of Mexico, UCLA, the Sorbonne. I am afraid I was not a good student.

I seldom attended regular classes. Eventually, each school discovered this and invited me to go away."

"You used the libraries a lot, I expect," Charlie said almost indifferently.

"Yes. Señor, it is understood that you may want to ask me questions."

"Did Mrs. Rice tell you she hired us?"

"No, señor. Don Carlos told me this."

"Did he also tell you why?"

"The little girl, Lori, saw something that frightened her very much. It worries her mother. And Señor Tony is very unhappy with my presence here."

In exasperation Charlie asked, "Are you willing to simply clear up any mystery about yourself? Why haven't you already done it?"

"Señor, there is no mystery. From the beginning, I have stated what I desire—first to Don Carlos, then to anyone who asked."

"And what is that?"

"To own the valley. When Don Carlos lies beside his mother, then I shall own the valley."

For a long time, Charlie stared at him in silence, disbelieving. Finally, he said, "And you think Don Carlos will simply give it to you?"

"*Sí.*"

"Why?"

"I cannot say, señor. No man can truly say what is in the heart of another."

Charlie felt the hairs on his arms stirring and turned to Constance. She was signaling. No more, not now. Not yet. Abruptly, he stood up. "We should go."

"Thank you," Constance said to Ramón. "We really should go now."

He walked out with them. The night air was cold, the sky very clear, with more stars visible than they had ever seen in New York State. A crescent moon hung low in the eastern sky, its mountains clear, jagged. The gorgons were lost in shadows now. But the moon would sail on the sun path, Constance thought, and set over the highest pinnacle and silver light would flow through the openings. . . .

"Good night, señor," Ramón said softly, and left them.

They did not speak until they were in their room. "May we have coffee?" Constance asked Manuel. There were many more books to read, magazine articles to scan.

"It's blackmail," Charlie said with satisfaction when Manuel had vanished. "So what does he have on Don Carlos?"

Constance gave him a disapproving look. "That's too simple."

"Maybe. But I've found that the simplest explanation is usually the right one. He's too damn sure of himself. It must be something pretty bad."

She moved past him to stand at the window. She would have to be out at sunrise, she was thinking, when the sun would appear above the tumbled rocks of the stream and light up the gorgons with its first rays. Something nagged at her memory. They had looked up the rough waterway, not really a waterfall, but very steep, the water flashing in and out of the granite, now spilling down a few feet, to pour over rocks again. It was as if the sunlight, the moonlight had cut through the cliff, opened a path for the tumbling water. The memory that had tried to get through receded.

Manuel brought their coffee and they settled down to read. A little later, Charlie put down his book with disgust and started to complain, then saw that she was sleeping. He took her book from her lap; she roused only slightly and he took her by the hand to the bedroom, got her into bed. Almost instantly, she was sleeping soundly. He returned to his books.

He would poke around in the library and if he didn't find something written about Wyandot by someone who had not idolized him, he would have to go to Denver, or somewhere, and search further. Wyandot and his past, that was the key, he felt certain. Blackmail. Find the leverage and confront both blackmailer and victim and then get the hell out of here. He nodded. And do it all fast.

The next morning, he woke up to find Constance's bed empty. He started to get up, then lay down again, staring at the ceiling. She had gone out to look at the formations by sunrise, he knew. He waited, tense and unhappy, until she returned quietly, undressed, and got back in bed. He pretended to be asleep and in a short while he actually fell asleep again. Neither of them mentioned it that day.

She insisted on going to the gorgons again in the afternoon. "Take some books along," she said in an offhand manner. "I want to explore and I may be a while." She did not look at him when she said this. Today they planned to ride horses and eat sandwiches and not return until after sundown.

He had binoculars this time, and before the afternoon ended, he found himself bird-watching. Almost angrily, he got to his feet and started to walk among the gorgons, looking for Constance. She had been gone for nearly two hours. Abruptly, he stopped, even more angrily. She had asked him to wait, not come after her. He glanced about at the formations; it was like being in a red sandstone forest, with the trunks of stone trees all around him casting long black shadows, all pointing together at the other end of the valley, pointing at the spillway the stream had cut. It was too damn quiet in here. He found his way out and stood in the shade, looking at the entire valley lying before him. The late sun turned the cascade into a molten stream. He was too distant to see its motion; it looked like a vein of gold in the cliffs. He raised the binoculars and examined the valley slowly, then even more slowly studied the spillway. He swore softly and sat down in the shade to wait for Constance and think.

When she finally appeared, she was wan and abstracted. "Satisfied?" he asked, and now there was no anger in his voice, only concern.

She shook her head. "I'm trying too hard. Want to start back?"

Manuel came with the horses, guaranteed gentle and safe, he had assured them earlier, and he had been right. They rode slowly, not talking. Night fell swiftly after the sun went down. It was nearly dark when they reached the house and their room again. Would they like dinner served in their room? Manuel had asked, and, after looking at Constance, Charlie had nodded.

"Can you tell me what you're doing?" he asked her after Manuel had left them.

"I don't know."

"Okay. I thought so. I think I'm onto something, but I have to go to Denver. Will you fly out in the helicopter, or should we plan a couple of days and drive?"

"I can't go," she said quietly, and added, "Don't press me, please."

"Right. I'll be back by dark. I sure as hell don't want to try to fly in here blind." He grinned with the words. She responded with a smile belatedly.

He summoned Manuel, who nodded when Charlie asked about the helicopter trip. "*Sí.* When do you want to go?"

And Manuel was not at all surprised that he was going alone, he thought grimly after making the arrangements. Constance went to bed early again. He stood regarding her as she slept and under his breath he cursed Deborah Rice and her father and Ramón. "You can't have her!" he said silently.

The managers had been in the swimming pool; others had been in the dining room and library. Constance finally had started to gather her books to search for someplace quiet. Manuel gently took them from her. "Please, permit me," he said softly. "It is very noisy today."

She had had lunch with Deborah Rice. Tony was coming tomorrow, she had said, and he was both furious and excited. He had something. There would be a showdown, she had predicted gloomily, and her father had never lost a showdown in his life. Deborah was wandering about aimlessly and would intrude again, Constance knew, would want to talk to no point, just to have something to do, and Constance had to think. It seemed that she had not thought anything through since arriving at the Valley of Gorgons. That was the punishment for looking, she thought wryly: The brain turned to stone.

She was reluctant to return to her rooms. Without Charlie, they seemed too empty. "I'll go read out under the gorgons," she said finally. At least out there, no one bothered her, and she had to think. She felt that she almost knew something, could almost bring it to mind, but always it slipped away again.

"*Sí,*" Manuel said. "We should take the Jeep, señora. It is not good to ride home after dark."

She started to say she would not be there that long; instead, she nodded.

Charlie had been pacing in the VIP lounge for half an hour before his pilot, Jack Wayman, turned up. It was 7:15.

"Where the hell have you been?" Charlie growled. "Let's get going."

"Mr. Meiklejohn, there's a little problem with one of the rotors. I've been trying to round up a part, but no luck. Not until morning."

He was a fresh-faced young man, open, ingenuous. Charlie found his hands balling, took a step toward the younger man, who backed up. "I'll get it airborne by seven in the morning, Mr. Meiklejohn. I'm sure of it. I called the house and explained the problem. You have a room at the Hilton—"

Charlie spun around and left him talking. He tried to buy a seat on another flight to Pueblo first, and when that failed—no more flights out that night—he strode to the Hertz rental desk.

"I'm going to rent a plane for Pueblo," he said, "and I'll want a car there waiting. Is that a problem?"

The young man behind the desk shrugged. "Problem, sir. They close up at seven down there."

"I'll rent a car here and drive down," Charlie said in a clipped, hard voice. "Is *that* a problem?"

"No, sir!"

By quarter to eight, he was leaving the airport. He felt exactly the same rage that had swamped him at times in the past, especially in his final years with the fire department, when he knew with certainty the fire had been set, the victim murdered. It was a cold fury, a savage rage made even more dangerous because it was so deep within that nothing of it showed on the surface, but an insane desire, a need, fueled it, and the need was to strike out, to lash out at the criminal, the victims, the system, anything. He knew now with the same certainty that the pilot had waited deliberately until after seven to tell him he was stranded in Denver. And he was equally certain that by now the pilot had called the valley to warn them that he was driving, that he would be there by midnight. And if they had done anything to Constance, he knew, he would blow that whole valley to hell, along with everyone in it.

"Manuel," Constance said when they arrived at the gorgons, "go on back to the house. You don't have to stay out here with me."

"Oh, no, señora. I will stay."

"No, Manuel. I have to be alone so I can think. That's why I came out here, to think. There are too many people wandering around the house, too many distractions. If I know I'm keeping you out here, waiting, that would be distracting, too. I really want to be alone for a few hours."

"But, señora, you could fall down, or get lost. Don Carlos would flay me if an accident happened."

She laughed. "Go home, Manuel. You know I can't get lost. Lost where? And I've been walking around more years than you've been alive. Go home. Come back for me right after sunset."

His expression was darkly tragic. "Señora, it is possible to get lost in your own house, in your own kitchen even. And out here, it is possible even more."

"If you can't find me," she said softly, "tell Ramón. He'll find me."

"Sí," Manuel said, and walked to the Jeep unhappily.

She watched the Jeep until it disappeared among cottonwood trees that edged the stream at the far end of the meadow, and only when she could no longer see it did she feel truly alone. Although the mornings and nights were cold, the afternoons were warm; right now shade was welcome. She selected a spot in the shade, brushed rocks clear of sand, and settled herself to read.

First a history of the area. These were the Sangre de Cristo Mountains, named by the Spanish, long since driven out, leaving behind bits and pieces of their language, bits of architecture. She studied a picture of petroglyphs outside Pueblo, never deciphered, not even by the first Indians the Spaniards had come across. Another people driven out? Leaving behind bits and pieces of a language? She lingered longer over several pictures of the Valley of the Gods, west of Colorado Springs. Formations like these, but more extensive, bigger, and also desecrated. She frowned at that thought, then went on to turn pages, stopping only at pictures now: an Oglala Sioux medicine lodge, then the very large medicine wheel in Wyoming, desecrated. The people who had constructed the medicine lodges could not explain the medicine wheel, she read, then abruptly snapped the book shut. That was how history was written, she told herself. The victors destroy or try to destroy the gods of the vanquished, and as years go by, the gods themselves fade into the dust. The holy places that remain are turned into tourist attractions, fees are charged, guided tours conducted, books written about the significance of the megaliths, or the pyramids, or the temples, or the ground drawings. And when the dust stirs, the gods stir also, and they wait.

She began to examine a different book, this one done by a small press, an amateur press. The text was amateurish also, but the photographs that accompanied it were first-rate. The photographer had caught the gorgons in every possible light—brilliant sunlight, morning, noon, sunset . . . moonlight, again, all phases. During a thunderstorm. She drew in a sharp breath at a picture of lightning frozen on the highest peak. There was one with snow several feet deep; each gorgon wore a snowcap. The last section was a series of aerial pictures, approaching from all directions, with stiletto shadows, no shadows at all. . . . Suddenly, she felt vertiginous.

She had come to the final photograph taken from directly above the field of gorgons at noon. There were no shadows; the light was brilliant, the details sharp and clear. Keeping her gaze on the picture, she felt for her notebook and tore out a piece of paper, positioned it over the photograph. The paper was thin enough for the image to come through. She picked up her pencil and began to trace the peaks, not trying to outline them precisely, only to locate them with circles. When she was done, she studied her sketch and thought, of course, that was how they would be.

She put her pencil point on the outermost circle and started to make a line linking each circle to the next. When she finished, her pencil was in the center of the formations; she had drawn a spiral—a unicursal labyrinth.

Slowly, she stood up and turned toward the gorgons. She had entered in the wrong place before, she thought absently, and she had not recognized the pattern. Knowing now what it was, it seemed so obvious that she marveled at missing it before.

She walked very slowly around the gorgons to the easternmost pillar. Facing the valley, she saw that the low sun had turned the stream to gold; the shadows at her feet reached for it. She entered the formations. There was a right way and a wrong way, but now the right way drew her; she did not have to think about it. A step, another.

She did not know how long she had been hearing the soft singing, chanting, but it was all around her, drawing her on, guiding her even more than the feeling of being on the right path. She did not hesitate this time, nor did she retrace any steps. Her pace was steady. When the light failed, she stopped.

I could continue, she said silently in her head.

Sí, Ramón's voice replied, also in her head.

Will it kill me?

I do not know.

I will go out now.

Sí. There was a note of deep regret in the one syllable.

It doesn't matter how I leave, does it?

No, señora. It does not matter.

She took a step, but now she stumbled, caught herself by clutching one of the gorgons. It was very dark; she could see nothing. There was no sound. Suddenly, she felt panic welling up, flooding her. She took another step and nearly fell over a rock. Don't run! she told herself, for God's sake, don't try to run! She took a deep breath, not moving yet. Her heartbeat subsided.

"Please, señora, permit me." Ramón's soft voice was very near.

She felt his hand on her arm, guiding her, and she followed gratefully until they left the formations and Manuel ran up to her in a greater panic than she had felt.

"Gracias, Madre! Gracias!" he cried. "Oh, señora, thank goodness you're safe! Come, let us return to the house!"

She looked for Ramón to thank him, but he was no longer there. Tiredly, she went to the Jeep and got in. Although it was dark, there was not the impenetrable black that she had experienced within the formations. They swallowed light just as they swallowed sound, she thought without surprise. She leaned back and closed her eyes, breathing deeply.

At the house, they were met by a young woman who took Constance by the arm. "Señora, please permit me. I am Felicia. Please allow me to assist you."

Manuel had explained the problem with the helicopter and she was glad now that Charlie was not on hand to see her drag herself in in this condition. He would have a fit, she thought, and smiled gratefully at Felicia.

"I am a little bit tired," she admitted. "And very hungry."

Felicia laughed. "First, Don Carlos said, you must have a drink, and then a bath, and then dinner. Is that suitable, señora?"

"Perfect."

Charlie was cursing bitterly, creeping along the state road, looking for a place where he could turn around. He had overshot the private road, he knew. He had driven over forty miles since leaving Pueblo, and the private road had to be eight to ten miles behind him, but there was no place to turn. He had trouble accepting that he had missed the other road, the neat sign warning that this was private property, a dead end, but it was very black under the trees. And now he had to turn, go back even slower, and find it. It was fifteen more minutes before there was a spot flat enough, wide enough to maneuver around to head back, and half an hour after that before he saw the sign.

No one could work with the New York Fire Department and then with the police department as many years as he had done without developing many senses that had once been latent. Those senses could take him through a burned-out building, or into an alleyway, or toward a parked car in a state of alertness that permitted him to know if the next step was a bad one, or if there was someone waiting in the backseat of the car. He had learned to trust those senses without ever trying to identify or isolate them. And now they were making him drive with such caution that he was barely moving; finally, he stopped altogether. A mountain road in daylight, he told himself, would look very different from that same road at night. But this different? He closed his eyes and drew up an image of the road he had driven over before—narrow, twisting, climbing and descending steeply, but different from this one, which met all those conditions.

This road was not as well maintained, he realized, and it was narrower than the other one. On one side was a black drop-off, the rocky side of the mountain on the other, and not enough space between them to turn around.

"Well, well," he murmured, and took a deep breath. The sign had been moved. He was on the wrong road. This road could meander for miles and end up at a ranch, or a mining camp, or a fire tower, or in a snowbank. It could just peter out finally. He let the long breath out in a sigh. Two more miles, and if he didn't find a place where he could turn, he would start backing out. His stomach felt queasy and his palms were sweating now. He began a tuneless whistle, engaged the gears, and started forward again.

"You know about the holy places on earth, don't you?" Don Carlos asked Constance. He had invited her to his apartment for a nightcap. Ramón was there, as she had known he would be.

"A little," she said. "In fact, I visited a couple of them some years ago. Glastonbury Tor was one. It was made by people in the megalithic period and endures yet. A three-dimensional labyrinth. I was with a group, and our guide was careful to point out that simply climbing the hill accounted for all the physiological changes we felt. Shortness of breath, a feeling of euphoria, heightened awareness."

Ramón's stillness seemed to increase, as if it were an aura that surrounded him and even part of the room. If one got close enough to him, she thought, the stillness would be invasive.

"I saw Croagh Patrick many years ago," Don Carlos said. "Unfortuantely, I was a skeptic and refused to walk up it barefooted. I've always wondered what that would have been like."

"The labyrinth is one of the strongest mystical symbols," Ramón said. "It is believed that the evil at the center cannot walk out because of the curves. Evil flows in straight lines."

"Must one find only evil there?" Constance asked.

"No. Good and evil dwell there side by side, but it is the evil that wants to come out."

"The Minotaur," she murmured. "Always we find the Minotaur, and it is ourself."

"You don't believe that good and evil exist independently of human agencies?" Ramón asked.

She shook her head.

"Señora, imagine a pharmacy with shelves of bright pills, red, blue, yellow, all colors, some sugar-coated. You would not allow a child to wander there and sample. Good and evil side by side, sometimes in the same capsule. Every culture has traveled the same path, from the simplest medicines to the most sophisticated, but they all have this in common: Side by side, in the same medicine, evil and good dwell forever intertwined."

"I have read," she said slowly, "that when the guru sits on his mountaintop, he increases his power, his knowledge, every time a supplicant makes the pilgrimage to him. In the same way, when children dance the maypole, the center gathers the power. At one time, the center was a person who became very powerful this way."

Ramón nodded. "And was sometimes sacrificed at the conclusion of the ceremony."

"Did you try to lure the child Lori to the center of the gorgons?" Her voice sounded harsh even to her own ears.

"No, señora."

"You tried to coax me in."

"No, señora. I regretted that you stopped, but I did not lure you."

"Don Carlos is a believer. Why don't you use him?"

"I wanted to," Don Carlos said simply. "I can't walk that far."

"There must be others. Manuel. Or the girl Felicia. There must be a lot of believers here."

"Perhaps because they believe, they fear the Minotaur too much," Ramón said.

"And so do I," she said flatly.

"No, señora. You do not believe in independent evil. You will meet your personal Minotaur, and you do not fear yourself."

Abruptly, she stood up. "I am very tired. If you'll excuse me, I'd like to go to bed now."

Neither man moved as she crossed the room. Then Ramón said almost too softly to hear, "Señora, I was not at the gorgons this evening. I have spent the entire evening here with Don Carlos."

She stopped at the door and looked back at them. Don Carlos nodded soberly.

"Constance," he said, "if you don't want to go all the

way, leave here tomorrow. Don't go back to the formations."

"You've been here for years," she said. "Why didn't you do it a long time ago?"

For a moment, his face looked mummified, bitter; the expression changed, became benign again. "I was the wrong one," he said. "I couldn't find the way. I felt it now and then, but I couldn't find my way."

There was a right way and a wrong way, she thought, remembering. A right person and a wrong person. "Good night," she said quietly, and left them.

She stood by her windows in the dark, looking out over the valley, the lake a silver disk in moonlight, the dark trees, pale granite cliffs. "Charlie," she whispered to the night, "I love you." She wished he was with her, and she closed her eyes hard on the futile wish. Good night, darling, she thought at him then. Sleep well. When she lay down in bed, she felt herself falling gently into sleep.

Charlie pulled on the hand brake and leaned forward to rest his head on the steering wheel, to ease the strain in his neck from watching so closely behind him with his head out the open door. Suddenly, he lifted his head, listening. Nothing, hardly even any wind to stir the trees. All at once, he admitted to himself that he would not be able to back out in the dark. The backup lights were too dim, the road too curvy, with switchbacks that were invisible, and a drop-off too steep, the rocky mountain too close. He had scraped the car several times already, and he had stopped too many times with one or two wheels too close to the edge or even over it. He had thought this before, but each time he had started again; now he reached out and turned off the headlights. The blackness seemed complete at first; gradually, moonlight filtered through the trees. It was all right, he thought tiredly. He could rest for a while and at dawn start moving again. He pulled the door shut, cracked the window a little, and leaned back, with his eyes closed, and slept.

When Charlie drove in the next morning, Constance met him and exclaimed at his condition. "My God, you've been wrestling with bears! Are you all right?"

"Hungry, tired, dirty. All right. You?"

"Fine. Manuel, a pot of coffee right now and then a big breakfast, steak, eggs, fruit, everything. Half an hour."

Charlie waited until they were in their room to kiss her. She broke away, shaking her head. "You might have fought off bears, but you won. I'm going to run a bath while you strip. Come on, hop!"

He chuckled and started to peel off his clothes. She really was fine. She looked as if she had slept better than he had, anyway. Now the ordeal of trying to get back seemed distant and even ludicrous.

Manuel brought coffee while he was bathing; she took it the rest of the way and sat by the tub while he told her his adventures.

"You really think someone moved the sign?" she asked incredulously. "Why?"

"Why do I think it, or why did they do it?"

"Either. Both."

"It was there this morning, back where it belonged. I think Ramón didn't want me here last night. What happened?"

"Nothing. That must be breakfast." She nearly ran out.

Nothing? He left the tub and toweled briskly, got on his

robe, and went to the sitting room, where Manuel was finishing arranging the dishes.

When they were alone again and his mouth was full of steak, he said, "Tell me about it."

Constance took her coffee to the window and faced out. "I don't know what there is to tell. I had a nightcap with Don Carlos and Ramón and went to bed pretty early and slept until after eight." She came back and sat down opposite him. "I really don't know what happened," she said softly. "Something important, but I can't say what it was. There's power in the gorgons, Charlie, real power. Anyone who knows the way can tap into it. That sounds so . . . stupid, doesn't it? But it's true. Let me sort it out in my own mind first, okay? I can't talk about it right now. What did you find?"

"Enough to blow Ramón's boat out of the water," he said. At her expression of dismay, he added, "I thought that's what we came here for."

There was a knock on the door and she went to answer it. Deborah was there, looking pale and strained.

"All hell's about to break loose today," she said when Constance waved her in. "Charlie, I'm glad you're back. Father's in conference, and then he's sending his associates to Denver to get together with company attorneys or something. And Tony's due in by two. Father wants to clear the decks before then for the showdown. You're invited. Three, in his apartment."

An exodus began and continued all day. The helicopter came and went several times; a stream of limousines crept up the mountain road, vanished. The loud laughter was first subdued, then gone. Yesterday, the managers had all been supremely confident, clad in their invisible gray suits; today, the few that Constance had seen had been like school-boys caught doing unspeakable things in the lavatory.

And now Charlie was probably the only person within miles who was relaxed and comfortable, wholly at ease, watching everything with unconcealed, almost childish interest. They were in Don Carlos's apartment, waiting for the meeting to start. Tony Wyandot was in his mid-forties, trim and athletic, an executive who took his workouts as seriously as his mergers. He was dark, like his father and sister, and very handsome. Constance knew his father must have looked much like that at his age. He had examined her and Charlie very briefly when they were introduced, and, she felt certain, he knew their price, or thought he did. After that, he dismissed them.

Charlie sat at the far edge of the group, watchful, quiet. Ramón stood near the windows, also silent. Carl Wyandot entered the sitting room slowly, leaning on his cane, nodded to everyone, and took his leather chair, which obviously had been designed for his comfort. And Deborah sat near him, as if to be able to reach him if he needed help. She and Tony ignored Ramón.

Tony waited until his father was seated, then said, "I asked for a private meeting. I prefer not to talk business or family matters before strangers."

Charlie settled more easily into his chair. Tony would do, he thought. Direct, straight to the point, not a trace of fear or subservience; but neither was there the arrogance that his appearance hinted at. Equal speaking to equal.

"I doubt we have many secrets," his father said. "You hired detectives and so did your sister." He inclined his head fractionally toward Charlie. "Go on."

Tony accepted this without a flicker. "First, I am relieved that you've ordered the reorganization study to commence.

I'll go to Denver, naturally, and stay as long as it's necessary. Three months should be enough time." He paused. "And I find it very disturbing that you've already signed papers about the dispensation of the valley." His level tone did not change; he kept his gaze on his father, but the room felt as if a current had passed through it.

His father remained impassive and silent.

"You have sole ownership, and you can dispose of your property as you see fit," Tony went on, "but a case can be made that this is an unreasonable act."

Deborah made a sound, cleared her throat perhaps, or gasped. No one looked at her.

"I did not believe that you could be so influenced by a stranger that you would behave in an irrational way," Tony said, his gaze unwavering. "That's why I hired the detectives, to find out exactly why you were doing this. And I found out." He paused again, in thought, then said, "I think we should speak in private, Father. I did find out."

"Just say it."

He bowed slightly. "Ramón is your son. The trail is tenuous, not easy to find, but once found, it leads only to that conclusion. He came here and claimed his share of your estate, and that's why you're giving him this valley."

This time, Deborah cried out. "That's a lie!"

Tony shook his head. "I wish it were. I had my agency check and double-check. It's true. Father, you were trying to keep the past buried, protect us, yourself, and there's no need. You provided well for him over the years, took care of his mother, saw that he had opportunities. You owe him nothing. A yearly allowance, if you feel you have to, but no more than that."

Ramón had not moved. Constance glanced at him; his face was in deep shadow, with the windows behind him.

She recalled her own words: The brighter the light, the darker the shadow. Deborah was twisting her hands around and around; she looked at Charlie despairingly, and he shrugged and nodded.

"Father," Tony said then, his voice suddenly gentle, "I think I can understand. There's no record of the marriage of your father and mother. You were illegitimate, weren't you?"

For the first time, Don Carlos reacted. His face flushed and his mouth tightened.

"But don't you see that it's unimportant now?" asked Tony.

"Haven't I provided for you and your sister?"

"We all know you've been more than generous. No one disputes that."

"And you would turn the valley into—what did you call it, a corporate resort? Knowing I detest the idea, you would do that."

"Not right away," his son said with a trace of impatience. "Places like this are vanishing faster all the time. You can hardly find a secluded spot even today. I'm talking about twenty years from now, fifteen at least."

Don Carlos shook his head. "The business will be yours. I have provided a trust for Deborah. Ramón can have the valley. Do you want to pursue this in court?" His face might have been carved from the granite of the cliffs. His eyes were narrowed; they caught the light and gleamed.

He would welcome a fight, Constance realized, watching him. And he would win. Tony flinched away finally and stood up. He had learned well from his father; nothing of his defeat showed in his face or was detectable in his voice when he said, "As you wish, Father. You know I would not willingly do anything to hurt you."

When he walked from the room, Deborah jumped up and ran after him. Now Charlie rose lazily from his chair, grinning. "Is he really finished?" he asked.

Don Carlos was looking at the door thoughtfully; he swung around as if surprised to find anyone still in the room. "He isn't done yet," he admitted. "Not quite yet."

"Congratulations," Charlie said, still grinning. "A masterful job of creating a new heir. I would not like to be your adversary."

The old man studied him, then said in a quiet voice, "Are you exceedingly brave, or simply not very smart? I wonder. You are on my land, where I have numerous servants who are, I sometimes think, too fanatically loyal."

Constance was looking from one to the other in bewilderment.

"Let me tell a different story," Charlie said. "A group of people arrives at the top of the cliff, where the stream starts to tumble down into the valley. Two Mexican men, two Mexican women, a child, a white man, and an Indian guide. They can't take horses down that cut, not safely, so they hobble them up there and go down on foot. Looking for gold? A holy place? What? Never mind. A fight breaks out and the white man and child survive, but when he climbs back out, the horses are gone, and from that bit of thievery, he gets the idea for the whole story he'll tell about bandits. It works; people accept his story. And now his only problem is that he can't find the valley again. He dies without locating it again. Why didn't he kill the child, Carlos?"

Don Carlos sighed. "Please sit down. I want a drink. I seldom do anymore, but right now that's what I want."

Ramón mixed drinks for all of them, and then he sat down for the first time since the meeting had started.

Don Carlos drank straight bourbon, followed by water. "Have you told Deborah any of this?"

"No."

"It was as you guessed," Don Carlos said finally. "I was back in the formations and didn't even hear the shots. I came out and he was the only one; the others were lying in blood. He raised the gun and aimed at me, and then he put it down again and started to dig graves. I don't know why he didn't shoot. He said from then on, I was to be his son and if I ever told anyone, he would shoot me too. I believed him. I was five."

"He killed your mother," Constance said, horrified, "and your father."

"Yes."

"How terrible for you. But I don't understand what that has to do with the present."

Don Carlos shrugged. "How much more have you guessed, or learned?" he asked Charlie.

"He couldn't find the valley again, but you did. I suspect there was gold and that it's under the lake today." Don Carlos nodded slightly. "Yes. You took away enough to get your start, and later you bought the valley, and the first thing you did was dam the stream, to hide the gold vein under many feet of water." Again the old man nodded.

Charlie's voice sobered when he continued. "Years passed and you preserved the valley, until one day Ramón appeared. Was he hired as a servant? A business associate? It doesn't matter. He read that history and looked at the waterway and drew the same conclusions I did. You felt that the gorgons had saved your life, that there was a mystical connection there. And he found how to capitalize on it." He was aware that Constance was signaling, but this time he ignored it and said bluntly, "I have as much right to call you Daddy as he does."

Don Carlos smiled faintly and lifted his glass, finished his bourbon. "You're a worthy adversary," he said to Charlie. "Will the others unravel it also? How did you discover this so quickly?"

"Ramón left a good trail, just hidden enough to make it look good, not so much that it can't be found. He did a fine job of it." He added dryly, "If you spend enough money, you can make the world flat again, enough to convince most people, anyway. I spent only a little bit and learned everything Tony's detectives had uncovered, and it hit me that if a man of your wealth really wants to hide anything, it gets hidden. I didn't believe a word of it."

Constance looked at Ramón in wonder. "You left false evidence that makes it appear that you are his son? Is that what you did?"

"Sí."

"When?"

"For the last two years, we have been working on this."

She felt completely bewildered now. "But why? What on earth for?"

"I knew Tony would investigate Ramón," Don Carlos said. "As soon as he found out I intended to leave the valley to Ramón, he would hire investigators to find out why. I tried to come up with something else, but I couldn't think of anything different that he would accept as a good-enough reason. He won't talk in public about his father's illicit sex life. I don't want a fight or publicity about this."

"And if you told the truth," Constance said in a low voice, "they could press for a sanity hearing, and probably win." She felt a wave of disgust pass through her at the thought of the hearing, the taunting questions, the innuendos.

"They might have won such a hearing," Don Carlos said just as quietly as she had spoken.

"And maybe they should have had that chance." Charlie sounded harsh and brusque. "This valley is worth ten million at least, and you're giving it away because he says there's power in the gorgons. Maybe Tony should have his chance."

"Señor," Ramón said, "come to the gorgons at sundown today. And you, señora. This matter is not completed yet, not yet." He bowed to Don Carlos and Constance and left the room.

They stood up also, Charlie feeling helpless with frustration. "We won't be able to make that," he said to Don Carlos. "Give him our regrets. We're leaving."

"We'll be there," Constance said clearly.

Don Carlos nodded. "Yes, we'll all be there." He looked at Charlie. "I ask only that you say nothing to my daughter or son today. Tomorrow it will be your decision. I ask only for today."

"You're not even offering to buy us," Charlie said bitterly.

"Mr. Meiklejohn, I am extremely wealthy, more than you realize. But over the years, I have learned that there are a lot of things I can't buy. That was a surprise to me, as it must be to you, if you believe it at all."

Charlie's frustration deepened; wordlessly, he nodded and stalked from the room, with Constance close behind him.

"That was brilliant," Constance said, walking by Charlie's side along the lakefront.

"Yeah, I know."

"We're really not finished here." She was not quite pleading with him.

"Right."

She caught his arm and they came to a stop. "I'm sorry," she said. "I have to see it through and I can't say why."

He nodded soberly. "That's what scares me." He never had doubted her, never had thought of her with another man, never had a moment's cloud of jealousy obscure his vision of her. And he knew she felt the same way about him. Their trust in each other was absolute, but ... He knew there were areas in her psychic landscape that he could not enter, areas where she walked alone, and he knew that when she walked those infinite and infinitely alien paths, the things that occupied her mind were also alien and would not permit translation into his mundane world. Standing close to her in the warm sunlight, a gleaming lake at one side of them, luxurious buildings all around, cars, helicopters, computers, servants by the score available, he felt alone, abandoned, lost. She was beyond reach even though her hand was on his arm.

He lifted her hand and kissed the palm. "It's your party."

She blinked rapidly. "We should go back to the house. Tony scares me right now."

They stopped when Tony and Deborah came into view, heading for the area behind the boathouse. Tony was carrying a rifle; Deborah was almost running to keep up, clutching his arm.

She saw Charlie and Constance and turned to them instead. Tony continued, stony-faced.

"What's up?" Charlie asked pleasantly.

"He's going to do target practice. Kill time." She laughed with a tinge of hysteria in her voice.

"Well, I'm looking for a drink," he said, so relaxed and quiet that he appeared lazy.

She walked with them, studying the path they were on. "Tony's so much like Father. It's uncanny how alike they are."

They all started a few seconds later when a shot sounded, echoing and chasing itself around the granite walls of the valley for a long time.

"He's as violent as Father must have been when he was younger," Deborah said as they started to walk again. "More so maybe. Father is said to have killed a man back in the twenties. I don't know how true it is, but it doesn't really matter. People who tell the story know it was quite possible. He would kill to protect his interests, his family. And so would Tony."

"So would I," Charlie commented.

Constance shivered.

Another shot exploded the quiet and then several more in quick succession. It sounded like thunder in the valley. They paused at the house, listening, feeling the vibrations in the air, and then entered.

The fountain splashed; the red tiles on the floor glowed; an orange tree in a pot had opened a bloom or two overnight and filled the air with a heady fragrance. It was very still.

Deborah paused at the fountain and stared at the water. They had started up the wide stairs; her low voice stopped them.

"When Tony and I used to come here, we just had each other; we were pretty close in those days. He was Lori's age when he . . . when something happened out there. He wouldn't talk about it. He was ashamed because he ran and left me behind, and everything changed with us after that.

Just like with Lori. I don't think he's ever gone back. And he shouldn't go back. That target practice . . . he claims an eagle has been snatching chickens. He says he'll shoot it on sight." She bowed her head lower. "How I've prayed for an earthquake to come and shake them all down, turn them to dust!" She jammed her hands into her pockets and walked away without looking back at them.

In their room Constance watched silently as Charlie unlocked his suitcase and brought out his .38 revolver. She went to the window then. "Charlie, just for a minute accept that there might be some force out there, some power. Tony said places like this are vanishing, remember? He was more right than he knew. They are. What if there are places where you can somehow gain access to the power people sometimes seem to have, like the inhuman strength people sometimes have when there's an emergency, a fire, or something like that."

He made a grunting noise. She continued to look out the window. The sun was getting low, casting long shadows now.

"If people can manipulate that kind of power, why don't they?" he demanded.

She shrugged. "New priests drive out the old priests. New religions replace the old. The conquerors write the books and decide what's true, what's myth. Temples are turned into marketplaces. Roads are built. Admission is charged to holy places and the gum wrappers appear, the graffiti. . . . But the stories persist in spite of it all. They persist."

She looked at him when she heard the sound of ice hitting a glass. His face was stony, unknowable.

"When we lose another animal species," she said, almost

desperate for his understanding now, "no one knows exactly what we've lost forever. When a forest disappears, no one knows what marvels we might have found in it. Plants that become extinct are gone forever. What drugs? What medicines? What new ways of looking at the universe? We can't really know what we've lost. And this valley's like that. Maybe we can't know what it means today, or even next year, but it exists as a possibility for us to know someday, as long as it remains and is not desecrated."

He picked up the two glasses and joined her at the window, where he put the glasses on a table and took her into his arms. He held her very close and hard for a minute or two and then kissed her. "Let's have our drink," he said afterward. "And then it'll be about time to mosey on downstairs." And he tried to ignore the ice that was deep within him, radiating a chill throughout his body.

Manuel drove them without a word. He was subdued and nervous. Ahead of the Jeep was a Land Rover moving cautiously, avoiding the ruts in the tracks, easing into and out of the holes. Deborah and her father were in it. Also ahead of them was Tony on a horse, in no hurry, either. He had a scabbard with the rifle jutting out.

Manuel stopped near the stream where he had parked before, but Deborah drove her father closer to the formations and parked within fifty feet of them. Manuel got a folding chair from the car and set it up; he placed a large Indian blanket on the back of the chair and then looked at Deborah with a beseeching expression. She shook her head. Silently, he went back to the Jeep, turned it, and drove toward the house. Tony was tying his horse to a hitching post near the mound of the graves.

Don Carlos walked slowly over the rocky ground; there

was a line of sweat on his upper lip when he reached the chair and sat down. No one offered to help him, but they all watched until he was settled. Probably, Charlie thought, they knew better than to try to help. If he wanted help, he would ask for it politely, matter-of-factly, and unless he did, they waited. A worthy adversary, he thought again. He had no doubt that Don Carlos had killed, maybe more than once, and that he would not hesitate to kill again if he had to. Don Carlos knew, as Charlie did, that the world was not always a nice place.

Tony drew nearer. He and Charlie eyed each other like two alley cats confined in a too-small space, Constance thought, watching everyone, everything closely.

She heard a faint singing and glanced about to see if the others were listening too, to see if Ramón had approached from behind the gorgons. Charlie's expression of lazy intention did not change; no one moved. They didn't hear it, she realized. The singing was more like chanting, and louder. The earth rolled away from the sun and caught the light in the stream at the far end of the valley: a dagger of golden light slicing through the cliffs, pointing the way.

It was time. She touched Charlie's arm. When he looked at her, she said softly, "Don't let them follow me. Please wait. I'll be back."

The ice flowed through him, tingled his fingers and toes, froze his heart. He nodded silently. Their gaze held for another moment, then she turned and walked toward the entrance of the gorgons. He had known this was her part, just as she had known; he had been braced, waiting for this. He had not known he would be frozen by the icy fear that gripped him now. She did not look back at him when she reached the right place. She took another step and was out of view. He let out his breath.

A right way, a wrong way. Her pace was steady this time, unhesitating. It was as if the wrong way was barred to her, as if she was being channeled only the right way. The chanting was all around her, inside her; it had an exultant tone.

I'm here, Ramón.

Sí, señora. I was waiting for you.

Sunlight flowed between the highest pillars, spilled like molten gold downward, touching the path before her. Then the sunlight dimmed and the shadows became deep purple. She continued to walk steadily.

"Look!" Deborah cried, and pointed toward the top of the gorgons.

For a second, Charlie thought he saw a human figure; it changed, became an eagle. That damn story she had told, he thought angrily. When he looked back at the others, Tony was at the scabbard, hauling out the rifle. The twilight had turned violet, the shadows very deep and velvety. Charlie watched Tony for a second; very soon it would be too dark to see him. He drew his revolver and fired it into the air. Deborah screamed. Tony straightened, holding the rifle.

"Drop it," Charlie said. "Just let it fall straight down and then get back over here."

Tony walked toward him with the rifle in the crook of his arm.

"Put it down," Charlie said softly.

"I'm going to shoot that goddamn eagle," Tony said. His face was set in hard lines, his eyes narrowed. He took another step.

"No way," Charlie said harshly. "My wife's in there and I don't want any bullets headed anywhere near those formations. Understand?" Tony took another step toward him.

Charlie raised the revolver, held it with both hands now. His voice was still soft, but it was not easy or lazy-sounding. "One more step with that gun and I'll drop you. Put it down!"

He knew the instant that Tony recognized death staring at him, and the muscles in his neck relaxed, his stomach un-clenched. Tony put the rifle down on the ground carefully and straightened up again.

"Over by your father," Charlie said. He glanced at Don Carlos and Deborah; they were both transfixed, staring at the gorgons behind him. Tony had stopped, also staring. Deborah was the first to move; she sank to the ground by her father's chair. His hand groped for her, came to rest on her head. He took a deep breath and the spell was over.

"It's going to be dark very soon," Charlie said, hating them all, hating this damn valley, the goddamn gorgons. "Until the moon comes up, I'm not going to be able to see a damn thing and what that means is that I'll have to listen pretty hard. Tony, will you please join your father and sis-ter? You'd better all try to make yourself as comfortable as you can, because I intend to shoot at any noise I hear of anyone moving around."

Deborah made a choking noise. "Father, please, let's go back to the house. Someone's going to be killed out here!"

Tony began to walk slowly toward them. "You shouldn't have interfered," he said. He sounded very young, very frightened. "I would have ended it."

"Tony, I'm sorry. I'm sorry I brought them here. I wish I'd never seen them, either of them." Deborah was weep-ing, her face on her father's knee, his hand on her head. "This isn't what I wanted. Dear God, this isn't what I wanted."

Charlie sighed. He felt a lot of sympathy for Tony

Wyandot, who had come face-to-face with something he
could not handle, could not explain, could not buy or control. In Tony's place, he would have done exactly the same
thing: try to shoot it out of the sky, protect his property, his
sister and father, his sister's child. He would have brought
the rifle, but he would have used it, and that made the difference. Don Carlos would have used it, too, if he had decided it was necessary. He had seen Tony take defeat
before, with dignity, but this was not like that. He knew
that no matter what else happened out here tonight, Tony
would always remember that he had not fired the rifle.

Tony reached his father's side and sat on the ground,
with his knees drawn up, his arms around them. The crisis
was over.

The light had long since faded, and with darkness there had
come other changes. Constance did not so much think of
the differences as feel them, experience and accept them.
Her feet seemed far away, hardly attached to her, and her
legs were leaden. Each step was an effort, like wading in
too-deep water. The air had become dense, a pressure
against her that made breathing laborious. She walked with
one hand outstretched, not to feel her way, but almost as if
she were trying to part the air before her. She saw herself
falling forward and the thick air supporting her, wafting her
as it might a feather, setting her down gently, an end of the
journey, an end of the torture of trying to get enough air.

Señora.

I'm here, Ramón.

Sí.

It is very hard, Ramón. I'm very tired.

Sí. But you must not stop now.

I know.

Another step. It was agony to lift her foot, to find her foot and make it move. Agony to draw in enough air and then expel it. And again. She was becoming too heavy to move. Too heavy. Stonelike.

"I have to stand up," Don Carlos said. "I'm getting too stiff."

"Do you want to go to the car?" Charlie asked. "You could turn on the heater." They could have turned on the lights, he thought, knowing that even if it had occurred to him earlier, he would not have done it.

"No, no. I just want to stand for a minute and then wrap up in the blanket."

"Father," Tony said then, "let me take you back to the house. Keeping vigil in the cold can't be good for you."

"I'm all right," his father said gruffly. "It won't be much longer, I'm sure."

"Father," Tony said after a moment, "don't you see how they're manipulating you? Ramón obviously offered Meiklejohn and his wife more than Deborah agreed to pay them. This isn't going to prove anything, freezing our butts off out here in the cold. Meiklejohn," he said in a louder voice, "I'm going to the car for a flashlight. I intend to go haul your wife out of there and be done with this." There was the sound of shoes scraping rocks.

Charlie sighed. "Tony, knock it off, will you?" he said wearily. "You know I won't let you do that or anything else."

"Sit down, Tony," his father said. It was a father-to-son command, a voice that expected to be obeyed.

Silence hung over them all. "Whatever you say," Tony finally agreed. "This is the stupidest thing I've ever seen."

Charlie loosened his grip on his revolver. Tony was vacillating from the kid who had had his universe shaken to the middle-aged man who could not allow himself to embrace a new belief system, and it obviously was a painful jolt with each switch. He had tried to destroy it and failed; now he had to work even harder to deny it. Charlie couldn't stop feeling that Tony was more in the right than his father. So Constance and Ramón would stroll out eventually, and what the hell would that prove? He scowled into the darkness. Meanwhile, he intended to preserve order in the cosmos.

There were more stars every time he looked up, as if veil after veil were being removed; he never had known there were so many of them. The moon hung over the house, fattening up nicely night after night. And what if she didn't come back? He checked the thought, but there it was, fully formed, articulated in spite of his efforts to suppress it.

What if she found something after all? Something so wonderful that she couldn't turn her back on it. What if the power she was looking for turned out to be malevolent? He closed his eyes for a moment and then looked at the moon again, trying to make the jagged edge turn into mountains instead of badly torn paper.

She had not completed a movement for a very long time. She had started another step, but it seemed not to end, no matter how she struggled. And now she could hardly breathe and the lack of air made her head feel as distant as her feet and hands, and everywhere in her body there was pain, more pain than she had known she could endure.

Will she die?

I do not know.

She didn't know how hard it would be.

One never knows that.

But you did it.

Sí. Over a long period of time. Each time, the way one has gone before is easier.

You took the photographs of the gorgons, didn't you?

Sí. And I told Manuel to make certain you saw them.

Twenty-eight pillars. A lunar month. This is very holy, isn't it?

Most holy.

And one must start at sunset and arrive in moonlight. Is that right?

That is correct.

She's taking another step. Actually, she hasn't really stopped yet. But it's so slow and so hard.

She forced her leg to move again. Another step. Each step now was a victory in slow motion. So much resistance to overcome. Again she saw herself falling, floating down, down, and she yearned to rest in the heavy air, not to move, not to hurt. Another step. The chanting was in her bones; she wanted to chant, too, but she had no breath. The image of herself letting go, falling, was becoming more real each time it came back. It would be so good, so good to let go, to let the heavy air float her to the ground, where she could rest.

"What on earth will he do with the valley?" Deborah asked. "Not a resort or anything like that. But what?"

"He'll start a school," Don Carlos said. He sounded faint, his voice quavering a bit.

Charlie thought of Ramón teaching kids how to walk among the gorgons. His hands clenched hard and he consciously opened them again, flexed his fingers.

"What difference does it make?" Tony demanded. "Let

him do what he wants with the rotten valley. I sure don't intend to spend any time here ever again."

Charlie nodded. The denial was complete. Tony had saved his soul the only way he could. Everyone was clearly visible now that the moon was almost directly overhead and brilliant. The dimensions kept changing with the changing light, he thought. Right now, the valley looked as wide as a plain, and the house close enough to touch. His eyes were playing tricks. He had slept so little the night before, and the altitude was strange.

For nearly an hour now, he had been fighting the idea that she really would not come back, that when it became daylight he would have to go in after her, and he would find her huddled at the base of one of those pillars. Twice he had started to go in, and each time he had forced himself to stop, to wait. He got up and stretched and started to walk toward the meadow; anything was better than sitting on the rock much longer.

When I was a little girl, I was so certain that if I could be Beauty, I'd recognize the nobility of the Beast with no trouble at all. How I wanted to be Beauty.

I am sure you recognize evil very well.

Not as well as I should. Is this an evil thing, Ramón? To let her walk the path in ignorance, is that evil?

You are not ignorant.

But I'm here and she's there alone.

That is your choice.

No. I can be one or the other.

There is no other, only the one.

Now she knew she had to stop; she could not go on. She shuddered. She put out both hands so that they would break her fall. And she heard her own voice very clearly, "Another step, Constance. One more. Come on!"

One more. Suddenly, she was dazzled by silvery light. It struck her in the face like a physical substance and she could see out over the valley in all directions. She laughed.

At the hitching post, Charlie turned and came to a dead stop; even his heart stopped. In the center of the formations, on top the highest of the gorgons, were two figures, Constance and Ramón, shining in the moonlight. He felt the world swim out from under him and caught the post for support, closed his eyes very hard. When he opened them again, the figures were gone. He raced back toward the gorgons. When he got there, Ramón was emerging, carrying Constance.

Gently, he transferred her to Charlie's arms. Charlie watched him walk to Don Carlos and lean over him. It was very clear in the moonlight. After a moment, Don Carlos stood up.

"I didn't ask for this," he whispered, and his voice carried as if he was shouting. "I made no demands, asked for nothing."

"It is given," Ramón said. "Now we must get the señora to the house and to bed."

"Is she going to be all right?" Don Carlos asked.

"*Sí.* She is suffering from shock right now."

And Don Carlos moved without his cane, Charlie realized. Constance stirred and pressed her face against his chest. She sighed a long, plaintive breath.

Are you sure, señora? You don't have to go back now. You can stay here.

Oh no! I give it all to you, Ramón. I don't want it. I told Charlie I'd come back. That's what I want.

You can never give it all away, señora. Some of the power will cling to you forever. Some day perhaps you will come home again.

She took another deep breath, inhaling the familiar smell of Charlie's body, and she let herself go, let herself fall into the sleep she yearned for. Charlie walked to the car with her in his arms, almost blinded by tears he could not explain or stop.

TORCH SONG

CHARLIE HAD FINISHED cutting up the apple trees he had felled back in February. Delimbing, debranching, disjointing, disarming—he grinned—at least sawing them into manageable lengths; he surveyed with satisfaction the mess he had made. "Get 'em before the sap rises," his neighbor Hal Mitchum had advised, "and you can burn the wood come fall." They were old, tired trees that yielded too little to stay and caught every disease known to the apple kingdom, and worse, they threatened the well-being of the half dozen new ones he and Constance had planted. He had gotten them before the sap rose, and then rain and snow had alternated week after week and Constance had said, "Charlie, you can't just leave them all spring, all summer. They'll be covered with brambles and weeds the day after spring comes. And you can't drag them out after the daffodils are up," she added in a way that warned she meant it. She had planted the daffodils and probably knew where each one was, when it was due.

"Why don't you just hire someone to come in, do the job, clean up, and be done with it?" he said, mimicking her very well. He should have answered, Because you don't hire someone every time there's a little job to do, not when you're supposed to be retired. But she would have nailed him on that one; there had been a couple of pretty lucrative jobs he had done in the past six months.

He started down the slope toward the barn to get the tractor fired up, find a chain, start hauling the butchered trees to less sacred ground. Slipping and sliding on a layer of snow over a layer of ice that rested uneasily on a layer of oozy mud, he made his way without a glance toward the house until he had nearly reached the barn. Then he stopped when he saw a man emerge from the barn and another one watching his progress from the back patio.

He shifted the chain saw and continued to walk. City men, dressed in topcoats, the nearer one in shiny black shoes that definitely were not meant for snow and ice and mud.

"Hey, Charlie," the man at the barn said. "Carl Pulaski, remember me? We met twelve, fifteen years ago."

Charlie had never seen him before. "You just dropped by for a little visit?"

"Sort of. In the neighborhood, remembered you, knew you were around here somewhere. I'm with ATF, you remember?"

Charlie passed him to enter the barn. He glanced around swiftly but couldn't tell if anything had been moved, touched, or added. Pulaski followed him in.

"Gee, Charlie, Mr. Meiklejohn, I'm sorry you don't recall our meeting. That would have made this easier." He held out ID.

"Yep, Carl Pulaski, says so right there," Charlie murmured after a glance at it. He headed for the rear of the barn, where coils of rope and lengths of chain hung on pegs. "Thought you guys were all south for the winter— Waco, someplace like that."

"I'm in the area on official business," Pulaski said stiffly. "My associate and I want to talk to you."

"Well, I'm pretty busy right now. Like to get that wood hauled before it snows, rains, or sleets, or all three. Why don't you tell me what you want, and I'll remind you that I'm not official anything these days, and we'll both be able to get on with our work."

"Why are you on your high horse, Meiklejohn? You know you can make this as hard or as easy as you decide."

"See, Carl, when I was a wee lad, my mother taught me that if you want to pay a visit, you ring the doorbell and wait for someone to answer it. If no one shows up, you go away. You don't go snooping around outbuildings."

"We're investigating the Fircrest fire, Charlie. We need to talk to you."

Now Charlie studied him with interest. Pulaski looked frozen. His face was lean and very red at the moment. About fifty, give or take five, bareheaded and gray, pale blue eyes; he looked very earnest, sincere, like an accountant about to tell you how badly you screwed up your tax forms last year.

"What about the fire?" Charlie asked. "I know what was in the papers. You can probably still get them at the library."

"Let's go inside the house and talk," Pulaski said with an edge in his voice. "My feet hurt from the cold, and my hands are numb."

Charlie shrugged and nodded. He led the way, secure in his heavy boots now that the ground was level. Pulaski had trouble with his footing. At the patio, the second man waited. "My associate, Cy Gorman," Pulaski said, starting for the sliding door. Gorman kept his hands in his pockets.

"This way," Charlie told them, and led them to the back

porch entrance, where he began to pull off his boots. He looked pointedly at Pulaski's feet, and the agent took off his shoes. Gorman's shoes were clean; he had had enough sense to stay on the walk, which had been cleared about a hundred times that year. Inside the back hall, Charlie hung his jacket on a peg; they kept their coats on.

He took them to the living room, where he poked a smoldering log into life, added another one, and drew aside as both agents crowded closer.

Gorman was softer-looking than Pulaski, and younger. His face was pudgy, pink from the cold, and he took in the room and Charlie with darting glances that didn't seem to linger long enough for anything to register. He was blond, with thick dark eyebrows that looked pasted on.

"Anytime," Charlie said, settling into his morris chair. He motioned toward chairs, the sofa. Ashcan, the cowardly gray cat, had gone rigor mortis–stiff when they entered the room, had blended invisibly into the covering of an over-stuffed chair. Now, when Pulaski approached, Ashcan moaned and fled. Pulaski pretended not to notice, but his lean face tightened and became sharper, as if he suspected Charlie had set him up for a fright. He took off his topcoat and tossed it on the couch, sat down, and stretched out his legs toward the fire. Gorman, still standing on the hearth, shrugged out of his coat and held it. They used the same tailor, Charlie decided, and the tailor had stock in charcoal worsted. Even the ties were the same inoffensive blue-gray.

Deliberately, Pulaski said, "We're conducting an official investigation of the arson fire at the Fircrest Nursing Home during the night of March tenth. Where were you that night?"

Charlie shook his head. "Wrong approach. See, first you tell me why you're here asking questions, why ATF is involved and not the locals, and then we'll see if I can give you answers."

The other one was mute, Charlie thought then. Actually, he thought dumb, then changed it, because no one in his right mind would suggest the ATF could do anything dumb at the moment, not with tanks and heavy artillery out in force in Waco. Gorman was watching him closely, not moving, not speaking. Charlie decided to ignore him. Instead, he watched Pulaski wrestle with an interior dialogue.

At last, Pulaski said, "I'm going to give it to you straight, Charlie. We looked you up; we know your record, your background, your years as an arson investigator, then homicide, everything that's public knowledge, and more. There are mixed feelings in the agency about you, your reasons for quitting on fires, where they say you were very good. Problem is, we got a tip three days ago, a woman from the nursing home who called to report that she saw a man toss something in a car trunk that night, minutes before the fire broke out. A white car. She got three of the numbers, and the computer came up with a match for your license. That's why we're here. Where were you that night?"

"My license and how many others have those numbers?" Charlie murmured. "She called you in Washington? Not Werner Kolb over at Fircrest?"

Pulaski glanced at Gorman before he answered. "Yeah, she called us."

"That's some savvy lady," Charlie said. "Course, you guys have made it big in the news department; that might explain her knowing about you. Got her on ice?"

Pulaski set his mouth in a firm line. "I'm asking the questions, Charlie. What about Wednesday night?"

"Here."

"With your wife, I suppose."

"I think I had a dancing girl in that night. You're sure the caller was a woman?"

This time when Pulaski glanced at Gorman, Charlie was watching to catch the signal, too. A slight shake of his head, easy to miss, easy to spot now that he was looking for it.

"Loosen up, Charlie," Pulaski said. "This is a preliminary, that's all. Someone calls in a tip, we check it out. You know that."

Charlie shook his head. "Uh-huh. Like the FBI checking out a tip on a local shooting. Give me a break, Pulaski. You got a whispery voice on the phone with a phony tip, you did a background check, and three days later here you are. You don't have the caller; you don't even know if it was a man or woman. What are the other dates you're interested in?" He was satisfied when Gorman's eyes widened, then narrowed.

"We haven't mentioned any other dates," Pulaski said altogether too fast.

Charlie stood up. "You'd better move a bit away from the fire," he said to Gorman. "Your britches will scorch there."

Gorman took a step away from the hearth. "They said you were quick," he said, breaking his long silence. His voice was thin and high. "You figured we're looking into serial arson fires?"

"I figured," Charlie admitted.

Gorman nodded, then, keeping his gaze on Charlie, he said, "Give him the dates."

Pulaski rattled off five dates, the first one a year ago in February. "Can you prove where you were on any of those nights?" he demanded when he'd finished.

"If all those fires started between three and four in the morning, probably not. Can you?"

"No one said when they started," Gorman said quickly.

Charlie was glad then that Pulaski was doing most of the talking; Gorman's voice was already an irritant. He shrugged and glanced at his watch, checked it against the mantel clock, and nodded. "Gentlemen, it's been interesting. Now I'm afraid I'm going to have to ask you to get the hell out of here. Chores to do, you know how it goes."

Pulaski got to his feet, crossed the room to pick up his coat, and put it on. "It isn't just arson fire; it's also murder. Four people have died, others injured, some of them seriously, including two firemen, millions in damages. . . ."

"Will you consent to a polygraph test?" Gorman asked.

Charlie gave him a look of disgust. "No." He said to Pulaski, "You picked him too green. Toss him back out in Wyoming to ripen on brush fires a year or two." This time, Gorman's face flushed, and there was a gleam for a moment in Pulaski's eyes. "Come on, out the way you came in, or you leave your shoes here." He walked before them to the kitchen, out to the porch, and watched Pulaski put his shoes on, tie them. They left without another word; he watched until they rounded the side of the house, and then he went to the living room, where he continued to watch until they appeared in the driveway, got in a black Chevy, and drove off. Pulaski drove.

By then, Ashcan had come out from hiding, and Candy was in the living room sniffing around, first the hearth, then the chair where Pulaski had sat, the couch. Charlie watched the orange cat as she stood on her hind legs to smell the couch cushion.

Slowly, deliberately, Charlie opened his fists and flexed

his fingers. Those sons of bitches, he thought, believed their cock-and-bull story.

Constance sometimes pretended that the community of Fircrest had built the recreation center just for her. It was not a big establishment as such things went, but it had a good pool, and a good gymnasium, where she conducted self-defense classes for women three times a week and twice a week worked out with several women who were almost as good as she was in aikido. Very satisfactory, she thought that morning outside the low, sprawling building. She felt extraordinarily good, as she usually did after a workout, and there were crocuses pushing up through a crust of snow at the edge of the sidewalk. The air was cold and the sky threatening, but the crocuses knew their business, knew when it was time to melt their way through whatever lay above them.

She pulled her scarf closer to her wet head and hurried to the car. She was starved, and Charlie would be hungry after wrestling with those trees all morning. She hoped he had spent the morning getting them out of her orchard. If he hadn't, she thought, grinning at the idea, she would nag until he did. He could be so stubborn. Oxtail soup, she thought then. She had some in the freezer. She was humming by the time she completed the ten-minute trip home. Snow lingered in the fields across from the house, under the evergreens in front, in sheltered nooks and crannies, but the air smelled of crocuses and spring.

All three cats met her at the door. Candy complained hoarsely, Brutus stalked about looking furious, and Ashcan looked as if he feared she might kick him. "Don't do that," she scolded. She had never kicked a cat in her life and by now he should know he was safe. She hung up her jacket and took her scarf to the kitchen to dry, walking through cats as if they weren't there; she stopped inside the kitchen door. Newspapers were scattered across the table and Charlie was scowling at them.

"You're looking for a garage sale," she said. Then she saw a headline: NURSING HOME FIRE. And he was as furious as Brutus, she realized. His eyes had that strange, flat agate look, and his jaw was tight, his back rigid. "What happened?"

"Sit down," he said, "and I'll tell you."

She forgot her hunger and sat at the table with him and did not interrupt as he told her about his visitors. Then she said, "Cy Gorman. Wait a minute." She went up to her office on the second floor. Charlie began to refold the newspapers. He was finished and had them back in the recycle bin by the time she returned.

"A forensic psychiatrist," she said, moving past him to get the soup from the freezer.

"Might have known," Charlie muttered. "A goddamn shrink. He looked like one, acted like one. No offense," he added darkly.

"None taken, since I'm not a goddamn shrink," Constance said. She was a psychologist, retired more or less, just as he was retired more or less. They were the busiest retired people she had ever heard of. She put a bowl of frozen soup in the microwave. She had made the soup on the woodstove, which even then had the house a touch too warm, but for thawing and reheating, it was microwave every time. She returned to the table and sat down again. "What are you going to do?"

"Nothing. They think they've got a case, let them prove it."

"Have you talked to Werner Kolb yet?"

He shook his head. "They've already got to Werner, told him to dummy up," he said.

"Probably, and if he stalls you, you'll know it for a fact and I'll get Marion to set up something." Charlie gave her a look and she shrugged. Marion had been in her class last year. "Did you see the expression on Werner's face when she put that football player down at the exhibition? He'll talk to you."

"To you maybe," Charlie said, and he knew he was simply being contrary, but he seemed powerless to stop himself. Talk to her, talk to him, same thing. He remembered the exhibition Constance and their daughter Jessica had put on; he would never forget that.

The microwave dinged, and Constance got up to stir the soup; she returned it to the oven, then brought out placemats and bowls, a loaf of bread and butter. Charlie started a pot of coffee. Of course, he wasn't going to do nothing, he thought savagely, but damned if he knew where to start. Arson fires that went back more than a year. *They* had the manpower, the equipment, the necessary information. Same method each time? A letter of warning, or a gloat after the fact? A calling card left at the scene? It wasn't merely that they had all started around the same time of night, either; arsonists often started their fires between midnight and dawn. But something tied them all together, and they knew what it was. And if they had looked up his record, talked to people, they knew he wouldn't take this without fighting back.

"I think they are stymied and see this as an excuse to get you to work on their case for them," Constance said.

He wished to hell she wouldn't do that, apparently follow his line of thought, and even complete it. "Is it soup yet?" he asked coldly.

It was, and they sat down to eat and didn't talk now. Constance finished first. "Good soup," she murmured. Then she said, "If you have the dates, we can find out where the fires were from the computer database."

Charlie pulled his notebook out and opened it to the last entry, the dates Pulaski had rushed through. Constance studied them and then stiffened.

"Charlie, where is that letter you got last winter? You know, the threatening letter?"

He put down his spoon and left the table. He knew exactly where it was, in the file labeled "Threats." Not the same date, he thought, hoped, when he pulled out the folder and extracted the last item he had filed there. The letter was postmarked in New York City on February 11 of last year; the first date he had jotted down was February 10. He returned to the kitchen and put the envelope on the table between them. They both knew the contents: words cut out of a newspaper, pasted on a sheet of lined paper. There had been no fingerprints on the letter, and only smudges on the envelope. The letter said: "You will feel my pain."

Constance did not touch the letter; she looked at the postmark and then at Charlie. "I'm scared," she said softly.

He got up and went to stand behind her chair, put his arms around her. "Take it easy, honey," he said, and kissed the top of her head. Her hair was still moist and fragrant. "We don't know that it's connected. Some nut out there wanted to get my goat, that's all. How many letters like that do you suppose I have in that file? Dozens, starting way back."

She did not relax. "If someone's been planning this for over a year," she said, "time's on his side. We don't have a clue about what else he might come up with."

"Then we'd better get moving," Charlie said, and kissed

her head again. "Enough of this lollygagging about. I'll go start on the computer."

She cleared the table, put the dishes in the dishwasher, and finally opened the envelope and read the message again. "You will feel my pain." It was connected. She knew it was. That had been step one. The tip to the ATF offices step two. Four people had been killed in the fires, many others injured. Suddenly, the house felt cold.

"Good heavens," Constance said when Charlie appeared later holding a printout with dozens of entries.

"Right," he said. "A fireman's job is never done." He had a map under his arm that he now spread on the table, and they began to locate the sites. At first, Charlie penciled them in with small *x*'s, but after a moment Constance left to get a jar of dried beans; then they continued, placing a bean on the name of each town and city in the northeastern part of the country that had reported fires on the dates Pulaski had provided. Buffalo, a two-bean city; Poughkeepsie; New York City, too many to fit on the map; Middletown; Pittsfield . . . After several minutes, Charlie straightened and grunted. Slowly, he began to remove the beans. He left four.

"September fourth, 'ninety-two," he said in a low voice. There were nine entries. After locating them all, he put a bean on Utica. "December seventeenth." Seven entries. He put a bean on Norwich, New York, and drew back to regard the map.

Six beans, six fires, and the most distant one—Danbury, Connecticut—was less than a hundred miles away. The beans might have marked a deformed wheel, with Fircrest in the center.

"I don't blame Pulaski and his crew," he said. "I'd have come here, too."

Constance made a note of the towns and then gathered up the beans silently. They would have to verify them, she knew, but no doubt the list was right: If you're making a noose, you make it tight enough not to slip off.

That afternoon, they drove over to the Fircrest Nursing Home. It was a three-story gray-stone building, built in 1889, a school originally, a prison for a short time, a government building during World War II, vacant for many years after that, and refurbished as a nursing home seventeen years earlier. The stench of recent fire was in the air. He hated that smell more than anything else he could think of.

Dense shrubbery would have screened a car from view here on both the first and second floor, he decided, driving slowly past the front of the building. From the third floor, only the top part would have been visible, no license plate, no trunk opening. On the side of the building he had already passed was a paved parking area, and beyond that were high evergreen trees. He drove around the other corner. Both sides of the building had columnar evergreens five feet from the stone, a screen for the inhabitants, allowing them to open windows, get some air, and still have privacy, but also blocking their view of the street. He continued to creep along the street to a drive that went in behind the building, no doubt a continuation of the other one that went to the parking lot. Here a tall streetlamp would have cast enough light, he thought, but again the shrubs and the angle indicated that no one from inside could have seen a license plate.

"You're not going in, are you?" Constance asked in her most neutral voice.

"Nope," he said. "Just wanted to see. When I get a lawyer, we'll come back and take pictures, prove a point."

She gave him a sharp look. "Have you figured out why anyone would try to burn down a stone building?"

He whistled softly and entered the driveway. He stopped the car at the center of the rear of the building and they both gazed at it. The back part had been expanded at some point, and the expansion had been made of wood, which was charred, and in some places burned completely away as high as the roof. The burn pattern formed steep, jagged peaks, like the stock market at its craziest. From here, they could see that the interior had been gutted.

Before Charlie shifted gears to start driving again, he saw in his rearview mirror an ancient blue Ford pull into the driveway. He turned off his motor and waited. The car pulled in close and Werner Kolb got out, came to his window. In his bulky jacket, he looked like a moving barrel.

"Charlie, Constance, how you folks doing? Thought I saw your car heading this way."

"It got away from you, didn't it?" Charlie said, nodding toward the building. "How the devil did it get up there so fast? Somebody take a blowtorch to it?"

"Pret near, I guess. We figure it was gas in a sprayer, a paint sprayer, or the kind you use for trees, something like that."

"Someone's living dangerously," Charlie muttered, thinking of gasoline under pressure. "The others like this?"

"Same pattern, far's they can tell. I'm not supposed to be talking to you."

"Figured that."

"Well, I told them they were barking up the wrong tree, but that's not what they wanted to hear. Told them how you come over to the station couple times a year, talk to the boys, give them pointers, all that, and they said that could be part of the pattern, keeping your hand in, irresistible urges or something. Told them if anyone's crazy around here, it ain't you."

"Where were the others?" Charlie asked.

Werner told him; it was the same list Constance had already written. "Gotta go," Werner said. "Marion's always complaining it takes me longer to go out and buy a jug of milk than it takes the cows to make it. See you around, Charlie." He started to move away, stopped, and drew an envelope from his pocket. "Oh, 'most forgot. You might want to look this over." He handed it to Charlie, waved to Constance, and turned to leave.

"Hey, Werner," Charlie said as he ambled away, "I owe you. Next time you have a benefit, I'll come twice."

Werner chuckled and kept walking.

A sprayer. Charlie thought of Pulaski in his barn, examining his sprayer, sniffing it, maybe photographing it. Constance put her hand on his thigh as he started to drive and after a moment he covered her hand with his. He wondered if she knew how bad this could get. When she squeezed his leg, he knew she did.

When they got home, Candy met them, demanding explanations in a raucous voice, her tail upright and quivering in indignation. Ashcan begged to be forgiven. Charlie eyed him moodily; that cat never had been able to shake his Catholic upbringing. In the kitchen, they found Brutus asleep on top of the warming oven of the wood cookstove. They ignored him; what it would take to break him of that habit would be having his tail catch on fire.

"The classic question now is, Do you have any enemies?" Constance said. She went to the freezer to contemplate packages and packages.

Charlie snorted. "Does a vulture have bad breath?"

She closed the door empty-handed. "I think three to six months would be long enough to consider, don't you?"

He waited. He had taken the papers from the envelope Werner had handed him.

"I mean before the first fire, of course," she went on, gazing past him absently. "But I simply can't think of anything you did in that period that would bring a response like this." She tapped her lips with her finger. "Maybe six months is too short."

"Go for the last thirty years," he said, and started to scan the six fire reports with the details that never made it to the daily papers. Now he simply looked them over; later he would read them thoroughly. February 10, 1992, Danbury, Connecticut: a movie theater. March 28, 1992, Middletown, New York: a strip mall, one shopkeeper killed. July 9, 1992, Pittsfield, Massachusetts: two warehouses destroyed, one watchman killed, one transient. September 4, 1992, Utica, New York: a paint factory burned down, a vice president killed. December 17, 1992, Norwich, New York: a high school damaged. March 10, 1993, Fircrest, New York: a nursing home. He tossed the reports on the table. "I'm going out to finish that damn wood," he said.

She nodded. He could always think better if his body was in motion, or at the very least his hands. Now he would fool around with his trees and think. She read the reports and then began to pace the kitchen, the living room, and finally upstairs.

When Charlie came in, it was getting dark, and although the temperature had been dropping steadily, he was sweating. He sniffed: lamb, green beans, tomatoes, lots of garlic and onions. "Aye, and it's a good woman you are, Constance," he said.

"God knows I try," she said demurely. He swacked her bottom as she walked by him.

"What's all that?" he said, pointing to many papers on the table—faxes, from the looks of them.

"Shower, change, relax. I'm about to have a glass of wine, and when you come back all dewy fresh and fragrant, you can have some, too." This time when he reached out to give her another pat, she caught his wrist, and he knew she could have put him down in the middle of the floor if she had wanted. Instead, she drew his arm around her waist and kissed him. She stepped back and shook her head; her nose wrinkled. "Just as I thought. You are in great need of a shower."

Laughing, he went upstairs to shower.

"Now," she said later, showing him the faxes while he sipped his wine. "I kept thinking of all the work you did last year, all white-collar crimes. Those men will never go to trial. They'll deal with their companies, pay fifty cents on the dollar, and retire."

He nodded. He had come to the same conclusion.

"And I tried to think of all the people you've made angry around here over the years. A very long list," she added gravely, "but not enough for anyone to retaliate this way. You have a knack at winning poker and you might make some of your buddies sore, but this sore? I don't think so."

He nodded, keeping his expression as serious as hers, enjoying this.

"So I called Loretta Halliday," she went on, startling him. "I got a list of people who were released from New York State or federal prisons for the three months before the first fire. Another long list, I'm afraid."

Charlie stared at her, awed. He had planned to get that list, but it had not occurred to him to call and just ask for it. Loretta Halliday had been on the state corrections board for as long as he could remember, and she was a dragon. "What in God's name do you have on Loretta?" he asked. "I might want to use it someday."

"Now, Charlie. I simply told her you received a threatening letter and refused to take it seriously, but that I did. Since she thinks men are such idiots, that seemed a logical approach. She was very cooperative."

He laughed and drained his glass. Besides, he might have added, Loretta knew the information was available to anyone who wanted to dig a little.

"The trouble is," she said, "I don't know many of these people from a long time ago, from when you were still with the police. It's going to be up to you to sort it all out."

By the time Constance had dinner on the table, Charlie had culled thirteen names from the list. In each case, he had been the investigating officer, the arresting officer, or had testified in court, often all three. He was gazing at his short list moodily when Constance called him to dinner.

"Ah, memories," he said, putting his list on a table by his chair. Then he demanded, "Why is it when you cook, I have a lapful of cats in here, and when I cook, I have the kitchen full of the damn beasts?"

"I feed them before I start," she said, "as I have told you more times than I can count."

He made them wait, he thought, tossing Brutus off his lap, so they could have table scraps, which was the natural order of things.

He did not mention his short list during dinner, and only

when they had coffee and a leftover apple kuchen did he say almost casually, "I think I know who it is."

She put her fork down. "You're kidding!"

He went to get his list, and then said, "These struck me as possibles." He pointed to the first name. "John Scovotto used a knife and he got caught. Bad temper, very bad. Acted on the spur of the moment, a flash of rage with an irresistible impulse to kill. I don't think so." He pointed to the next name. "Lincoln Trowbridge liked a baseball bat, drug stuff. Nope. Gary Thomson, armed robbery, several times, I believe. He forgave me on the spot. The way he saw it, he was doing his thing and I was doing mine. Reasonable sort of fellow. Barbara Jelinsky killed her pimp in a fight. Not her style—arson, planning." He went on down the list, remembering all of them. . . . He paused at one and said thoughtfully, "I considered him a bit longer. Wade Lee. He killed his wife, her mother, and a neighbor who happened to be in the wrong place, wrong time. Then he set the house on fire. After insurance, and really stupid. Too stupid." He shook his head and pointed again. "Don Flexner. He was plenty sore, but he couldn't plan far enough ahead to get a bus transfer." Finally, he pointed to a name he had skipped over.

"Peter Eisenbeis," he said. "A great-looking kid, tall, blond, blue eyes, football type. A real planner, too." He could tell from the alarmed expression on Constance's face that she remembered him.

The look of fear vanished; her face became expressionless, and she asked in a low voice, "When did they release him?"

"December tenth, 'ninety-one."

They were both thinking about the anonymous threat: "You will feel my pain."

God, Charlie thought suddenly, all this was making him feel old. Thirteen years ago, yet he remembered as if it had happened last week. Pete Eisenbeis had scoped out a warehouse on the East River, not far from where his girlfriend lived. One Friday afternoon, he had gone there to apply for a job and, application in hand, had roamed the building with no one paying much attention. At four, an armored truck arrived and at the same time a fire broke out in half a dozen places at once. The kid had walked up to the truck just as the guard on the passenger side opened his door and stepped out. The kid had shot and wounded him, had taken his place, and the truck had sped off. With all the confusion of alarms, fire equipment arriving with sirens blaring, workers rushing around, the truck was lost.

Charlie had found Pete's prints on the application, on a door facing, a metal girder, and he had gone through the neighborhood with his description and had come up with a name, Peter, and his girlfriend's name, Marla Sykes. No one approached her; they waited. Two days later, Peter Eisenbeis returned. Charlie should not have been involved in the chase, but he and the stakeout were trying to decide if they should wait outside the tenement or go in after him, when Marla and Pete reappeared; he was carrying a baby. He spooked, shoved the girl and baby inside the car, and raced off. Charlie's car was the one that hung on his bumper through the Upper East Side. By then, other cars were converging, and the kid crashed his car. He was barely injured, a few scrapes; the girl was hurt slightly more. The baby was thrown thirty or forty feet and suffered massive brain damage. Pete was sent up. The baby lived, but he would have been better off if he hadn't, from all accounts.

"You will feel my pain."

"They didn't find the money," Charlie said, remembering. Pete had taken them to the spot where he'd hidden the truck, out on Long Island. They had found the driver's body chained to a water pipe in a bathroom of an empty house; he had suffered a heart attack. Pete swore he had left everything in the truck. His plan was to get Marla, take the cash, and get out of the country. At least $280,000 in cash vanished, and millions in checks, paper of various kinds.

Constance was thinking of the two youngsters. Marla had been seventeen, Pete nineteen. Her mother had told her to get out with the baby; Pete said he did it for her, for their son, so they could have a life. The public defender took a plea bargain for him: twenty-five years. But now he was out. She rubbed goose bumps on her arms.

"Hey," Charlie said softly, taking her cold hand. "At least we have a place to begin, more than we had a couple of hours ago." He was grateful she didn't tell him to take this business to Pulaski. He could imagine the pitying look on that lean face, because he was certain he had worn such a look many times when a suspect cried, "I've been framed!"

When Constance went downstairs the next morning, Charlie was making blueberry waffles, whistling. Water droplets still clung to his crinkly black hair; it was hard to tell the droplets from the few gray hairs. She liked his hair, she was thinking, pouring coffee, when the phone rang.

They listened to a woman's voice explaining why she wouldn't make it to the aikido class that morning. When she finished, Constance said, "I'll give Sandy a call and have her take over for me." Sandy was good enough to lead the group, she had decided during the night as she lay staring into darkness. Charlie had been up and down several

times and she had been awake every time he left the bed
without a sound.

"I don't think so," he said, at the counter, taking a waffle
from the iron. "Look, perfect, is it not?"

She agreed. He gave it to her on a plate and poured in
more batter. "I'm going to be on the phone all morning.
Pete's probation officer, where he reports, what he's up to,
what he did in the jug, where Marla is now . . . stuff like
that. You might as well be doing the usual thing. Let them
worry that we're not taking any of this bullshit seriously.
Okay?"

She nodded, her mouth full.

He was on the phone in his little downstairs office when
she left for the recreation center, and he was on it when she
returned two hours later. She waved to him from the doorway and he nodded, listening. He looked tired, she thought
with dismay. Now and then, she caught him in a certain
light, in a certain pose and realized that he was growing
older before her eyes. Most of the time, such thoughts
never came to mind; he was young in every way she could
think of. But in fact, he was getting gray, and at the moment he looked tired. He hung up and regarded her with
those strange, flat eyes that he sometimes showed her, and
she knew it wasn't just that he was tired; he also was
frightened.

She held her breath for a moment, then grinned and said,
"I think a workout was just what I needed. How'd you
make out?"

He shook his head. "I shouldn't have let you go out
alone. I'm acting like a fool, honey."

"Why? What happened?"

"Nothing. I began to think: If our guy is really Pete
Eisenbeis, what hurt him most? Going to prison or losing

his lover and his child? I don't want us separated until we see this through. Okay?"

She could feel his fear radiating out to her, enveloping her. She nodded wordlessly and went to him at his desk, held his head tightly against her; he wrapped his arms around her and drew her even closer.

"He's dropped out of sight, broken probation," Charlie said, the words muffled against her breast. "He's out there somewhere, maybe watching us, watching you."

Dear God, she thought. Oh dear God!

The phone on the desk rang. He drew back and picked up the receiver. "Yeah," he said, then listened and made a note or two. "Right. I'll call if there's anything else. Thanks, Brian." Brian Possner was an investigator he sometimes used in New York City.

"Let's go sit down and I'll tell you what I have," Charlie said. "Hungry?"

She shook her head. Hand in hand, they went to the living room, where he sat in his morris chair and she in the wing chair, close enough that they could touch each other.

"Okay," he said. "He got out and two days later turned up at Marla's place. She has a house down around Tuxedo Park, been there all these years with the boy. She said she sent him away, and no one's laid eyes on him since. He's skipped, probably with two hundred eighty grand. She hasn't heard from him. That's for openers. She married Steve Boseman a year after Pete went up, and a year later Boseman was killed. They figure he was in the drug game or numbers; it had the marks of a gangland killing—hands tied behind his back, shot in the back of the head. He was dumped in a creek and drowned a few miles from where they lived. She's been alone since then. But she visited Pete once a month all the time he was in the pen."

"Why? If she married someone else . . ."

"Don't know. We'll ask."

Constance nodded. Crazy, she was thinking.

"What I thought we might do," Charlie said, "is take a little spin over to Utica and then down to Norwich. If you're really not hungry yet."

"We can get some lunch along the way," she said. "I'll change first." She was wearing sweatpants and a sweatshirt, running shoes. He thought she looked good the way she was.

She drove. It was less than an hour's drive to Utica. He directed her to Grant Street, where the paint factory had burned down. And it would have burned to the ground, Charlie knew; it had been made of wood. Explosions, toxic fumes, roiling, poisonous smoke . . . The site had been cleared and fenced. This was an industrial area with ugly gray buildings and trucks, ugly gray slush, a railroad siding. . . . A road led around back of the property; the fence was new. Anyone could have parked within a hundred feet, walked in, sprayed the place, tossed the match, and out.

He directed her past a hospital, past Utica College, onto State 12. Another good road, she thought, driving. All the places had been on good roads, accessible. Rain started to fall. Don't freeze, she ordered. Just don't start freezing.

In Norwich, an hour later, they drove around the high school building. The gymnasium, an annex, had been destroyed; the school building had been saved.

Constance stopped for a bunch of teenagers who couldn't decide if they wanted to cross the street or not. They didn't seem to notice that they were getting wet.

Charlie scowled at the kids. He'd be leaning on the horn, he thought, and they'd flip him off and make him even madder. He'd end up yelling; one of them would pull a gun. . . . They moved out of the way and Constance edged past them; they didn't seem to notice the car. She turned to circle the school again, and Charlie touched her arm.

"Let's go find something to eat," he said. This was a bust. The school would have been a cinch at three in the morning. A quiet neighborhood, everyone sleeping. Something was nagging at him, and he couldn't get at it. Something was screwy, he thought, then realized he was thinking like an arson investigator. What was behind the fires? Not killing anyone, not a spectacular show. He couldn't have hung around to watch, he thought, or said—he wasn't sure which, because Constance made a sound that sounded like agreement. A stranger in a small place like this would have been noticed. Even in Utica, around the warehouses, no stranger would have gone unnoticed. And Fircrest? Forget it.

Constance interrupted his train of reasoning. "What you should do," she said grimly, "is find us the quickest way home, without going over mountains on narrow roads."

He looked at her questioningly.

"The rain's starting to freeze," she said.

By the time they reached their driveway, three hours later, the car was riding on ice like a hockey puck. Charlie let out his breath as she pulled into the garage. "Ya done good, babe," he said.

She gave him a mean look. "I'm just about ready to faint from hunger. You cook."

That night, Charlie dreamed of the fire, his fire. He was in the endless corridor, where every doorknob burned his hand as the fire roared behind him, forcing him on until he couldn't breathe and his knees were buckling. He woke up, to find Constance's arms around him. He drew in a long breath, another, and said, "Thrashing about a bit?"

"A bit," she said.

He was soaking wet, the way he always was after that dream. "Shower," he mumbled, pulling away from her. A moment later, as he stood under the hot water turned on full force, her shadow fell on the glass door; she opened the door and stepped in beside him.

"Wanton hussy." He reached for her.

"Damn right," she said.

Charlie hated it that he never could sleep later than seven, but there it was. They had remade the bed last night, and the last thing he remembered was seeing Constance turn the clock away. She intended to sleep late. He grinned; on the whole, he felt better than the few hours of sleep warranted. He was whistling as he made coffee and fed the cats. Constance was right; they stayed out from underfoot as he scrambled eggs. He took his plate to the table and only then glanced out the glass doors to the patio, and he stopped whistling. Iced in. Ice coated everything. He turned on the radio for weather news.

When Constance came down at nine, at first he thought her radiant smile was for him, but then he saw that she was gazing past him at the world turned into fairyland.

"Oh," she said, and went to the door.

"And good morning to you, too," he said huffily.

A thin coating of ice glistened on every blade of grass, every twig, every tree branch; already it was starting to drip diamonds. The weather forecast said it would be gone by noon. If he could go out there with a giant heat machine, he thought, he'd do it, and it would be gone now. He continued to watch her at the door, and when she turned away finally, whatever it was on his face changed her smile into an expression tender and private. Charlie didn't think anyone on earth but him had ever seen that look.

"I'll make you some scrambled eggs," he said. "I'll even bring your coffee."

She nodded and sat down, then eyed the table curiously. He had brought out the road map, a calendar, his notebook, and the faxes of ex-cons' names, and she couldn't tell what else.

He brought coffee and went back to the counter near the sink. "Onions, cheese?" he asked.

"Everything. I'm starved."

He laughed and began breaking eggs, enough for both of them; he was starved again, too. When they were both eating, he said, "I looked for a pattern for the dates—zilch. Two on a Saturday, one on Tuesday, and like that. No pattern. And they're spread out over the months, too. Not the first week, or the last, just sort of random. No pattern there, or in the intervals between fires." Always look for patterns, he had advised rookies in training. But you don't always find them, he now added.

"So, what's the plan?" she asked, motioning toward the papers he had pushed to one side.

"First, I want to see the other sites, just to check them out. I don't know what I'm looking for, to be honest. Then, a visit to Marla."

"You think he might be hanging around her?"

"Maybe," he said soberly. "I hope to God he is."

He would take his gun, she knew, and no doubt Peter Eisenbeis would be armed. Slowly she said, "Charlie, listen a minute. You know a lot of people, and most of them will be like Werner, on your side. An APB on Pete might catch him in a day or two. You don't have to do this by yourself."

"The people who really count won't be like Werner," he said. He had already considered this; he gave her an abbreviated version of where his considerations had led him. "First, he skipped out on his parole officer, so they already have a bulletin out. Second, he might lead them to nearly three hundred thousand in cash and millions in paper, so they're looking. Third, even if they get him, I'm not off the hook, because he's bound to have as good an alibi as mine, or better. Fourth," he finished, "they already think they know who torched those buildings; they aren't looking for anyone else." What they were doing, he knew, was sending flocks of agents out to every location, asking questions about a white car, a stocky man with dark hair turning gray, flashing his picture. . . .

"So where do we start today?" Constance asked when he became silent.

"Toss a coin. We can go over to Pittsfield and on down to Danbury, and Tuxedo Park, or we can go down to Middletown first and then Marla. Can't do all three sites in one day and still get to Marla, I'm afraid. I thought we'd pack a suitcase, pile up in a motel tonight, then hang around Tuxedo Park tomorrow and ask a few questions."

"It will be mountain driving all day if we go to Middletown," Constance said, and he said, "Right." They decided on Pittsfield and points south. An hour later when they started, the ice was gone, and most of the lingering snow with it.

Charlie drove today, mostly on the interstates, and too fast. "Pittsfield," he said as they neared the town in Massachusetts. "Two adjacent warehouses, one furniture, the other a wholesaler for craft supplies. Two dead, a watchman and a transient, who apparently sneaked in and went to sleep." Soon they had entered a district of warehouses and car lots. Again the building sites they were looking for were closed off with a new fence, and again access would have been simple without the fence. Just warehouses with loading docks, drives, parking areas, a road behind everything, fields behind that, and nothing in the way of anyone with a sprayer filled with gas. He could have been heading out U.S. 7 before an alarm went off. What he couldn't have done was hang around and watch the show.

Charlie was tempted to skip the next one, but since he was driving on U.S. 7, and Danbury was on the way, he headed for the theater site. It would be the same, he thought, disgruntled, pondering the question of how Pete had been able to find such ideal places in such a short time. Had he drawn a circle on a map and worked only within the circumference? It looked like it. What he would give, he thought then, to find such a map with Pete's prints all over it, with each town circled in red. . . .

"You don't suppose he knew any of those people who died, do you?" Constance asked. She was looking at the descriptions of the victims: a shopkeeper in Middletown, fifty-eight, lived there all his life; a chemist who had lived in Utica for twenty years, vice president of the paint company. The transient had been twenty-four, bumming around after serving in the navy for four years; the watchman, sixty-four. . . . She gave it up. Charlie didn't bother to respond. He didn't suppose.

The theater in Danbury was constructed of brick and wood; it had been repaired, the first of the buildings to be burned, the first one fixed again. It would have been the biggest challenge, too, Charlie thought as he drove through an alley behind the building. On the other side of the alley was a medical complex with a large parking lot, and a Methodist church on the corner, but the alley was narrow, and this was practically in the center of town. He must have driven exactly where Charlie was edging along. This was the only place where he had run any risk at all. But at three in the morning, who would be up looking? He suspected Pulaski would be concentrating on Danbury, maybe going from house to house, betting on the theory that someone was always up and looking. The fire had not done as much damage here as in the other buildings they had inspected. Pete had been learning on the job. By the time he hit the warehouses in Pittsfield, he had been a real pro who did not take risks.

An hour and fifteen minutes later, they checked into a motel in Tuxedo Park and got directions for Cedar Falls, which turned out to be a hamlet a few miles to the west. Charlie nodded as he drove through Cedar Falls: a supermarket with prices posted in the windows, and a smaller, more discreet grocery without signs in the windows, an antique shop, a few small houses set back off the highway. A Porsche and a Cadillac were in a gas station being serviced. A fine Victorian house partly hidden by trees had a sign swinging in the breeze: CHELSEY HOUSE.

"Restaurant," Constance said. "Look at the size of that parking lot!"

The road narrowed when they left the tiny town: a slender black snake frozen in motion. The woods were dense here; the only indications that there were also houses were the many driveways that vanished among trees and shrubs. Most of the entrances had gates or chains. Some of them had signs with names. He spotted the name Boseman with a sigh of relief. That driveway had neither gate nor chain, but it wound among trees just like the rest, to a large, handsome split-level house with a lot of windows and a turn-around at the front entrance.

"Well," he said, "little Marla struck it rich."

She could have used a yardman, Constance thought as they went to the front door. The grounds were unkempt, overgrown with shrubs and flower beds that had been neglected for years and were a mass of decaying flower stalks, weeds, and leaves. Seedling maples had been allowed to grow, crowding one another, all spindly.

The door was opened by a young woman who looked surprised to see them. "Oh, I was expecting someone else. What do you want?"

"Can we talk?" Charlie asked pleasantly. "We're looking for Peter Eisenbeis."

She started to close the door; he held it open. "I don't know where he is," she said sharply. "I told them that already."

She was slender and pretty, dressed in jeans and sneakers and an oversized white sweater. Her hair was black and long, caught up in a ponytail tied with a red ribbon. She looked almost exactly the way he remembered her from thirteen years ago.

"Mrs. Boseman—Marla—Pete's in very serious trouble. I have to find him before it gets even worse." His voice was gentle; he made no motion to push the door open.

She looked from him to Constance, back. A slight frown appeared on her forehead as she studied him. "Who are you?" she asked, nearly whispering.

"Meiklejohn. I arrested Pete thirteen years ago."

"Why did you come here? What's he done? I told you, I don't know where he is!" She stepped back from the door.

They followed her into the house. "Let's just talk," Charlie said. "Maybe you know something and just haven't thought of it."

She shook her head but made a vague motion toward an arch on one side of the foyer they had entered. Inside the house, the same lack of attention showed that was evident on the grounds; there was dust on a sideboard near the door, and an empty vase, also dusty. A pale blue rug that was deep and soft was also dirty, with a trail of footprints embedded in it. The room she led them to was spacious, with twin sofas, many chairs with damask covers, everything dirty, dusty, uncared for, all the expensive furnishings untended. She waved toward the sofas, and she perched on the edge of a chair. Almost immediately, she stood up again.

"I have to do something," she said. "I'll be right back." She hurried from the room, and after a moment Charlie and Constance followed. He kept his hand in his pocket, where he had put his .38.

They trailed after her up a short flight of stairs and saw her enter a room. Moving without a sound, they went to the open door, and now they could hear her voice; it had softened and sounded musical.

"Honey, I won't be long, and Roy will be here any minute. He's running a little late today, he said. Do you want me to put on a movie? . . . *Beauty and the Beast* again? . . . How about *The Canterville Ghost*? I'll just raise the chair a little. Here we go. . . ."

She continued to speak in a soothing, comforting tone. Looking through the doorway, Charlie could see the boy, her son, an elongated figure on a reclining wheelchair—so thin, he hardly raised the sheet. For a second, he looked bald, but then Charlie could see pale, fuzzy hair. His head appeared oversized for the thin neck; his arms on the sheet were skeletal, and he did not make a sound. The elaborate wheelchair was near French windows leading to a balcony, and a mammoth television was against the wall opposite his bed. A round maple table and a single chair were close to the bed. Silently, Charlie drew back when he felt Constance's fingers on his arm. They returned to the living room and sat without speaking until Marla reappeared in the arched doorway. The sound track of a movie was barely audible.

Before Marla could enter the room, the doorbell rang, and she ran to open it. "Roy, thank God! He's had a terrible day, and he's so tired."

A large man walked past the arch, his head cocked as he listened to Marla. "I think if you just let him soak for a long time and then give him a massage, maybe he'll relax enough to eat something." Her voice faded as they passed out of sight.

A minute later, she was back, and this time she sat down. "I'll tell you what I told the others," she said. "And that's all I can tell you."

She was as rigid as a department-store mannequin. Her white-knuckled fingers clutching the chair arms looked frozen.

"Pete came here a day or two after he got out," she said in a low, fast monotone. "I told him to leave and he did. I haven't seen him since and I haven't heard from him."

Charlie held up his hand. "Not quite so fast, Mrs. Boseman."

"Don't call me that," she said sharply.

"All right," Charlie said. "But you see, we really do need to find Pete. Mind if we look around a little, just to make the record complete."

She jumped up. "You think he's here? I'm hiding him?

I told you, we had a fight and I threw him out. Be my guest, help yourself, look. I'm going to make Nathan something to eat." She left the room swiftly, without a backward glance.

When Charlie stood and glanced at Constance, she shook her head and walked out after Marla. He started to explore the large house.

Constance followed Marla to the kitchen and stood back out of the way as she began to prepare food for her son. The kitchen was spotless. It was ultramodern, with a cooking island, stainless steel everywhere, white tiles, white appliances, all gleaming. An adjoining room that overlooked the back of the property held a television, comfortable chairs with russet-and-green covers, a dining table and chairs. That room looked used, as if this was where she spent her time. Half a dozen fashion magazines were on a sofa, jewelry and garden catalogs.

Marla was cutting up cooked carrots; she put them in a commercial blender and whirred them briefly, added milk and whirred them again, and scraped them into a small plastic bowl; she tasted the puree, added salt and a half teaspoon of sugar, stirred, and tasted it again. She put a lid on it and began to cut up potatoes to repeat the process. The food had the consistency of cream. A piece of well-done steak was next; she blended it with stock until it was like a thin soup. When the dinner was prepared, she put the bowls into a microwave.

She washed the blender and made a milk shake with frozen strawberries, a banana, half an apple, milk, and a scoop of ice cream. She poured it into a plastic glass and snapped on the kind of top used for toddlers just learning to drink from a glass. She put it in the refrigerator.

Finally, she looked at Constance. "What are you, an investigator for the health department or something?"

Constance shook her head. "It must take him longer to eat the food than for you to prepare it. Will he eat much of it?"

Marla seemed to sag, then straightened again and walked to the table across the room. "He eats enough," she said, gazing out the wide windows.

A long ramp went to the back of the yard; there was a concrete walk that curved around bushes and trees. Thick, high shrubbery screened the entire back; no other house was visible. The back section looked well tended, with several raised flower beds. "You work out there?" Constance asked.

Marla nodded. "He likes to be outside, watch me plant things, weed, pick flowers."

"Why do you stay here, so isolated? It must be lonely for you."

"Boseman did that to me," Marla said after a moment. "I can't sell the house, or his car, or anything. I can use it for as long as I want to, but I can't sell out. I'm stuck here. He did that."

"What about Boseman?" Constance asked. "How on earth did such a man enter your life, yours and Nathan's?"

Marla went to the window and pressed her forehead against the glass. "Funny," she said. "No one ever asked that. They asked everything else, but not that." She glanced at Constance, who had moved to stand beside her at the window. "He got the gun for Pete, and the car; he knew all about it. Later, when Nathan was in the hospital, he came around, to collect what Pete owed him, he said. I told him to go talk to Pete. He wanted to make out with me. You know? And I said no. He asked what it would take and

I said a ring, the piece of paper, the whole works. He laughed. But then he said, 'Why not?' I thought he meant it, but he had me sign papers, and after he was gone, I found out what I'd signed. We can stay here, I can drive the Buick, but nothing's mine, except the Datsun. His mother gets it all the day I leave." Tiredly, she added, "I'll stay; it's a good home for Nathan, better than anything I could afford."

Constance wished Marla would sit at the table so she could sit across from her and study her face as she spoke. The profile told her nothing. Her sweater was a very fine cashmere and the earrings were dangling garnets. Not cheap, but not insurable jewelry, either. She didn't look destitute, Constance decided, and got no further than that with her examination.

"At first," Marla was saying in a low voice, "he thought I knew where the money was, where Pete had stashed it, and he thought he'd get me and the money sooner or later, but when he saw that I really didn't know, he began to change. He taught me how to drive and bought the little Datsun for me. He wanted to take a trip, a late honeymoon."

"Ah," Constance said thoughtfully. "So he didn't object when you continued to go visit Pete."

Marla gave her a sharp look. "He wanted me to go. He thought Pete would tell me someday."

"How did Pete take it when you got married?"

"Look, we thought he was going to be up there for twenty-five years. He knew I couldn't keep Nathan without help. He was all for it. 'Take him for all you can,' that's what he said."

"And you kept visiting him all these years," Constance said. "Why did you, Marla?"

She shrugged. "You think I haven't asked myself that more than once? Habit, maybe? The only guy I felt safe around, maybe? I met a girl who makes jewelry. She showed me some pieces she was taking to show her husband. He's in for life. Anyway, it was neat stuff, earrings, necklaces, things like that. She gave me these," she said, fingering an earring. "I told her she could sell jewelry like that and she said no way. She had three kids, a full-time job, and lived up by Saranac Lake. She never even saw New York City. So I bet her I could sell it. I took a few pieces down to SoHo and sold them, and she gave me twenty-five percent. It was like fate gave me a break. If I hadn't been going to see Pete, I never would have met her, and others like her. I'm a jewelry rep—can you believe it?"

Constance nodded, but before she spoke, Marla faced her and said angrily, "You want to know what a bind is? Let me tell you. It's when you have a sick kid and no money and have to get a job, but if you leave him to work, the state will take him away and put him in an institution so he'll get the kind of care he needs. That kind of care would kill him. That's a bind."

"The state pays for his medical care, doesn't it?" Constance said, not so much a question as a statement of fact.

"They have to. They did it to him; they take care of him. Someone like Roy an hour or two a day, and respite care. You know what respite care is? I get a day and a half off each week. At first, I wouldn't leave even that much. They were just looking for an excuse to take him away from me, claim I was neglecting him, something like that." Her cheeks flared as she spoke rapidly. "I fainted a couple of times and the doctor said it was stress, that I needed to get away now and then and that no one could hold it against me. It was my right. If I got sick, they'd take him

in a hurry, and if I didn't have some time off, I'd get sick.
Sheila showed up with her jewelry about then and I was in
business. I take my respite days all at once, five, six days
in a row, make my rounds, take the jewelry down to New
York, and next month do it again. Nathan hates it, but I figure he can put up with someone like Roy for a few days if
it means I get to keep him with me the rest of the time.
And it does."

"That's a terrible burden to shoulder alone," Constance
said. "Why didn't Pete tell you where the money was, help
out that way?"

Marla went to the hallway and cocked her head, listening. No sound came from upstairs. "He knew they'd be
watching for me to come up with money," she said scornfully. "That would really have been stupid." She stayed by
the hall door now, still listening.

"I suppose so," Constance said. "It just seems so unfair.
Did he think you'd get back together when he got out?"

"Yeah," Marla said after a moment. "He thought so, and
I guess I did, too. He said he had a few things he had to
take care of first, and we had to be cool, not lead anyone
to the money, just wait for the right time and then take off
for Spain. We talked like that, and it was like having a
dream over and over. You know? You hate to wake up because it's such a good dream. I used to take Nathan's pictures to show him, and I told him how Nathan was getting
along. Pete knew all about him. But when he walked in and
took one look, he said we'd have to put him in a hospital
or an institution. We had a fight. I kicked him out and he
stayed out. I guess he got the money and went to Spain or
somewhere like that."

Constance shook her head. "We think he's still hanging
around. How did he get here from Attica? He got out on

the tenth and came here on the twelfth. Where was he those two days?"

"He didn't say," Marla said coldly. "He called me from the bus station in Tuxedo Park, and as soon as Roy got here, I went over and picked him up. The next day when Roy got here, I took him back." She added bitterly, "He slept on the sofa that night."

She stepped into the hall to listen again, and this time when she came back, she checked the wall clock in the kitchen. "Look, why don't you and your husband just leave. I told you he came here and then he went away. That's all I know. I haven't seen him or heard from him, and I don't expect to. I've got to go up and see to Nathan and feed him some dinner. Just go away."

Almost as if on cue, Charlie entered the kitchen then. "Ready?" he asked Constance.

She nodded. "We'll come back tomorrow," she said to Marla. "Just a few more details we need to clear up. It shouldn't take long. Is this Roy's usual time? Between three and five?"

"Get out of here!" Marla cried. "Just get the hell out of here!" She hurried across the kitchen and punched in numbers on the microwave, turned it on.

Charlie took Constance by the arm and they walked through the house to the front door and left. Neither spoke until they got inside the car and were heading back out the narrow black road. Then Charlie asked, "What was that all about?"

"She's lying," Constance said. "I'm not sure yet how much, or when she turned the lies on and turned them off. She alternated, I think. But she most certainly is lying."

"You sure?"

"Yes indeed. She claims to be living in poverty and yet

she's wearing a five-hundred-dollar sweater and earrings that cost about that much. And she called you my husband, but no one mentioned anything like that to her at any time. Did we?"

He squeezed her thigh lightly.

"Okay," he said when they were in their motel room. "Change of game plan. We can't see Marla until after three, and there's no need to ask too many questions around these parts, so let's breeze over to Middletown in the morning and come back here in the afternoon."

She eyed him narrowly. "You turned on Roy's talk switch?"

"Sure did, but you first. Give. Or do you want something to drink first?"

The motel room was a minisuite, a king-size bed on one side and a little sitting room on the other, with a sofa, two chairs, and a low table, where Charlie's feet now rested.

"Drink," she said, getting up to cross the room to their suitcase and a shopping bag. She took a bottle of wine from the bag and held it up for him to see. "No expense account, no room service. Right? I came prepared."

Then, as they sipped wine from water glasses, she told him in detail what Marla had said. "My problem," she said when she finished, "is that I know she was lying, but not about what or when. For instance, I think she noticed that I had appraised her earrings, and she came up with a story that sounded plausible at the moment but really isn't. A woman scraping by with three kids doesn't give away jewelry that would bring in hundreds of dollars. And that sweater, not what you wear in the kitchen pureeing food. Splatters . . ." There were other things not quite right, she was certain, but she needed time to sort them out. "Your turn."

"Roy lives on the road between Cedar Falls and Tuxedo Park," Charlie said. "He knows everyone in the county. He thinks she's a saint and she's blind to the truth about the boy. She gives him parties, puts up a Christmas tree, the whole thing. He has the brain waves of a vegetable, according to Roy, who is a hospital orderly, by the way. Up until two years ago, they didn't have the ramp, and she carried him downstairs to take him outside, gave him his baths, and had in a handler when she had to go out, and for the five or six days she takes off. That's what he says he is—a handler; the kid's past therapy. A couple of years ago, the boy began to grow, until she couldn't lift him. Roy stops in there every morning, gets the boy out of bed and into the wheelchair, and goes back later to give him a bath and get him back in bed." He poured himself more wine and stood at the table, swirling it in his glass. "It's been hell for her," he said quietly. "She's done it all alone."

Constance knew he was remembering the day of the wreck, when the infant Nathan had been thrown out of the car. She made a motion as if to reach for him, but, oblivious, he returned to his chair.

"So," he said, "Roy was there the day Pete arrived. She went out and brought Pete back. The next day, while he was giving the boy his bath, she said she had to go out again, that Pete was leaving. They were fighting, he said, yelling at each other. Everyone in Cedar Falls probably saw her drive by with Pete; they all knew the ex-con was there, and they were afraid he might stay. They saw her drive back without him. Roy says if she sneezed, the whole town held its breath for fear they'd catch whatever she had. She scandalized them the first time she showed up at the supermarket with food stamps. She was a loner from day one and is still a loner. Roy thinks she has a boyfriend out there on the road, hopes she does. He said she comes home with presents now and then, but she doesn't confide in him, hardly even talks to him except about Nathan. She's real close with money, does things herself or lets them go for the most part, and she nurses the cars along. He says she takes the gangster car, Boseman's Buick—they call him Grossman around these parts—out on the highway to keep it running well, because that's her emergency car for when Nathan has to go to the hospital for a checkup or something. He's had about a dozen operations over the years, and he has seizures. Other times, she drives a little red Datsun that's twelve years old, Boseman's wedding present. Everyone in Cedar Falls hates that Datsun. They don't think a person like her should be allowed to live in a big, expensive house and let it go to ruin, and drive a heap like that around to shame them all."

His voice had gone very flat. "So there it is. Pete came and Pete went away. I think we're back to where we started from, honey."

They were both silent then until Constance asked, "How much does this room cost?"

"Ninety per. It's off-season. Why?"

"I don't know. It's just that if she's so broke, how can she afford to stay in motels every month, eat meals out for five or six days? How much money could she be making with that jewelry? It seems she must be spending it all just to survive on the road."

"If it's her therapy, maybe she figures it's worthwhile even if she loses money," he commented.

She felt a twinge of annoyance with him. Someone had paid for that ramp, she thought, and the expensive wheelchair with a motor. The state didn't provide that kind of chair. And the pricey sweater and earrings . . . and insurance for two cars, utilities for a house that size . . . Even as she thought this, she felt disgust for herself rising. So what if Marla had a rich friend? Or what if she was into something illegal herself? Her devotion to her son was real; her care in preparing his food, her steadfast refusal to surrender him to anyone, to risk losing him, that made up for a lot. She had no doubt that Nathan would have died long ago without her constant attention.

A few minutes later when Charlie said maybe they should think about food pretty soon, she agreed readily. No more brooding about Marla and Pete, she told herself. Think food thoughts, she added, remembering the Victorian house they had seen. Not being on an expense account did not mean they had to eat at McDonald's, she also told herself, and she suggested aloud that they should call Chelsey House for a reservation.

The restaurant was as good as they had expected; Constance had sweetbreads. Charlie said he wished she wouldn't do that and she said at least she never made the dish at home, and he said she should wait until he was out of the country to eat it at all.

It was close to 9:30 when they left Chelsey House. Charlie drove to the supermarket, stopped, and gazed around Cedar Falls. There was a dim light in the market, another, dimmer light in the grocery store across the street from it, and a light at the service station. The antique store was dark. No one was in sight.

"What I'm thinking," he said, starting to drive again, not toward Tuxedo Park, but back up the road toward Marla's house, "is that it was too public, the way she got rid of Pete. A fight for Roy to hear, driving through town, where everyone would be watching, dumping him and coming back, knowing she'd be watched all the way. She could have stopped, let him get out and hop in the backseat, scrunch down out of sight."

"Where are you going?"

"Just looking. This sure is a dark road, isn't it?"

Dark, narrow, with occasional lights showing from houses that were not visible, the road wound uphill more steeply all the time. He slowed down and grunted in satisfaction. "I thought so," he murmured, and made a turn to the right onto another narrow black road. After winding about for a bit, this road led downhill. A few miles later, there was a well-lighted intersection at State Highway 17. The information sign said that I-84 was four miles to the left, Tuxedo Park three miles to the right. Charlie turned right, and within minutes they were back at their motel in Tuxedo Park.

"Escape hatch," he said. "Thought there might be one. So our boy Pete could have gotten in that big black Buick and been gone without anyone ever suspecting he'd been around."

There had been nothing in Marla's house to indicate that he had ever been there, but Pete was smart—he would have erased his tracks thoroughly. Charlie thought of upper New York State, Pennsylvania, New Jersey, Vermont, Massachusetts, Connecticut. . . . He could be anywhere out there, secure, waiting to make his next move. Marla would be in touch with him, he felt certain. She would tell him they were sniffing around; they had done exactly what he had wanted them to do. Pete was toying with them, and there wasn't a thing he could do about it, except follow where the trail led, knowing that Pete had planned it this way, that the trail might be mined, booby-trapped a dozen different ways that no one could anticipate and avoid. Time was on Pete's side and he had enough money to carry out whatever plans he had made during his thirteen years in hell.

The drive to Middletown the next morning was quick and easy. The sun came out and all traces of winter were gone; that was deceptive at this time of year, Charlie had learned, but for now, today, the early spring made him cheerful. He found the strip mall without any trouble, and they drove behind it to look, as they had done with all the other buildings. This strip had a dozen shops—shoe store, florist, Chinese restaurant. . . . Charlie's good humor faded as he studied the rear of the long, narrow structure: cement-block construction, metal window frames, barred windows. There were a few pallets leaning against the wall, two Dumpsters, a few stacks of cardboard boxes strapped together . . . and nothing that would burn more than ten minutes. Yet a shop had been destroyed, the owner killed. Mervin's Novelties, he remembered, and made a sharp turn at the end of the alley to drive by the front of the mall. No Mervin's Novelties. That business had not rebuilt. Although the mall was open for business, there were few cars, few pedestrians. He pulled into a parking space and studied the layout of the strip mall.

"I see how the fire got inside," Constance said, reading the report about this fire. "The back window to Mervin's shop was open; gasoline was sprayed in. He was in the rear section of the store."

Charlie nodded, unhappy with it. You can't burn down a cement-block building, he thought grumpily. You don't leave a window open at three in the morning, even if it is barred. You don't sleep through alarms and get burned up when the outside door is a few steps away.

"Let's buy a flower and ask a question or two," he said, nodding toward the florist shop. "For Auntie Geraldine." The shop was in the space where he had expected to see Mervin's Novelties.

"Hi," Charlie said to the woman in the florist shop. She was quite round, with iron gray hair and a pleasant smile. "Maybe we can find something in here, honey," he said to Constance, and then turned to the woman. "We're on our way to Monticello, her aunt's birthday, and thought we should pick up something, since we left her present on our kitchen table. I left it there," he said woefully. "Guy I know said there's a novelty shop around here somewhere, but we can't find it."

"I'll just look around," Constance said, peering at a birthday card. She replaced it and picked up another one.

"Well, people always like flowers," the woman said. "A nice arrangement? Or a garden bouquet?"

"I don't know," Charlie said. "Is there another mall like this down the road? Maybe the shop's in a different one."

"You said a novelty shop. Like trick lapel buttons that squirt you? Whoopee cushions? For her *aunt*?"

"Is that what he meant?" Charlie said, aghast. He took a step backward.

"Well, if it is, the shop's gone. Used to be that space where your wife is looking for a card. I expanded when Mervin got burned out last year."

"Gone," Charlie echoed. "Burned out?" He looked around. "You, too?"

"No, hardly any damage in here, but his shop was destroyed. He died in the fire, poor man."

"Gee," Charlie said, and leaned in closer again. "Really? Right there?"

She nodded, then said in a low voice, "He must have

been dead drunk. They say he opened his back window and fell asleep on the floor, never woke up. He was a lech," she added, and pursed her lips. "Some of the stuff he had, well, pornographic comes to mind, but maybe others didn't see it that way. Well, I'm not saying he's paid for his sins—that's not up to me to judge—but he's gone, and that's for sure."

"I can't imagine what my good buddy was thinking of, telling me to go to a place like that with my wife! Junk like that! What kind of stuff did he handle?"

"Oh, inflatable animals, lions, even a dinosaur, inflatable beds, anything you could blow up, he had. Dolls. Dolls with . . . you know, parts? Real junk. He had an inflated woman in his window for about a year, looked like a maid, you know, the high heels, little tiny skirt and apron, cap, everything. People would stop and pretty soon they'd be laughing, but some of his stuff wasn't funny, I don't think. I told him all that gas was dangerous, but he wouldn't listen to anyone, not him. You know gas explodes and spreads the fire something awful when it gets too hot."

"Gas," Charlie repeated. "He kept gas in there?"

"You know, for blowing up the balloons, the animals and people, all that. Real dangerous to keep gas around."

"It's surprising that he could manage a business, what with chasing and boozing. . . ."

"Oh, he chased, all right, but he wasn't a real drinker. That's why it was surprising that time. But why else would he have stayed after the fire started? Unless he was out cold," she said triumphantly. "Never went home that night. Got himself a bottle and started in and didn't quit until he passed out. Just that one time, and that one time's the one time the place catches on fire. Makes you think, doesn't it?"

"What do you mean he never went home? You mean he slept in his shop?"

"Just that one time ..." she started again, and again made his head spin.

He tsked tsked. "Makes you think," he said. "Sure does." He looked at the rear of the shop, where Constance was reading another card. "Honey, just pick one, will you? Aunty Geraldine can't see it, anyway."

"It has to be right," Constance said primly; she replaced the card and picked up another one.

"We all think he had a girl in there. He had these books and magazines he kept locked up, and sometimes he'd pull his shade down and put the 'Closed' sign up, and we knew he was in there with someone, probably showing her dirty pictures or something. He closed early that night, but he didn't leave."

Charlie stared at her in disbelief. "That one time ..." he said. She nodded vigorously. "What did the police say about *that*?" he asked in a hushed tone.

Now she drew back and looked at Constance. "I don't guess anyone mentioned it. You know, his wife, Shirley, I mean, what was the point in hurting *her*? She had enough to put up with when he was living and chasing, no cause to bring her more grief." She was watching Constance.

"Honey," Charlie called sternly, "if you're not through in two seconds, I'm leaving without you."

Constance marched to the counter and put down a very large card with a red velvet rose. "And that box of chocolates," she said, pointing.

"That's fifteen dollars!" Charlie exclaimed.

"If you hadn't left the birdcage on the table, we wouldn't have had to stop to buy anything. Pay the lady."

A block away from the shop, she opened the box of

candy and handed him a piece, took one for herself. They began to laugh.

"Birdcage!" he said.

"This is the one time that . . . I can't do it." She laughed harder.

"That one time was the one time that . . ." He sputtered to a stop and ate the chocolate.

After a moment, he said, "I think it's a break. Someone might have seen something that night."

Traffic was not bad, but still he had to pay attention. It was Sunday, and drivers who had not touched a wheel all week were out flexing muscles that were stiff and uncooperative. A Dodge passed him doing eighty and then slowed to fifty a car length ahead of him. Two other cars were dawdling in the passing lane. A U-Haul passed them on the right. Telephone, Charlie was thinking. He needed help. He spotted a gas station and diner and left the highway.

At a pay phone outside the diner, he dialed Brian Possner's number in Manhattan. A machine answered, as he had known it would, and he said, "Meiklejohn. I'll call back at one. Answer the damn phone then." It was ten minutes before twelve, giving him plenty of time to decide exactly what to tell Brian.

His smile was beatific when he turned then to Constance. "Know what occurred to me out there on the dieway?" He took her arm and steered her toward the restaurant. "Ten percent of roughly six million smackeroos. Reward money for recovering the loot from that job Pete pulled thirteen years ago. You want a Danish with coffee? Let's live it up, kiddo."

In a booth, sipping coffee that was very bad and nibbling on a Danish that was good, he made notes for Brian. "Keep her in sight," he muttered. "From three until five every day, get any phone number she might call. . . ."

"And through the night," Constance said. "She could leave any night in the Buick. Who would know? Nathan won't tell."

"You think she'd leave him alone like that?"

"She does what she has to do for the greater good," Constance said.

He made another note. This would get spendy, he knew, but eventually Marla would lead them to Pete. He wrote again in his own peculiar shorthand: "Find out who was in the novelty shop with Mervin, when she left, what shape he was in, when he opened the window, or if she did." No doubt she was afraid of publicity, afraid to come out with it, but she could be found, questioned. Not by him. He was determined not to give Pulaski a clue about where he was heading with this. His guys would be all over the place showing Charlie's pictures, describing his car; they'd know he was snooping around, too. He might have gone too far already with the woman in the florist shop, but that was done; he doubted that she suspected she had been questioned. But he couldn't go back. Ten percent of six million, he thought. Worth the risk of keeping the ATF in the dark.

"I don't guess we could get a list of all the artists she deals with, the shops where she sells the jewelry," Constance said thoughtfully. "She mentioned one woman, Sheila, who gave her the idea, and who has a man in Attica for life. What if Pete is staying with someone like her, upstate somewhere?"

Charlie shook his head. They couldn't even throw such a wide net, much less follow through—contact all her clients, investigate them all. There were federal and state agencies who could, but he wasn't part of them. Marla had to lead them to Pete. And she would, he added. She would. It was nearly one. He left Constance to go make his phone call. As he walked, it occurred to him that if he had an hour alone in Marla's house, and if she kept records, addresses, he would find them. He tried to dismiss the idea and dialed Brian's number.

When Charlie pulled up to Marla's front door, Roy's station wagon was already there, still ticking as the motor cooled. They had watched it drive by from a driveway down the road, had waited two minutes, and followed. Marla opened the door almost instantly. She was wearing a heavy sweatshirt, and she stepped out onto the front stoop, pulled the door closed after her.

"You can't come in," she said. She sounded hoarse and looked as if she had not slept. "You got Nathan too upset yesterday. We were up all night. You can't come in and do it again." She drew in a quick breath. "I called a friend this morning, and he said to tell you about him, about us. I don't have Pete here, and I don't know where he is. He won't come back. I told him I have a friend and he won't come back! I see someone every month. Up by Lake Champlain. He has a cabin up there where we stay." She was hugging her arms about herself as if she was freezing.

"His name, Marla," Charlie said.

"Scott Breckinridge. He teaches at Bennington and he has an art gallery. People come there to bring jewelry for me to take to New York, and then we go to his cabin. I go out to meet with other people during the day, and back there at night."

"Where's the cabin? When did this start?"

"Benson's Landing, in Vermont. I met him years ago. You think that's so awful, that I have a man, a boyfriend?"

She flushed angrily. "Well, that's how it is. Now just go away and leave me alone!"

"I think it's perfectly normal," Constance said. "The only strange thing is why you don't get together on a more permanent basis. A few days a month isn't much."

"I can't!" Marla cried. "I can't take Nathan out of the state! You think Vermont would pay for his operations? For a therapist for him? Hah! And Scott can't just leave his job. He has tenure! He can't just walk away from it."

"Does Breckinridge use the cabin when you're not there?" Charlie asked.

She shook her head. "Maybe in the summer."

"Did you tell Pete about him?"

She shrugged and muttered, "Yeah. I knew he'd understand how it's been with me, and he did. He said I needed a little attention, a little fun, but then he blew, after he got out."

She opened the door behind her and tilted her head, listening. "Look, I told you all I'm going to say. Now leave me alone. I won't talk to you anymore. If you come back, I'll call the police or something." She laughed bitterly. "That's a joke, isn't it? Me call the police on you!" She opened the door farther and stepped inside, closed it softly behind her.

Back at the car, Constance asked if he wanted her to drive and he said yes. Marla was hoarse because she had been up all night reading to the boy, he was thinking. Roy had said she did that, read to him for hours at a time when she claimed he was upset. Roy said there was no way to tell if he was upset or not, or even if he could hear what she was reading, but she thought it helped him through bad times. He said each meal took two hours, and she chattered away all the time she was spooning baby food into his mouth and wiping off most of it when it dribbled down his chin. She chattered, he had said, even while she was changing his diapers.

Charlie slumped in his seat and gazed ahead and saw nothing of the scenery they passed, nothing of the traffic that Constance navigated through. They didn't talk now. She always knew when not to talk.

At home, they ignored the cats and listened to the answering machine messages; Charlie instantly forgot what the messages were. If any had been important, he would have noticed, he thought, and sat down to call Breckinridge. When he hung up, he said, "Tomorrow. He'll meet us at the cabin at three. He gave me directions." He looked at her. "I feel prickly."

"Me, too." It had been too easy, she thought then. Why had Marla told them anything? She could have slammed the door.

"She got orders from Pete," Charlie said softly.

"We turn left at the sign for Benson's Landing," he said the next afternoon, watching for the sign. He suddenly thought of the distances out west, drive two days and not leave Texas, ten hours to get across Oregon, a lifetime to travel from southern to northern California. All the distances in the northeast were child's play comparatively. The drive from home up here to Benson's Landing had been only two and a half hours. He saw the sign, two miles to Benson's Landing, turned left, and checked the odometer. One mile and turn left again, then watch for Breckinridge's sign.

There was more snow up here than they had seen all day, and now they could see the lake, with pale patches of ice against dark water. His next turn was onto a gravel driveway that wound through pine trees to a gray cabin. The lake was a short walk through the woods. The air smelled good.

"We're so early," Constance said. It was 2:30.

"I figured he'd probably get here before three," Charlie said. "Give us time to look things over before he shows up."

They had both worn boots, not knowing what to expect in this area, but the drive was clear of snow, as was a walkway bordered with pale, round rocks that led to the cabin door. The structure was of unpainted cedar that had weathered to a nice silver gray. Patches of thick pine-needle carpeting showed through the snow, melting its way to the light. Constance went to a window and peered in; the shade was drawn halfway down. Kitchen, with a gas stove, scant cabinets . . . She wrinkled her nose. And a dead mouse. Two dead mice. She drew back just as Charlie yanked her arm, jerked her away from the house and into the snow, where she staggered to get her balance. He kept his hand tightly on her arm and pulled her farther away.

At that moment, another car crunched on the gravel drive, and they turned, to see a Land Rover come to a stop and a short heavyset man get out.

"Breckinridge," he said. "You're early." He was carrying keys and walked quickly toward the house.

"Don't go near it!" Charlie called. "Stay back."

"What?" Breckinridge paused. "What's that?"

"Gas," Charlie said. "Stay back." He stopped and picked up a large rock and heaved it at a window. Almost instantly, the smell of gas was in the air. "Where's the main?" he demanded.

Breckinridge looked stunned. "You broke the window!"

"Where's the goddamn gas main?"

He pointed to the side of the cabin and Charlie strode off in that direction. Constance and Breckinridge followed. "I need a wrench," Charlie snapped.

Constance ran back to their car and opened the trunk. There were always some tools there. She found a wrench and hurried back with it. Charlie turned off the gas. He glanced around the back of the cabin, but the snow was too deep for any rocks to show. Silently, he went back to the front and lifted another rock.

"For God's sake, you don't have to do that," Breckinridge cried. "Just open the door." He started to go to the cabin door and Charlie caught his arm.

"Don't even think of touching that door," he said darkly, and pointed. A narrow strip of metal was visible at the bottom of the door. Breckinridge backed away; he looked confused.

Charlie broke another window, took a rock around back, and broke a window there. The smell of gas was sickening all around the cabin. They went to stand by the cars.

"What are we going to do?" Breckinridge asked helplessly.

"Wait a while and then open the back door. Is there a key for it?" He took the key from Breckinridge's fingers.

"*He* did this! My God, he tried to kill me!"

Charlie grunted, thinking of the unbroken snow at the back of the house, some of it drifted up over the doorsill. If that door had been opened, booby-trapped, the snow would have been disturbed, he decided, and went around to unlock the door. First he examined the frame, the single step, the door itself, and finally he inserted the key and turned it. A light wind was blowing, would be blowing through the house, he knew, and a lot of gas had already been released, replaced with fresh air. Enough ventilation?

He decided it was, and he pushed the door open and quickly stepped back as a cloud of poisonous air rushed out.

He waited ten minutes before he entered the cabin through the back door. It stank of gas, and would for quite some time, but it was no longer a primed bomb. He stopped to examine the front door: solid wood, like the back door, with weather stripping, a good tight threshold, and a narrow strip of metal nailed to the door on the inside, bent to fit under it. Inside the door, a metal plate was like a deadly welcome mat. It would have done nicely, he decided, and opened the door carefully, using a handkerchief, watching for a spark. If one came, he missed it, but he felt certain that it had sparked, and if the door had opened an hour ago, the house would have gone up in a gas explosion.

Constance had followed him in through the back door and now took his hand without a word. Breckinridge approached cautiously. He was pasty-faced.

"Keep your hands in your pockets," Charlie told him. He squeezed Constance's hand and released it. "You'll have to go to the nearest phone, in Benson's Landing, I guess, and call Bruce Wymouth over in Albany. I don't know anyone in the FBI in Vermont. Tell him what we found here, why we came—checking out a tip that Pete might have holed up in the cabin—and tell him that we haven't called in the locals yet."

After she left, Charlie pushed open the doors to the bathroom and bedroom, both empty. Bedding was in a jumble on the bed; Breckinridge looked away in embarrassment. "Let's go sit in your car and wait," Charlie said. "Smell's giving me a headache."

Breckinridge led the way, his head bowed, hands deep in

his pockets. At the car, he said, "I won't say anything until the FBI gets here."

Charlie shrugged. "Suit yourself." They got in the Land Rover, where Charlie slumped down in the passenger seat and gazed at the cabin broodingly.

After a short silence, Breckinridge said, "She's so pretty." Charlie made a noise, and Breckinridge went on. "She's only thirty. All the trouble she's had and only thirty now. I'm forty-two," he added. "She's the first girlfriend I ever had ... real girlfriend." Then, haltingly, fragmenting it, jumping around in time, he told it all.

She had been coming to Bennington for a couple of years before he met her. One of his students had made a necklace and earrings and wanted to put a price tag of a thousand dollars on the set; Marla had said six hundred, and they came to his gallery for an opinion. He did appraisals, he said. He had said two hundred. Two months later, Marla had dropped in to tell him she had gotten six hundred, and they had gone out for coffee. He mentioned the cabin a month or so later, and they had met here, and she had stayed all night. ... He trailed off.

She hung around his gallery for a few hours and the artists brought their pieces to her, he said a few seconds later. He always came out first, fixed things up, bought wine, things for dinner, made a fire, then she came. He was sure no one suspected that he was letting her use the cabin, that he met her there.

"She's so paranoid," he said unhappily. "She's afraid someone will accuse her of being an improper mother or something and take Nathan away from her. I tried to talk her out of the notion, but that's what she believes. So I had her for a few evenings a month, and those were the happiest times of my life."

"You've broken up?" Charlie asked when the silence continued this time.

He nodded. "Not altogether, but . . . I asked her to marry me. I told her I'd pay for a hospital, that she didn't have to worry about that. I said she could move up here, we'd get a house. . . . She walked out and I didn't see her for three months. Then I went down there, to her place. She was furious that I showed up, but she let me in, and I saw Nathan. She didn't have a minute for me all afternoon, through the night, and the next morning she made me leave. She read to him nearly all night," he mumbled. "All night. I could hear her voice outside his door. I begged her to start coming back the way she used to, and finally she said she'd spend a night in the cabin, and that's what it's been like for a year now. But I'd be happy to have her one night a year, if that's all I can have."

Charlie probed a little, and Breckinridge obliged with answers. Then Charlie asked, "What did she say when she called this time?"

"I knew about Pete," he said. "She said you thought she knew where he was, that you were making Nathan miserable, making her miserable, and she had to tell you about us, make you believe her. I told her to tell you." For a moment he looked defiant. "I don't care who knows. I never tried to keep it a secret. I would have danced in the streets if she had let me talk about it. I want to marry her," he said miserably. "I haven't seen her since January! We had that blizzard in February; she couldn't get here. I call and leave messages; she doesn't even have time to talk to me."

They both turned to look when a car pulled into the driveway. Constance was back. She got out of the Volvo, carrying a cardboard tray with three styrofoam containers.

"Coffee," she said. "We may have a little wait."

She sat in the backseat and they drank the coffee. In twenty minutes, a car pulled in, then a second one. They went out to meet the feds.

Six men emerged from the two cars; five of them were nameless, and they went straight to the cabin and entered, carrying little satchels, cases of various sorts. They looked like a flock of doctors making a house call on a head of state. The sixth man introduced himself. "Robert Chelsky," he said. He looked as if he belonged out on a whaler, as if he had spent most of his years at sea, where the salt spray and wind had chiseled his face down to the bare essentials and colored him red. He took their statements, made notes, and then snapped his notebook shut.

"We'll know more what to ask after we've gone over the cabin," he said with a heavy New England accent. He studied Charlie. "Eisenbeis has been out for over a year. Took you a while to get interested in tracking him down."

"I've been out of touch," Charlie said. "Just found out recently."

"Um. All right. Mr. Breckinridge, I reckon you'll want to stay and cover up those windows. Maybe we can turn on some heat in the cabin and talk a little. Mr., Mrs. Meiklejohn, if you want to leave, there's no reason not to. Long drive back down to your place. Appreciate it if you keep this quiet for now."

"Trust me; we will keep it very quiet," Charlie said gravely. He shook Breckinridge's hand, pitying the wretched man even more than he had before. He suspected that Chelsky would find out when he lost his first baby tooth before this night was over.

In the car, Constance asked, "Do you think he knows about the ATF investigation?"

"Probably not."

"Will the FBI tell Pulaski about this?"

He laughed. "Does the dog tell the cat?" He patted her leg. "Want to make a note of some dates before I forget them?" They both knew he would forget nothing of what Breckinridge had said, but she got out her notebook and he filled her in.

She studied the dates thoughtfully. "He proposed in September of 1991. December twelfth, Pete showed up at her house. On December twentieth, Breckinridge showed up. She agreed to resume their relationship on her terms and has had access to his cabin ever since. You don't think Pete's been there all that time, do you? With Breckinridge there one night a month, too?"

"Maybe he hid under the bed," Charlie said. Now, he thought, the big guns would go after Marla's contacts, her clients; there would be a list. He began to ponder the problem of how he could get his hands on it.

"I bet he hasn't been there at all," Constance said after a long pause. "Until last night, anyway. It's too far from Marla's place, and there's no telephone in the cabin. He certainly wouldn't have gone into town to use a phone, too public."

And they are in touch, Charlie finished silently for her. He said, "You know, it really doesn't take both of us. We could take turns staying home, tending the fire." This time, she patted his leg.

That night, holding a book that she was not reading, Constance worried. Had the trap at the cabin been step three? First the threatening note, then the tip to the ATF, next an explosion and fire, possibly another death. If Breckinridge had gotten there first, he would have been killed; Charlie would have been found on the scene of another fire with another body. Step three? But there had been no guarantee that Breckinridge would open that door. It might have been her, or Charlie, who . . . She shivered. "It hadn't mattered," she said under her breath. "He didn't care who got killed."

Charlie put down a magazine he had not been reading and said, "Listen."

She didn't hear anything.

"Wind," he said in disgust, and stood up.

Now she heard it. It was March, and a certain amount of wind could be expected, she thought but did not say. He hated high winds; he got twitchy. The cats hated the wind and they got twitchy. So now for a day or two, they would all twitch at her, she thought in resignation.

"What are we going to do next?" she asked.

"Not a damned thing we can do but wait," he said, still listening to the rising wind. "Wait for Brian to check in, or for Pulaski to show up with a warrant, or for Chelsky to come around and ask polite questions for twelve hours, or for Pete to make his next move."

Twitchy, she thought. Waiting was going to be very hard.

All day Tuesday, he stayed busy doing something or other to the car in the garage; she didn't ask what. And she stayed busy doing something with apples in the kitchen; he didn't ask what. Late in the afternoon, he sniffed at the woodstove, where she was stirring a very large pot of something. "Umm," he said, and put his arms around her, nibbled at her neck. She turned and nibbled at his earlobe. The first time she had done that, thirty years earlier, he had growled, "What the hell are you doing?" and she had said, "Stimulating an erogenous zone." A second later, he had said, "I'll be damned!"

Now, thirty years later, he was still surprised. She pushed the kettle to the back of the stove, closed a damper most of

the way, and arm in arm they wandered upstairs. Outside,
the wind shrieked and the rain pelted down.

Wednesday, the cats were all snapping at one another.
When Candy came in drenched, he reached for her, a hu-
manitarian gesture—he just wanted to dry her off; she
snarled and hissed. Brutus watched him through evil, slitted
yellow eyes. Ashcan slinked around, hiding behind a chair,
behind the couch, underfoot, whimpering. Constance
snapped that the apple butter was tasteless, and she fussed
around adding spices; he had to take the spark plugs out
and put them back in before the car would start. The gutter
had filled up with spruce needles that had blown like snow,
and he had to get the ladder out and clear the channel; he
came in as wet as a human could get without having been
dumped in the ocean.

"That doesn't happen if you live in a decent apartment
building," he said coldly, removing layers of wet clothes.

"You're dripping on the floor," she said, just as coldly.

They both stopped when the telephone rang and Brian's
voice came on. Charlie raced to pick up the phone. Constance finished making the coffee she had started and got
out the bottle of Irish.

They sat at the kitchen table when he hung up. He sipped
his coffee, raised his eyebrows, saluted her with the cup,
then drank again. "Ah," he said. "Okay, first Marla," he
said then. "Chelsky and company paid a call yesterday.
Stayed two hours. As soon as they left and Roy showed
up, she got in the Buick and went tearing out to the interstate, down the highway to an exit with a gas station and
phone, ran to the phone, then turned and got back in the car
and raced home. No call. She hasn't shown her nose since."
He took another drink of the Irish coffee, savoring it. "The

real scoop is on Sal Mervin," he said then. "The guy with the novelty shop." She nodded. "They found an empty bottle, scotch, and the story is that he drank until he passed out; then he got up to open a window later and passed out again. Trouble is, his widow says he couldn't drink more than one mixed drink or maybe two during a whole evening or he fell asleep and was out for twelve hours at least. He was on allergy medication, and that along with alcohol put him out fast. Anyway, a passing cruiser checked the mall at midnight and the window was closed, lights out."

She said doubtfully, "He could have come awake enough to open a window? But what was the woman doing all that time in a dark shop? Sleeping?"

He gave her a look. "Come on. Try this. For some reason, Pete had to get rid of him. He goes to the shop, gives him a couple of drinks—" He ignored her skeptical look. "Anyway, Mervin passes out and Pete unlocks the back window so he can open it from outside later, and he leaves."

"Every time you said 'Pete,' you could have said any other name that occurred to you," she pointed out. "What you mean was, someone did this, someone did that."

He scowled, but she was right—it was too iffy. No stranger could have counted on Mervin staying asleep with only a drink or two in him. Would Mervin have been chummy enough with an ex-con to tell him he couldn't drink? He stood up and took his cup to refill, just coffee this time. Why hadn't Pete just hit him in the head and been done with it? It wouldn't have tied in with the serial fires, he told himself. The arson murder was meant to be laid at Charlie's door along with the others. If the trap had been sprung at Breckinridge's cabin, that would be on his head, too.

Thursday was not quite so twitchy; the wind had died

down again. The cats all went outside and spent most of the day in the sun; Charlie fooled with his fly rod in the basement, and Constance pretended to answer mail, pay a few bills, but she accomplished little. The thought nagged at her: They were missing something. In the basement, Charlie thought in annoyance that there was something right over there, just out of sight; if he could turn his head fast enough, he would have it.

Chelsky called and then dropped by on Friday morning. "Just need to fill in a few details," he said, shrugging out of a heavy plaid jacket. He had taken off his boots and left them outside the front door; he pulled on felt slippers. "March," he said, "hard month. Too hot, too cold, blizzards, wind. You sure can't count on anything in March."

Without comment, Charlie led him to the living room, where Chelsky took a chair close to the fire. "Nice," he said. "Smells good in here. Apples, cinnamon, cloves. Like the apple butter we make back home."

"Would you like some coffee?" Constance asked. "It won't take a minute." Charlie gave her a look. She was falling for the nice "just home folk" line. Chelsky said coffee would hit the spot.

"What can I do for you?" Charlie asked brusquely.

"Reckon you could do a lot, but what you'll do is pretty much what you've already decided on." Candy appeared and sniffed his feet, then jumped onto his lap. He stroked her. "Way I see it," he said, gazing at the comfortable fire hissing in the fireplace, "you either started a lot of fires and you're aiming to pin them on Pete Eisenbeis or else he started them and is doing a pretty good job pinning them on you." He glanced at Charlie; his eyes were a sparkly blue. "Mrs. Boseman says you're crazy," he added.

"You get around," Charlie commented.

"Yep." He gave it two syllables. "Why don't you just fill me in on Pete, Mrs. Boseman, all of it, from day one."

Charlie shrugged and told most of the story.

Then Chelsky started asking questions. Constance brought coffee and he added sugar and cream to his and went on asking questions. Why Eisenbeis, not one of the other cons who got out about the same time? How long did the drive to the cabin take? Had he known Boseman? How long had they been at the cabin before Breckinridge arrived? Had anyone touched anything inside the cabin? He was thorough.

In the middle of a question, which already had been asked and answered, Charlie held up his hand. "You didn't find Pete's prints, did you?"

"Nope. Not a one." He started to say something else, but Charlie shook his head, thinking.

"How tight is that cabin?" he asked after a moment.

"Good and tight. Cold up there, windy. It's tight."

Charlie visualized it: solid doors, all that weather stripping, storm windows, bedroom and bathroom doors closed. Now he remembered the gas stove with one burner on less than a quarter turn.

"The fireplace damper was shut down, I suppose," he murmured.

Chelsky nodded and remained silent.

"It could have been set up anytime—a week ago, a month ago, anytime since the end of January," Charlie said at last. "Not aimed at me, but at Breckinridge."

"Looks like it," Chelsky agreed. "Would have passed as an accident more than likely. It would have burned to the ground, isolated like that, old wood." His eyes were twinkling again as he asked, "Haven't been chasing around Vermont the past six weeks, have you?"

"Nope." But Charlie was thinking. There was something, something elusive that he should have noticed.

Abruptly, Constance stood up. "If you don't need me any longer, I should put on some dinner." She hardly waited for the agent's polite response as she hurried to the kitchen, where she stood rubbing her arms, chilled through. Step three was yet to be taken. The cabin wasn't it; that was simply opportunistic, unplanned as far as Charlie was concerned; he just happened to be on the spot. Step three had him at the center.

Chelsky stayed another half hour. As soon as he left, Charlie came to the kitchen muttering, "No one, absolutely no one believes Pete's anywhere in the state, maybe not even in the country."

"Charlie," Constance said from across the kitchen. Her voice was low and charged, intense. "There has to be one more fire, doesn't there?"

He stopped near the table. "Go on."

"Breckinridge would have opened that door whether you turned up or not."

He nodded.

"He was meant to die. But his death wouldn't have had anything to do with the serial fires. It was separate." Step three was in the wings, she thought, planned, ready. She said, "It has to be something bigger, something so incriminating, you won't be able to get out of it. They'll arrest you. You can't prove a negative, that you didn't set the fires, and there's no one else, not really."

She was thinking out loud, Charlie knew. Softly he said, "And then what?"

"Remember the note: 'You will feel my pain.' Prison won't be enough. I'll be killed, or disabled." Suddenly, she went white. "Jessica!" she whispered.

"Just sit still," Charlie said. He had taken Constance to the living room and stirred up the fire, added a log. He felt as clammy as she did.

"She's coming home next month," Constance said in a strained voice. "And he's so patient." She started to get up. "We have to call her, tell her not to come."

"We'll call her, but not at midnight, their time. What I'm going to do is make us an Irish coffee; later I'll do one of my famous omelettes." When he started for the kitchen, she got up to follow him; she stood within reach as he brewed coffee and then rooted around in the cabinet for the Irish. "You want whipped cream?" he asked. His voice had returned to normal; until that moment, he hadn't realized how forced it had been minutes ago. She shook her head.

He stopped fiddling with the Irish and cups and took her into his arms. "Ah, honey," he whispered.

"That's the worst thing, isn't it?" she whispered back. "Having your child threatened."

He nodded and then kissed her neck and returned to the coffee. "Let's sit down and talk it through," he said. "We're missing something. It's nagged at me for days."

That wasn't right, she wanted to say; they never talked it through until they had more to go on. First he had to think and think, and then they talked. She bit her lip, and they went to the living room with their Irish coffee.

"Let's start with Pete," he said after a moment. "He's up for thirteen years, plenty of time to plan anything. Maybe she took him clippings, anything she came across concerning us." He was thinking of the article that had appeared about Jessica when she was selected as a Rhodes Scholar. She was in Oxford, due home in April. The article had spelled it out. He shook himself. "So he gets out and two days later he turns up at Marla's house."

"Why two days? Why not go there directly?"

"He had to collect the money and stuff."

She shook her head. "Marla had the money. I told you. She must have been careful about how and when she spent any, but she had to have it. The television alone cost over a thousand dollars, and the custom bed, the wheelchair. . . . Did you look at it? It's custom-made. It will make a bed; that's why she could have Nathan in it from morning until evening. And that sweater."

"Breckinridge? He has money."

"Some of that stuff predates him. Just think of her other expenses, insurance for two cars, utilities. Heating that house must run over two hundred a month. She had to have the money, Charlie. She only works four or five days a month, remember? Then one day in New York. She simply isn't handling the kind of jewelry that would bring in that much money with so little effort."

She had told him, and he had dismissed it, he realized. He had seen the disarray, the dirt, the lack of yard care, no help with housework, no help with Nathan except what the state provided. . . . So, he thought soberly, Pete lost his girlfriend, his son, and the money.

Constance started to say something, then stopped, seeing the look on his face. She sipped her Irish coffee. He had forgotten his, on the table by the side of his chair.

"She observed all the holidays for Nathan," he said finally. "Put up a Christmas tree in his room, decorated for Halloween, gave him a birthday party every year. Complete with balloons. Roy said they floated around his room for days, until she got tired of them and took them out."

Constance gazed at him. Balloons, she repeated to herself. Helium balloons? If they floated . . . "Oh," she said then. "Mervin's shop. He kept tanks of gas for balloons."

"Maybe," he said slowly. "Maybe." The nagging feeling of having overlooked something was gone, he realized suddenly. "I wonder if Mervin had a butler to go with the maid he kept in his window," he said softly.

"Charlie," she said with a touch of exasperation, "where is this going? What are you getting at?"

Gazing at the fire, speaking in a low voice, he said, "Pete called and she made him wait until Roy was there. People got a good look at him; they knew who he was. Roy got a good look at him. What if Pete stayed alive just long enough for her to tape a real fight, and that's what Roy heard the next day? Suppose she had the inflatable butler all ready for the next act, Pete's jacket on it, a cap, and away she went, past the gawkers in Cedar Falls, up the road, nearly to Tuxedo Park, to make the time right, and then she stabbed Jeeves and deflated him and drove back alone. But Mervin knew what she had bought."

"If she was a regular customer, she probably rented helium tanks now and then, left a deposit, gave her name and address," Constance said after a moment. "He probably talked to her a lot. She could have known about his allergy medicine."

They were both silent for a time, considering. "Poor Pete," Constance said then. "She punished him every time she went to Attica, didn't she? Pictures of Nathan, stories about him, her marriage to Boseman, her car . . ."

The real bind, Charlie thought then, was sitting on a quarter million dollars and spending it a nickel at a time because otherwise they might haul her in for questioning, put Nathan in a hospital or a home of some kind.

"She's obsessive about Nathan," Constance said in a low voice. "She'll do whatever she has to to keep him with her, and punish those who hurt him."

"Crazy," Charlie said under his breath. He got up to make an omelette, thinking that they had not even a shred of evidence. Chelsky had not taken seriously his suspicion that Pete was carrying out a vendetta. How much less likely was it that he would believe the saintly Marla could entertain evil thoughts?

What if he, Charlie, had become obsessive? he thought suddenly, and stopped grating cheese. What if the arsonist was someone else, someone not connected to Pete and Marla? A nut out there with a real or imagined injury, getting revenge. Slowly, he returned to the job of making dinner, more shaken than he would have admitted. He had nothing but a gut feeling about Marla and Pete, he admitted to himself; she could be exactly what she appeared to be—a devoted mother nursing a hopeless invalid child.

They ate the omelette, delicious as it was, without comment. Constance pushed her plate back fractionally, got up for coffee, and then said, "What do you suppose she talks to him about for hours and hours every day?" When Charlie looked blank, she said, "You told me Roy said she talks to him all the time, while she's feeding him, giving him a drink, cleaning him up, and each meal takes about two hours. Up to eight hours a day, more? What can she find to talk about?"

Charlie thought about the things *they* talked about, trivialities for the most part: spruce needles in the gutter, emerging crocuses, what the cats had been up to, neighbors, their daughter and her future plans. . . . Trivial, but necessary. The real punishment of solitary confinement was having no one to talk to. People needed to talk.

"Let's think about this," he said.

She brought coffee for both of them; they pushed their plates aside and thought about it.

* * *

The next afternoon at 5:30, Charlie made the turn onto Marla's driveway and slowed to a stop long enough for Constance to get out and vanish into the shrubs. He continued to the house. "If it doesn't work," he had said, "I'll leave and accidentally tap on the horn, and you hightail it back to the road. In any event, in exactly ten minutes, you be back there. Right?"

She had nodded. And now she was out of sight. He parked and went to lean on the doorbell. Constance ran lightly to the rear of the property, zigzagging in the overgrown brush. There was a board fence separating the front and backyard. She didn't even try to find a gate, test for a lock, but simply pulled herself up and over the fence, then trotted to the first door in the rear. Locked. The next door was locked, and the kitchen door. Without hesitating, she ran to the end of the balcony outside Nathan's room and jumped up a few inches so that her fingers caught the edge, and again she pulled herself up and over the rail and crouched down.

"Look," Charlie was saying to Marla at the front door, "I know you sent lover boy to booby-trap the cabin. Okay? I mean, that's a given. Let's get on to something else."

"I told you to get out or I'll scream for the cops."

"Scream, doll. Scream. But first think about ten percent of six million dollars. Want a calculator?"

Constance felt too exposed on the balcony, even though she was keeping low, hiding behind the rail as much as possible. Too open. If anyone happened to glance this way ... The sliding door had a drape closed over it, but light came through; she would be silhouetted. She covered the last few feet and stood against the house at the side of the window. The screen door slid without a sound when she

nudged it. The glass door was locked. Charlie had said
there was a security bar, but probably it wouldn't be in
place this early; if it was, he had said she should leave.
They would find another way. She pulled a strip of metal
from her pocket and worked it into the tight space between
the door and facing. She had practiced at home. Charlie had
shown her exactly how to do it. . . . She had to start over
when the metal strip jammed. This time, she felt the lock
click, and she let her breath out.

"Marla, stop playing dumb," Charlie was saying harshly.
"We're talking big time here. I want a piece of it, and I intend to get it. I'll split with you. I'm generous. But first we
agree that Pete's just a little detail that we can dispense
with. Right?"

"You're crazy! I told them you're crazy. I don't know
what you're talking about!"

The glass door moved; the bar was not down yet. With
the door open an inch, Constance stood there listening.
Roy's voice sounded very distant; there was the sound of
rushing water. Swiftly, she opened the door and slipped inside, hesitated only a moment behind the drape, and then
darted across the room to the table where Marla sometimes
worked jigsaw puzzles or sat and read. She knew exactly
where everything was; Charlie had made her a map. She
had the backing off the tiny listening device before she
reached the table. She pushed the device into place at
the top of a leg, where it joined the tabletop. Roy's voice
sounded louder.

"Okay, buckaroo, that's it."

She ran back to the sliding door and out just as he entered the room, carrying Nathan. Very gently, she pulled the
door closed, then the screen door, and in a crouch she re-
traced her steps across the balcony to the edge. There was

the ramp; Charlie had said maybe she should use it, but they had known it would be too exposed; she ignored it again. She swung her legs over the edge of the balcony and dropped to the ground.

"Honey, we do it my way or I'll send you up exactly like I sent Pete up. The kid will be a number in a hospital. I want Pete, doll, and I want him bad. You know where he is. We deal. Sooner or later, we deal. I'll be in touch."

"I'm calling the FBI. I'll tell them you threatened me, threatened to burn down the house if I don't give you the money. We'll see who goes up." She slammed the door.

When Charlie stopped at the end of the drive and Constance opened the passenger door and slid inside, he was breathing harder than she was. He put his arm around her and drew her to him for a moment. "Okay?"

"Fine. Done." She pulled back and stripped off rubber gloves. Her hands were hot. "You know, Charlie, if you would work out with me a couple of times a week, you'd be in much better shape."

He wanted to slug her as much as he wanted to kiss her. He shifted gears and started the drive home. Done, he thought. The tape recorder and receiver were in a waterproof box in a shallow depression at the edge of the driveway, hidden by a log. Every day, Brian would retrieve the tape and put in a new one. Brian didn't want to know more than that; Charlie didn't plan to tell him more. Illegal as hell, he knew, and done.

On Sunday, Brian's colleague delivered the first tape, made on Saturday. After twenty minutes of listening to it in Charlie's office, Constance left the room, looking stricken. Charlie listened for another twenty minutes before he had to turn it off. Prattle of the sort a loving mother mouthed to a two-year-old. "What a good boy you are. . . . One more bite. . . . It's chicken breast, your favorite. . . . Oh, the sun was so good for you today! You're getting a suntan. . . . Just a sip, that's right. Strawberry milk shake, isn't it yummy? . . ." Her voice was low and musical, lilting. There was not a trace of impatience in it.

He joined Constance in the living room. "It's going to be tough. She's telling him what they'll do next week, next month."

"We don't have to listen together," Constance said. "We can take turns, half an hour at a time, something like that." She stood up. "I'll go."

Charlie went out to make himself a drink.

"We'll put in a new flower bed," Marla's voice was saying happily when Constance turned the tape player on again. "Remember all those catalogs we got last winter? We'll use them and pick the prettiest flowers we can find. One more bite now, a little one. That's good. . . . I'll tell Roy to take you out every day if the weather's good. He'll do that, and you won't even miss me. . . . I think there's just a little more of the milk shake, hardly even a mouthful. . . . You have such an appetite! . . ." Constance closed her eyes; she felt stiff and rigid as the voice went on and on, rising and falling. Then it was Charlie's turn, and she went to the kitchen, where she found a martini waiting for her. She drank it gratefully. She should start some dinner, but she did not move.

"Honey, come here," Charlie said from the doorway a few minutes later.

She followed him to the office. He had turned off the tape player and now turned it back on. Marla's sweet voice filled the room.

"I'll just cut off those roses right at the ground and that's where we'll plant our seeds. The roses will go in the trash. No funeral for flowers, you just haul them away if they die. You remember what a funeral is, don't you? That's for people, not plants. Oh, look, no more chicken! . . ." Charlie turned it off again.

"Nathan knows what a funeral is," he said. He sounded remote.

"She could have buried a bird, or a cat or something," Constance said faintly.

Charlie looked at his watch. "Let's go buy another tape recorder. I want to tape segments like that so we won't have to listen to the whole thing ever again." He took the tape from the player and put it in a wall safe. "Let's eat while we're out. I sure as hell don't want to cook."

"Neither do I," she said.

At dinner, she said, "It's like free association, what she says. One thing reminds her of another and off she goes. Eventually, if she keeps on, she'll tell everything, but we'll never be able to use any of it for any purpose."

For their purposes, it would do just fine, he thought, but she was right. Legally, it was useless. He said, "I think I goaded her enough yesterday to make her change her time-table. She'll want me off her back sooner rather than later."

That night, listening, he knew he was right.

"I know you hate it when I have to leave," Marla said. "And my regular days are coming up next week, but I'm afraid I'll just have to. It won't be for long, I promise, and not tonight. Tonight let's watch *Beauty and the Beast*. I think that must be my very most favorite movie." The tape went dead momentarily.

It was voice-activated but did not record electronic sounds, Charlie's supplier had told him. "How does it know?" he had asked, and the man had said mysteriously, "Magic."

He listened to Marla giving Nathan a drink of water. It took fifteen minutes and she prattled, then finally said good night. She would be in later to see if he wanted anything.

The tape went through the morning and into the afternoon, when Brian had lifted it and replaced it with a new one. It took Marla an hour and a half to feed Nathan breakfast and she said nothing worth retaping; then Nathan took a nap, and when she was back, she told him they would go out to the balcony. Charlie cursed when her voice faded out.

Later, feeding Nathan lunch, she said, "You have to eat a little more if you want to grow big and strong like your father. He was over six feet tall, and you're going to be that tall. I can tell."

Brian brought the new tape the next day and Constance called Charlie to listen to a segment she had retaped. "Time to go to work," Marla said, laughing. "What do you think? Six hundred? I think I got six hundred for that one. Isn't it ugly? So six hundred. And four hundred for the pin. When that FBI guy asks my clients what kind of business I do, won't they give him an earful! I'm the world's greatest saleswoman! See this? It's tigereye. Isn't that a nice name for a stone? You can see the light in it, just like an eye. I think eight hundred, don't you? . . . Maybe that's too much. That would be three thousand eighty dollars. My cut . . . seven hundred seventy . . . I guess that's okay."

"She began talking about buying him a cowboy hat then," Constance said. "What in the world was she doing?"

They listened to it again. "I think she's settling for twenty-five cents on the dollar," Charlie said finally. "She sells something for a hundred, says she got five hundred,

and pockets twenty-five percent of that. No questions asked
about her income; she has records, and happy artist clients,
and probably fake receipts for shop owners in New York.
My God, she could go through the whole schmear that
way." He glowered at the tape.

"The FBI will interview her contacts and they'll all come
on like boosters," he said aggrievedly. Then he said, "But
that means she has the money within reach, in the house!"

"The figures she was using don't add up," Constance
pointed out. Then she said, "Oh, it doesn't really matter
when or even if she sells anything, does it? Not if she's
making up prices, paying off her clients with stolen money,
collecting commissions on sales she might or might not
make."

"Twenty-five cents on the dollar," Charlie growled.
"God, she is crazy!"

And very smart, Constance added silently.

Marla talked about her mother, on the streets of New York,
she said, just where she belonged. She talked about her father, whom she had never seen, about Breckinridge, a fat
little toad. She talked about the weather, about Nathan's
hair coming back in so thick, just like his father's used to
be. Drivel, Charlie thought in disgust, listening to her read
the descriptions of flowers from a catalog. Throughout the
day, he had retaped no more than a few minutes and had
listened to hours of drivel. Constance took his place and he
left to do something about dinner; it was his day to cook.

It was six o'clock Monday evening, and they were listening to the tape that had been made of Marla starting Sunday
at three through Monday afternoon, when Brian had put in
a new one. It made Charlie nervous to be a day behind all

the time, hearing today what she had said the night before, no clue about what she was doing at the moment.

"Charlie!" Constance called. He hurried back to the office, where she was rewinding the second tape recorder. "She was reading from the catalog and he fell asleep, I guess. She just came back on." Constance pressed the play button.

Marla said gaily, "Oh, I thought you might be awake by now. I can't come too close. I stink like gas. I'll just take a shower and be right back."

There was a pause. Constance held up her hand. Then Marla was back. "Now I'm decent again. Did you have a good little nap? Roy will be here pretty soon and I'll make you turkey. And asparagus. You love asparagus! Tomorrow when I go out, I'll get some new library books, something we've never read . . . and groceries. We're almost out of ice cream. . . . And I have to put gas in the Buick, and check the oil and the tires. It would be terrible if I had road trouble, wouldn't it? There are car jackers out there, just waiting for a woman to have trouble in the middle of the night. Did you know that? I wonder which would be worse, a car jacker or a cop. Anyway, it won't happen, because I'll have the Buick checked out. . . . I know what I want to read next. . . ."

Constance turned off the machine. "She talked about stories and then Roy came in. Charlie, she serviced the Buick today, and yesterday she smelled of gas."

He rewound the tape and played it again. Hours more on the tape, he thought then, and it was after six now. With few exceptions, they had to listen to it all in real time. They couldn't finish with this one before midnight. Too late? Right now she would be in with Nathan, feeding him, talking, talking. Call Chelsky, tell him everything? He shook his head. He didn't know where Chelsky was, how long it would take him to arrive, or if he could persuade him to come out now, tonight. And for what? He didn't even know if there was a reason to call for help. He went to the door. "I'll rustle us up a sandwich or something. You keep listening. Okay?"

She reached for the on switch. Roy was there; she fast-forwarded the machine until she caught Marla's voice again and listened until Charlie came to the door and motioned for her to turn it off.

"Anything?"

She shook her head.

"Come on out, take a break," he said. He waited and they went back to the kitchen. "What I'm going to do is go down there and grab the new tape the minute she turns off Nathan's light. Eight, eight-thirty, about then. I'll listen to it in the car. Be back around ten. And that's just about all we can do right now." When she started to object, he said, "And I want you to get on the pipe to Chelsky. Run him down if you can and tell him what we think is going on. If he doesn't call back in an hour, go after Bruce Wymouth up in Albany, and if he's not available, as a last resort try to get Pulaski." He put a sandwich in a plastic bag as he talked, and kept a second one on a paper plate. "You know the old saying, Eat and run. 'Fraid I'm going to run and eat. Made a couple for you, too." He glanced around as if checking whether he had forgotten anything, and then he said casually, "Of course, no one's going to believe you."

"Probably not," she said. "But someone might be curious enough to come around. Especially if they realize you're out somewhere."

"Especially," he agreed.

She gave him one of her looks that sometimes made him

think he was as transparent as a crystal skull filled with spinning gears in rainbow colors.

"Charlie, when you don't show up again by eleven or twelve, do I tell Chelsky or whoever it is that you're keeping the vigil at Marla's house?"

He was pulling on a heavy jacket and stopped moving for just a moment, then grinned and said, "Honey, Brian has a cellular phone. If I decided to do anything like that, I'd call you. Honest." He was ready to leave. On the way out, he said, "Try not to give them the tapes if possible."

"Resist torture to what point?"

"It won't get too serious before I get back. You can hold out."

She walked to the garage with him, watched him back out and leave, and then locked the door and returned to the kitchen. It felt empty and cold. She called the numbers Chelsky had left with them and left a message on a machine with the first call, and left the same message with a man who wanted to know why she wanted Mr. Chelsky. Then she took a sandwich to the office and turned on the tape player again.

She couldn't eat and listen to Marla, she realized after only a minute or two. She put the sandwich down and listened to the sweet voice cajoling, laughing, lilting as Marla fed bite after bite to her son. Then Constance stiffened and turned on the other tape recorder.

"That toad called again. I don't know why he doesn't catch on. But he's dumb, even if he is a teacher. If he knew how much we hate hospitals, he'd never say that word again. I know what's good for you. Just look how you're growing. . . . Hospital! I know how much you hated it there, how mean they were to you. I won't see him ever again, I promise. I won't go near him again. . . . I put just a little cinnamon on it, exactly the way you like it. . . ." She began to talk about getting a motor home, a little one, and the vacations they would take.

At ten minutes before eight, Chelsky called. He asked for Charlie.

"He isn't here," Constance said. She drew in a deep breath and then said swiftly, "We have vital information you should have immediately. We think there will be another fire, probably tonight. We prefer to talk to you about it, but if you can't make it, then I'll call Bruce Wymouth in Albany."

He was skeptical and he kept asking where Charlie was, when he would return, where they thought a fire might happen. She cut in sharply. "Mr. Chelsky, those fires never started before three in the morning. There's time for someone to get over here and talk about this and maybe avert a disaster. If you can't or won't come, say so, and I'll call Bruce Wymouth."

"Now, Mrs. Meiklejohn, don't get in an uproar. I didn't say that, now did I? Happens I'm in Albany myself. I could take a run down that way. You expecting Mr. Meiklejohn back soon?"

"Around ten or eleven, or he'll call," she told him, and he said he'd be there at ten, or a little after.

She ate her sandwich; the bread had already gone too dry. Then she ate an apple and drank a cup of coffee and finally started to listen again. How could Marla keep it up? That pleasant, cheerful prattle, on and on and on. Laughing over nothing, pretending he understood, responded. Constance began to pace the office, and she thought suddenly that she simply couldn't stand this any longer. She clenched her fists and after a moment sat down again.

When she took a break later, she made a pot of strong

coffee. This would be a long night, she thought despondently. She had copied only two sections of tape since Charlie left; both of them had to do with hospitals, how everyone wanted Nathan in a hospital, how much they hated them. Slowly, she returned to the office and rewound the machine a little and listened again.

". . . and there won't be any more talk about that. But they'll think of something different. They just don't give up, do they, honey?" Constance rewound it farther back. "I'll make them stop talking about putting you in a hospital. I'll wave my magic wand and there won't be any more talk about that. . . ."

Marla went on talking about magic, about fairies who lived under flowers. . . . That's what she would start checking out of the library, she went on very happily. Everyone loved fairy tales.

When Chelsky arrived at ten minutes past ten, three other men entered with him. He introduced them: Carl Pulaski, and his assistant, Larry Dell, and his own colleague Stan Lehman.

"Where's your husband?" Pulaski demanded before he had his coat off.

"I'm not sure," she said. She pointed toward the hall closet and let them hang their own coats.

"When did he leave?"

She ignored him and said to Chelsky, "I have to start at the beginning for this to make any sense."

He nodded, but Pulaski demanded harshly, "Mrs. Meiklejohn, I want some answers, and I want them now!"

"Seems she wants to talk to us, if you'll just let her," Chelsky said in a mild way.

She nodded. "I have a map on the kitchen table. It will be helpful."

Pulaski's face was a tight furious mask, but he followed when she led the way to the kitchen and he remained silent until she told them what she and Charlie had surmised about Marla. Then he snorted.

"She's been investigated more than once and there's nothing. Where's Meiklejohn? What's he up to now? I'm warning you, if there's a fire tonight and you don't cooperate, you'll be an accessory."

"He's watching Marla's house."

"Do you mind if we look around?" he said gratingly, and started for the back door.

"Do you have a search warrant?" she asked coldly.

"No. Not yet."

"Then you can't look around."

He reached for the wall phone, and she said, even more coldly, "And don't use the phone. Charlie will call any minute now."

He jerked his head at his assistant and they went out the front door. Constance watched them, and when she turned back to Chelsky, she caught a glint in his eye that looked suspiciously like a sparkle of silent laughter. He leaned over the map without comment.

The phone rang and she snatched it up. "Hi, honey," he said cheerfully. "You have company?"

"Mr. Chelsky is here, and Mr. Pulaski," she added when he reentered the kitchen.

"Everything under control?"

"So far."

"Okay, put on the speaker phone. Let's chat."

If she had had to reveal the tapes, she would have said so; they both understood that. When she turned on the speaker phone, his voice sounded as if he were in a deep mine. He told them he was at Marla's keeping watch and he suspected that she would venture out to set a fire that night.

"Could use some backup," he said blandly.

"You know we can't do that," Chelsky said. "Not with no more than we have."

"Come on in, Meiklejohn, and let's talk," Pulaski said harshly.

"I think he's getting a search warrant," Constance said then. Pulaski glared at her.

"Uh-huh. You got a bug in place yet, Pulaski?" He didn't wait for an answer. "I'd guess not yet. I'll call back in half an hour or so, give you time to put things in place. Talk to you later."

"Charlie! Wait a minute," Constance cried. "If she tries to leave, can't you block the driveway? If she has the gas—"

He chuckled. "Honey, I'm afraid Brer Pulaski might claim I was out salting the mine or something. And she'd claim she was out to get a breath of air. Hang in there, kiddo." He hung up.

Chelsky asked questions about Marla; she answered. They all drank coffee, and after a prolonged silence, Chelsky glanced at Pulaski. "You boys have a car down anywhere near Tuxedo Park?" Pulaski shrugged. "Neither do we, I guess. Not familiar with your roads around here. How long you suppose it'd take to get a car or two in the area?"

Pulaski motioned for Chelsky to go to the living room with him. They left together and murmured inaudibly. When they came back, Chelsky said to Constance, "Problem is, if your husband's telling the truth, won't do much good to have an APB out on the Volvo, now will it? I mean, he wouldn't try to follow anyone in a white car like that. You happen to know what kind of car the other fellow's driving?"

She didn't know.

He motioned to his companion, Stan Lehman. "Why don't you bring in another phone in case we decide to make some inquiries?"

Lehman went out as silently as he had remained since arriving. He was a tall young man who never seemed to take his gaze off Chelsky. They went to the living room together and spoke in low voices when he returned.

Charlie called again at twenty minutes to twelve. "Speaker phone," he said. Constance felt a tremor pass over her at the sound of his voice. "Listen up, guys," Charlie said over the speaker phone, sounding as distant as the man in the moon. "Find out where the kid has hospital treatments, where she takes him for checkups. I think that might be the target." He hung up.

"Hospital!" Pulaski whispered. "My God, is he going to burn a hospital?"

Chelsky snapped at Lehman, "Find out."

"Not just checkups," Constance said then. "Where he had surgery within the past few months." She was shivering.

Chelsky eyed her narrowly and then nodded to Lehman. "Get on it."

"His hair is just now growing out again," Constance said. "He has seizures, and sometimes they operate to remove a blood clot or something."

They waited. In various combinations, the four men went to the living room and spoke in low voices, returned.

Finally, Charlie called again. "She's leaving," he said. "We're keeping with her. Be back on as soon as she hits the interstate." He disconnected.

"Mrs. Meiklejohn," Chelsky said, "if you can sort of

point me in the right direction, I could probably work your coffeemaker just fine."

She stirred. But she had made a pot. . . . It was empty. She started a fresh pot, grateful to Chelsky for giving her something to do.

Charlie slouched in his seat while Brian drove. He stayed far enough behind the Buick not to alarm her, and now and then he drove with his lights off. He was good. He stayed with her. Charlie called home again. "Heading north on I-Eighty-seven," he said. Pulaski wanted to know what they were driving. He hung up. But he was worried: It was early for her to be heading out. How far did she intend to go? He kept his eyes on her taillights. Somewhere with a hospital where Nathan had been operated on. He kept hearing her soft, musical voice: "Such beautiful hair, and they shaved it all off. My poor baby. But it's coming in thicker than ever. Just like your father's. They won't do that to you ever again. I promise you. After tonight, they'll never hurt you again."

She held at seventy miles an hour. Traffic began to ebb and flow, growing heavy at each entrance to the interstate, thinning again. Suddenly, Charlie straightened and pressed the redial on the phone. Brian said, "There she goes." She had turned onto State 23.

Charlie reported in. "Anything about the hospital yet?" he asked. Chelsky said there wasn't, and asked where he thought she was going. "Don't know," he said. He gave them the number of the cellular phone and then said, "Constance, you okay?"

"Yes," she said in a low voice. "You?"

"Sure. Oh, oh. She's going to turn again, or pull over or something. Hang on." She was signaling a turn, and now his stomach began to hurt. "She's on State One forty-three," he said in a flat voice.

He heard Constance make a soft noise. "Take it easy, honey," he said softly. "We'll know more when she gets to I-Eighty-eight. You still have a lot of company?"

"All of them, four guys," she said, and she sounded perfectly normal.

He grinned. "I'll be back in a couple of minutes," he said.

Marla was going to his house, taking the route he used, the quickest way from her place to his. He bit his lip. There was little traffic on 143; Brian had to keep farther back than he liked. Could use a little backup, guys, Charlie thought darkly. He called Constance again in a few minutes. They were about ten minutes from the interstate. Constance answered his first ring.

"Honey, if there are cars out front, maybe it would be a good idea to get them in the garage, or around back, out of sight."

"Thought of that," Chelsky said. "We're moving them now. We'll turn off lights, make it look like it usually does this time of night."

Marla turned left at I-Eighty-eight and then made the next turn onto the county road that led to his house. Brian hung back as far as he dared; he was muttering under his breath, and driving without lights half the time. When they passed the house, it looked like a house should look at 1:30 in the morning: an outside light on the front stoop, a dim light from an upstairs window, empty driveway. Marla drove past slowly, then speeded up a little.

"Don't turn on anything yet," Charlie snapped into the phone a minute later. "She's turning around, making another pass."

Chelsky said very calmly then, "Meiklejohn, don't touch the brakes. If she's suspicious, the brake lights will give it away."

"We'll pick her up here," Pulaski said, "just as soon as she goes by." He and the two aides hurried to the garage.

This time, she slowed to a crawl as she drove by the house, then came to a full stop for a second at the boundary where a ditch separated the property from Hal Mitchum's.

Charlie was speaking into the phone throughout, worried. She had pulled too far away before they had been able to make a turn and resume the chase. Her lights were distant and fading fast. He saw a car pull out of his driveway and go after her, but he was cursing softly.

"See what she did out there," Chelsky said to Stan Lehman, who had come back in and now went scurrying out. He returned with a sprayer.

"It was in the ditch," he said.

Then Charlie was back on. "We lost her," he said in a harsh voice. "We're on this side of a train with Pulaski; she's on the other.

"Where?" Chelsky asked, looking again at the map on the table.

"About seven miles from the house, four miles from the interstate. Pulaski will head north with me; his guy will go south with Brian as soon as we hit the interstate again." He sounded very grim. "Pulaski's holding a gun on me," he added. There was a choking sound close by, and Charlie said, "Well, then take your damn hand out of your damn pocket."

"Easy, easy," Chelsky said. "We'll have people on the interstate as soon as possible."

Charlie hung up.

* * *

Chelsky was on the kitchen telephone, speaking in a low voice; Stan Lehman was on the cellular phone, arguing with someone. Constance sat at the table, feeling helpless. Lehman made some notes then and disconnected. "Got it," he said.

Over the past five years, Nathan had been treated in two hospitals in New York City and had had surgery in one in Albany last November.

"Let's go," Chelsky said, and they ran to the garage. Constance was at his elbow when he reached the car. He hesitated briefly, then yanked the back door open, and she got in. Lehman drove; Chelsky stayed on the phone.

In the other car, Pulaski listened to Chelsky and relayed the message to Charlie. "Children's Hospital, Albany. If this is a wild-goose chase, Meiklejohn, I'll have your ass."

"Just shut the fuck up. Address."

Pulaski told him and he snapped, "Get on the phone, someone to lead us in, tell us the best route to take."

Pulaski began speaking again.

Charlie watched taillights, drew close enough to see if it was a black Buick, passed whatever it was in front of them, and then did it again. Traffic was light, but as they got closer to Albany, it picked up. Pulaski made a choking sound again when Charlie swerved and passed a semi. "No sirens," Charlie snapped. "No fanfare, no fire trucks. Understand? She'll spook and take off for parts unknown to dump the gas. God only knows what she'll burn then."

"Right," Pulaski said, and repeated the message into the phone.

A few miles out of Albany, they picked up an escort—two unmarked dark cars, a Chevy and a Dodge, one to lead, the other to follow. Pulaski kept the phone line open now and the three cars left the interstate and headed for the hospital.

Two blocks from the hospital, the lead car turned down an alley, and the following car passed them and continued out of sight. "We stop here and you drive," Charlie said. "You're a doctor on a call. Park near an entrance, get out, and go into the hospital. I'll duck down out of sight in case she's already around watching the place." She was cautious, he thought, paying no attention to Pulaski's objections as he stopped at the curb. "Another doctor arriving for an emergency—she probably will accept that, but she knows me. Now."

They changed places and Pulaski drove into the parking lot near a side entrance where several other cars were parked. There was a Buick there, but it wasn't hers. Pulaski got out, stretched, and walked to the entrance, into the hospital.

The hospital was close to the street in the front; the ambulance entrance was on one side, well lighted. Here in the back, the parking lot was lighted with a few lamps, and had great shadowy areas, with cars scattered here and there, clumped near entrances, some all the way to the far edge near the sidewalk. The other side of the building was flush with the sidewalk. It would be back here, he thought grimly—if she came at all.

He had been too busy driving and searching for her to worry until now that they might be in the wrong place altogether. Maybe they had made a false assumption and she was heading for another warehouse, a school, the governor's mansion. He eased the car door open and slipped out, keeping low. She would drive by, make sure it was safe, maybe drive by more than once, and then . . . She wouldn't enter the lot, he thought; she would park out on the street, walk in, ready to run back to the car and take off as soon as she tossed a match.

How many agents were already there, in parked cars, in

the building, across the street? He couldn't see anyone, but he knew they were there. They'd better be there, he thought grimly. A car drove in; a man and woman got out and hurried inside the hospital. He heard another car leaving. A nurse came out, smoked a cigarette, and reentered. Another car pulled in, parked. No one emerged this time. He didn't move.

He eyed the building; what she'd do was park over on the street, walk around the block maybe, approach from this side, spray it and light it, and have only a dozen feet to the car to cover. They hadn't come down that side street; he didn't know if the Buick was there or not.

The building was old and shabby, brick and wood, lots of wood on windows and doors, and a lot of dead ivy clinging to the bricks. It would carry fire to the roof, he knew. A couple of wooden benches were near the entrance, no shrubbery, no place anyone could hide, just a walkway around the building, and the parking lot. His ears had become attuned to the night sounds now—traffic out front, an occasional car on the side street, a light wind rustling in the dead ivy. Then he heard a different sound, soft footsteps, and he carefully looked around the back of the car, into the parking lot. At first, he thought he was seeing a boy with a backpack, but it was Marla, dressed all in black—jacket, jeans, shoes, a black visor cap pulled low. She was walking openly through a drive lane, making no attempt to stay hidden behind cars, and she looked like a boy going to work late. Then figures appeared from parked cars, and others from the building, and he heard Chelsky's voice.

"Stop there, Mrs. Boseman."

She was holding the wand of a sprayer, Charlie realized; the backpack was a sprayer tank. Don't anyone shoot, he prayed. Marla hesitated, raised the wand, and then continued toward the building.

Charlie went cold all over when he heard Constance's voice. "Marla, you have to stop now. If you don't, someone will shoot, and you'll die. Who will care for Nathan if you die?"

Marla swung around, aiming the wand toward the car where Constance stood. Charlie began to move quietly then. Her back was to him.

"You!" she said in a low, harsh voice. "Now he'll know what it's like to see someone you love crippled, hurt."

"Marla, if you spray me, someone will shoot. The sprayer will explode if it gets hit. You'll die. No one will watch out for Nathan, see if he's making progress. Who else will even notice if he's getting better? They'll let you see him, visit with him, make sure he's getting things he needs."

Charlie was nearly close enough. Don't spray her, he prayed. Don't do it. Don't.

"Who else will read to him, Marla? Who will tell him about the flowers? No one else believes he can understand. They won't read to him, talk to him, but you will be able to. They'll let you see him."

"You're lying!"

"If you're dead, he'll die, Marla. You're keeping him alive. You know that."

Charlie knew others were moving, too, although he didn't take his gaze off Marla, off her hand holding the wand pointed at Constance. She had something clutched in her other hand.

"He'll miss you, wonder if you've forgotten him, if you're ever coming back. No one will even tell him that much, because they don't think he can understand. He'll suffer, Marla. He will."

Charlie jumped then. He threw one arm around her neck and grabbed her hand on the spray wand. As she tightened her finger on the trigger, he forced the wand down; gasoline sprayed on the pavement at their feet. She raised her other hand, and he swept it back in a brutal, swift motion. Something fell with a clatter. Abruptly, she relaxed; her whole body seemed to lose tone, and her hands hung limply at her sides.

"I have to go home now," she said. "He's waiting for me."

Charlie held her while someone came and removed the backpack sprayer gingerly. She didn't resist then or when two agents took her by the arms and led her away. He took a step toward Constance, who was running to him. They held each other hard, not speaking.

Then Chelsky tapped Charlie on the arm and cleared his throat. "This yours?" he asked. He opened his hand to show them a disk, the size of a silver dollar. He opened it, a locket, with Constance's picture in one half and Jessica's in the other. They were both wearing *gis*, their martial-arts clothes. Marla must have been at one of their exhibitions, he thought with a chill. The last one had been over a year ago.

"It's what she dropped," Chelsky said when Charlie shook his head. "That probably would have done it, that and the sprayer at your place." He started to walk away, then said, "You folks go on home. You need a ride?"

Charlie shook his head. "Brian can take us."

"Someone has to go take care of Nathan," Constance said, facing Chelsky.

"We'll see to him. He'll have to be put in a hospital to-morrow."

When Constance turned back to Charlie and took his

hand, he saw tears gleaming on her cheeks. Brian took them home and no one said a word all the way.

The next morning Charlie left Constance in bed and he and Brian drove down to Cedar Falls to collect the Volvo. He went on to Marla's house after Brian headed back to New York. He retrieved the tape recorder hidden by the driveway and parked behind several other cars; Chelsky met him at the door. It appeared that an army was going through everything inch by inch.

"They took the boy to Children's Hospital this morning," Chelsky said. "We found the money, certificates, checks, all that's left. And a map," he said heavily. "Every arson neatly circled. Few other things, but that's the big one."

Charlie shook his head. "I'd go dig up the roses out there," he said, motioning toward the back garden. That was the big one, he thought.

It was late afternoon before Charlie returned. Constance met him at the door, examined him closely, and said, "You look terrible."

"I have a right," he said. He told her about the money, then said, "Pete's body was under the rose bed, along with an inflatable butler. The kid's in the hospital."

They went to the kitchen, where he poured himself a shot of bourbon and drank it down. "About the money," he said then. "Had a talk with Chelsky. I think if we recover expenses, that'll be okay. Don't you?"

She nodded. "And the rest?"

"Oh, I don't know. Children's Hospital, something like that."

She kissed him.

He needed a nap, he said, and she said she would help him take a nap, and they went upstairs, just to nap, they both understood, but it was nice to fall asleep holding her, being held by her.

Two weeks later, Chelsky called and asked if it was okay to drop in, since he was in the neighborhood. He took his boots off outside the door and pulled on his felt slippers; then he settled into a chair before the fire. "April showers," he said. "Not too bad, though."

Constance brought in coffee.

"The boy had a seizure couple days ago," Chelsky said, gazing at the fire. "He didn't pull out of it this time. They couldn't save him."

No one spoke for several moments. Finally, Constance asked, "And Marla?"

"They told her last night. She hanged herself in her cell."

The silence stretched on and on. Chelsky stirred his coffee and put the cup down again.

"You came all the way down from Vermont to tell us," Charlie said.

"I reckon," he said slowly. "It'll be on the news later on. Just thought you should know first." He stood up and said more briskly, "Guess I'll pass on the coffee. Things to do." They walked to the door with him. "Sometimes it's hard," he said. "Sometimes it surely is hard. You both take care now." He shook hands with Charlie and then kissed Constance on the cheek. "You take real good care now."

They went back to the living room. On the table by the cup of untasted coffee was the little bug Constance had put on the table in Nathan's room. Charlie picked it up and regarded it and for a moment he heard that soft, sweet, musical voice. From the look on Constance's face, he thought she was hearing it, too. There was nothing they could say. *Sometimes it's hard,* he thought, and she nodded.

More stunning mysteries by

KATE WILHELM

JUSTICE FOR SOME

After her husband's death, Judge
Sarah Drexler goes back to California
to see her father, visit her moody son
and pregnant daughter, and consider
an offer to run for Oregon State Judge.
But then her father dies suddenly, and
a detective is murdered. When one of
her children turns up a suspect, Sarah
is caught between her love for her
family and her loyalty to the law.

DEATH QUALIFIED

A *NEW YORK TIMES* NOTABLE BOOK

Out of the law for five years, Barbara
Holloway is still "death qualified"—still
able to defend clients in Oregon who face
the death penalty. Her lawyer father's
request to take on a new case brings her
back to the arena of a small-town courtroom, where she will have to find the truth
in a nest of lies, gossip, chaos, and love.

THE BEST DEFENSE

Attorney Barbara Holloway is content in her
blue-collar neighborhood diner in Eugene,
Oregon, where she regularly brings her laptop to work. But then she is approached by
the sister of a woman charged with killing
her own child. When she finds herself up
against a smear campaign of unimaginable
proportions, Barbara realizes that even
the best defense may not be enough.